THE

LITTLE

TIME

ALLOTTED

US

LAURA PAQUETTE

IBSN:

979-8-9883950-0-3 (Paperback)

979-8-9883950-1-0 (E-Book)

979-8-9883950-2-7 (Audiobook)

Dedication

To memere and pepere, Aunt Kathy and Uncle Ralph.
I know you'd be proud, but I still wish I could see your face when I handed you
the book.

Part I

Let me forget you, and everything is true.
    The Earth is the flat center of the multiverse,
    the prison of my mind has a marvelous view,
    and love is not a curse.

    I will not remake you as muse;
    you are not a caricature,
    a pile of bones to pin up and display as I choose.
    But what were you here for?

    My love, if I forget you, I'm finally free.
    Good and evil are mere words untethered from reality,
    I grant the world no guarantees.
    I am the monster I was meant to be.

    This weakness of memory is my sentence.
    Though my bones are dust, my casket has rust,
    though the tired stars burned through their light,
    I will love you—the only true repentance.

"Amnesia" Aidan Riley, 436 Dìqiú Hòu

Khair's First Death

She was drowning.

She didn't know who she was or why she felt suspended, weightless in a liquid so dense she couldn't move, but that came second to the drowning bit. With each breath, tasteless, knotty fluid flooded her mouth and stung her eyes.

A lock clicked.

"Don't free her," a young woman said.

Her breathing sped. She swallowed more icy slush, sucked in more with each breath, but didn't drown. It must be oxygenated, but not nearly enough. If she controlled her breathing, the heterogenous jelly stung a little less in her dry sinuses, but her eyelids drooped and sound faded. She couldn't thrash or escape, but she kept her breathing ragged—better to be panicked and awake than return to the endless night.

What was out there?

Her prison grated against the floor without any vertigo inside. A ship? Spaceship or seaborne. Either way, something was wrong. Otherwise, there was nothing in her world but the pressing darkness so total it took on an amorphous off-black color that shined in the corners.

"Look at her heart-rate, she's suffering." The man sounded old enough to remember the first intergalactic flight back when they drank recycled urine and couldn't travel at lightspeed, but deferent somehow. Not a family then, military, corporation?

"It's a dream." The woman's voice softened. "Remember her as best you can and let her rest."

The ship shook like a child's present.

Where were her weapons? She should probably ask who she was, but that wouldn't matter if she suffocated or got vaporized. She had to bust out and hope she was in fighting condition: her mind's voice was middle-aged, steady enough under pressure but that could make her anything from a mom to a manager so depending on how deep into that middle age thing she was, she might pop a hip or something. If not, she'd capture the woman for leverage, break a few fingers, maybe kill—

She screamed but there was no sound, though thick bubbles popped centimeters from her face. Pain seared from the base of her skull into her brain, so intense that if she had known her name, she would have forgotten it again.

What makes your life more valuable than hers?

That robotic voice in her head must have been what electrocuted her. The watcher's presence felt like a knife between her ribs; every thought irritated the wound.

My bad. She did not mean that whatsoever, but she wanted to send something instead of just being laid out for this stalker. ***Let me out safely and I won't hurt anyone.***

No answer.

No? I'm supposed to be best buds with the people that stole my memories and locked me up so I can't even move, can barely breathe?

They didn't do that; it was me and my organization. Observe, listen, and hold off the assumptions. Your ship is breaking up in the atmosphere, if they release you, you don't have time to be wrong.

"Look, she's awake," the man said. "And Taivan said—"

"He had a concussion, he wasn't thinking clearly," the woman said.

The man said nothing, and her heart pounded.

Something beeped outside.

"I'm sorry, Jiao," the man said.

Her cave exploded with static white light. Too much, too close. Passing shadows would have overwhelmed her as she regained her body, rejoined society, and became human again.

This body of hers was not in fighting condition. Despite appearing healthy, she was in a hospital gown, trapped in a doctube filled with snot colored plasma, metallic anklets on both feet, with no piercings, scars, or tattoos to indicate who she was. Chunky gunk receded into sidebars. The door opened. There was no difference in temperature or humidity as the goop slopped off, but this air had enough oxygen.

She floated toward the ceiling and bounced off to test over-eager muscles. Her hamstring cramped. How long was she imprisoned?

Nope, no time for introspection. Red lights flickered, and a shelf ripped loose from the wall, scattering edged surgical tools that bobbed in midair.

The man, unarmed and wearing an antiquated bubble suit with tinted mask, hit a button on his wrist-control link to electronic equipment, networks, and other wrist-cons. Her anklets magnetized to the ground. She bent her knees to soften the landing, but her heels bruised.

She raised her hands slowly, trying not to get distracted by the long windows around the beige infirmary, where the ship's ginormous wings blocked any view of space. Fire burned over the wings. Was that supposed to happen? They weren't smoking, but maybe there was no smoke in space?

Whoever she had been, she certainly wasn't a scientist.

"Give me your wrist-con," she said to the man, Sergeant Batu from his name plate. "I'll fly out on a life-pod, and you'll never see me again."

"You're not leaving," Jiao said.

Batu was average height and gaunt, leaned on his back foot—she could wrestle the wrist-con off him and use its map to find the life-pods.

Pain swelled in her head, burst, scattered down to her toes. She buckled and fell. When it stopped, the digitalized voice didn't say why she got zapped, but it clearly only appreciated its own violence.

She stood and measured herself against Jiao, an admiral by the golden rank on her chest. They were about the same height but she had fifteen kilos on Jiao, with broader shoulders and arms visibly muscled even at rest.

The admiral was far too young for her rank and looked like she forgot how to sleep. Still, she was beautiful: silky black hair pasted in a military grade bun, delicate features set in a frown, wearing a sleek pilot's suit that showed off a sinewy frame, a classic Mustang Dragoon 2587 strapped in a shoulder holster under her right armpit.

A prism buzzed in her head when she looked at the pistol. All the pain originated from one place so it was probably hardware, something a bribed doc could slice out. Otherwise, it'd be a race between her pummeling Jiao, and Jiao drawing her revolver.

She bet on herself. Jiao was a lefty, a slight advantage. But the spring and coil of her muscles promised power and the flesh on her knuckles was new, hiding scars. If she picked her moment—

Heat flashed. She blinked. Found herself on streaked sanitized tiles, elbow scratched, gown torn, heart racing as if to escape a black hole's event horizon.

You just died. Next time, it'll be permanent. Do not attack anyone.

Tears welled in the corner of her eyes, but she blinked them back and tried to even out her breathing. Her chest throbbed.

She could mimic Hannibal's double envelopment in three-dimensional space or instill Temujin's discipline to prevent a weeklong feigned retreat from becoming a real loss. But whoever was in her mind could kill her at any time, and there was absolutely nothing she could do about it.

She understood Jiao's gun. So, she tried to clear her mind of violent escapes, though she couldn't scrub them all, and looked the admiral in the eye. Daring her. Jiao could kill her, but she'd have to shoot a kneeling woman with green glob in her hair.

Jiao stared back, eyes hardening, lips pursed, thumb stroking her pistol. The admiral flipped the holster open.

She should probably beg, but if the shuttering, overheated cabin was any indication, they were goners anyway.

"You're needed at your post, Admiral," Batu said.

Jiao's hand didn't move.

"Shoot me or don't, you'll regret it either way." Her voice wasn't nearly as authoritative as Jiao's but flecks of slime clung in her throat. Pretty badass last words, though. She was probably too old to care, but with hair shaved on both sides and short on top, clearly, she was the type of old that didn't realize it was old.

The original quotation was better, but you're welcome. I can help if—

Definitely doesn't make us even.

"Cuff her and keep her close," Jiao said. "Don't bother finding a rebreather. There's no time, and she's not worth your life."

Maybe not. All she knew about herself was that her memories lay in a gray fog that should clear with sunrise, and if her memory was wiped she had accepted it as a stay of execution.

She drummed over her heart. "Mercy, I've no defense against such wit."

Jiao didn't even roll her eyes. "Hurry, Batu. You'll be safest if you buckle up in the Haven within two minutes."

"What about the life-pods?" A ship this big would have them, and they were much safer than the Haven emergency shelter.

"Taivan used them up to absorb missiles once our shield went down." Batu waved her down a bland hall. He might be strolling through an absent neighbor's pasture for his haste, while the craft shuddered, gravity lapsed, and condensation dripped down the walls.

Fat help seatbelts would be when they blew up. "You have anything to drink?"

He stopped at a custodian's locker stuffed with everything from hammers, flysuits, comm parts, and a candy wrapper. "Do you need to drink?"

"Need isn't the point." But based on her tight bladder, she still had human requirements. She didn't feel modified beyond some chip in her head turning her to a shock toy, could walk and talk and trust her senses.

How do you know? To know anything with certainty, we first have to doubt everything we know.

When she burned, she wouldn't ask the flames if they were real. ***I know I'll be an alcoholic by the end of your next sentence.***

You act as if that's an accomplishment. And whether the sensations you view exist or are mental perceptions, you—

I'm about to sing off key, then learn to throat sing off two keys, and I'll only get more annoying from there.

"We'll drink on the ground." Batu found handcuffs with a short chain that connected to the ankles. "May I?"

"Nope, not my style." She winced, shocked on a lower voltage, and held out her hands. "But I'm adaptable. Just don't tie my ankles."

He double cuffed her wrists with the ankle bracelets. Was all this necessary? Her mind had been executed, so she'd been mediocre at best and incompetent enough to get caught. But hey, she had abs so not too shabby for forty-something. Maybe thirty-nine.

Batu led her to a narrow, waist high tunnel. She squeezed into it. The hot, thinly-carpeted floor blistered her knees and palms as she crawled. She pushed out, breathing heavily as she tried to expel hot air, and landed in the Haven's circular room with padded walls. Air conditioning blasted over an obnoxiously peaceful symphony. There was nothing but a window roof and a medkit with emergency rations, but the ship's walls were thickest here.

She claimed the medkit and lathered aloe on her knees. "Why's Jiao more concerned with me than blowing up? Did I kill her family or something?"

Batu's shoulders tensed, face inscrutable behind his dark helmet. "No."

"Am I her mom?"

He laughed.

Fine, she was only about fifteen years older than Jiao, darker skinned and with a vastly different face, but it's not like she knew the father. Or if this was her unaltered face.

"Then what did I do? This is pretty extreme. Maybe it was a mistake, and it was supposed to be Jiao? She's not one of us." Taivan and Batu were Mongolian names, and she was Mongolian too if she recognized that. Jiao wasn't.

"Yes, she is."

"So, either I committed genocide, a stunningly impressive assassination, or I annoyed the wrong people."

"Sit down!" Jiao's voice blasted over the ship's intercom.

One vote for annoying.

Batu sat against the wall, metal straps unclipping to hug him. She tried to follow, but fell on her ass. The floor tilted and she slid until a seatbelt clamped around her.

"How many people could I have possibly killed? Millions? Billions?" No reaction. "It couldn't be trillions? Shiiiiiit. Logistically, that's impressive, but... shit. How'm I still alive?"

She couldn't remember anyone she'd killed. So, her seething stomach worried about the super-heated cabin and not dead strangers.

What are trillions of people compared to your glorious self?

Who did this cheap chip of silicon think it was, prattling along, its ode to its own goodness hammering her head? ***Yet you make me seem the zenith of humility.***

"I don't think I did that," she said to Batu. "I must have just lost. A POW."

The last historical event she remembered was a Mongolian uprising against the People's Republic of Greater China. She didn't know who won. Jiao could be PRGC, but Batu wasn't a prisoner. Maybe Batu was a collaborator, and she was a nationalist.

Whose ship was this? Scum lines and water residue in swirling cleaning patterns stained its white walls, with no pictures. A military vessel, now without a shield or life-pods. Who was after them?

The intercom stayed dead.

"You were not a great person," Batu said, almost cheerful.

"Then why free me? If I was supposedly a great pilot, I don't live up to the hype."

The medkit flopped to the floor, bouncing so often it barely noticed the growing gravity.

He clutched his seatbelt. "I don't think so."

Pressure built in her ears.

In the window, the pink sky darkened to a blood red and vibrant orange. They were inside a fireball.

Was that doubt thing a hint? Maybe I'm not here? Fire glowed and its bands of different colors wrapped around the ship like flowered garlands. If this was a virtual reality, the simulation would end soon. If not, it'd still end soon. ***Get me out of here and I'll give you an equal favor.***

Why do you want to live, anyway?

There'd been nothing pleasant in her five-minute life: no colors but white and yellow-green until the fireball. She was hungry and stiff and barely dressed, with a taser in the head. ***What's going on? These lunatics wouldn't wake me just to poof out.***

It is absurd. The context makes perfect sense: gravity and pressure and fuel combustion are constant, but you need more—

Thank you for giving me my reason to live. Spite. Didn't seem enough. Not in some flimsy, moral, nonsense way, just not worth the effort.

"So why wake me? What happened?" She meant, "why do I matter to you?"

"Taivan said so," Batu said. "Jiao—Admiral Jun—wouldn't want to. He'd only say it if it was necessary."

Jun Jiao was definitely a PRGC name. Maybe they were PRGC mercenaries and there'd been some imperial schism? She waited for the rest, Taivan's plan to save them for a long, profitable, stress-free life. But Batu was finished. "Who's Taivan?"

"Shut up!" Jiao yelled over the intercom as streaks of blue darted over the glass.

She rested against the trembling wall, though her head pattered against the soft panel. "What's my name and the year?"

"It's 532 Dìqiú Hòu." Half a millennium from Earth, and she'd no knowledge of the last twenty-some years, but beyond that, only her personal history was lost. It would have been easier for the enemy to lobotomize her than to unravel her from history. If they hadn't, they wanted something from her. "You went by Khair."

Your nom de guerre, a mockery meaning 'Love.' Leave that name.

I know my own language, thanks.

She would've sensed the name was a lie, but it wasn't terrible. Certainly better than say, Sorghaghtani, and she'd gone from a captured bride to one of the most influential people in Terran history.

Their trajectory snapped. There was no engine hum, no jolt of air as the wings shifted, just the whoosh of fire.

They spun down. The force pinned everything to the wall, pulled her cheeks back, pulled tears from stinging eyes as sweat gathered in a crease in her gown. Batu hummed, sounded like a choking motor. The light outside was only blue now, not crystal sky, but space waves, dark, ethereal, washing over their craft in time with the blood rushing in her veins.

It was beautiful. The pounding in her stomach waned, the remaining chittering only the nervousness of meeting an old friend after years apart. She never should've left that dreamless sleep. Khair was ready for this reunion, though the road between was long and potholed.

Batu wretched. She fought a losing battle against nausea while gravity crushed her shoulders and spine.

You're not some avenging spirit, right? Khair was probably dreaming through doctube hibernation, but no harm asking. *I'm not about to go to hell?*

It hesitated without demurring. *The greatest suffering is to do evil.*

You're one of the people that brought us down, aren't you?

"Batu?" Jiao said over the intercom, earlier arrogance evaporated. "I'm sorry." Their velocity halved, died.

The ship slammed the ground and wobbled as it skidded.

Khair lurched against the belt, bruised her ribs and bloodied her nose against her knees. Her ears buzzed, barely hearing echoing blasts.

Outside the windows lay solid ground. She laughed, muscles aching as they unclenched, delirious with pain and so dizzy she could barely see, but she kept laughing while she hiccuped and gagged. Then she saw Batu lay limp.

The only thing she felt was warm blood and relief.

How Not to Make Friends

FOR HALF A MOMENT, Khair considered helping Jiao from the wreck. Thankfully, that bad idea waifed off with the smoke and Khair escaped with only a cough. There was no punishment; either the voice was connected to the ship, and she was free, or it wasn't programmed with a duty to save.

Outside, on frosted alien ground, Khair examined the ship. It was shaped like a crocodile, a big, triangular head and a long round body, with the red and blue Khanate flag on its side. The ship's airbag had deployed around the hull. It was discolored and distorted now, a smear of flattened clay behind it. At least there'd be no angry populace—they'd left the middle of nowhere fifty kilometers and three wrong turns back.

Winds rushed over her. She pulled her paper gown closer, tearing the back more. After the ship stopped burning, she'd salvage it, but now, she stared up at the dim prick of light and wondered what was so wrong with the sun. Was it really blue, or just so weak it barely squeezed through the atmosphere?

The gravity was too light, air thin, this planet either too far from the sun or else with an atmosphere that didn't retain enough heat. No sign of people.

No one would know when she died here.

At forty years old, Khair should be able to compare this gravity to home's, reminisce of lost pets now that she was without even insects, dream of home-cooked meals to fill her empty stomach. Instead, she wrote 'Help, I'm Hungry and TRAPPED.' Feeling inadequate, she added an exclamation point.

"What am I doing?"

She just wanted to hide in a crowd celebrating Nadaam, the summer holiday that would never happen here. Someone would play the deep morin khuur, but she wouldn't know the tune, would scour thousands of bright deels and broad hats without recognizing anyone.

You didn't have to take my childhood friends, my family. Is my ghost that terrifying?

Nothing.

"I know that voice was real. You shocked me! I'm not completely wacko. You could've left me a coat!" She circled the ship for an overhead shelter. If it was on fire, even better.

Jiao had landed them on a thin cliff, saving them kilometers of damage. That kid was either vain or a superhero. Had been, anyway.

The ship's lower half was crunched but the passenger deck was intact, though a hole the size of a city block was blown through the side. That a ship the size of a sideways skyscraper had landed with only a chintzy metal patch was near miraculous.

Indeed, you should wonder if you're indebted to a higher power. Or if you were spared without reason and—

Just shut up. Shut the fuck up and stop acting like I owe you anything!

It didn't miss a beat. *Watch your language, there's people nearby.*

Khair looked around. Apart from the ship, smoke huffing from its corpse, there was no life. Not a single bug or weed. She scanned for tracks, but the granular, pale silt didn't even have a thistle. From this cliff, she could see for kilometers; there was no water, or glaciers, or icebergs, or clouds, or swamps of rice.

Where?

In the ship you abandoned.

Now it was just playing. **Fuck you.**

The intruder shocked her. She swore in surprise and the tingling burn reverberated stronger than before. Which made her swear again, and again, and again, till she could do nothing but hold her head with twitching fingers.

Dirt stuck under her nails, her lungs refused to expand, and her eyeballs felt like they'd explode. Most combat injuries caused shock; she should elevate her legs, try to keep warm. But that would require moving.

Khair didn't speak until she ironed out her hate. "What was the point of that demonstration of power, oh great bastion of morality?"

Just making sure you can be trained. Good doggy.

Her cheeks flushed. **Who are you?**

You have other concerns.

Her throat was dry as desert sand. If she didn't find water in the ship, she'd have to trek downhill. But if the valley was this rocky, she couldn't dig a well. Dew should condense to water as night turned to day unless it was too cold, but how long was a day here?

There's water in that ship. People to help you survive if you give up a little safety for the common good—at least until your tyrant Leviathan rouses.

Clearly, you're not a machine, you're too in love with your own voice. Even if you're as awkward as an AI, Computer Chip. No, too long, I can't be bothered to think about you that long—just Chip.

Why did she have to name it, like it would be with her forever?

It showed a livesteam of Batu. The picture layered over her vision, a thick spider's web where she could focus on the strands or the image beyond. The vision was clearer than human sight, from a strange angle—a security cam. It itched.

Batu climbed out of the Haven through the hot tunnel, ignored an exit despite the glowing arrow path. Hadn't that poor sucker died already? He must have lost consciousness.

Save him yourself.

It panned across the twisted hall to a sleek, coffin-sized, rust-red doctube like the one she'd woken up in. On its side, vitals chirped and various modes offered lightyear sleep, life-finding assistance, or short flights, but the front was clear. The man inside wore space clothes: a tight gray suit with geometric patterns on the collar and cuffs, boots in matching busy design.

He was the most handsome man she'd ever seen. Yes, the options were herself, another woman, and a geezer who hadn't taken off his mask, but that didn't change that this man had a patent on the ideal male physique. This explained why everyone was so googly over Taivan.

Show me where he is.

It snorted, buzzing through Khair's nose.

It led her to a different exit and made her scale up a warm ladder. When she yanked herself inside, she expected to face down an inferno, but beside wisps of smoke, the ship only seemed messy.

"Taivan!"

Don't yell, the structure's compromised.

It survived—

Ceiling pieces crashed through the floor in front of her, banging through half a dozen levels before an explosion shook the floor and a rush of sparks and flame leapt out.

Fu—n.

Khair sprinted through the halls, hurdled mangled steel and warping floors, almost overtook her navigator's directions. Pushed down giddiness at moving this fast, almost skipped.

The instructions changed constantly as bits collapsed.

She sweat so much it was a second skin. Fire frothed deep below, ever closer. Heat swelled and thickened the air to an oppressive, tangy roux, objects dimmed into their surroundings.

Can you fix my vision?

No, but I can keep you conscious.

It buzzed, too faint to hurt. She ran faster, past signs the ship was lived in—all quaint and flammable. Wooden furniture and cloth tablecloths and landscape photos that almost tipped toward pleasant, but whose edges curled and crinkled.

The fire wasn't impressive; there was no great wall pressing toward her, just huddles of orange crouching over the oven or dancing about the walls on hidden wires. But it'd be enough.

How hot was fire? Why was some orange, red, yellow, blue? Maybe they could set a controlled fire to put out—

Pay attention and slow down. You're almost there and your lungs aren't ruined yet.

This guy better be into older women.

Or what?

She had no comeback and pretended to wait out a distant explosion. **If I'm going to die badly, hit the off-switch first.**

No response.

She found Batu and Taivan's doctube across a three-meter gap in the floor. It widened every moment she hesitated. Fire crackled beneath. Electric blue sparks sizzled and stinging smoke billowed from the chasm.

At least it'd be instant. She backtracked, raced forward, and leaped across, stumbling on the edge but falling forward. Batu helped her up, his hand clammy, strong, and fleshy.

She squeezed his hand to see what another person was like and released him. "I've got him, get out."

"What about Jiao?"

"Probably dying terribly, which is why we should leave."

Batu shook his head. "No, she's too smart, too good. She's not dead."

"How does being smart—" she coughed and waved at Batu to exit.

Jiao saved your life with this landing.

She was trying to save herself. Great effort. But she failed. That's no reason for me to join said failure.

Batu took off his helmet and extended it to her. His face was burned almost beyond anything human, hair gone, features smoothed into nonexistence, skin puffed with red ridges of still burning coals.

He bent to his knees, joints cracked, and the floor bent beneath him. "Please, Khair."

"Get up Gramps, stop making it weird." **Tell me you see Jiao's corpse.**

There's no footage of the cockpit, but I can take you to her without dying on the way in.

No promises on the way out. **Good thing I don't remember anything I loved, cause then turning into a charred shish-kabob would really suck.**

"I'll save your admiral if you'll answer my questions when I get back."

No.

"Yes, good." Batu pushed Taivan's tube toward the exit.

She passed wall after fireproof wall as she descended, as if a skittish pilot built the ship. Bumps of marred steel warped its bulkheads and decks. The engines squealed below and shook the floor and loose debris kept falling, biting at her in its death throes like a beheaded snake.

Batu's helmet stifled sound, made her flinch at everything, whirl around in fighting stance to face a swaying wire. Steam fogged her visor. The inconstant rhythm of her breath pounded in her ears and made it more erratic.

Fun fun fun.

She removed the helmet as she reached the cockpit, its floor kissing the ceiling in the front. A meter separated Jiao's head from the roof.

Jiao raised her pistol. Khair dove up the stairs as a projectile popped against the stairs without a trace. What was that ammo? Guess they didn't make Mustangs like they used to.

"This isn't how we make friends, sweetie," Khair yelled to make sure she was heard.

Jiao flicked the pistol's selector switch.

"Whoa, whoa! We got off to a bad start. So. Is 'Jiao' pronounced Jow or Gee-ow or—" Another shot obliterated the stairs below her feet.

They really did not make Mustangs like they used to.

"Batu sent me! You're trapped and you can smell smoke, so if I wanted to hurt you, I'd leave."

"He has a bad heart, he couldn't survive—"

"If you don't believe me, fine, I'll take Taivan for myself."

Debris shifted and Jiao slapped the floor to cover her shriek. "Don't try anything funny."

"Tough luck for me, because I'm hilarious."

Jiao's right leg was severed at mid-thigh, the wound closed with glue from an empty bottle, a tourniquet tied seven centimeters above the cut. Her left leg was flattened between the floor and control instruments.

"I have to cut it off. Find me painkillers." Jiao rummaged through a fallen first aid kit for a second tourniquet. She slipped it high on her left leg, almost to her hip, and twisted the windlass until it couldn't finish another rotation.

Khair didn't see any pills, and if she had, she would've taken them. "Do you have big ol' longswords or laser swords or something?" Laser swords hadn't existed twenty years ago, but someone should have invented them by now.

Jiao reached for a bloodied flathead screwdriver with jittering fingers.

Khair hid a gag behind a cough. ***Can you help keep me from hurling on this kid?***

A revulsion to blood was programmed.

You don't have fancy speak for 'sometimes blood is necessary'?

You've forfeited nearly all privileges, and even some rights.

Khair spat bile.

Jiao watched her with furrowed brow, her disgust not the fascinated horror that made people flock to mummy exhibits, just simple repugnance. "What do you want with me?"

"To leave you, but the stalker in my head said no."

Jiao weighed her with such a caustic gaze she almost felt bad for not shrinking from it. Part of the ceiling fell, piling more weight on Jiao's leg. She gasped, choking back whimpers, and reached with the screwdriver for something under the co-pilot's chair. It was out of reach.

Khair grabbed it, a curved handle with a red cord around the bottom. "Where's the edge?"

"Turn the top to the left."

You have to let me. Jiao can't cut her leg off with a flathead, and much as I want to, it won't go through her femur.

Pity trickled, like for a rabbit mangled in a snare. *Go on.*

Khair twisted the handle, expecting flashes of memory or fireworks in her stomach. A thick slab of a blade popped out. The handle snapped around her hand with horned knuckles, protecting her hands and turning her fist into a weapon.

The revolver clicked behind her.

"I'll take that." Jiao's voice trailed off.

"You need me to carry you."

She tapped the first aid kit.

"Then we're right where we started: you wanting to kill me, and me giving you sad puppy eyes."

"Drop the sword and don't step closer."

Khair shook her hand to free it from the sword, but it stayed clasped around her wrist. "You can't do it, JJ, you don't want to—"

Evidently, she did.

Puppeteers

"ERROR: HUMAN TARGET."

Khair laughed as Jiao's eyes widened. Jiao shouted "override!" Misfired again. She hit the gun's handle and aimed at the ceiling above Khair.

Khair leapt up the stairs as rubble collapsed between them, and flattened herself against debris as shots pitched past with a dull pop. Loose wires sparked.

The end of the tourniquet in Jiao's hand caught fire. She hit it against the floor, but flame belched up the healing oil. Jiao untied it and threw it into the pit. It roared, and the cabin teetered with a swirl of smoke.

Only this hall fastened the cockpit to the ship, and half its roof was jumbled on the floor.

Let me leave.

Jiao set her jaw and loosened her remaining tourniquet—didn't dare untie it, just a little slack to ease her passing.

Khair watched. The cabin jounced in the breeze; she should escape. Especially when there was nothing impressive about it, Jiao didn't have many options, but to accept death without complaint or pleas or apologies....

You should memorialize this.

It hesitated. She'd been sure Chip was a person, but now it seemed more like a computer grasping for an old file than a person scrambling for words to mitigate death.

"Death be not proud, though some have called thee
mighty and dreadful thou art not—why are you walking away?
She'll die alone or with me. Which do you think she'd prefer?

"Stop." Taivan descended the stairs, his rumbling bass hypnotizing her.

He could walk into a room and the walls would thank him for it. He wasn't tall, but he didn't need to be. Whatever his injuries, he was hale now, movements graceful as a ballet dancer and muscles to make a wrestler jealous. Amber eyes and long lashes, flawless skin, artfully messy hair, razor jawed... she was very much staring, though fire spat at them.

Jiao fixed her tourniquet.

"Batu has the doctube outside, but you need to stay with me that long." Taivan looked to her, and her mouth dried. "Which name did you take?"

She only knew her pseudonym. "Khair."

His eyes narrowed, and he turned to Jiao. "Khair, then. Rip out a wire."

She sliced open the wall to find one that wasn't oozing acid and handed it to him.

Jiao cringed as she reached over, grabbed Taivan's arm, bluish around her fingernails. "You can't trust her. She doesn't even care about Batu anymore, there's—"

"I need you to stay still. You'll get cut more if you move." Taivan wiped the wire clean and tightened it around Jiao's still buried leg, the wire twisting into her skin.

She seethed and leaned into his shoulder. "It was a bad sacrifice, Taivan. Everyone counting on us, and...." Her voice caught, and she couldn't go on.

He raised her head and kissed her forehead so briefly they barely touched, too chaste to be into each other. Though maybe that was the time constraints. "They made their choice. But I need you, okay? Your legs are in bad shape, don't look—whatever it is, we'll make it right. We'll make it all right."

She pressed her spasming leg down and closed her eyes.

He grabbed the pilot's instruments over Jiao's leg. Khair did the same, and together they strained against the wreck.

It didn't move.

"The sword is always a great option," Khair said.

Taivan switched his grip on the wreck, set his feet, puffed out his chest and pushed back his shoulders. Khair wiped her palms. They lifted it a few centimeters.

Jiao ripped her leg back.

Khair spewed slop. Half Jiao's flesh had stuck inside. Her suit melted to what skin remained, bone peeked from blackened flesh, and her foot was sideways.

She wiped vomit from her chin and followed Taivan as he swept Jiao over his shoulders.

"Do you know the way out?" Khair asked.

"Not yet," he said.

You there, sucker? I gotta get the love of my life and my archnemesis outta here.

I can't see a way out, but most of the cameras are down.

How many walls between us and outside?

One, but you're hundreds of feet off the ground.

Like a baby's foot, or an elephant's? No matter. Khair cleaved her sword through the wall and kicked out an opening. Taivan was too busy trying to find a position that didn't make Jiao fuss to be impressed.

"Batu!" He yelled. "Send the doctube!"

Batu, on the ground, spoke too quietly for Khair to hear, and the machine zipped in a circle, then stopped where it started.

"How do I do that?" Batu yelled.

The winds swept the dust in impatient circles so Khair couldn't see how far they'd plummet.

"Use its life finding function," Taivan said. "The directions are on the side."

There was no sound of movement.

The ship shivered. Below, engines burned, and the floor softened. "If we die because he's denser than a rock, I'm going to—ow! How's it my fault he can't read the instructions?"

Taivan raised an eyebrow. "Must be hereditary."

"Yeah, proba—he's not my father!"

He can't tell you about your past. You'll be punished.

Taivan didn't answer, but that was answer enough.

The man who'd knelt and begged minutes ago? He'd barely remembered her name. "You're teasing. Why him? Was my mother blind, or a science experiment victim? Maybe he's a really good cook, but even then—"

"Just a minute more," Taivan whispered to Jiao.

Khair watched Batu between the dust waves sweeping over frosty dirt and tried to imagine the life they'd had. She almost loved him then. Her life-pod in this abyss, tied to her by an accident of birth that bound them unconditionally.

But he'd let this happen.

He got those scars somehow.

She couldn't think, couldn't move. Batu traced the instructions and sounded out the words.

Not helping you, but you couldn't know that.

That flickering hope whiffed out.

You'll hear countless renditions of what happened, all accompanied by demands from people who claim they loved you, or could free you, or will hurt you if you refuse.

Good thing she wouldn't refuse.

I can show you footage in context from multiple angles, court transcripts, physical and circumstantial evidence. But you have to choose to believe the hard truths and act accordingly.

It talked like it wouldn't always be around or she might graduate this. She had to be clever, keep this loser talking—get it bragging. **Don't worry, I'm sure you're the best puppeteer.**

It snorted. *You can't hate your father for giving up on you when you're incorrigible.*

She blinked. Well, guess that couldn't be true 'cause there weren't hours of film confirmation.

Taivan and Jiao hadn't noticed the tug-o-war in her head. Jiao grimaced, nails digging and tearing fabric, while Taivan held her hand and reminded her of every brave thing she'd ever done. Khair had saved both their lives, but she was ignored as expired cans in a survival shelter.

The doctube dashed to them in a perfectly straight line, not slowing until she'd ducked so it didn't knock out her teeth.

"Systems damaged. Battery failing," the machine chirped. "Expect delays and—"

"Override!" Taivan lay Jiao in the 'tube, its lid down so it formed a walled stretcher. When Khair hopped in, it sunk a few centimeters.

"That would be unwise at—"

"Override, and return to last position." Taivan squeezed in, the 'tube wavering.

The doctube zoomed to the ground, decelerated just shy of terminal velocity, and gently sank into the land. Batu helped Taivan out and prepped the machine for healing mode without looking at her.

Khair tottered out over the side, buried her face in the wasteland, and discovered her overlords had not robbed her of her ability to cry.

Man is Wolf to Man

KHAIR CRIED UNTIL SHE couldn't stand to lie on cold pebbles any longer. She sat up, shivering, wiped her eyes, and searched the countryside for something cheerful but there was nothing but elephantine gray, wrinkled mountains, and a too-close cliff.

She flexed her memory.

Khair floundered with historic events. There were touch stones she could recall and prod around until she remembered or guessed well.

Her own history was a void.

Yet her skills remained. There must be a difference between physical experience and learned skill. Could she trick the—

Not unless you want to get rebooted.

"The doctube should have radiation tablets and a water purifier." Taivan told Batu, without turning from Jiao. "Try to find anything useful thrown from the ship."

"Khair should come," Batu said.

Taivan nodded as he tried to cut off the leg of Jiao's suit. Jiao wanted him to go with Batu. He said leaving her like this would be the dumbest thing since attacking Japan in typhoon season. Khair settled in to watch when Batu gingerly tapped her shoulder and gestured her to follow. She did. But only when Taivan stopped talking, waiting for her to leave.

"You should remember chores," Batu said.

"Collecting dead wrens from around the windmills to see if they were fresh, cleaning the barn's radiation filter, chopping wood all day for rustic furniture in someone else's spaceship." It was a category like colors or food without associated recollection.

Something exploded in the ship. Khair hopped back, hands raised, while Batu stepped in front of her, holding her back. His hand was rough and cold against her arm. He took his hand back, rubbed it against his pant leg.

"Pretty sure memory loss isn't contagious," Khair said.

He said nothing.

"Take me home." She tried to make it sound a demand.

"Maybe we'll find birds here that taste like wrens."

Her chest tightened. "You're not even here for me. When I was locked up, you freed me for Taivan's sake."

"He'll get us home. Come on, you'll be happier if you work."

"I'd be happier if you were useful as spoiled milk." But she followed him.

She tried to make herself a mental sanctuary, imagined things that warmed her: old puzzle games solved by hand, wrestling a motorcycle while the engine growled and wind rushed past, betting on horses to see the pretty beasts and handsome riders though she didn't like the smell, drinks so strong she didn't have to smell them.

I don't have to kill you if you poison yourself.

And thus went Socrates. That thought was out of place, yet it came automatically.

Ha. He thought knowledge was intrinsic, so clearly, he never met you.

That would've slid off any kid in a playground, but school kids could fight back. **I know stuff. I'm probably some sort of Sun Tzu, and my army of concubines will—wait. That did not go great, at least for the concubines.**

Two women killed to instill discipline had been lauded as a triumph, but it seemed excessive now. Khair tried to rub feeling back into her hands. **Did you make me dumber?**

You don't need to know.

Heat flooded back. **You didn't—**

Don't flatter yourself; we removed data, but we didn't touch your ability to extrapolate. At least, not intentionally. So what? Your intellect didn't make you a better person, and your ignorance isn't an excuse.

Her fingers tingled. She needed to run, to fight, to escape this cold, this body. Khair bounced on her toes, hands rising to protect her face in a fist and claw, a hybrid of meticulously experimented cultures and centuries. Her own fighting style; she had that, at least.

Batu's eyes widened, and he hurried away.

Chip warned her with a dull static, slapped her as she dared a timorous jab. Khair hit her own head and sat, warming her hands under her arms, conjuring everything she wanted to experience again.

The sound a baseball made cracking off a wooden bat, the smell of leather and fresh cut grass, snapping peanuts and blowing gum, heat steaming off the dirt.

Was that her fondness, or Chip's?

Sparring in loose clothes without gloves or helmet, bruises flowering in every color, hardened shins, grins through a cut lip.

Take a hint.

New hobbies, then. Lounging in a recliner watching cheesy samurai—*no*—console racing—*insurgents use chatrooms*—masked dances—*you're not concealing your face* (so this was her face)—going to concerts—*or going anywhere dark and crowded.*

So I can't do anything but what, become a recluse and wait to die? Swim laps in an old folk's home and hope to cramp up before the sleeping lifeguard notices?

You can't do anything where I can't shock you.

Well, I gotta shower. Wait, will you watch?

I'll ensure you don't harm our investment or hinder our interests. Rest assured, I've no personal interest in a toothless enemy.

Skin to skin on silk sheets, lights dimmed and the air perfumed, out of this cold and dirt, the windows darkened, someone strong but faceless with his arms wrapped around her in as graphic an image as she could create for some privacy in her own mind.

Chip snorted. *Even without me, you couldn't pay someone enough.*

She glanced at Taivan as he gently eased Jiao in the doctube, and couldn't argue.

Don't you have more pressing concerns?

Sure, let's blab about universal truths no one has discovered after millennia of effort. Let a hundred flowers bloom; let a hundred schools of thought contend.

It was a PGRC revolutionary slogan, and Chip's references had been Western. If she didn't get it, she may be United Oversight for Democracy, bureaucratic busybodies who regulated tech—like this mind swipe thing and whatever gun had shot them down—which in their minds qualified them to run the multiverse.

When Khair didn't get shocked, she hopped up and skipped before stopping herself, and joined Taivan.

Maybe you should have studied things that are actually happening instead of all this abstract nonsense. Do you even know who I was?

You're authorized to know you're an enemy of peace. Nothing more.

That means nothing. Maybe I'll do the same thing because I don't know any different.

Chip's throat tightened, silently agreeing.

What about the PRGC, the Andromeda Khanate? Did you bother learning that? Just the Khanate name made her heart beat faster.

I'm learning.

I could explain every major battle in the formation of the People's Republic of Greater China, how it had kindled and fizzled out until a piece of it surged in the Andromeda Khanate, engulfed the outer rim, and swelled past the old hearth. Catch up.

"Did we win?" She asked Taivan. Jiao was tucked away in the doctube, a piece of her suit, skin attached, folded at its head.

"When?" He tried to use the water pump to get water from the air.

"Against PRGC."

"Yes." He adjusted a valve, tested it, and hit the side.

"Take that, Jiao. Are we being chased?"

"No."

But UOD was tracking them through her.

"So," Khair said. "If the ship's stored fuel hasn't blown up yet, it'll burn for days." The ship's warmth was alluring, but its degrading plastic poisoned their lungs. "We'll need to find energy, primarily protein, ideally fried in dough, and warmer clothes. If we gotta be cold, we oughta be in Ulaanbataar, see pretty girls at the ballet, huh? Or the dinosaurs."

She knew two things about Taivan: their shared heritage, and he had wanted to free her when the ship failed.

"I thought you'd prefer a monastery now." The water pump broke in Taivan's hand and when he tried to screw it back, it shattered. He laid the shards on the doctube, palm bleeding, wrapped his hand with scraps of Jiao's clothes.

Batu returned empty-handed, apologized to Taivan, then sat beside the doctube watching lights blink. The glass had darkened, so the only trace of a person was the one-and-a-half-smiley-faced progress bar.

"Will it heal her?" Khair asked Taivan.

"This first time should heal the burns. But she'll need a doctor to set the bones, another session in the 'tube to heal it straight, then physical therapy."

"And her reflexes?"

"She can fly if we get her a ship."

"How long will it take?"

He massaged his injured hand. "A couple days for her, not much longer for me to wrangle a ship."

Find me water. Preferably a beachy cove with a great view of the sunset.

There wasn't a sunset; one moment the sky was blue with a needle of solar light, the next it was black with half a dozen reddish moons looming. The air was slightly colder, but the winds took the night off.

Don't presume to give me orders.

I bow at the throne of your benevolence, oh great khan of khans, bequeath upon your supplicating servant—

Enough. There's no water nearby.

"Do we have transport?" Khair asked Taivan.

"Only the doctube."

Batu was her dad. Jiao liked her for target practice. But who was she to Taivan—and who was he? "What are we doing? You need all the help you can get, Robinson Crusoe."

She covered her mouth to take it back. Chip had added that name, not controlling but inhabiting her. For what, an insult neither she nor Taivan got? *I could give a half-baked crap cake who that is. Stop playing, I'm behaving.*

Taivan looked at her as if she were an exhibit at the Intellectual Museum.

"You don't want me here, do you? Am I their slave or yours?"

The closer you get to him, the tighter your chains.

"You're a child," he said.

She glanced at the sword, blinking past a burst of pain. "And Batu, what's he? Jiao can rebuild her leg, but he's left looking like that?"

She didn't care about Batu any more than she'd care to wear a string bikini in this weather, but she cared how Taivan treated broken things.

"He can use the 'tube any time, but I won't force him to for my viewing pleasure."

"Look," Batu said. "There's a new light."

It was a green rectangle with a white plus sign on it. Jiao was visible in a dim light now, closed eyes fluttering, hair loose, face childish as she contorted in pain.

"It's on energy saving mode. It can be solar, aeolian," seeing Batu's look Taivan added, "wind, or battery powered. Switch it here. Let's get pieces of the ship for shelter, sleep on warm pieces until Jiao recovers."

Taivan and Batu collected scrap, but Khair decided it'd be against child-labor laws to help and stayed at the stained glass doctube. She stared like it was a hallowed relic, barefoot and contrite, not daring to touch it. "Remember the good ol' days an hour ago when you almost shot me? Fun times."

The prayer went unanswered.

"How do people live like this?" Khair said.

Standing around, alone, while everyone else works to survive? They don't.

She'd done her part and gotten nothing except the opportunity to see Jiao all bleary-eyed. And get shot at. Between the two of them, Jiao was more useful. Taivan would choose her and Khair would be alone, or worse, saddled with Batu. Though maybe two-legged mutton wouldn't be so bad if she cooked it right.

No. She wouldn't grub and grind and commit cannibalism for a few more moments of misery.

Shock me or don't, you'll regret it either way, fucker.

Khair grabbed the sword, the chilled handle enveloping her hand as she activated the blade. Taivan said 'override' to the pistol but didn't aim it, standing sideways to present a smaller target but otherwise still.

"I wondered how long it'd hold you, anda." An anda was a brother of choice but also signified a political alliance, almost like a platonic marriage. He might be bluffing but he held the pistol with a relaxed grip, a slight upturn in his lips.

"What are you talking about?"

He flicked a switch on his wrist-controller. "I don't know how long we have and it won't work again, but the chip is blocked. We're what's left of the Andromeda Khanate. Do you remember?"

"I guessed." She didn't raise her sword, but didn't let its tip dull in the dirt.

"Our fleet was half destroyed by a solar storm before a battle with UOD—United Oversight for Democracy—after our world, Irmeg, became unviable. We were nearly overrun."

'Our world,' how easily he said it. She tried to imagine it. "Andromeda," named for a beautiful offering, the galaxy nearest mankind's cradle, a purplish disk fraying at the edge. "Khanate," forged first with bow and spur but remade calculating angles on nuclear-operated cannons. And "Irmeg." Too insignificant for any annals.

"You were my best captain. Wanted by half the universe, but there were no easy choices and everyone was on those lists. Except Jiao. So, you volunteered for their Mercy Mission to save our lives."

She almost laughed. "I'm the hero then? Somehow, I doubt that."

"Your choices were surrender, restart, and return to your people, or get blown up."

She almost asked what she did to piss everyone off, but she knew so little of the world, didn't want her first impressions to be what she'd ruined. "Who are you?"

"I'm Jinong Borjigin Jochiin Taivan, and I'll reclaim our nation. Help me, and I'll get you back your memories." Neither Jinong nor Borjigin were names, it was a title and clan: claiming to be heir of the old imperial line.

Hence why the self-appointed galactic police were after them.

Static chaffed at the back of her neck. "And our nation's gonna be what, the universe's worst sandcastle? Why here?"

She didn't ask about her memories because he couldn't—or wouldn't—get them back. And Chip would rummage around the lost minutes.

"We needed to land fast, and I have allies here."

Maybe the discomfort wasn't from Chip. "It's a lot of work for no guarantees and a high chance of death. Why bother?"

Taivan shrugged, the nonchalance not touching his eyes, his gaze all but flaying her. "I told Batu we'll make a better world for our people where we have means and freedom to help each other. Told Jiao we'll give what's left of PRGC a community run honestly, efficiently, where everyone has a place to improve themselves in service. I will strive for that."

So, he was a dream merchant. At least he knew his people better than most commanders, but he only had two.

"And I'll strive to live forever," Khair said. "But here we are. Don't sell to me. I don't even know what I want."

Disdain wrinkled his mouth. "You've nowhere to go. Neither do they, really, but I'd rather they were happy." He realized she was still waiting. "Because people still remember Temujin. Xander, Dracul and Mehmed—"

"And we remember..." She tried to think of someone in Temujin's family that wasn't famous for war or getting killed, a friend. Did he have friends? His anda, until his execution. "Polo. We can visit other people's lands that are already safe and pretty."

"He did nothing for his people."

Taivan must've been a real cute kid or his parents would've left him on the side of the road. "I can't even name Dracul's country. It's gone. And no one cares."

"Our kingdom doesn't have to last forever; it just has to work for us." He ignored the batting wind, as comfortable as if in his jinong parlor. "I've seen laws that shouldn't be, laws corrupted, laws left unenforced. That machinery rusts, but no one notices. It's left for us to rule ourselves in the little time allotted us and let the people after us do the same."

Look on my works, ye mighty, and despair. Khair stiffened, waiting for the dark, but it didn't come. *If you think violence can be a virtue, kill him and prove it; we'll put you on parole.*

The sword in her hand nodded approval. "That's it? We fight and reign and die?"

What do you think 'reign' means in a country without law?

Chip showed her war—she tried to focus past, but the footage darkened on her eye, more than mere vision, it filled her periphery, stank, screamed, squirmed.

She couldn't take it anymore, this stranger in her head, being a stranger to herself. *I'll kill him, just stop!*

The vision faded. Taivan stood a step closer, eyes narrowed and pistol ready. She gave him an obviously fake smile and though he nodded, he kept studying her.

Finally, he holstered the gun. "We can't do more, and I won't do less."

She slashed out his leg.

He howled and crumpled, blood spurting out of the stump above his ankle.

She hadn't really meant to, but the sword was spoiled otherwise. Better than killing him, and it hurt enough for him to remember he was mortal with the tech to put it all back.

That wasn't the deal.

Close enough?

Taivan bit his lip till it bled, blanching, squeezing the wet flesh Khair couldn't look at. Bright blood, inconstant flow—it was an arterial bleed. She might have killed him. She hauled him by his collar to the doctube, collecting the amputated foot and carrying the boot.

"No." He moaned, as she scanned the doctube's directions. "Can't fix it, let Jiao—"

"It can heal her leg, but can't reattach your foot?"

He nodded, eyes distant.

"Shiiiiit."

Unpayable Debts

Before General Jebe—Arrow—earned that name and rank, he'd been Temujin's enemy and shot his favorite horse from under him. But Temujin was merciful. Upon Jebe's defeat, he'd been inducted into the army. When Jebe's later success made Temujin wonder if his general would attempt to usurp him, Jebe raced to pay homage with a hundred horses of the same caliber as the one he'd slain.

All for the insinuation of disloyalty.

What could she give Taivan for this?

Help me save him.

Already, Taivan's lips turned blue. One hand clutched the stump, the other forearm dug into his thigh. Dirt turned to mud beneath him.

Batu dropped a sheet of metal and raced to them, his hands replacing Taivan's as the younger man's strength sapped.

Khair held the dismembered foot away from her. The neatly cut boot filled with blood burbling from the entombed ankle. She tossed it away, and the calf deflated as it drained, flat tissue coiled around the bone like a fallen tree's rings.

This is a deserved, proportionate response.

Maybe the universe was better off without him, but she wasn't.

I'll do ten good deeds if you help me. Nothing crazy or dangerous or—

Batu aimed Taivan's pistol at her. "Why'd you do that? You shouldn't be able to do that."

Despite not being daughter of the year, she didn't want to cut down the man who had known her since birth. She tried to drop the sword, but the handle encased her hand. "A misunderstanding?"

"Batu," Taivan said. "Help."

Batu's hands shook, but he stuffed the revolver in his belt—cringy gun safety—and pressed on Taivan's leg.

Should I write a thesis about why I don't want one of three people I know to die? Or would you prefer me to murder an injured man who trusted me?

Oh. He'd called her his anda when her father wouldn't claim her.

You trying to save the murderous object of your lust was not ideal.

It may not be the platonic Ideal of 'the good,' but it's about as good as I get. It hadn't mentioned Plato, and Khair never would have studied that. This nerd's knowledge was leaking into her brain.

Since he's the only person you've cared about—defining 'care' loosely—I'll temporarily dull your blood revulsion.

Dandy.

Khair used Jiao's discarded wire tourniquet around Taivan's calf. Cross contamination could wait, this bleeding wouldn't. She tied the tourniquet as tightly as the windlass allowed. Blood still oozed through. What was she doing wrong?

You'll have to cauterize it; get to the ship.

Taivan's cold hand squeezed her wrist, his eyes, wide and black, searching hers. He let her go.

When she stood, Batu stepped in front of her, so close she wiped his spit from her face when he spoke. "I'm going with you."

"We need a piece of metal heated to orange, red or white is too hot."

Batu motioned for her to march ahead and kept one hand on her shoulder. "You shouldn't have done that."

"Dunno. Had my reasons."

"He was your friend. Stop here." He pointed to an open doorway in the ship, humid heat emanating, condensation on the metal the first water she'd seen.

"It's too hot to touch." Otherwise, she'd lick it for the moisture.

Batu's pout softened to something resembling fondness, making his face more macabre. "Watch." He pulled his sleeves over his hands and tore off a bent strand of metal. "The cloth's like a big oven mitt."

When they returned to Taivan, he was having a slurred conversation with the stars, calling names and ranks, trying to save people who weren't there.

"Hold him down," Batu said.

Khair held his hand, unsure she had the right to do anything more.

"Anda?" He closed his eyes. "Good."

Help me contact the Khanate, their doctors—

Chip snorted.

I need someone!

The Andromeda Khanate is completely dissolved. Any remaining factions compete for resources and control. Chip spoke as if were only soldiers, but there'd be farmers, teachers, engineers, hospitable families.

"Okay, Batu," Khair said. "You have to—stop!"

"Don't worry, I've done this plenty of times." He held the brand to skin in second long bursts, not overlapping the scarring rows, not touching the sharp edge of bone or bothering the flap of skin on the side.

Taivan whimpered and writhed, tried to push Batu away, but she pinned him.

"How much longer?" Khair asked.

Batu moved to a different section. He held the metal there for three seconds, glowered at the instrument. "I have to heat it again."

"Hurry."

Without Batu, it was silent except for Taivan scratching the dirt and the simmering fire. But the world had a presence in the stillness; no wind, no tides, no motion, but an oppressive presence blanketed the vast tundra desert.

Or you're realizing how small you are. There was something that, with only slight distortion, could be mistaken for pity.

I'm a solid 1.78 meters.

Think about who you want to be before you throw yourself behind him again. Jochiin lies well. And it's natural to believe the people you depend on. But see how he's affected the world, look outside yourself—

We know truth not only by reason, but by the heart.

Khair quoted a philosopher Chip knew but hadn't referenced. She should've kept the evaporating distance between them as an extra knucklebone up her sleeve, but there was no point. She would never win.

If Chip felt any concern, none slipped through their connection.

'The heart is deceitful above all things. Who can know it?' Therefore, 'listen to advice and accept instruction, and you will be wise.' Or ignore me and I'll restart you until this experiment becomes feasible or we determine there's no fixing you.

Her jaw tightened till it hurt her teeth.

"Jiao?" Taivan's first conscious word. His voice yanked her from her head, but it was a moment till she could reply.

"She's fine. Besides needing a personality transplant."

Taivan let himself lose consciousness. She watched his chest's steady rhythm and ensured her own foggy breaths steamed out in a mostly constant rate.

If she were brave, she'd threaten Chip back; in this cold, she should be able to bear the electric burn. If she was only risking death or pain, she might. But she couldn't be erased again, realize who Batu was or who'd cut off Taivan's leg again.

Having a second chance sucked. One choice could ruin a life, but there was still a hope for what might have been. She would wreck a dozen lives.

Batu returned and finished sealing the wound. A fragile bind, but any more would burn the healthy tissue.

"Do you think we should keep watch, or rest?" Batu could barely keep his eyes open.

"You rest. I have something I have to do."

Batu shook his head. "I don't need a lot of sleep, and I don't want you awake alone."

"I could've cut off his head." And she'd be free. No, she would have only outlived her usefulness.

"That doesn't help. What do you need to do?"

Khair tapped her head. "Fight."

We're enemies now, but that's not my preference. Don't do anything stupid.

Chip's voice was an automated alto—probably a woman—with no decipherable age, no accent, but it pronounced words stiffly, probably through a translator. UOD wanted an untraceable spy, yet Chip indulged in inside jokes, even believed it was helping her, and disagreed with its masters. Chip and UOD were not the same.

Khair ventured from camp and walked along the cliff's edge by the reddish tint of the moons. She wouldn't get lost, not when the ship puffed like a chain-smoker.

Too late, this is necessary. And that's all we do—according to Spinoza, since you love quoting others without thinking for yourself.

I've referenced theories of thought, not cults of personality, and you couldn't refute them.

She wandered down the cliff, footing secure though the ledge thinned. There was nothing to grab if she slipped, but as her heart sped, her vision sharpened and the pressing cold retreated. Her bare legs and feet had numbed.

How could I dare? Chip's insides felt slippery with not quite guilt, but similar murkiness. Time to gamble. ***I thought you lot were supposed to love your enemies?***

Chip had quoted Christian texts, Khair quoted them back.

Chip said nothing. The silence wasn't colored by emotion or infringed by foreign thoughts. Khair had not expected it to work that well. If she ever became an evil overlord, she'd be sure to test future lackeys and screen out those with independent interests.

She studied the ledge as the sky darkened. The soil's chalky smell faded, and the dirt darkened, grain richer than on the surface. Khair rubbed it between her fingers, tasted it. Not a great texture, should've waited for real food.

Her arms swung, she ambled by the edge. The cliff went on forever, the ground so far down it was invisible, but she felt so unkillable she could hop off and float back.

Khair threw a rock and watched it tumble. These rocks differed from the porous sponge and shale slates up on the plateau, with a glistening edge that rubbed off on her hands: charcoal. Wasn't that wood somehow? A dusty rock, and here was evidence of life. She grinned. Things were greater than the sum of their parts.

Then she felt it. A storm of emotion and calculation swirled over everything, washing out any tracks Khair might decipher.

Fuck you. You sit in safety and torture me when I try to survive. You pathetic, boring spectator. Push me to murder, then act like your hands

are clean 'cause I'm the one blood-spattered. But I would have outlived my usefulness if I had assassinated him, right? Whatever I was, you're no better.

Might as well say it before she got rebooted into a sniveling fool.

Something revved, charged like the air before lightening, but she wasn't hurt. *Thank you for reminding me of my duty. However, given I'd consider killing you to be a mercy, you'll forgive me if I refrain.*

She kept walking like she could escape this conversation.

For the record, I would have freed you had you killed Jochiin. Jochiin's—

His name is Taivan. Maybe she should jump off this cliff. If she felt some of Chip's emotions, Chip might feel some of hers. No, not worth it.

Regardless. Not all my actions were necessary. You have one free question, as long as it's not classified.

You think I'll take a bribe to soothe your bruised conscience?

Say no then. Its attention wavered. Here was her entire life, and it was less interesting than what, a popcorn break?

What do you—not UOD—want with me?

Seriously? Not 'what was my family like,' or 'how can I apply for asylum on another planet,' or—

My family doesn't electrocute me.

"Khair! There's—" Batu's scream was silenced.

She couldn't see him on the plain, but sprinted up the hill. She'd run the other way, but there was nowhere to hide and she couldn't outrun whatever had reached them so quickly. Their best chance was making a stand together.

By the time she'd crested the hill, feet numb and bleeding, air stinging her face but muscles warm, Batu was gone. A smudge of dried, brown blood marked where Taivan had been. There had been no shots, no screams, no trace of them in the sky or on the horizon. They must have been overwhelmed instantly.

Find them. When it didn't respond, she added 'you know you owe me' then 'please.'

There were no treads; the sword and revolver were gone.

I can't see them.

There was nothing. Nothing but the burning ship and Jiao's untouched doctube, its facade dark except for the low battery warning and two loading smiley faces.

The Heroic Art of Groundless Hope

YOU COULD'VE WARNED ME. *Who was it?*

Ask your admiral.

Khair paced before the clicking maroon doctube, exposed feet so frozen her weight should shatter them. The ripped paper gown didn't hold warmth and when she pulled it tighter, the tear broadened, now barely clinging to her shoulders. She did pushups to warm up, though it only made her sweat.

She could leave Jiao. No, they'd need a pilot, eventually.

To answer your earlier question—

No, sit there and feel bad.

Jiao was in no fighting condition. She wasn't a threat. Khair just didn't want to deal with someone who hated her, though that was 98% of her options.

She poked around the doctube, only muttered "I'm too old for this" once, and kicked it twice before it opened.

Taivan and Jiao snuggled inside.

"That's cozy," Khair said. Except Jiao's leg looked like a raw steak, and Taivan's calf ended in a burned roast. Okay, she was hungry.

Taivan sat up and wrapped his arms around Jiao, shielding her from the wind while his fingers grayed. Jiao leaned against him.

"What happened? 'There was no horse left for Batu?'" The euphemism used when a young Temujin fled a raid, leaving his wife to be kidnapped.

Taivan worked a muscle in his jaw. "I can save him. He can't save me."

"Who was it?" Khair said. "And why didn't they check the 'tube?"

"It's against intergalactic law to meddle with one." Jiao piled healing goop on her leg, the limb convulsing every time the wind blew off the medicine.

"So, it's against intergalactic law for you to hide there," Khair said.

"And?" Taivan said.

"They could have stood outside and waited for us to get out," Jiao said. "They may have taken Batu as bait."

"Yeah, yeah." Khair circled the tube. "You tried to sacrifice him already, and it didn't take, so here's round two."

"That's not what I said. We have to acknowledge our limitations." Jiao held Taivan's hands, shaking like a volcano about to erupt.

Wait, were there volcanoes here? Didn't appear to be, which was a shame because ash was good for the soil, steam provided water, and raining lava could kill them before they froze.

"We won't be able to help him until we've found water, food, fuel, and warmer clothes," Jiao said.

"There's nothing here," Khair said. "No resources, no advantage in the terrain, no volcanoes, and some idiot crashed our ship."

"The planet isn't terraformed, but there are people here," Jiao said. "The resources are there."

Khair gestured at the blank wilderness. "You're a sneeze from shock, but go ahead, Princess."

Jiao stiffened before shoveling more gunk on her leg. Huh. Maybe she had grown up poor enough to fantasize about selling a kidney, or been aristocracy in a failed state.

"You should rest," Taivan said to Jiao. "The tube hasn't been charging, it won't last. If Batu was grabbed by who I think, he's with my allies. He'll be fine."

Allies he wouldn't trust with his life.

"Let me make you a prosthetic first," Jiao said.

He squeezed her hand. "You don't have any tools and I need you at your best. Rest."

"Don't worry," Khair patted Taivan's shoulder as he climbed out. "I'll give him a piggyback ride if things get rough."

Jiao's face remained impassive, but her knuckles whitened. "You're not as valuable as you think you are."

"Night night." Khair tried to close the tube, but hit the wrong buttons before Jiao hit her hand away and did it herself. "The killjoy's gone. What now?"

"Be kinder to her."

So, he was stalling. "I know you're a would-be-conqueror with two followers and one leg, but I assure you, you can do better."

He smirked and looked down, blinked, expression neutral when he looked up. "You're supposed to be our diplomat."

"I'll grovel to the powers-that-be later, but she ain't one of them. Have a plan yet?"

"We'll use the doctube's life-finding mode and push it towards whatever's closest to conserve energy."

That barely qualified as an idea, much less a plan, but she didn't have a better one. Taivan flicked a lever on the doctube's side. It glowed yellow and rose until it hovered at her waist.

"That's gotta use energy," Khair said.

"It's a thousand kilograms in standard gravity, and we have kilometers to go." Taivan leaned against it, compensating for his right leg that ended five centimeters below his knee.

She pushed it, telling herself she went slow to make sure Taivan didn't trip. But her breathing deepened. When the 'tube hovered past rocks, it slowed, then jolted forward as if it actually rolled over them, and it seemed heavier on the hills.

She pushed it a hundred meters, another hundred. There was nothing ahead, no proof of progress. Her chest ached with shallow breaths, her bare feet slowed to a shuffle, and Taivan stooped over the 'tube, adding his weight.

The gritty night air took so long to reach her lungs it seemed to lose its way. Still no signs of water or clouds, the arid sky as thirsty as the tundra below.

"I hope you can plan a galaxy better than a rescue." She tried to hide her panting.

"Planning is easy. None of it matters until it's carried out." He snorted. "Though the plans have to change now that I can't walk right."

She blushed, told herself to leave him be, but couldn't stand the quiet. "At least you've got the fuzzy politician answer down."

"I won't explain my life's work while I scurry around looking for half my retainers. What's left of them, anyway."

That ship should have had more people, hundreds more. Better to distract him. "Less to worry about if we faint, right?"

The veins in the arm he leaned against stood out. "Save your breath."

For what?

The doctube slipped free as it rolled down a bump. Taivan tried to catch it, put his nonexistent foot down and fell, howling as his wound opened. The doctube kept rolling. She let it, less work for her, and it stopped fifty meters away.

Taivan's leg oozed dark sludge, the burned wound coagulating. He stayed face down, frozen except for the deep drawl of his breath.

She shook him, the fibrous muscle of his shoulder hard and cool as the terracotta army. "Anda? Boss—"

He held his hand up.

He screamed—there was no anguish in it, it was a war cry—and tried to stand. His shaking leg refused to move. Taivan punched the ground, cracking a jagged rock and opening a gash on his knuckles.

And he wept. He hid his face but his shoulders shook and there was no muffling the sound.

"Uh…" Khair tried to rub his back, but he hit her hand away, though at least that dampened his cries. She crouched beside him, ground too cold to sit. "Am I supposed to give you a moment? I would. But there's nowhere to go."

You got a joke?

Chip's embarrassment churned Khair's stomach, her only previous image of him a gray, flat wanted poster nothing like the moving, three-dimensional being. *Leave him alone.*

I can't leave him.

He was so young, not halfway through his twenties. So foolish, believing he could change this ever-expanding universe. Everyone depended on him, and without allies, weapons, tech, all he had was strength and the appearance of it. And he'd lost it.

He didn't lose it. You did this. Which, strangely enough, is one of the better things you've done, though your motivation was severely lacking.

"Taivan?" She barely heard her voice. "We'll get Batu. Jiao will recover. And between us, these suckers will line up to kiss your feet—foot—actually gross. But this isn't over."

Taivan cried for a minute more and lay inert. She poked him to make sure he wasn't dead, and he flicked her hand away. Finally, he cleaned his face, frost on his eyebrows.

"Obviously, that never happened." His voice was deep and raw, his eyes swollen.

"Obviously."

"I have to sit on this 'tube. If you need a break, tell me."

She'd never ask. "Jiao does seem a little heavy. Let's lighten the load."

He rolled his eyes, but his bleached skin regained color. "It'll only get colder in the morning when the winds start, trade Jiao's pilot suit for that hospital gown."

Or he wanted to see Jiao, someone he cared for. Even if when he held her, it hadn't been close enough to qualify as cuddling. "Hm. Chivalry is dead; I love this time. Let's wake your girlfriend and steal her clothes."

"We're not together."

Khair opened the doctube, hiding a dorky smile. Jiao sprung up, grabbed for her missing pistol, bit back a cry, and leaned on her good leg. Her burns were already healed. Which was obvious, since her pants were now cut-offs.

"Easy, JJ," Khair said. "There's no one to kill yet."

Jiao huffed and stiffened when she saw Taivan, who made a grimace seem a genuine smile. "If there's still juice in the 'tube, it's your turn."

"You need it more. Can you lend Khair your suit? We'll be walking for a while."

Jiao blinked. "Turn around."

Taivan did as he was bid.

Jiao nodded to her.

"Really? Taivan's prettier." Khair looked away, untied the hospital gown and extended it behind her back. Cold seeped into her bare skin. "You just like being bossy."

Jiao handed her the suit and climbed back into the 'tube, the tattered gown tied with a neat bow. "Don't wake me unless there's something important."

"Not for minor things like hypothermia."

"You are allowed to say one thing that's not sarcastic." Jiao shut the 'tube before Khair could reply with something sufficiently snarky.

Khair contorted into the too-small suit, but within a few minutes it fit perfectly. It didn't warm her, yet somehow her exposed face, hands, and legs to mid-thigh were colder by comparison.

On her right sleeve was a wrist-controller that displayed her temperature—35.3 C and dropping—blood pressure, pulse oxygen—92%—and a dozen other factors. Including a projected life expectancy of 127 minutes.

There were "Stories" and "Games" tabs. Apparently, Jiao liked horror, tragedies, and engineering games. The latter sounded scariest.

"Don't touch that," Taivan said.

Khair pointed the wrist-con at the doctube. "Why, is there a weapon?"

"It's not yours. And it was an order."

She raised an eyebrow. "And where am I in this chain of command? Because until I get a paycheck, I'm freelance. In the meantime, you get to explain your reasoning. The horror."

"It is exhausting to question everything."

Khair flinched as Chip stiffened, grudgingly agreeing. "I'm sure your conquered people will be much more amenable."

A ghost of a grin crossed his face and vanished again. "That's why I'll have seven layers of bureaucracy insulating me from the public."

"Any chance this comes with a map or snacks?" She poked buttons that seemed important.

An obscenely high-definition image of younger her and Jiao standing back-to-back on a ship's deck, enemies surrounding them, blazed from her wrist.

The Crime

If you watch that, I have to kill you. "Have to" not "will," but Khair couldn't care about whatever constraints Chip was under, not when she could see her past self as clearly as if she stood before a mirror.

Khair stared with her mouth half open as if watching the ocean march out, wave on giant wave, as a tsunami formed. She didn't spit out the dirt blown into her mouth, just blinked, mesmerized by every pixel.

A younger but still ancient Batu was there, face scarred, fighting alongside a dozen equally decrepit warriors. Probably dead.

Taivan was resplendent in a silk scarf, with a warrior's thumb ring, and a jade crown. His weapon was a black flag with a silver wolf and red deer, the pole a spearhead, the same animals stenciled on his body armor. Ham-fisted, to wear and fly his nation's mythological origin. But even years later, some of the pressure in her head relented.

He'd stood a meter from her, looked to her, expecting her help. Truly been her anda.

Jiao held a short-barreled semiautomatic ZAX rifle, and hid behind a wall as Khair covered her from the corridor, completely vulnerable.

"It was the day the Conqueror died." Present-day Taivan said softly, stepping closer to her.

Their enemy was there. In a mixture of armor and weapons, half a dozen different uniforms, various armies gathered and funded by United Oversight for Democracy. Chip's goons.

"After he died," Taivan said. "You could've gathered an army, but you pledged to me, and I pledged to you. I offered you a planet, but you refused."

Tell him that's enough.

Khair barely recognized herself. Dressed to die in a sleeveless hoodie and baggy trousers. She wore two pistols but held the axe from the "in case of emergency" glass and wore a demon mask—not festival quality papier-mâché art, a toy pumping fake blood.

Her hair was thrown into a haphazard ponytail, her sleeve tattoos a mosaic of drunken mistakes. She'd been taller, buffer, a little fatter back then. Though her face was obscured, there was no fear in her stance.

"I was crazy." It was the most respectful thing she'd ever said.

Taivan nodded.

She exhaled softly. Was that her? Did she want it to be? Whoever else that person was, she'd been sure of her purpose.

The thin air chiseled a crater in her chest. "Turn it off before Chip kills me."

Taivan double tapped the wrist-con, and the image vanished.

Here's my question. You and UOD could've executed me. Why was I worth saving? She said it too quickly, a kid begging for a treat, but her face was too windblown for her blush to show.

It hesitated. *Assuming it doesn't endanger the victims, everyone is worth saving.*

Bull. I didn't ask about anyone else.

You were available, notorious, and more suggestible than Jochiin.

I was weak. And you took advantage.

"I didn't look worse than you," Khair said to Taivan. Sure, her mask was tacky, but was that worse than trying to seize the galaxy?

"I wasn't keeping score." His voice was light, words clipped, making sure he said nothing that got her electrocuted.

"No, you let our enemies do that."

"You'd wronged me, needed the anda oath to feel safe." He steadied himself and held out his hand to her. "But there's no more debt between us."

Shouldn't there be more? He thought he found her selling point: his friendship. Gallingly, he may be right. His hand waited, strong, with healing callouses.

But she didn't take it.

He kept his hand extended. "Coloma City's a few hundred kilometers away. I'll send you the coordinates if you think you can make it. But I hope you stay."

It's your duty to stay, to mollify him before he destroys this world.

How can I have a duty to a world that's done nothing for me? Her world was Chip, Taivan, Jiao, and they were up for 1st, 2nd, and 3rd place in 'Khair's Least Favorite People' contest.

The people here only deserve to live if they serve you?

She snorted. Taivan's eyes narrowed, and he lowered his hand.

Hate Taivan, but you people are no different, remaking the universe in your image, except he's brave enough to do it openly.

Taivan sent her Coloma's location with a muted ping, a 3D overview of a sprawling city, everything foreign but the guns on the walls. No water between them, no transport stations or inns or restaurants. There were camps but they moved, nomads she'd never catch.

Your duty depends on what the world needs, not what it offers you. He doesn't understand that.

"The chances of you reaching Coloma are negligible," Taivan said.

There it was, the choice that wasn't a choice. Manipulative witch. But he'd meant something to her once and a vestige of it remained in her brain chemistry, stronger than any bioengineering feat. "Start walking."

He nodded without deference. "I need a ride or I'll get worse."

"Fine."

He sat on the doctube and she pushed him along.

You've never defended UOD.

'Never?' Your memory isn't good enough for that claim.

Her feet left blood droplets on the ground, barely visible. The frost—too full of limestone to drink—drew lines in her soles, and pebbles stuck in the softened ridges, grating with every step. Strips of moist, paled skin shed from her toes, leaving an exposed, embarrassed red.

You expected me to help people.

Calluses crusted the top of her palm. Her purplish, swollen fingers stuck to the doctube's handle, permanently bent as if her brain signals froze on the way down.

I read the map and gave you moral reasons as well as pragmatic ones.

The breeze awoke with the sun. The barely illuminated rocky pillars formed crouching chimeras in the gloom and sent the skittish wind running, tumbling into hidden crevices and swirling over hills. It beat her, the respite between strikes as fearsome as the blow. The suit that held back the night's languid cold failed against this renewed assault.

I could save your life and it wouldn't be enough; you have to make me a monster to justify this.

No response.

On the doctube, Taivan pulled his limbs into his suit and tied off the ends to keep in warmth. Her suit made her give up what little sweat she had, dabs caked at her wrists and drizzled down her legs.

I wish we didn't do this.

The words lifted a burden from Chip's spine, but it was an incomplete revelation and within a breath that weight tumbled down again. Chip paced along the precipice of despair, Khair's mind strapped to it.

Khair kept walking, legs working automatically, but her mind stalled, thrashed, a deer stranded in a tar pit. As hope dimmed, Chip embraced disappointment with a consoling familiarity and stepped back from the ledge.

Whoever you're punishing died. You're spitting on a corpse.

Her ears and nose had stopped stinging long ago and feeling leeched from her cheeks. That last throb of pain fought to keep its dominion, a chill dug into her skull and nested there. It burned as a film of frost stretched across her face.

You did nothing.

Khair slowed.

While Chuluun, the supposed conqueror, exterminated and enslaved peoples, mutilated the genome, hid IEDs in toys, you did nothing.

Her stomach tried to liquify itself. *Unless I'm greatly mistaken, my name's not Chuluun.*

He had a council of seventeen generals. You were the only one who didn't sign a petition suggesting more effective methods of war.

She laughed as warm relief flooded. The sudden movement cracked the iceberg floating on her face and sent avalanches of pain down to her teeth. *One missing signature and everything's my fault?*

It wasn't the only attempted reform, just the last. Everyone involved, excluding blood relatives like Taivan, were catapulted into space.

We were having an affair?

Not if you were older than fourteen.

She couldn't push the doctube anymore.

I shouldn't mask it with words like 'genocide'. Shang Mei, twenty-six years old, nursing home attendant and petty drug dealer to care for her young son, Ling, and infant daughter, Yuxi. After you won the battle on their street, her children were killed in front of her and she was sold, fate unknown. Kang Chao—

I'll die before you finish that list.

There were alleviating factors. Other things to deal with after battle, security, supplies, friendly casualties, interrogations. Maybe the petition has a hidden clause that would make things worse, like eradicating puppies or worshipping slow computers.

Except there was nothing worse.

No, screw that. She wasn't a bad person, could be free if she'd killed Taivan, but she hadn't. It was war.

War? Chip's stuttering anger burned Khair's stomach. *Fight soldiers instead of civilians, I promise you, it's harder.*

She couldn't free her hands from the doctube's handle or pry her feet from the ground. She leaned against the 'tube, driving it a meter, but still her legs didn't move, so she only rolled herself out until her knees hit the ground.

Too bad you can only die once. There was no mockery, no hatred, merely a hunter calculating how much to winnow the herd before winter. *Real justice would have you die 84,981,126 times, feel the deaths of 84,981,126 loved ones. Restore those lives that are gone.*

Maybe Chuluun had done good, too. There was always upheaval with change, maybe it'd been society's growing pains before it metamorphosed to something worth the strain.

No.

Her mind fogged, synopses firing into a nebulous void, illegible in this storm. Air didn't reach her lungs. It stung in her mouth, wheezed through her nose, but she couldn't get enough. Her pants drew in less air with each hiss, expelled it quicker. She tried to stop struggling and let it end but her body refused, heaving, clawing, inhaling diluted oxygen and greedy for more.

Turn me off. Or take control, just please be decent with me.

You found out you have no moral backbone, so you give up all agency to a stranger?

Great Blue, she couldn't even surrender correctly.

"Khair?" Taivan slid off the 'tube to stand.

She shook her head.

The sun glittered as an unblemished sapphire, so worthless she could look at it without squinting. Being catapulted out there would've been a good end. To march to a death she chose, with friends, to escape this labyrinth below even if only on melted wings.

"Why didn't I sign it?"

Taivan blinked. "You were in the field."

"And no one else was? I fled. It—I looked brave on that screen, but... why did you put me in command? I was obviously a liability, you—"

She jerked. Her palms blackened where she held the 'tube, and orange tresses scarred her feet where electricity escaped.

It was you. You could've walked away at any time, or fought for the defenders.

Taivan shook her, tore her hands from the 'tube.

She pushed him away. "You'll get shocked."

He grabbed her with his other hand, held her so tightly she half expected him to smother her. When he didn't, she embraced him, her head against his chest. "You won't be like him, will you?"

His heart beat faster beneath her ear. "I hope not."

Skull Breaker

KHAIR WOKE IN THE same spot she'd been shocked in, the grounded doctube beside her shielding her from the sandpapery winds. Taivan slept with his arm draped over her, her head against the thick synthetic wool on his chest. The cold demanded it, but she didn't mind.

Her fingers were reduced to bags of pus with brittle, yellowing nails, and her purple toes darkened as if dabbed in soot as mothers did to convince spirits their baby was an animal not worth haunting.

An animal would've been put out of its misery by now.

Frost hung on Taivan's eyebrows and long lashes. His cheeks were purple, green, every color a person wasn't supposed to be. The tip of his nose and the center of his chapped lips were black.

He gave off so little warmth, she'd think he was dead, except he covered her hands with his own. His breath hitched, eyes fluttered open. When he saw her, his breath stopped and his eyes teemed with disgust. Even when he recognized her underneath the mess that was her face, a hint of revulsion remained.

Was it for her past self, or this castrated version?

Taivan groaned when he scanned their surroundings. The doctube's panel was blank. Their ship burned beyond the planet's curve, smoke still visible, but they'd never reach it. The unmoved rocks gave no reprieve.

He tried to push himself up, but the effort spun his eyes back. He tried for a minute more but never opened his eyes, and she didn't trouble him, idly murmuring for him to rest.

Why walk on and leave bits of their feet behind when they could fade into the night? She burrowed against him.

We've all been half in love with easeful death, but the people who took Batu are coming for you. You have to move.

Khair did not move.

Get up.

Her suit overworked itself; she was hot. With this tech, what'd she been worried about? She'd be fine, rest and heal by the time she woke.

I can't help you if you lie there.

Fine by her. Even if she laid flopped like a pancake flipped too soon, she felt better than she had since the crash. But Taivan, well enough to stop shivering, hoarsely protested his nightmares.

She shook him. He only continued his mutterings. Khair dragged him to the doctube and dumped him inside, but chunks of slushied gel splashed out. She tried to pull him out, couldn't. She yanked out a lighter Jiao to help with Taivan, but Jiao lay strewn on the dirt, unconscious.

A sensor on her suit must've turned on a sauna function—if that sauna was located in the core of a sun, and the sun was exploding. And this stupidly cut suit made the cold worse. She couldn't get accustomed to it with her extremities exposed. She tried to take it off, but her swollen fingers couldn't free her.

Keep the suit on.

No, Chip sat at a desk monitoring the thermometer, without even a window to see what the world was like. Khair checked to make sure a second sun hadn't crested the horizon.

I may not be experiencing the same thing, but that doesn't mean I don't understand. Chip spoke slowly, enunciating each word. *If you're undressing, you're nearing the terminal stages of hypothermia. Wake the others. You'll have to flag down the kidnappers and bargain for medical attention.*

Blah blah, she had to get off this suit. But it wouldn't budge. She screamed and kicked whatever was closest—Jiao, though she didn't stir—losing a chunk of her toe. The wan, spectral flesh stuck to Jiao's hospital gown.

Khair vomited hot, stinging bile as pain surged through the missing flesh and blinked out within a nanosecond.

How much time do I have?

She couldn't wake Taivan or Jiao. No reason for them to count their mottled, flaky extremities as they shriveled off.

The locals will be here within two minutes.

Not what I meant.

This ugly world wasn't as drab as she'd first thought now that she wasn't factoring in pesky things like survival. Nothing so regal as the stark rings of Saturn, or the intricate pattern and swirling storms of Jupiter, or the nostalgia of an idyllic Earth that was never truly tamed. But this new world, its rock formations of arches and spires, orphaned cliffs and granite umbrellas all sparkling with frost... they might've had a life here.

Jiao squirmed, blinked with dilated eyes, scraped green starch from her face.

"It's a dream, kiddo, sleep," Khair said.

Jiao snuggled closer and relaxed, her soft breathing slowed to a hibernating rabbit on life support.

You have no right.

It's a kindness now. It wouldn't even the scales, but that didn't matter. The snobby pilot and scheming prince would lie with her for eternity. She might as well get comfortable.

Dying lucid would be kinder. Living kinder still. Tell her the truth; she might live if she makes peace with the locals.

Khair wrapped an arm around Jiao's, her arms bare since she'd given up her clothes. "Actually, you're about to die. What a shame I'm being nice now."

"Shhh." Jiao pulled Khair's arm farther, the joint protesting. Khair winced and tapped her side, but Jiao seemed to think she was a blanket, so she wiggled free and repositioned herself.

It was still better.

Whatever.

She wasn't quitting. There was nothing to do. No fuel for fire, the doctube was dead, she didn't have the strength to move. No brave, villainous last stand. Don't glance at Taivan or listen to Jiao breathe, just focus on the sky's dancing lights.

Machine hums pulsed from the horizon, the pulse shortening as it approached. Psychological warfare, nothing more than making an arrow whistle, or making pyramids from the skulls of people beyond that indignity.

Joke's on them. She didn't care anymore.

The pulses became a screech.

A person popped from a craft that appeared as the door opened, then disappeared again. "Your friend's healing." By his voice, it was a man around the age he may still be a boy.

A green and gold mask and a fluffy hat concealed his face; nothing showed but tufts of red hair and weary blue eyes. The costume was padded pleat so thick it doubled as armor.

"Nifty equipment for healing," Khair said without moving.

He had a fan shaped axe on his back, a saber on his hip, and an automatic rifle so primitive she didn't know the model slung over his shoulder.

"You can play dumb and die or come with me and live. I have beef hash and brisket waiting and I'll enjoy them either way."

"Vodka?" She'd haggle down to hot chocolate.

"I'd give your comrades a few minutes before the damage is irreversible."

She offered her hand to the man so he could pull her up, but he ignored the dying limb. "Why're you helping us?"

"Gives me an excuse to get outside, and now you owe the queen a 'life debt.'" He made quotation marks with his mittens. "Slavery, really."

Hey, I'm not the only baddie here, help me out.

"But no worries, Khair." He said her name like it meant he knew her. "I've seen three scenarios in which you survive the week. Though there's six you die, usually because you try to fight and I break your skull against the doctube."

Potential Skull Breaker was healthy and armed, while Chip wouldn't let her punch air. Even if he tripped and impaled himself, she'd still freeze.

She raised her hands. "Let's skip that one, Skull Breaker."

The Necromancer

SKULL BREAKER LET HER board his cloaked ship without searching her for weapons or tying her. Jiao revolved through states of consciousness and Taivan, with a body fat percentage of approximately zero, was down for the count and left in the doctube.

Breaker lay his weapons in the cockpit and turned the small busing ship's temperature down so her frozen skin didn't thaw. A medical consideration or to keep her weak? If Chip knew, she wasn't speaking.

Breaker gave her warm liquid in an IV bag, insulated so she couldn't warm her hands. "Drink slowly. And anything you dirty, you'll clean."

He entered the cockpit and locked the door between them. The passenger section had no windows, a dozen seats without cushions faced each other, a low ceiling forced her to sit. There was a door beside the cockpit, loose and squeaking. Breaker yelled at her to sit when she checked it.

This wasn't an expensive ship. He must not be important, probably wasn't loyal to whoever had sent him.

"You're the expert and all," Khair said. "But slaves with their valuable extremities sound better than poor stumpy ones."

She'd end up chained to some sucker her soldiers had sold.

"Not while they're alive."

Khair couldn't tell if he was kidding.

She squeezed liquid on her finger and sniffed it. Bleach smelled more appetizing. But she drank it, weak alcohol that couldn't decide if it wanted to be minty or lemony. It burned through her throat and stomach, so she guzzled it.

Now her head was floaty. A placebo? Drinks didn't drunkify people that fast, unless he drugged it.

"It's called a 'life debt', right?" She yelled to make sure he heard. "So how much is a life worth? Because saying Batu's life is worth as much as mine is crazy."

His snort carried through the intercom. "He does seem worth at least three of you."

"What? Nooooo." The minty thing was great. She licked it off her fingers. "Do Taivan and Jiao have life debts?"

"If we save your life, you owe it. As in, even though I save you and the state of Albion scolds me for wasting fuel, they claim your labor."

The ship skimmed over the land, moving so smoothly Khair couldn't gauge their speed until they zipped past a bump. Too fast to jump out. There was little to ground her, no windows, walls empty except for scraps of glossy paper where posters had hung. The ship had no smell but their unwashed, smokey hair and skin, silent except for a gargled comm system.

"If we're worthless, drop us off somewhere. Like the tropics. Or a restaurant."

"If paradise was around the corner, we wouldn't live here."

Why did they live here? Sure, there weren't many planets in habitable zones, but life in space was an option. "Do you have a life debt?"

"Worse. I have family."

"And—" The craft spun, pinning her against the wall. It slowed to a gracious stop once she'd been silenced.

He opened the door between them. "I'll send Taivan in the 'tube and carry Jiao." She cared about them, she really did, or would've, if that drink wasn't weighing down her bladder.

"I'll guide you to the rope. Follow it inside. Move quickly." He checked the IV bag and rubbed his temple. "If you can walk straight."

"Who're you?"

"Aidan, with lots of titles." He opened the squeaky door and threw a long coat at her. "There are foot wraps if you can fold them over your feet."

"Small feet?"

He glanced to her feet, which had almost doubled in size. "Compared to a yeti."

She grumbled incoherently as she flung the yarn corners over her foot, leaving large gaps exposed.

Aidan wrestled the door open against the wind. Before her lay a weathered rock staircase hewn in the mountain, with ropes tied to the top and fastened to poles on the way down. Desiccated corpses littered the stairs. The cold rushed back and her blood slowed to drivel. On top of the staircase was an unadorned entrance with only light to beckon her.

She wanted to refuse, but could only shake her head.

He gripped her wrist and jumped out. "If you die, you won't hear open mic tonight at Grace's Pub. Everyone loves democratization until you're listening to a drunk howl, thinking she's Jihan Shafik reborn."

"Maybe I should stay on the ship and use a bathroom."

"Go on the ground. Holding it will make you colder."

She gestured to the skintight suit she was wearing, and he shrugged. "Guess you'll miss open mic."

Khair stepped out, that first step across the threshold, stealing her breath. She couldn't loosen her suit. Aidan untied the knot at her neck, then turned her around to face the wind.

"If you don't know how, figure it out."

She wobbled as she squatted and struggled to stand again. Her piss froze instantly. She didn't feel warmer.

Aidan flipped through music on his wrist-con. She tapped his shoulder. He kept scrolling but she poking his arm until he grabbed her hand without looking, twisted painfully, and tied the knot on her suit without looking, making it close automatically.

How come he was that fast? She must be drunk or dying.

"Stay close." Aidan dumped a rope in her hand and strode on ahead, Jiao over his shoulder.

The mountain was steep. Its stairs were irregularly spaced and caked with ice, its waterlogged rope frozen. One foot-wrap ripped open, and the other untied in her slow haste. Within a minute, Aidan was three flights ahead.

Her legs shook, but she kept moving, using brightly coated corpses as markers.

"Didn't have to leave 'em here," Khair said. "Probably had people they loved, probably, and gloves!"

She pulled on a corpse's mittens, but they were frozen to the hand, and its wrist broke off. She cradled it to her chest to hide it, but then it looked like she had three hands, so she threw it, waving goodbye as it bounded down.

"Sorry."

She counted stairs but stopped after three. Tried to take two at a time, but fell, cut her toe, the corner of the unraveling foot wrap a sieve of blood. Her arms dragged her up two more craggy steps before they quit.

Aidan waited on one knee, still holding Jiao up from the frozen ground. "You're five steps away. Get up."

Khair aimed her thoughts at Chip, waiting for taunts to spur her, but the one time she wanted that loser's company, it was gone.

Aidan disappeared into the mountain.

She swallowed. Well, she didn't want to wring herself out to spend a few years chained in an icebox anyway, and she'd emptied her bladder so her corpse wouldn't reek. But she couldn't convince her pattering, rebellious heart to rest.

She relaxed against lumpy stone, gazed at the world below. It looked still and safe: there were no crackling storms, no rampaging beasts, just a tranquil icy sea. Yet it'd bested her. Batu, Taivan, and Jiao too, though they got to live.

Hopefully, they'd collect her body. Burial didn't matter, but she wanted someone to care.

Aidan hauled her to her feet. She couldn't contribute anything more than to direct her fall, so she landed across his shoulders. He staggered under her weight but reached the summit.

"There's a time for weight lifting and a time for cardio. You should try the latter."

"Cardio smardio. If you lifted weights more, there wouldn't be a problem."

A tad ungrateful, but he was kidnapping her.

He let her down inside the shelter and pulled a lever so a rock fell to lock them in. The sudden warmth almost put her to sleep.

She sat in a large cave with dim lights, a rack of bathrobes, wool socks, a corner stuffed with crude medicine. Taivan's doctube hovered, charging beside a sealed door. Jiao lay unconscious beside one of three metal panels raised from the dirt floor. The walls and ceiling were rock graffitied with desert scenes and hastily censured pubescent classics. Her ribs ached as she laughed.

Aidan signaled to a camera high in the corners, an automatic rifle tacked beneath. One panel slid back, revealing a pool as large as a bed with steam wafting off it.

In space and her old country, water was precious, practically sacred. Given the scarcity, it should be here too. The steam was collected, but the pools smelled defiled with herbs and salts, which didn't dampen out that fine abandoned morgue aroma.

Nurses rolled Taivan's doctube out through the door. She couldn't see what was beyond the door from her angle, and no sound crept through.

Aidan checked Jiao's vitals, carelessly putting two fingers on her neck, tilting her head to check her ears before laying a ventilator mask over her head. He ripped off her hospital gown.

Khair stumbled toward him, fists balling. But he looked at Jiao like an antique sports-car, padded her dry with a towel and draped it over her, then wrapped her hands and feet. He hooked her into a blood warming system. Khair swallowed and shifted away from the countless needles.

"She'll live." Aidan loosened his own damp suit. Beneath his mask, his face was young and pallid, with frizzy red hair and a trimmed beard. "She gave you that suit. It doesn't fit you. Why?"

"So I'd survive to push her doctube somewhere safe." Khair couldn't remove the suit, so she rolled up the sleeves.

He undressed beside his weapons, ignoring her unhidden appraisal. He was too lean for it to be entirely by choice, his chest scarred with ritual cuts, limbs long so he had a reach advantage. Not exactly good looking, features severe, pimples on his forehead, but his trimmed beard and toned legs weren't unappealing.

He eased into a pool. "Throw me Jiao's wrist-con."

She did. Aidan guessed her code and searched her music, settling on classical piano in the minor key. He aimed it toward Jiao.

Khair stepped into his pool, still in her suit. She sucked in her breath. The water reached her chin and brought back feeling, reminded her of her forgotten bruises. Her frozen skin burned. As soon as she could, she peeled off the suit and lay against the wall, weightless, inhaling hot steam.

"There's medicine in the water, but it takes time," Aidan said.

She grit her teeth and forced her head underwater, holding her breath as long as she could.

Aidan sighed and washed his face, heedless of splashed water. "I'm getting a doctor. Don't hurt Jiao, it won't increase your value."

He dressed and left.

She should look for an escape. But she'd have a better chance when she was healthy, so she stretched her legs and paced the pool, then doggy paddled to test her arms. When Aidan still hadn't returned, she learned to swim and lapped around until there was a whirlpool.

She was bobbing in the current when he returned in uniform: a black vest with polished buttons, a white shirt with rolled sleeves, a black beret, and a green kilt. She would laugh, but he carried his crescent axe.

A girl was with him. She was never-seen-the-sun pale, red-haired and blue-eyed like Aidan, but plump, hair abandoned to its curls, a dozen piercings in her ears.

"You're young for a doctor," Khair said. If this kid was twenty, she'd dance naked outside.

"Impressive, huh?" She wasn't wearing gloves or doctor's gown, sporting a plunging floral dress and practical shoes.

"If you're good."

The kid winked. "Good enough for you. Get dressed. Aidan will take care of Jun."

The trek between the pool steps and the towel rack seemed a marathon, and she got dizzy picking up a fluffy bathrobe. The doc led her out the door, waving her along as if the new world below the stairs wasn't a big deal.

It was.

Half a dozen trains cut through the cavern below, the tracks surrounded by grass, though the rest of the city was stone and brick. Plastic balls of lights hovered and gravitated toward clusters of people. Crowds wandered through shops dressed in short skirts and sleeveless shirts and sandals despite the wind squeezing through the walls. It smelled of chocolate and whiskey, tobacco in hookahs and honeyed perfumes much too strong.

"Where's the slave block?" She tried to say it as a joke, but she didn't step any closer to the city.

The doc sighed. "He told you?"

Children ran through the street, hitting each other with hockey sticks and tossing a crying girl's garishly colored doll. They were sensibly dressed in sweaters and shawls and felt boots, some in knitted veils, some in kilts and leggings. Though the adults looked like they were on rations, the kids had full faces.

"How were you gonna keep that a secret?"

Craftsman worked in open shops on green marble and blue porcelain cutlery, wooden sculptures so smooth they seemed metal, bronze lanterns with neon glowing latticework. The shops and houses were one connected red rock, distinguished by their bright doors.

The girl shrugged. "I'm just the doc, and occasional necromancer."

Without explanation, the doc offered her a wheelchair from a closet. Khair accepted, and it moved by itself.

She rolled past pubs and coffeehouses, women inside watching jets race or arguing over politics. On the street corners, anyone with an instrument joined their neighbors, bagpipe or synthesizer playing beside a stick and box drum.

No one with a collar, no one in chains. Armed soldiers roamed, but they stopped traffic for children to cross the road.

The men outside the pub bowed their head as they passed. Maybe they wanted an excuse not to look at her thawing face, but that was an odd consideration toward a slave.

"Not a bad view, eh?" The doc said. "Whiskey, cinema, baklava, old women with stories, young men in uniform, it's a good life."

She slowed to stare up at mosques and museums, colleges and cathedrals. How old was this civilization?

An unleashed beast snapped at her.

Khair threw herself back so hard she would've tumbled out of the chair if the doc hadn't caught her. "What's that?"

There were canine influences in it, but it wasn't all dog, its back sloped and lighter on its feet.

"The latest failure in animal husbandry. But they're cute and make good pets, so people keep making them."

It knocked its head against her wheelchair and nuzzled her leg before the doc shoved it away with both arms, and only then since the not-dog allowed it.

How could she escape this?

"Guess I wouldn't be allowed to ride one?"

The doc grinned. "Why not? We have bigger beasts."

If she'd stepped back in time, it would be less of a shock. None of the cultural influences were familiar, and it was its own thing too, doctors extracting medicine from poison glands of glowing octopi-spider, engineers competing to recycle alien waste onstage, people loaning their skills and stories out at libraries.

She stiffened at an open-air jail in an eerily empty square.

The doc took her to an isolated room in a quiet, guarded wing of the neighborhood. There was nothing inside but a locked cabinet and a reclined couch with a clear coffin-shaped apparatus hanging overhead.

"That's to reconstruct the damaged tissue so you don't look like a plague victim," the doc said. "I get to do my thing first."

"What's your thing?"

The kid dumped her onto the couch and rolled away the chair. "Cell regenesis."

"That's a big word for me. I'll pass."

The doc unlocked the cabinet and pulled out a needle thick as a thumb. Nope. She'd been thinking violent thoughts with Aidan and Chip hadn't done anything, Chip was jammed. She could nab a guard's weapon—no, she had to let them fix her. And how was she supposed to slip out when there was a concert on every corner?

The doc flicked the syringe and tied a rubber strap around Khair's bicep. "I'll give you a cookie if you don't scream."

"What—"

The doc jabbed the needle. Khair backhanded her and yelped. The doc stumbled away, lip bleeding. "You made me miss the vein. And this," she waved to her face. "Unsanitary." She slapped off gloves, scrubbed her face—looking at herself longer than necessary—and found new gloves. "Do that again, and I'll stick it in your ass."

"Why isn't there a pill equivalent? Unless you slept blindfolded through med school."

"Bloody well could've." The doc sprayed clear liquid on her arm, dabbed off blood, and tried again. Khair managed not to hit her.

"You're welcome." The doc punched a button on the couch and the coffin dropped around her. Khair covered her face as a gray gas puffed in, and she blinked too long, and....

She woke on the couch, unrestrained, alone, her fingers and toes their proper color. She touched her nose and ears. They were soft and healthy again.

A note was taped on the door.

I'll be back soon. Don't break anything and don't try to get high. There's nothing fun, anyway.

Sophie

Khair hopped off the table and rattled the doorknob.

It wasn't locked.

Time Machines Can't Solve Everything

KHAIR STARTED OPENING THE door when Sophie flung it open, almost flattening her.

"You're up," Sophie said. "Taivan and Jiao are doing well, safe together."

Amateur kidnappers. It'd be easier to escape since they weren't separated. "What now? Aidan promised beef and vodka. Or something like that. Being gassed isn't great for the memory."

Sophie smirked. "That's what did it, not the voices in your head."

"Seems like you know as much about that as I do."

"More, predictably. Do you think we would let you walk around if you weren't tamed?" She leaned against the table. "I thought rescuing people for labor would score easy points, but people groaned about it so your friends are officially free. But you? Still hated. Still, there's not been an execution recently and I don't like the precedent."

Khair tapped the translator on her suit's wrist-controller, and said, very slowly: "Is this broken?"

"Aidan didn't tell you I'm queen, did he?" It wasn't a tech malfunction. Sophie's voice carried in an easygoing tone, without accent.

"In what universe does that make sense?"

"Aidan's older, he should've inherited—he didn't tell you we were siblings? He's adopted. Anyway, his existence fluctuates, and he's mopey about it, so we made succession matrilineal."

Khair flicked her forehead to see if she was dreaming. Nope, she'd destroyed her evidently limited brain cells for nothing. "Okay, so I don't... what are these drugs?"

"No one told you about time?" She checked her schedule. Khair's translator wasn't authorized to read the foreign script. "We've voting on an IQ voting threshold in an hour. Don't ask, you'd fail. So, before humanity left Earth, Ivan Ito invented a time-machine, the Arc Dilator."

She paused with a please-question-me grin. Khair didn't respond.

If Sophie was truly queen, she didn't do house calls. She wanted something. And since there were millions of mercenaries, it had to be the tech in Khair's head.

One invader was enough.

"UOD claimed to protect universal rights, but they serve Ito's interests with the time-machine, containing its impact, and stopping anyone else from making their own machine. That's what happened to my parents."

"Aidan's always disappearing, and UOD doesn't help. So mom and dad tried to make their own machine to protect him. They could have done it, I saw their notes. But their machines exploded. With the same problem based on the color of the explosion, even though mom double checked after dad's attempt. Their notes got fried too, all our systems went down for two days; people froze to death. So Aidan abdicated, people complained, and now women inherit everything."

Sophie wasn't lying, she was grief crazy. "The only solution."

The doc straightened, barely up to Khair's chin. "You're a blight on humanity, don't patronize me. Look around. Five hundred years ago, we hadn't left earth. Now we travel at lightspeed and remake planets. How? Because this universe is the graveyards of other 'verses."

No. Chip might be MIA, but she was a UOD agent and some of her knowledge remained. Her association with 'The Time-Machine' was innocents with flowers in their hair and nothing in their heads, and the subterranean monsters that fatted and hunted them. It wasn't real.

"I'm sorry," Khair said. "My substandard IQ prefers proof to hearsay."

Nope, nope, let the crazy ruler get drunk on her elixirs of life until they poisoned her.

Sophie pressed a button on her wrist-con. "Keep filibustering. I might be awhile." She gestured for Khair to sit.

The only seat available doubled as a knockout chamber, so she refused.

"There's no pretty picture or single chart," Sophie said. "It's years of circumstantial evidence and teasing out a dozen possible implications of recently discovered theorems. I can trade you that if you let me study your brain."

"No chance." Aidan had known things about her he shouldn't have, had known Jiao well enough to figure out her wrist-con password though they had never met. But there were easier, better explanations.

"Could you take me back before all this?" Khair gestured to her own head. She wouldn't understand the theorems and couldn't trust Sophie, but something wasn't adding up. Though, some of it might be Batu blabbing in an interrogation.

"No. No one knows where the Arc Dilator is, and if I try to build my own, UOD will assassinate me."

"Then how is Aidan supposedly traveling?"

Sophie shrugged. "That's one of the many mysteries I'm trying to find out."

Or was she just refusing to say?

"I will say this," Sophie said. "Time always moves forward. Even when we bend and distort it, it'll unknot itself, eventually."

Khair paced. Maybe it was true. If UOD was powerful enough to selectively wipe her memories, maybe they were powerful enough to manipulate time. Better to overestimate than underestimate her enemies. After all, given enough time, anything that wasn't impossible would happen, eventually.

She just wished it had happened to someone else's time.

"If you want to study my brain, you can," Khair said. "As long as my skull remains firmly closed, and you explain everything you're doing in layman's terms. You have me for a week. Then, me and my buddies get a free ride out to whatever passes for a resort town around here."

"Sure."

Khair crossed her arms, flexing, which might have been threatening without the cartoon bandages. "I'll need that publicized, in writing. Assuming you have a free press."

"I have a nation with an atmosphere almost too thin to retain heat on a planet with barely oxidized soil and salinized water. These fools can't be allowed to choose their own demise and celebrate that failure."

"So I can't take your word for it."

"Where would you go? The 'verse forgot you but if you remind them, they'll hate you again. I'll give you a new face, new name, a commission to honorary captain or some nonsense if you let me run tests that'll save literally countless lives."

A life beyond Chip's reach was tempting. But Taivan would never be satisfied here and so this city would descend into war. Besides, Sophie's promises were worth less than an expired coupon.

"Let me talk to my people about it."

Sophie rubbed a wrinkle from her dress. "That's a no, isn't it? Let me restart: I'm studying your brain. Would you prefer your head to be attached or—"

Khair kicked out Sophie's leg and smashed her elbow across her jaw as she fell. Khair pressed her knee into the kid's stomach, pulling up on her shoulder to increase the pressure. "Trade my life for yours."

"They muzzled you. You can't—" she screamed as Khair leaned into the hold. Sophie raked her nails through a pressure point on Khair's wrist. "Guards!"

Khair punched Sophie's neck as the kid drew a tiny pistol from her sleeve and snapped the wrist that grabbed it. A knife sliced into Khair's side. They screamed together.

She gagged at her own blood. The hole in her side was so small, she had to be okay. Seven centimeters deep would kill. How long was that knife? She was next to that healing contraption, she had to be okay.

The door opened and soldiers rushed in. Khair rocked under a second shank, grabbed Sophie's hand before she could be stabbed again.

"Freeze!"

Khair reached for Sophie's knife, but she threw it to the soldiers. Khair pressed her thumbs to Sophie's eyes. "If you move, I'll crush your queen's skull." Sophie tried to buck her off, jostling that imbedded knife, but Khair kneeled on her elbows. "Let me go."

Sophie poked a finger into Khair's wounds, twisting deeper into her side. A parasite eating through her. She blubbered for mercy that wasn't coming and leaned into Sophie's eyes.

Lights dimmed and blood bubbled down her side. Which distracted her from the soft pop and the kid's shrieks until clear fluid spurted into her mouth. Khair retched and pulled away, eyeballs stuck on her thumbs but attached to Sophie's head by fleshy cords.

Khair shook her hands, snapping the cords out and whipping her own face with them. Guards puked while commanders demanded updates on their comms. Khair slipped the deflated eyes off and tossed them at the dodging guards; they left a moist trail as they rolled and landed, so a fractured blue orb stared at her.

She vomited on the queen.

Sophie groped for support, found only Khair's hand. She squeezed it, swallowing, bolstering herself to speak clearly. Everyone leaned forward.

"Kill her!"

Khair jerked Sophie in front of her, bullets flying overhead, pieces of the wall falling, patients on the other side fleeing.

The soldiers stopped firing. They stepped back, watching the ceiling lights swing, rubble shatter beakers, the civilians they'd wounded cry and crawl. Their eyes betrayed them.

They were too used to peace.

She dove for Sophie's knife as their sergeant ordered them to switch to batons and charged. She ducked and stabbed the sergeant's chest. The other two stepped away. She grinned, wiped the man's blood beneath her eyes to convince them to flee since the room spun.

They did.

She doubled over, clutching her side. Accidentally looked at Sophie. Sophie groped for her eyes with one hand, cleaning her face with the other, calling for her bodyguards and magistrates and brother. She was no use dead, so Khair fought her up onto the doctor's chair before realizing none of the buttons were labeled.

Sophie kicked her chin.

Oh, she needed to heal, too. Forgot. When the room straightened, Aidan had entered. He glanced at his sister without changing expression and drew his two-handed axe with a spear on the end of the pole.

Khair stepped back, still hunched. "I could've killed her."

"Move."

Khair stabbed at him. He swatted the blow and slashed back, forcing her to the corner. She tried to grab the shaft, but he smashed the handle against her forehead. She staggered; he followed.

But she wasn't as weak as she'd played and as he lunged, she hit the handle aside with her wrist, bruising it, and stabbed at him.

He punched her back into his weapon's range. She parried a blow, weakened at its force. Blood dripping.

She'd just recovered, too.

Aidan stabbed at her head, but as she blocked, he pivoted and stabbed her foot, pinning her to the ground, and hit her back. She slipped and lay in blood. Khair tried to stand on her uninjured foot, but he stomped on her knee.

It cracked.

She moaned and tossed away her little knife.

"I might've won." Whatever Khair's other wounds, the cut to her pride was mortal. "If I wasn't dying when you stepped into the room."

He pried his spear from her foot.

Khair screamed and didn't bother hiding her tears. Displaced pain swam in her head.

Aidan picked up his sister and left Khair bleeding on the floor, locking the door behind him. "Push the red button."

She plastered her hand to her side and rummaged through the cabinet for bandages, or something she recognized. There was a wound patch with antibiotics, but as she ripped open the package, she tore the bandage. She used the stapler sitting on papers instead. Khair curled onto the healing table and poked the red button.

When she woke, her wounds were closed, and the pain was more a whisper than a howl. Batu sat on the floor. He looked like an Albion, wearing plaid pants and a turban, but at least she was allowed visitors. "You maimed that little girl. She gave us food and shelter."

Solitary wouldn't be so bad.

"She would've killed me."

Batu scratched his head. "Are you sure?"

She could almost hear Chip asking how she could be sure about anything. It'd seemed ridiculous. Now she wasn't sure if she dreamed in the 'tube, or lay drugged on the table, or hallucinated as she died. There had to be some way to know, not philosopher's babble on logical forms or experiments funded by interested parties, something tangible.

Chip would say the truth was independent of them. That—Khair could never get away from that thing, could she? She snorted. Soon enough, she'd be perfectly alone.

"Sophie said she'd kill me," Khair said. "I don't know if she really would've, but it seemed like it."

Batu nodded. "I believe you."

She nearly choked.

"You have to beg for mercy."

Khair massaged her aching side, worked her stiff knee and foot, proudly prodded her first scars. "I don't think that'll work." Her lip wobbled, though her voice was steady. "I did try this time. I could've killed her. It's not much, and maybe everyone would be better off if I had, but I didn't want to."

Was that any better?

"It'll work," Batu said. "You're good at what you do. She'll want you."

"Plenty of people are good at what I do, and most are on the better side of forty."

"Taivan and Jiao will protect you."

Khair scratched her fingers, their healed color strange in this stark light. "Doubt it."

Batu rattled the door in the room the soldiers had fired into, found it locked, and felt along the walls of both rooms, moving the cabinet. "We'll find an exit."

"You shouldn't be here. You should've retired somewhere, biking around bars, hiking up mountains, making a fool of yourself on social media. Or do you need your master?"

Batu wiped his hands. "You shouldn't speak to anyone like that."

She held his gaze a moment, looked away. When she'd discovered he was her father, she'd wondered how he'd let this happen to her. But with what she'd done, it was a wonder he was still here. "I don't deserve you. Dad." She said the last bit so softly she almost swallowed it.

"You know?" He raised her chin, searching her eyes. "Are you still there?"

"No. But—"

"But you know me." He hugged her before she could correct him. She embraced him back, warmer than she'd ever been. "There's so much to tell you. About your mother, our family, Irmeg."

Khair slowly disentangled. "I don't think I can take all that, probably don't have the time. But one story."

"That's why I stayed," Batu said. "You lost your memory and so when I died, they'd be gone."

Her mouth dried. "They're dead?"

"Gone." A gentler word, but that didn't change it. "Long time ago. Couldn't be helped. But before, you had two younger brothers and a younger sister, and your mom—"

Her stomach boiled. "How did they die?"

"That's not important."

"Yes, it is."

Batu held his fingers to still them. "The house collapsed in a blizzard, crushed a wire, and it caught on fire."

"Fuck." No enemy, no vengeance, no fancy little time machine to bring them back.

"They were perfect. Your mother, Tuya, was a veterinarian. You were apprenticed to her, good with animals, not with books, but she thought you'd manage."

She was wrong.

"Your brothers—"

A soldier opened the door. "He snuck in here! Mr. Batu, you're needed with Ms. Jun, she's coming out of the 'tube. Are we still giving the prisoner a visitor?"

The answer must've been yes, because after Batu shuffled out, his frostbite not as easily healed as his younger companions, Taivan entered.

"Just survive a few hours, and I'll take over this complex."

Acceptable Losses

KHAIR SAT ON THE counter. In the last few minutes, she'd learned time travel was real and her family was dead, but Taivan salvaging their lives still seemed impossible.

"Subutai scouted central Europe for a year," Khair said. "Then destroyed two armies in three days. I like that model. Gives us time to think about...." They'd kill her if Taivan didn't seize power. "Sow dissension and misinformation among the enemy, harry anyone competent, and quell the masses."

"It's arranged." He flicked a switch by the doorway, and the solid wall dissolved into a tinted glass window. "Albion was functional; I'm not sure it'll be after. If they were content, it'd never work, but who could be, stuffed in a cleft and left to rot?"

"People who like safety, warmed with tapestries and tea and tobacco, while their kids frolic unsupervised on the street. Don't count on their support."

Children were named for the fate their parents hoped for them. 'Taivan' meant Peace.

He smiled faintly, voice bitter. "They'll prefer conquest soon enough."

"If you want me to stop you, I can't."

"No." He stared out, enemy soldiers playing catch with kids or getting handsy with sweethearts. "In Lower Albion and in the corners here, they're scheming. This'll require less bloodshed."

"Or you could sell Sophie our services for pardons, buy time." If Taivan gained power in violence, no matter how just his policy afterward, people would wonder if he wouldn't overturn it again. Some would be cowed, but others may revolt.

"The girl you blinded? She prefers experiments to governance, if she even realizes there's a difference." Taivan watched people dine on silver, though there was little on the plate. "If they have all this, and still switch allegiances, there's no buying them. I'll have to terrify them."

"Can we get back to me staying alive? Maybe just escape first. If they're letting you wander, they're tailing you."

"Aidan's men are with me, yes."

"'With you' or with you?"

He gave a tired smile.

Aidan was his ally, probably the reason he came here. "Don't trust him. He stepped down for Sophie instead of holding out for you."

"He came back from another 'verse and Sophie was in charge. The prince's forced abdication is part of the people's discontent, gives us legitimacy."

"Gives him legitimacy. If he'll turn on his sister, he'll turn on you. And we don't have an army, they do."

"I did. Only a week ago." He almost continued, but screwed his jaw shut instead.

Khair paced, weaving closer and stopped when she was close enough to hold his hand, though she didn't dare. "Please, just convince Aidan to let me live. Sophie will listen to him."

"No." He dusted gravel from her shoulder. "I went to pick you up from UOD as agreed, and they tried to change the terms. I took you instead. My men covered the retreat."

A guard knocked. "Two minutes."

"I didn't ask for that." She had enough real deaths to answer for, she didn't need imaginary debts.

"Me neither. I ordered half to return with us, but they all held." He looked down. She shivered, pants ripped at the knee, with holes in her shirt. "Take out those staples."

The knife wounds in her side had healed, but blood trickled from the staples. She tried to rip them out, but they bent under the skin. Taivan handed her the extractor, magnetized pliers.

"Can't get blood on your suit yet?" Khair removed the staples and stopped the bleeding, though it left a thin, dark line that only smudged when she rubbed it with an antiseptic wipe.

"One minute," the guard said.

"That was twenty seconds. Can you even count?" Khair said. To Taivan: "If I was worth half your army, listen to me, anda. Don't waste their sacrifice. Let's make peace with Sophie and stay here."

Taivan fixed his tie and adjusted his fitted tweed suit. He didn't blend in, few were so well dressed, but it covered his prosthetic. There were no concessions to the Khanate, not even the thick belt that signified a free citizen or the thumb ring of a warrior.

She missed them, but she wasn't free anymore.

"It wasn't a sacrifice for me," Taivan said. "It was a down-payment on a better future for their families and their nation. I can't steal that."

"Yes, you can! They're not here, neither are their families, and what's a nation? Just the extended family—which is still not here. Help the people you can. Jiao, Batu,—"

"You?" He held out a bandage.

She took it. "I'm with you, aren't I?"

He held her gaze until she turned away to finish cleaning up. He turned, too. "If you stay with me, there'll be a show trial. Keep them busy and I'll do the rest."

"Fine." She ran her fingers across the scarred walls. "Taivan, one day, we'll settle somewhere like this?"

He tapped the window twice. It switched to a mirror, and he checked his reflection for something in his teeth. "I'll probably burn everything, but we'll give future generations a chance."

All this for the dead and strangers, and their world might not even improve? "For nothing more than your glory?"

Given the choice between an uneventful, long life, and a short one with unending fame, the great warrior Achilles had chosen renown. After death, the hero had moaned he'd rather be a living laborer than lord of the dead.

"Tell your handler it's not the only one willing to make the necessary compromises," Taivan said.

Aidan entered.

"Hold for two hours," Taivan said as he left.

Aidan tossed her handcuffs and a hooded mask. She put them on without protest. A crowd had gathered outside. Police shouted; the mob shouted. Khair shrank against Aidan but he shoved her forward as kids threw rugby balls at her, elders screamed idiomatic curses that didn't make sense in translation, everyone sang jaunty hanging ballads. Smoke prickled her throat, polluting the air. Were they burning her effigy?

Someone knocked against her, but Aidan yanked her along. This was the same crowd who'd made their children thank the waiter yesterday? Maybe Taivan had underestimated the current regime's popularity, or maybe knocking someone around was a universal pastime. But Aidan got her to her execution safely.

A door closed, and she removed the hood. Sophie sat in an austere wooden chair, the only object in the dusty room, her eyes covered with burnished plates. A shotgun sat on her lap.

Khair slowly raised her hands, squinting at the eye shields for a sign of how much Sophie had healed.

"The eye is mostly vitreous gel," Sophie said. "I can replace it, reattach the optic nerve and reconstruct the cornea, pupil, retina. You know what blinded me? Your bacteria covered fingers. Everything had to be scooped out. Our neighbors have replacements, but since our chief exports are minding our own damn business, I can't afford it."

How was a blind girl gonna shoot her?

"Nothing to say?" Sophie said.

"Compliments on your Hartford D7, that—no, not really. You were gonna kill me. But being blind seems worse than death. Do that and let me live with my horrible self."

Sophie jounced her leg, finger on the trigger like a fool. "I'm no fool. I know my people blame me when their loved ones cease to exist, when their neighbor has cuter kids, when I tell them they can't go out and freeze. I have my position by chance, so every chance incident is my fault. Your boy's building—has built—an uprising on it."

She snorted. "My people always loved their rebellions, but only after the martyrs are cold. But Taivan, he.... I was never enough. I have the perfect system. Look at everything objectively, don't even privilege my own opinion. But everyone thinks they're the exception."

She waved the gun; Khair ducked. "Anyway. I can return your memories if you help me stop him."

Sophie clicked her wrist-con and showed a villa of the red Albion rock filled with baubles for a dozen lifetimes, laughing people chattering among blooming vines, but Khair hardly saw it.

How could she refuse to be herself again? To remember what and who she loved, not as stories to be recited, but lives to be known. She hadn't been a monk, but she'd been a person, not a grotesque lab chew toy.

Sophie was no worse than Taivan: both warring against all for absolute control out of fear of death or insignificance—which was another death. Sure, some things here should be fixed. But beyond that universal law there was a particular justice fit to each nation written in their hopes and expectations. Sophie knew it here; Taivan would erase it.

Batu wanted her memories restored, he would accept her helping Sophie. And Jiao, for all she thought she was better, hadn't proven it.

"You're taking too long," Sophie said.

"Yeah."

"That's not an answer."

"Uh huh."

"Listen," Sophie said, but it sounded like 'please.' "I've only had a year, and it... I buried my parents. But since then, ask anyone. Tensions between Upper and Lower Albion are at an all-time low, rations are increasing. This place is worth saving."

Taivan had all but assured her he'd burn the world. But he'd risked electrocution to hold her frostbitten hands so she wouldn't suffer alone. And all those dead Khanate soldiers, her people—unless Taivan had lied, but no, someone had shot their ship down. Besides, there was no faking the raised hackles in his shoulders.

She didn't owe the Khanate her life. But Sophie didn't value her as Batu and Taivan did.

"Any chance I could think on this over a meal? I haven't actually eaten ever."

Sophie's face scrunched, but she held back tears. "Whatever Taivan offered you, I'll double it."

"I can't stop him." It seemed better than *won't,* and it was truer. Whoever history deemed right after time smoothed away the nuances, Taivan would win.

Sophie nodded curtly. "And if your princess's throat is on the line?"

Huh?

Two guards with bruised faces marched Jiao inside. She was red-faced and panted quietly, but her only visible injuries were a faint limp and scarred knees partially concealed by her ash gray skirt.

"Chuluun started his empire in Imger," Sophie said. "Just another warlord squabbling over politically insignificant planets. Until you captured Jiao's planet, Jungang ju, PRGC's old capital, and made a great example of it."

Jiao dissected Sophie with her gaze. "They were far stronger than you; surrender while you can." But it wasn't an offer.

"Chuluun slaughtered the royal family, except Jiao, who was supposed to be his concubine. You took her as your ward instead. Something about being amused she tried to fight when she was, what, twelve?"

Khair's jaw tightened. When she looked to Jiao for confirmation, Jiao stepped forward, held back by the guards. "Don't look at me like that."

"Help me stop Taivan or she dies. Then I bring in your father."

If Sophie had Batu, she would have brought him. "We've done no violence toward you, leave us alone and we'll forget this."

"Taivan needs our resources and loves his own myth. He won't leave," Sophie said.

Khair forced a shrug, not looking at Jiao. "Jiao and Batu have done nothing to you. Remember that the fall of Khwarezmia and the great slaughters there began with the murder of a peaceful envoy."

Kangaroo Court (With a Disappointing Amount of Marsupials)

JIAO TAPPED HER FOOT on a broken tile floor, as she'd done since Sophie left them alone in a cramped parlor, the emerald wallpaper yellowed, the furniture dragged off somewhere it wouldn't mold.

"Then." Khair waved the hand shackled to Jiao's. "We keep moving. Don't present a target."

Jiao's foot thumped louder. A crowd cheered above. The mock trial Taivan had warned about seemed full of the people calling for her death this morning.

"Taivan will—"

"You've talked nonstop for the past seventeen minutes and twenty-nine seconds. Shut up."

Taivan told her to survive two hours, but when should she start counting? "Then shoulder your share of the conversation."

"There's nothing to talk about."

She fantasized about choking Jiao until she changed her mind, but gagging wouldn't help their little chat. So Khair tapped her foot despite how hollow it sounded.

"I'm sorry," Khair said.

Jiao wiped dirt off her blazer, though she leaned against a wall with cobwebs in the corner. "You're sorry you have to live with it."

"That's not—"

"You apologized every time you saw me putting on concealer or fixing my dress."

Khair said nothing.

"I wanted to kill you, but I knew you'd do it yourself."

It was a relief when guards finally ushered them onto a trimmed field, pink rubber and limed lines circling the perimeter. The five-kilometer-long oval track had millions of people in the stands.

Flea sized camera drones silently hovered around them. Khair flicked one away. The floating marble returned unharmed.

It seemed like every Albion soldier was here. Half had axes, half sabers, a few had Terran guns from before ZAX manufacturers, so no centralized off-switch. All had flysuits and tinted eye protection.

If Taivan won the army's allegiance, there were enough soldiers to look menacing, but without armor a mob could tear them apart. If he'd armed the crowd, there were enough soldiers to fly up, shoot down, and kill their rebellion. Either way, a few zealots would get their way while millions of sensible people hid under crummy seats.

"We're bait." Khair didn't care it was obvious, she wanted Jiao to agree.

Jiao ignored her.

Sophie and a hundred ministers had box seats, their inflated image projected on a dozen screens around the stadium, else they'd be nothing but a smear in tinted windows. A German Shepherd pup—picked for cutesy points since it was too cheerful to have completed obedience training—guided Sophie onto a meter wide bridge without a railing. She stood a kilometer above everyone, her crosswalk spanning the kilometers between Upper and Lower Albion.

"My people." Sophie spoke softly but her voice carried, crisp and clear, through speakers. "We've suffered this last year, been tested almost beyond our capacity. But we've survived. By putting our duty and our neighbor before ourselves, we've persevered. And if we stay the course, no matter what happens to me, to your ministers or magistrates or soldiers, you will endure."

Sophie knew she'd lose.

"Some of you doubt my ability to lead you through this crisis."

She dropped the leash and stepped toward the edge. Her dog's whine echoed through the stadium and she almost tripped over him. The screens captured the concentration lines in Sophie's forehead as she flapped her arms, but the dog was in the center of the shot, its back paw centimeters from the edge.

She would kill a dog for sympathy? Asshole.

Jiao shielded her eyes from the lights, staring up at Sophie and not the projected image. "Where's the net?"

"I admit, I'm young, and difficult times have forced difficult decisions," Sophie said. "But doubt gravity before you doubt my devotion to you." She shuffled closer to the brink. The dog's back foot stepped into space before it pushed her back and made room for itself.

The screens scaled the distance between Sophie and the ground in painfully slow motion, panning over the mystified faces of the crowd. No nets.

Khair stepped out of the splash zone, tightening the chain between her and Jiao. Jiao didn't move. Khair yanked once, twice, then ignored, stepped back.

"If one of you could lead better, step forward, and so will I." Sophie raised one leg, wavering. "I can't hold forever. Ministers Pasha, O'Leary, Naguib, you've expressed displeasure in our current direction. Here's your chance."

The only response was awkward chewing.

Maybe Taivan had found a real opponent after all.

"No one? Yet you skulk in the dark, colluding with terrorists." Sophie pointed to Khair and Jiao. "These women have massacred across three galaxies and came here for the same purpose."

Their image projected on-screen. The cold fury deadening Jiao's eyes and twisting the edge of her lips would convince everyone they were guilty.

"But given the chance, we'll be lenient. Princess Jun Jiao, Mercy Mission Designation 7701, how do you plead?"

Khair sputtered. Designation? If they were gonna act like she was nothing but what UOD made her, then she was three days old, but—

Jiao stepped forward. "I deny the authority of this court and denounce the presiding judge. I am not your citizen and I was brought here to be enslaved despite committing no crime on this planet or any other, or in interstellar space."

The crowd fell silent, some glaring at Sophie. Slavery had been instituted for easy points and canceled almost immediately for the same reason. And it didn't hurt that Jiao looked like a hero.

"I am the pilot of the *AKS Bankhar*," Jiao said. "I won battles according to the rules of war. I accepted surrenders, rescued enemy sailors in life-pods and tended their wounds; I delivered humanitarian aid by my own coin in regions no one else could reach. If that's not enough, I dare you to tell me what you've done better."

The screens had split, Sophie and Jiao on either side, Sophie slightly higher, slightly larger, though obvious to anyone paying attention.

"The *Bankhar* was at the Battle of Orion's Belt." Sophie played to the screens, canting herself for a good angle, but the plates over her eyes couldn't hide her weariness.

"I wasn't there." Jiao used the magnification to steel her features and study Sophie.

"Your proof?"

The crowd was bored, background chatter rising, a poll on the screens displaying the popular 'guilty' or 'not guilty' vote. Jiao drifted toward 'not guilty.' Khair didn't.

Khair searched for an exit. The field gave her nothing: spongy blue-green synthetic grass over centimeters of impenetrably hard bedrock. The rubber track was softer than blacktop, but she couldn't dig through it even if she knew what was underneath.

"I suffered third-degree burns in the previous battle," Jiao said. "Helping my crew evacuate. If anything, it shows the difference between when I'm at the helm and when I'm not."

The lowest stands were two stories off the ground and even if Khair broke her thumb to free her hand from the cuff and scaled the wall without handholds—possible in this light gravity—there were soldiers in every aisle. By the glint of scattered light, there was a barrier between her and the stands, anyway.

"Mere hearsay." Sophie said, without a trace of the little girl asking the adults if she'd done a good job.

"There's time-stamped documentation in my ship." Jiao hadn't changed at all. Khair had assumed her squared shoulders, chin high nonsense was a mask, but if so, it was fused to her skin. "If this is anything more than a farce, take a few hours to confirm it."

There was nothing for a distraction. Khair couldn't reach the lights to start a fire, and the accessible ground sprinklers were useless.

"We've searched and found nothing," Sophie said.

There was no way to threaten the ministers. Beside the invisible barrier, it was a kilometer high and saturated with guards.

"Mò xū yǒu," Jiao had turned off her translator.

The crowd broke from their beer and baklava long enough to look it up, hissed and chuckled when their wrist-cons soldiered past their spelling errors. It meant "there must be something." The words that condemned Yue Fei, a general and poet who'd tattooed "serve the country with utmost loyalty" on his back years before being executed for treason since his competence embarrassed everyone else.

Sophie's wrist-con suggested a documentary with a pop-up holo of Fei's statute standing over his kneeling prosecutors that anyone except Sophie could see. The documentary's trailer played through the speakers. Sophie slapped it away, but people looked it up.

Seventy percent of the polled crowd judged Jiao 'not guilty.' It'd been too quick a swing. Though the support was for an innocent woman rather than Taivan or rebellion, Sophie, standing high on a ledge, was cornered.

"I was responsible for the Battle of Orion's Belt." Khair said, watching her image to make sure she wasn't hallucinating or being controlled by Chip. "I'm guilty. Jiao isn't. Any crimes she committed—allegedly—were done by me or with my gun at her head."

Sophie cocked her head a centimeter, movements controlled again. "If you're acting out of maternal obligation, I warn you, this incident will be investigated fully."

"Why would I lie for the kid? She hates me. I just don't want to die as a Memory Reboot."

The polls showed everyone knew Khair was guilty.

Sophie made a benevolent 'I tried' gesture. "The punishment should be death." But she waited to see what the people wanted. Must be how she held to power: yielding on trifling things and concealing everything important.

Khair's crimes played out around them. Millions of safe people wanted her dead after watching only seconds of her life, and the number grew as the footage continued.

Khair bowed to Sophie, looked down so she wouldn't see their faces, so they wouldn't see hers, so she wouldn't see what she'd done. "Did you have to traumatize the kiddos to feel righteous? Whatever they think, I'm too valuable to kill."

It wasn't fair. These simple, petty people were right.

The cuff between Khair and Jiao unlocked. A door opened behind them, leading to the stands, but Jiao didn't move.

"There's a split." Sophie was generous. The poll was shut down once it showed eighty percent wanted Khair dead. "I can't kill you, but nothing else is suitable. Blind chance will decide. Survive and we'll revisit your sentencing after we've seen the extent of your punishment."

Translation: while Khair lay half dead, Sophie would pick through her brain under the guise of tending her wounds.

The ground shook. Fifty meters away, the turf split, panels smoothly opening to sand beneath. Khair couldn't see what was there without getting closer. The screen above zoomed in and out of the sandy pit with a shaky cam, red scratches splicing the screen to roars and screams.

"Tasteful," Jiao said.

Some people cheered, others searched for the safety net or heralded snacks to distract themselves.

Khair raised an eyebrow and nodded toward the path Jiao could walk through. That one person wanted her alive was enough.

"No." Jiao glared as Khair grinned. "This doesn't change anything, I just don't abandon people to their death."

That one person happened to be herself.

"Hey!" Khair called to Sophie, then whispered to Jiao. "Do you know any poignant, classy insults for blind assholes?"

Jiao blinked into the camera.

"Blindy!" Khair yelled. "How about some weapons?"

Sophie nodded to the box and axes shot from the wall into the turf two meters from them. She flicked a button on her wrist-con. "Good luck."

Don't panic. We're through Albion's jamming, clearly, and it—

Quieter! Can you help or are you about to kill me for blinding that brat?

She'd moan about how she'd evolved beyond this later. Now, Chip's access to nearby cameras and scanners could buy extra minutes. For a full two hours. Or so Taivan had said, but that was a while ago. How much time was left? Maybe Taivan wasn't using standard time, but some planet where an hour was like three minutes.

She cut me off; she's a threat to my mission.

Khair spun her axe. "Think I can hit her?"

"No," Jiao and Chip said.

Khair hopped on her toes, the pressure in her mind subsiding as her muscles bore the load. **Where's Taivan?**

Off grid.

The lights turned off. Jiao stepped back on Khair's toe and touched her hand in amends as any polite Irmegian would, and froze, yanked her hand back. Sirens trilled. White light circled the stadium.

Are they looking for him, or—

Something exploded. Khair threw herself to the ground, covering her head and opening her mouth to protect her ears. The explosions continued, crackling down. She peeked up to see green fireworks. Lights flashed back on.

A crowned monster stood in front of them. It was six stories tall, its wingspan twice that, with the body of a lion, each paw the size of a spacious room, its human teeth blunt. But the horror was the lifelike human face: the skin texture, the undertones in its cheeks, the detail in its eyes where her reflection shrank.

It's the Great Sphinx.

The Sphinx's heavy head could barely look up. Light reflected off the golden diadem nearly blinded her. The sphinx was sandy colored except for a neon bracelet around each leg with constantly changing width: the odds it would crush Khair and Jiao with that leg, wagers in real time. The front right band broadened as she gaped.

There's been no bloodsport here, this was only used on other automatons.

So?

The drone pilots might hesitate before killing you.

I already lost the popularity contest, keep up.

"It's a machine. Your chip could hack it," Jiao said.

I can observe other sites, I can't interfere.

"No. You're the engineer. Can't you do some cross wiring magic to stop it?"

"I'm a pilot."

"Close enough."

"No, it's not!"

"You could've left and lived!"

Jiao glanced to Sophie, every bit the house cat confusing itself for a tiger. "Who does this travesty benefit?" But her mic was turned off, Sophie obliviously eating with her ministers and giving scraps to her dog.

"This injustice won't stop with strangers." Jiao yelled to be heard, but the crowd looked to Sophie, already believing whatever excuse would let them go on with their lives. "Even if the ship records were unsalvageable, there were daily reports of the war—"

"They can't hear through the barrier," Khair said.

The sphinx's head tilted down with a whir and it cackled, lasers in its eyes dotting on their foreheads.

So, apparently, you UOD suckers are into time travel. Any chance I'm in the future?

The sphinx stepped forward, projecting the noise of a bomber plane, covering fifty meters with one step, its bracelets oscillating. Khair ran away to buy time, but Jiao hadn't moved.

"If this is a peaceful protest, save it for a society with a soul," Khair said, hating herself for jogging back to Jiao.

Jiao twisted the axe in her hand.

"What is this, seppuku? Com'on Princess Samurai, it's cardio time for the next hour and fifty-eight minutes."

Can you speed up time or something? Wait, no! I'd get squashed sooner. There's a manual control panel on its belly, the main control is in a room below.

Jiao waited till the sphinx raised its foot, and sprinted forward, underneath it. She aimed the half-moon axe at the belly, though synthetic flesh and feathers covered the control panel.

Khair grabbed Jiao's arm. Jiao whirled and punched her nose. Khair cocked her fist until a shock buzzed at the back of her head.

"We're underneath it, if you bring it down, we're dead," Khair said.

It leaned forward and fell. She darted out the left side, diving out across the turf as its wing collapsed—both wings, Jiao alive on the other side. Khair rolled on the wing.

I may have made a small mistake.

The sphinx leaped up, wings gently rising. Khair grabbed a person sized feather, but her weight plucked it. She caught another as she skidded down toward the body, and pressed herself against the paneled metal of its wings, careful to keep her fingers from getting pinched.

I'm taking suggestions at any time.

It was almost fun. Wind rushing past, puny people gawking and pointing, marbles in her stomach, adrenaline making her light.

It wasn't exactly a smooth ride, its movements jerky, metal rattling, shell hot and sticky, reeking of smoke and fuel.

Not so fun anymore. Wind stung her face, the view specks of compressed color veering toward brown, her breath stolen, adrenaline poisoning her. Their flight a steady route to crush her against the roof, the machine quiet as its systems adjusted, its body cooling like a corpse newly dead.

She hacked her axe into the wing. Stupid, falling from this height was death. She crouched up, waited till the wing flapped up and jumped down onto its back, flying for a moment. Now, if it crushed her, it would snap its own back.

It was a machine.

Khair sliced into its back, pulled off a strip of plastic skin, and found the steel frame underneath. If she made a cubby—it spun. Too quickly for her to fall off, and too quickly for her to do anything else.

The sphinx straightened and lofted toward the roof. She squeezed with her knees and clasped fistfuls of squishy skin strips instead of tinsel feathers as she climbed toward its face.

There's nothing to hold on its head.

I'll hide in its nose.

It dropped. She screamed and lost her grip, fell into its shoulder. Pain surged through her wrist where she'd caught herself and warm piss leaked down her leg for the world to see.

I'll climb onto the underside of the wing, then drop down on Sophie's ledge. Chip didn't respond. **Are you gone again?**

Running calculations.

And?

For once, there was no mockery in its voice. *And it's a good time to pray to a merciful God.*

From this height, it didn't seem like there was such a thing.

She looked for a chance to jump onto a higher bleacher seat, but they flew around center stage, nothing below them but Jiao.

The sphinx flipped and dove back first.

Air rushed past. Her nails bled. All this to save Jiao, and Jiao would be a casualty of her own pride.

This is it? I offer my life and it doesn't matter. What was the point?

She could make out pebbles in the turf. People blurred to a single mass, but she glimpsed the split screen with disgusted despair. Jiao's face serene, though tension coiled in her forearms, Sophie's forced, queasy smirk at her minister's narration.

A far, far better rest than you have ever known.

She moved too quickly for her consciousness to keep up.

To Subdue Without Fighting

KHAIR WOKE WHEN A giant automaton smashed into the sphinx. She barely held on as the flipped sphinx righted itself and hovered just above the ground.

Taivan rode a creature three stories high with the body of a leopard and the head of a hooded cobra. He stood balanced at the shoulders, holding the reins like a pharaoh on his chariot.

The crowd cheered, thinking it a show.

Jiao scrambled to Taivan's beast, dodging green acid falling from the viper's mechanical tongue.

Khair slid down the sphinx's wings once the slope was gentle enough. Her feet sunk into turf and she managed three steps before she face-planted. She lay there long as she dared, massaging her popping ears and wiping away half-dried tears, wishing for a change of clothes.

The turf dipped and sprung as the giants moved. She raced to Taivan.

His rifle was slung over his longcoat, a sword sheathed on his hip, the battle already over—his right eye was bruised purple but hadn't yet swelled. Batu and Aidan must have helped, but they didn't fit in the spotlight.

"I warned—" Sophie stopped when a spear pressed to her chest and held her growling dog back. Her ministers kneeled with hands raised, only two loyal guards beside them. "O'Leary, Naguib, where are you? Did you—" her microphone turned off.

Khair fought nausea, stomach not realizing she was on solid ground.

"If you want to play with toys, I'll win." Taivan's bass voice filled the stadium. "But I'd rather reason together."

Sophie cleared her throat, the microphone functioning again. "We can speak in—" she was cut off.

People realized it wasn't an act, whispered, squeezed children to their chest, pointed to the open doors. But no one moved first.

"Join me." Taivan's creature kneeled. He swung down and landed harshly on his prosthetic, but kept a straight face.

He passed Jiao his scoped Hartford M23 rifle, not a ZAX, but decent enough. She immediately checked it was on safe and pointed it to the ground, so someone—perhaps an apologetic kidnapper—had taught her something.

Taivan passed Khair his saber and longcoat. He wore a bland suit, and a patterned jade scarf beneath. Green was Albion's color, and the scarf hung like a tie, but the intricate weave harkened back to a pectoral and seemed as royal as a crown. How easily he took on foreign embellishments. Did he have a self beneath?

Khair used the coat as a dress and tossed away her soiled clothes, rubbed her hands on grass, then spat on them to clean them.

Sophie walked to a glass-enclosed elevator, her wrist-con guiding her. Her dog ran ahead to sniff Taivan, circled him with a wagging tail and sat by his bad foot.

"You even have the dog," Sophie said, voice stripped without speakers to carry it, speaking to the space between Jiao and Khair.

Taivan cleared his throat, and she faced him.

"Whiskey, come." Sophie sighed when the dog didn't move. "Seems about right. How's Aidan?"

The stadium screens were blank, their words private.

"My ally."

Khair searched for soldiers under new banners, but the old guard milled around. The people watched, some rising halfway out of their chairs, others slouching into them.

If he starts killing people and you do nothing, you'll be held accountable.

And only a minute ago you whispered sweet nothings in my ear.

"I have conditions," Sophie said.

"A life under house arrest for facilitating slavery?" Jiao lay in the turf, digging her elbow and feet into the ground to secure her firing position. That prone position was most accurate and made her a small target but narrowed her peripheral range, so Khair wandered to her back. Jiao adjusted to keep her in view.

"For two weeks," Sophie said. "And we only captured you. We're even."

"Hardly," Jiao said. "Finish that trial."

Sophie laughed.

"You won, Jiao," Taivan said.

"There was no official ruling."

"Can I have my mic back?" Sophie addressed the crowd. "I confess there was no investigation. I assumed Admiral Jun Jiao was guilty by association." She tried to go on, but the mic cut off. "Good enough, I take it."

Jiao blushed. "I meant a real hearing."

"It'll only look worse if you protest," Taivan said.

"I'll be your vassal," Sophie said. "I know these people far better than Aidan cares to; I'll keep them docile and happy."

"You and the soldiers are coming with us."

Pay attention.

Khair had been petting Whiskey. And why not? Albion was taken. Still, it felt like she had heard too many horror stories after dark; there was no real danger, yet she squinted and flinched at every sound. Though that might be Chip's return.

"Bring Aidan with you." Sophie twisted a gaudy ring too big for her finger. "Minister Naguib's more reliable here."

"She convinced the guards to side with me," Taivan said.

"Figured. But she's the most competent and if she's in charge, her fate is tied to Albion's, especially with you overseeing." She snorted. "Unless you want to make an example of us, too. We really don't have great weapons, but hey, instead of butchering us by hand, go to my lab and split an atom."

Chip bristled, a cold shock down Khair's spine, but then a greedy longing. What now? The sense of getting on a ship and the shore shrinking away, Chip's pining to jump off and swim back. To go home.

You're American. UOD was an organization, not a nation. They recruited across galaxies. But they were founded by American President Ivan Ito, the

time-machine inventor, and still recruited heavily there. ***Bless my heart and
slap your momma, ya'll are—***

There is no America. Focus on Sophie's ring; it's emitting a signal I can't read.

"I have no intention of destroying Albion," Taivan said. "I need access to your
defenses and private networks."

"Yes, fine." Sophie crossed her arms, ring hidden. "What will you do with us?
We can plague you with partisan warfare if necessary."

"We'll capture the source of United Oversight for Democracy's power: their
time machine."

Khair gasped as Chip seethed, hit her with a long, weak blow. ***What do you
want me to do, stab them?***

Jiao coughed, but Taivan ignored her. "Can your people take Coloma City?"

Even if Prince Aidan had been popular with the soldiers, that was no guarantee
they'd follow General Taivan.

"No," Sophie said. "And they're well-connected with the ZAX trade routes."

Albion didn't have ZAX weapons though they were neighbors with Coloma,
and ZAX was the best in the business. Clearly the weapon profiteers were banned
here. If Taivan fought Albion's enemies, Albion might join him reflexively.

"Even if you took Coloma," Sophie said. "You couldn't keep it. But their
president Buck Davids is an honest dope, he's the weakness."

Heat pulsed through her head. *Seek out and aid Davids.*

No uproar for your UOD buddies, huh? Who are you?

"This wasn't the plan," Jiao said.

Sophie laughed, wringing her hands, ring out of reach. "For someone who
hates your old woman, you're standing by your conqueror just like she did."

"We weren't after UOD. There are more pressing concerns than an enemy half
a galaxy away," Jiao lowered her voice. "They would destroy us."

"They already have," Taivan said. "When they murdered our crew."

Jiao adjusted her scope. "Let's speak in private."

"I haven't forgotten our plans," Taivan said. "I know the PRGC remnant needs
a home more immediately than former Khanates. We'll carve it out for them, for
all our people. But we'll never build a safe haven if we can cease to exist at any
time. UOD took Aidan today."

Or had he outlived his usefulness?

Sophie slowly kneeled. Her puppy hopped to her, rubbed his head against her leg, and she stroked his neck, careful not to touch him with the ring on her index finger. That was the only ring that wasn't flawless, a dark indent on its side. A trigger?

Khair crept toward Sophie, trying not to spook her.

"If this is against your conscience, I'm sorry." Taivan kept the tone he'd used with Sophie, so businesslike he'd died of boredom and become a zombie. "Rule here if you can't follow me."

"Ten years gone just like that?" Jiao matched him, tone emotionless, but she tore her attention from her rifle to look at him.

Taivan's voice softened. "I'd rather you stay, but you're not my prisoner."

"How long do I have to decide?"

"However long it takes to mobilize their army. A day, probably. I'll come back for you after UOD if you'll take me."

"Don't stay," Sophie said. "Naguib owns this place, an outsider couldn't... fine, but there'd be considerable hand dirtying required."

"Or she's lying," Khair said. Very softly, so Sophie wouldn't know she was an arm's length away. "You should stay. Not just because I can't stand you, but these people would have a trustworthy leader, and you'd be safe."

Jiao's eyes narrowed. "I'll come. And we'll re-evaluate your plans to make sure no one's caught in the crossfire."

Taivan winked at her over Jiao's head. He turned to Sophie. "Is there anyone you trust with your life?"

"Death time already, huh?" She scratched her ring.

Khair grabbed her wrist and wrenched it free. "Spoils of war."

Taivan and Jiao exchanged glances, looking at her the way she sometimes looked at Batu. Ungrateful children. "Eh, not my type."

She hurled the ring, and it exploded on impact.

Chip flinched, but Khair moved. Absent gunfire echoed in her mind, body freezing, racing, ready to fight, trying not to let anyone see her react—no one had. Chip shoved back out of Khair's mind, away from this arena.

You could've killed everyone! Chip's mind felt like pulverized putty. So she overcompensated, took herself out of the equation and considered the big picture, where her struggles were too small for the frame. *Whether you meant it or not, you'd be guilty.*

If Chip could accidentally control her, how much power did it have?

Fancy voice Purity of heart is to will one thing, and I was purely concerned with none of us turning to pink mist, so I call it a win. Did that come through with an accent?

Chip ignored Khair and shook off her troubles like a dog coming in from the rain, but her feeling slipped off with it.

There would be no mercy now.

"Does she have anything else?" Taivan said.

"'Thank you, Khair, that was so timely done,'" Khair said. "And there's nothing electronic, though last time we fought she had hidden weapons, so maybe she stuffed a bomb in the dog." She opened Whiskey's mouth and waved away his breath. "Looks good."

"Try it again," Taivan said to Sophie. "I'll buy you working eyes and slaughter this city in front of you. Can I trust any ministers besides Naguib?"

Sophie hadn't moved from the ground, petting her dog. "They're loyal to the city, not me."

Taivan said nothing.

"Their families are watching," Sophie said.

"Wait—" Khair spoke, but it was Chip's protest. Khair grabbed Sophie's shoulder to steady herself, let go when she recoiled. Chip stumbled for words. Any help Khair could give was trampled beneath Chip's spinning wheels.

Taivan nodded to Naguib and the other ministers had a sudden case of split throat. Khair's blood revulsion had returned.

If you want me to rein in Taivan, you've gotta let me think. He won't listen to you. Besides your knowledge seeped into me, you're basically superfluous. Go nap, I—

1) You will no longer receive extra data, and since I'll continue to learn, you will not know everything I know. Was it a technological breach, or had a bored Chip broken protocol? *2) Regardless of what you know, you wouldn't act.*

Because nothing I could say would stop him. And despite your intention, they died, so how are you any better?

The magistrates were laid gently on the floor, more care taken with their corpses than the slash. They had seemed ancient alive, squinting at papers, fumbling with screens, but their limp limbs had a fresh vitality.

"It was quick." Taivan's voice didn't carry, speaking for Sophie's benefit—and Jiao's. Jiao watching through the rifle's scope, her finger on the trigger though the only people up there were their own.

Taivan lied. The ministers had thrashed before they lost consciousness, tried to staunch the bleeding before their hands were pinned down, reached toward old rivals already gone, croaked out words that never left the booth. A few had to be cut again.

"Are you done?" Sophie said.

The booth was silent.

Taivan surveyed the crowd without facing the bodies. For the first time in the bottom of this kilometers' high stadium, he seemed what he was: just one man. He spoke slowly so the translator wouldn't fumble over the tangled snarl of emotions, raised his voice to flatten them out until he boomed.

"I am Jochiin Taivan. I was Prince Aidan's ally and friend from before his sister usurped him, years before Coloma City and their ZAX Technology killed him today. I will care for Albion in his stead."

Without Aidan to confirm, no one believe him. They sat petrified, defiant, no more Taivan's subjects than before their magistrates were murdered.

"You'll be hungry and cold until you defend yourselves. Your enemies are my enemies. By the end of this month, they'll surrender to anyone who joins me."

Taivan turned to Jiao, but his words still reverberated through the stands to anyone who might dare join. "I'll reward your faithful service." To Khair: "And give you a better future than you could've dreamed." He turned to the crowd, eyes ablaze. "If you have to ask about safety or comfort, don't come." He showed his metal foot. "You may be maimed, you may die, but you've already locked yourselves in a tomb."

All his lies, and Khair believed every word.

What will a man like this do if he controls time?

The crowd sat in silence.

"I'll join," Sophie's voice didn't carry, but Taivan nodded and she tried again. "If you'll have me. I'm not much as a queen, but I'm still a doctor and would care for my soldiers in our service."

That'd be a trick.

"I'm supposed to believe you'd go from a queen to a lackey just like that?" Taivan said, microphone off.

"When I'm half out of my mind with pain and oppyin and don't even know which of my hand-picked guards put a spear to my heart? Hand me a gun and I'll start spraying, see how many of my people you kill. What else am I supposed to do?"

Taivan turned his mic on. "You've conspired against your own brother; the punishment should be death."

Sophie paled. "It's bad form to slay a teenager kneeling beside her puppy." She'd leaned into her youth, wearing a baggy dress with a much higher neckline than yesterday, forgoing makeup. It was hard not to pity her, but through great effort, Khair managed.

Ow!

Taivan didn't miss a beat. "For your brother's sake, we'll be lenient. Pledge your loyalty to myself, my officers, and our army."

She raised her right hand. "I solemnly swear..." she trailed off, but that was enough.

"So begins your parole." He drew a silver chain with a string of rubies, their luster distracting from the button on the back.

Her dog growled, but she swatted him and held out a shaking hand.

Taivan turned his mic off. "If you plot against me or fiddle with the clasp, you die."

"Or if it gets tangled in my hair, or malfunctions, I die. Did Aidan make this?"

"Hush," Taivan turned on his mic. "If you have a weapon, sharpen it tonight. If you need one, we'll take one. And if you forget who to aim them at, I'll remind you."

The lights died. People screamed, but there was no violence and resistance was impossible. Even half a kilometer from the stands, she heard the grumbled threats of the soldiers she'd stand beside tomorrow.

Part II

TOP SECRET! (If You Read I'll Use You As A Spaceship Launch Pad)

~~Dear~~ Journal,

Normally I'd mock people for this 'cause who are you to think your thoughts need to be recorded forever? But Batu acts like I'm someone I'm not, and no one else would care if I died. Except maybe Taivan because we got ourselves a real war now.

Seems like it anyway, but I've not exactly been sleeping and there's been pills, then getting zapped for pills though that's why I need them, so I don't know what the frickity-frack-cadillac is going on or what I should be doing.

Just heard something, gotta go.

I saw Aidan rummaging through the kitchen! Maybe I've gone full loony because no one else mentioned him but he was a ginger, so who else could it be? I scoped out Sophie's quarters, but he didn't show up. Also, I got bored waiting and since Sophie was working, I broke in to pet Whiskey.

That doesn't sound great in hindsight. But I can't wait around. I start thinking, then Chip gets mad or bored or power trippy and I can't do anything. Taivan's like a sun dragging us all in his orbit and unless I move fast enough, I'll always bend to his will. I chose him in Albion. My life revolves around him since I chose him over Sophie in Albion, all logistical chores (I know armies march on their stomach but imagine counting 'one thousand barrels of spam, one thousand one' all day), and even in my dreams I see him.

Jiao's worse. Even eclipsed, the seasons and tides of my life change to her demands, her silence. I offered her my life. Maybe for guilt or shame or pride, maybe love. But she didn't want it, so it was vain as a golden ship.

I'm going to Sophie's quarters and if she's not there, I'll take Whiskey.

Chip didn't let me take Whiskey.

-(I'll name you later, 7ᵗʰ day of 7ᵗʰ month)

It's 0200 and I want to watch a documentary about the Serengeti on beautiful, habitable Earth (did you know African elephants are bigger than Indian elephants but more skittish so make bad war beasts?). Chip won't let me, as if watching a crocodile will make me grow webbed feet.

Chip's replying, but it doesn't make the cut. This is mine and you with your worm sized brain (they only have ganglia) don't rate.

Anyway, I haven't described the war. There's probably no need for a Rashid al-Din or Xenephon nowadays, but it's better than watching a dozen women compete for the blandest man in the galaxy.

I'm aboard the AKS Sphinx, *a three decker sub-orbital space freighter converted to third rate passenger ship that, with guns mounted, has the audacity to call itself a tanker.*

We're on Planet Asa, our Albion soldier's home planet, which is like Siberia except instead of gulags and sad novels, there're igloo towns and terrible television.

Taivan leads us, his staff Admiral Jun Jiao, Minister of Public Development Enkhiin Batu, Minister of Health Sophie Riley, and Chief Keshig Aidan Riley—something between bodyguard and administrator. They're stiff titles, since that's all he can give. He offered to call me ambassador, general, minister of flattery, but I don't have a proper name to stick it to. I was his anda once. But that was because I needed assurances he wouldn't kill me. Now he calls me his baghatur, a valiant, honorable warrior.

~~I'm not sure if he's kidding.~~

The war started sorta by accident.

The Sphinx *was headed toward Coloma, an independent ZAX trade outpost that ZAX pretends to own (they're more East India Trading Company than Hunnu Mall). We broke down in a storm.*

We towed ourselves to the closest approximation of a village, a bunch of pits insulated with furs and silicon strips. I explored.

The pits—that's a terrible name, it's more like a lodge or sauna-house—were awesome. Dozens of connected room with low ceilings to keep heat, dry enough to keep any tech safe, warmed by the tandoor oven that cast a soothing orange glow over the icy exterior. Was this camp a permanent lodge, or a way-station? Did they travel in families, clans? Wouldn't be a bad way to live.

They weren't thrilled about a grumpy army parking in their yard. Batu haggled for repairs. He went into the Sphinx *to give gifts—don't know why; they hadn't shown hospitality—and found teenagers snagging souvenirs. They panicked and attacked him.*

Taivan heard it. Next thing you know, he has six kids old enough to think they're adults lying on the ground with broken bones, and apparently their crimes are such a grievous offense we declare war on the village and the entire region. These villages might not even constitute a state, they might hate each other. But we conscripted the six and moved on.

The campaign lets our untrained Albion pups play at war with minimum casualties, but it gives Coloma time to prepare. And why do we need Coloma? Their ZAX weapons, maybe.

And the war binds the men to Taivan: he forges orders from the enemies superiors to lead them into traps, uses our dated equipment better than the enemy can use their new gear, and makes overtures of diplomacy to muck it up and stake the letters on his flag like we're the wounded party. Our men may not love him, but they need him.

Chip, you're lucky, so sure of yourself. Please shut up and let me sleep.

(9ᵗʰ day of 7ᵗʰ month)

Chip, I saw your Earth.

It must be a flub since you said I wouldn't get more data, but this wasn't information, it was experience. I stood in your uniform, a camouflaged green though brown grass and gray sky surrounded me. Your comrades learned marksmanship beside me, laying on cold concrete and adjusting their iron sights, your winds only about sixty kilometers per hour. The food was cold and crumbly, with no staying power, but there was stale candy in the ration.

Why are you losing control?

(12ᵗʰ day of 7ᵗʰ month)

We burned another village. I can't see any pattern. Sometimes we kill anyone who looks at us wrong, sometimes we tend the enemy's wounds. The same soldier encouraged his buddies before battle, cowered when it started, threw back a grenade that landed at his feet and led the counterattack.

We train constantly. The Albions iron out mistakes till pride spurs them, makes them slip, confidence smolders until Taivan lights it again.

I tried to help with medicine, but blood makes me crazy. Can't even tie a tourniquet right—killed more of our soldiers losing them than anything else.

I—Khair, but in Chip's memories—walked down a Terran road, gravelly, hilly, carrying my weight in a badly fitted pack. The boots made my heels bleed, feet so swollen I didn't dare remove the boots on our breakfast break. Medics checked for trenchfoot after torrential rains. I pretended I was fine, kept hobbling till it got dark, and we stopped long enough for them to hand out more junk to carry.

My own feet hurt.

(18ᵗʰ day of 7ᵗʰ month)

Batu saved my life. Or stopped Taivan from doing something he shouldn't, so close enough with Chip. Towns banded together to protect a shrine or a show location or something. We weren't going to hit it, but they gathered there. Taivan said to destroy any building they shot out of, but spare anyone who kept the peace.

I stayed on the Sphinx, *supposedly guarding it. I asked Chip to show me the battle, but only because she always makes me watch.*

Taivan marched down the main street in a hazmat suit, surrounded by keshig. I don't worry about him despite their assassin drones (always aimed at him), chemical pulses (that incapacitate everyone exposed), and Iron Dome (it kills outside communication and controls the weather). Jiao covers him with air support and his men cling to him. But Batu fights with the keshig though Taivan says he didn't have to.

A soldier shot at Taivan from a hospital window, killing a man between Taivan and Batu.

Chip prodded me to stop Taivan. But if soldiers hid in a hospital, they made it a legitimate target.

The keshig dragged Taivan into a safe alley. He pushed them aside, pointed to the hospital window, would've gone himself except they blocked him. Batu moved first toward the sniper, half the keshig followed.

I grabbed the radio, but I had nothing to say and the Dome would've stopped it, anyway.

Then I wasn't me.

I blinked and found myself in a damp city, twisted skyscrapers dwarfing dilapidated brick palaces, medieval towers topped with candy-striped cupolas defying the cloudy sky. My team patrolled the streets—some smooth, others cobblestone, most landmine infested. Passing over clear bridges, through mowed parks, around cement roadblocks. Kids filmed us. I smiled at them, listened to them whisper in a language I'm only technically fluent in, and begged a foreign God they're only curious.

Then I was shot.

I, Khair, hadn't left the Sphinx, *but I felt my ribs break underneath Chip's kevlar. It took a moment for that city of onion domes and victory arches and refugee camps to fade. I still see it. Her presence burns through my lungs as I write.*

On Asa, Batu tried but failed to kick in the door. Another keshig threw his shoulder into it and fell in, shot dead before he hit the ground.

When we're ambushed and I'm forced to duck and let them shoot at me, or fight and hope Chip's in a good mood, there's not much fear. But I was outside the battle. My vision wasn't narrowed, adrenaline wasn't pumping. Just me and reality. Yet I wasn't there either, couldn't affect anything, split between the world I saw, and my barely comprehending mind, and all of it was incomplete.

Batu nearly shot the sniper, a young warrior with one arm in a sling, surrounded by those too wounded to flee, but an explosion shook the building.

Then Batu did one of the bravest things I'd ever seen: he slung his weapon across his back where he couldn't use it. He shouted that Taivan and Albion had won, it was over, time to tend the wounded, call in the medics, supervise triage, carry the dead to the mortuaries. The sniper stood there, frozen.

Batu asked the sniper if he wanted a smoke—for outside, of course.

Another explosion rattled the building, and the lights blinked off, replaced by greenish backups. The sniper flinched at the dark, then accepted a cigarette.

Taivan and the rest of the keshig burst in.

My fear filtered through Chip and back again, the feedback loop between us growing the storm. Chip wanted to kill Taivan. But she would've settled for me.

Batu explained to Taivan that the sniper was trying to lay down cover, but an explosion messed up his aim. Batu promised to punish his negligence. When Taivan noticed his keshig had already lowered their weapons, he smiled with bared teeth and promoted the sniper for such wounded bravery. The sniper was so stunned he didn't seem to notice the change of allegiance.

So Taivan spared the hospital and Chip spared me. But if she kills me, she doesn't have to spend half her life in my head, so I'm not making any plans.

I should want it to happen in my sleep. But no, when the time comes, 'let me feel the fog in my throat, the mist in my face' for 'I would hate that death bandaged my eyes and forbore, and bade me creep past'. Yes, those favorite words you hoard for yourself but I wake quoting them.

I've left tracks in your mind, too. My heavy metal doesn't bother you anymore. You're disappointed when I skip the sauna, and when I pass Sophie's room, you listen for Whiskey. How long until you love my people and hate yours? You idiots. You took my life, but you'll become me. So when I have to die, 'let me feel the whole of it in one fight more,' finally look you in the eye and haunt you like you haunt me.

(19th day of 7th month)

I saw Aidan in footy pajamas, standing over the sink with a head of lettuce in one hand and dressing in another. I asked him what he was doing, and he said "eating salad." Then I asked him why, and he said "because there's no pie."

Now I'm eating mint ice-cream alone, which is the worst kind, but the rest of the fridge is salted meat, pickled vegetables, sauces crusted over their caps, and milk on its expiration date.

I tried to ask Aidan about when he'd come back to make sure I'd seen him earlier, and he said it didn't matter, dying was terrible, and he didn't have a preference for any 'verse. He also claimed to have died trying to backflip from one elephant to the other. I said he was full of it, and he acted like I was the crazy one.

I told him to visit Sophie, cause you know, I kinda owe her—all I did was hurt her before she hurt me, why do I feel bad?—but he said it would look like a revolt.

Then he tried to find dessert, and I asked him if his tastebuds were always the same when he traveled. He got impressed at an original question, took out a notebook, and gave me a tally. Jiao was winning, but I had a lot. For some reason, Sophie didn't. Also, he said his tastebuds do change.

Then I asked why he hadn't checked in with Taivan. He said he heard that all the time and if I didn't say something interesting, he'd kick me out of the kitchen. I told him to flip off an elephant. Then I asked why Taivan trusted him since Temujin killed everyone who betrayed their liege, even if they defected to him. He said if Taivan hadn't told me, he wouldn't either. That's probably why.

(25th day of 7th month)

Woke up on a bunk. I sleep in a bed.

We're attacking the last stronghold/town in the area, Kolpol, basically an outpost of Coloma. Their news say Coloma's reinforcing them. Maybe.

Chip saw Taivan and Aidan scheming over a security cam and ordered me to send the recording to Coloma. I will.

Aidan wanted to blow up the town. Taivan said we couldn't waste the firepower, and it was more effective to leave people alive to scare others and strain resources. Aidan said we could blow up their news station. Taivan said their journalists helped us, spreading fear and discord, then laid out his plans.

He talked to Aidan as an equal, a lifelong friend. I thought maybe they were together, but no, Taivan never touched him and barely looked at him, he just prefers the company of a foreign traitor. That's not why I'm gonna give his strategy away, though. He knows I have a snitch in my head. What does he expect? ~~I'm a bomb set to detonate and no one cares.~~

They're nervous about Coloma's spyware. Our sensors can't tell if Kolpol's apparent missiles are real or dummies and we have limited missiles. We'll need boots on the ground to figure it out. Of course Batu volunteered, looking at me as if I'd join him. Why does he always risk himself?

(27th day of 7th month)

Spent the last few days in the hospital cause I didn't broadcast the tape of Taivan's scheming. Batu would be down there.

Chip tried to take me over to send the recording, and now I black out whenever she tries anything funny. Well, Batu's mission starts in a few hours, so I'm going to nap then—if I'm lucky, I'll sleep through it, and then Batu can explain everything when he's back.

***

Khair's body woke up.

Tamika Moore woke stretched out under a weighted blanket, a stuffed wolf tucked under her arm, and wearing nothing but someone else's underwear. Weird dream. She closed her eyes again. Not a dream she wanted, not when shift would start whenever Khair woke. Khair didn't sleep nearly enough, so neither did she.

Someone knocked on the door.

Tam hopped out of bed looking for clothes, heart fluttering over whatever emergency had caused this off-schedule summons.

"Give me a second, Sir!" That wasn't her voice, or even her language. She rubbed her eyes and noticed her hands were paler—she was taller, heavier, and had shorter, straight hair. "Or maybe a few minutes."

She drew in a deep breath, held it for four seconds, exhaled slowly. Tried to focus on what her senses could absorb, and ignore the fishhooks tearing at her stomach that wasn't her stomach. Fluffy blankets, the sea-green walls, the pyramid of soft, bright clothes in the corner, forested white noise Khair listened to when she couldn't sleep.

And the mirror, where she was now one of the multiverse's most hated war criminals. No point denying it. But even as she stared at Khair in the mirror, her mind rebelled.

So did her stomach.

She made it to the toilet at least, even if she tripped on the way there, her stride wobbly.

"Are you okay?" Batu, who must think she was his daughter.

"No." If she was in Khair's body, was Khair in hers? If so, Khair had Tam's wrist-con, could shock her at any time. No rules governed the treatment of Mercy Mission subjects except not to use them for personal gain, so none of Tam's coworkers would intervene.

A fair end, maybe, but not a pleasant one.

But she had tried to help Khair. Perhaps that was why she wasn't dead yet. No, Khair would have panicked in a dim cubicle, would have at least shocked her a few times. Khair was out of commission somehow, but was she still here, or dead?

And what had happened to Tam's soul?

Tam threw on Khair's favorite black hoody, and as the fabric passed over Khair's eyes, she saw through her own eyes—it must be her own, she wore her wedding ring. Halfway across the galaxy, her own body laid on a thin mattress, in a hospital dress, without a blanket. Tam blinked, and was back in Khair's body, Khair's room.

She tried the breathing exercise again, and tasted vomit.

"I'll be off soon, but I have a few minutes to make you mint tea with lots of honey," Batu said. "Or chamomile, to help your stomach."

She slipped into joggers and flushed the toilet. "I think I'll be here a while, thank you."

Is anyone over there? This is Sergeant First Class Moore. There's been some mix-up; I'm in 7701's body. I can give my ID number or any other verification.

No response. Tam brushed Khair's teeth, dressed, and sat on the bed like a kid waiting for a spanking. She had never been fidgety, but she tapped her fingers. Half an hour passed. Neither her comrades nor her superiors said anything.

She didn't fit her body well enough to work out, not yet anyway, but she couldn't sit still anymore. She cleaned. Khair was surprisingly neat, if only because she meticulously cared for everything, antique comics and model engine puzzles and dogeared cookbooks, so Tam couldn't complain too much when she found a decade old canned milk in the mini-fridge.

"What are you doing?"

Jochiin Taivan.

Tam had spent the last few years as a spy, the years before that as an Army linguist and interrogator; she could lie if she fooled herself into believing it was necessary. But she could never lie to anyone she loved. And though General Jochiin stood in front of her, taking up more space than a man his size should, her heart squeezed—no, Khair's—and her own mind drifted back to Zion.

All the flak he'd gotten when they were dating. He spent half the day in trade school and captained the chess team, she had college offers for hockey and basketball. But he was too sure of himself and too proud of her to care. Their wedding the day after graduation. And all the years the Army had kept them apart until he finally died five hundred years ago.

Five hundred years ago, the Chaplain would have told her to identify her emotions and unmet needs, consider the people around her, use mediative language. But between Khair's body misguiding her thoughts and her own borderline psychosis, she couldn't do anything but stand there holding wilted celery and an empty apple juice carton.

"It's time to support Batu," Jochiin said.

He didn't wait for her response, and led her down to his command headquarters, safe in the bowels of his *Sphinx* tanker.

A three-dimensional hologram of the battlefield projected over a round table, their soldier's vitals and missile capabilities projected on one wall, schematics of the enemy's equipment on the other. It was laid out almost exactly like a UOD control room, but that made sense; Chuluun had been a UOD mercenary.

There was no one there but Jochiin and Jiao. Jiao at least looked mission ready in her pilot suit, pistol included. Jochiin wore gym clothes and hadn't combed his hair.

"Are you sure you want UOD to see this?" Jiao said to Jochiin.

Khair's teeth clenched, but it was just a reference to the chip.

Tam spent most of her day at a walking desk, monitoring Khair. It should have been easy to fall into this role, but now these were her only set of eyes, without access to surrounding cameras, without her own space to ground her.

The world was distracting, everything from the chill, the strong coffee Jiao drank, Jochiin's cologne, her chair too high at the desk, the grating sound as Jiao scooted her chair from Khair, the corded muscle in Jochiin's forearms. The image wasn't as high-definition, and she couldn't pause it. Khair's eyes saw. But whose mind processed the data?

Seeing Jiao felt like missing a penalty shot in triple overtime.

"Batu's going out," Jochiin said. "She should be here."

"That won't mean much when I'm trying not to die of food poisoning," Tam said.

Jochiin looked to her, eyebrow raised. "We need to take Kolpol if we're to take Coloma."

She looked away. At least she could direct her vision. Choosing what to see was as important as sight itself.

"The keshig are en-route, keeping comms silence," Jiao said.

"Batu has his own comm. We can check in at any time?" Tam asked, as expected.

Jochiin nodded, expression cool. He didn't like it, but why? It could be dislike for the woman who chopped off his leg, but then why bring her along? Maybe it was stress.

"Aidan should have called by now," Jiao said.

"No one's vitals have spiked. Give them ten minutes." Jochiin touched two pieces of Kolpol's hologram wall and dragged out the ten-kilometer strip between. Dots moved along the wall as a timeline ticked at the bottom. Jochiin stretched out the image, copied it, and turned the duplicate's time to the day before, watched the two timelines on repeat.

"More guards, and different intervals," Jiao said.

"A 20% increase," Taivan said. "And the rotations are staggered by only eight minutes now. Aidan must be studying the new pattern."

"Hey Zanabazar, this is Michelangelo," Aidan said. Codewords, Zanabazar must be some artist.

Jochiin smiled. "I thought you all wanted Temujin?"

Tam tapped her finger. Even as a twenty-first century American, she knew Temujin as the real name of Genghis Khan, the man who killed so many people he changed the earth's atmosphere. And that without ballistic missiles.

"That was only when your plan was working," Aidan said. "You see the hiccup?"

"Noted," Jochiin said. "Can you see if the missiles are legit?"

"Not from this wall, and there's no way we can scale it without spreading outside our refractor's range."

A light refractor could hide a small team from guards if they stayed close and didn't get within five feet of a guard.

"Hold," Jiao said to Aidan, and turned to Jochiin. "We don't have an interplanetary ship anymore. If this fails, there's nowhere else to go. We're outmatched here."

Jochiin wiped sweat from his forehead. "We're outmatched everywhere. Khair, thoughts?"

Tam had been the one on patrol, never the one choosing who to risk. Khair's body leaned forward, strained toward a fight, the prickle running down her spine excitement rather than fear. Whatever tincture of Khair was left thought the Khanate would win. Tam believed her.

"Yeah, don't send my sixty-year-old dad with the scouts under the command of a random foreign mercenary."

"Let me bring air support, Taivan," Jiao said.

"There's not enough time." Jochiin brought Aidan back on. "Stick to the plan."

"Roger that, minimal improv." Aidan's comm went down, but he streamed the light refractor's camera so a live feed of his team's progress appeared over the hologram.

Aidan carried a knapsack and the refractor, while the rest of the team had nothing but a flysuit and sidearm. It would be too difficult to stay together with their flysuits, so they crept toward Kolpol. Mines littered the field before the fence. Batu claimed to have spent months in Explosive Ordinance Disposal before it got too technical for him and led the way.

Tam paced. Batu's pulse quickened, and his blood pressure spiked once when an ambulance went off inside Kolpol, but it regulated after the initial surprise.

By the time they reached Kolpol's wall, it was twilight, the horizon a shade darker than what the eyes had adjusted to: the most dangerous time on patrol. It was only an electric barbed wire fence. They could fly over it and the guard dogs to the missile launchers.

Aidan halted the keshig, readied his flysuit, and waited for the others to follow. Batu fumbled with his. Finally, the keshig jumped, propelled fifteen feet off the ground, and leaned toward the missile launchers.

Dogs barked, alarms screeched. Sleep-deprived, overly caffeinated Kolpol soldiers shot at the keshig as soon as they were visible, before even identifying them. Aidan landed on the other side, invisible again under the refractor, while Batu and the others zigzagged toward the missiles.

A soldier shooting at Batu collapsed with bleeding hamstrings. Aidan flicked the refractor off and stood beside the moaning young soldier, a sawed-off shotgun in one hand, a whip sword in the other, then disappeared again. "You get to live this time. But the rest of you?"

He reappeared behind a soldier, disappeared again as she swirled, and shot her knee.

"Tell him to focus on the mission," Jiao said.

"He's drawing their attention," Jochiin said.

Tam leaned against the wall, as far as she could get from the bullets firing. They echoed over the holo, but she couldn't hear them hit dirt, couldn't get that release when the bullet was most definitely past and not going to hit her.

Breathe in for four seconds, hold, breathe out. Thank God for every undeserved gift, beg for forgiveness, feel no relief. Hope anyway.

Batu reached the missile launcher and slapped a beeping identifier on it. "It's fake!"

Jochiin pumped his fist. "Good, get out of there."

Batu raced back toward Aidan and the refractor, but a Kolpol soldier threw up a jammer. The jammer spun once and detonated, its pulse incapacitating the flysuits and refractor—but also the fence. Everyone's vitals went black. Not dead, just all off-line.

They couldn't see what was happening in Kolpol except by holo, nothing but blue and red dots in a pixelated, gray city.

Tam approached the table, but kept a healthy distance from Jochiin.

"Surrender," Jochiin said over Aidan's comm, broadcasting to the whole team. "You've done well, live to fight another day."

"Thank you, General," Batu wheezed.

His comm turned off.

Jochiin shrank the Kolpol holo and brought up the buzzing Kolpol airport where the commercial jets had been replaced with dogfighters and bombers and troop transporters.

"Bring them back," Jiao said, voice thick.

Jochiin duplicated the holo and sent one to her, but kept his attention on the airport.

Jiao played Kolpol's local news on her wrist-con. A shaky camera recorded soldiers kicking and beating the keshig while the Kolpol officers explained to the crowd that everything was in good order. Batu tried to crawl away.

Tam slapped the table and swore. "Give them something, Taivan, make them stop this!"

She couldn't tell if she was faking; she never could once she took on a role.

"You're killing a Khanate Minister!" Aidan yelled, the only keshig on his feet, though hunched over, lip split. "He's the only one that restrains Jochiin Taivan. He's the only reason Albion is still here…" he spat blood, stifled terrified tears. "If you kill him, that monster will—wait. You don't know he's coming. I need to talk to your colonel! He has my sister, the Queen. I can't tell you everything, not unless you can promise you'll hit back. You have to punish him!"

The camera turned around to an elderly woman, but in the background, they still beat Batu. "Prince Aidan of Albion claims—"

"Turn off your equipment." Jiao called the journalist after Jochiin complied. "I'm Admiral Jun—"

"We know who you are, Princess. What made you fight for the people that murdered the PRGC royal line, and most of your home planet?"

Jochiin leaned forward slightly.

Jiao's nose scrunched, but she flattened it out. "Can the public see this?" The woman nodded, and Jiao set her pistol on the table. "When I was a child and a prisoner, Minister Enkhiin Batu defied his own people to keep me safe. I hope you will treat him as kindly in his imprisonment as he treated me, or I…" Jiao collected herself and looked to Jochiin. She turned off her translator and spoke to him in her heart language, which neither Khair nor Tam knew.

He saluted Jiao as if she were the superior.

She turned her translator back on and kneeled. "I am an Admiral. Minister Batu has an honorary position fitting his years of service, but serves as a sergeant. I will surrender myself in exchange for him."

The anchor bobbed her head. "Great! I don't really have authority for that, but everyone is looking toward that colonel. He must be the highest ranking. Hey, sir!" She waved at the officer, but Jiao hung up.

She nodded to Jochiin, glanced to who she thought was Khair. "Be good to Batu and don't disgrace us."

She left.

Jochiin brought the news and the Kolpol airport back up.

Tam, still smelling blood and dirt and gunpowder though the room smelled of pine cleaner, headed toward the door.

"Stop, Chip." Jochiin leaned back in his chair, Jiao's gun in hand.

"It's a bit of a jerk move to call me that." Tam used her best Khair intonation. "You know the whole mind-invasion thing is not one of my favorite subjects: that's either prehistoric animals, the history of warfare, or—"

"Shut up."

For a moment, there was silence except Aidan on the news, bubbly explaining about a supposed Khanate attack within the hour. The silver-haired newscaster was almost salivating at the thought of an attack on-screen, and kept trying to call Jiao to verify it.

Jochiin spun the revolver wheel and motioned for Tam to sit.

She could be shot just as well standing up, so she didn't move. Khair's legs had gone numb, anyway.

"Where is she?"

"I don't know. Some part of her must be here; she feels for Batu and Jiao in a way she didn't when she just woke up from the procedure."

All true, and it didn't hurt to have him wonder how much of Khair remained. But even with her lingering love, she might be dead. Love only grew stronger with practice, despite opposition or regret, and death was powerless against it.

If Khair's body was killed, would Tam return to her body? Or just die?

The news showed Kolpol officers checking Aidan's story. It appeared as if one third of the Khanate troops were marching toward Kolpol, but their stealth attacks were deemed suicidally inadequate, and the whole march was considered a feint.

On Jochiin's airport holo, little red dots raced toward the troop transport planes. Kolpol was launching a full attack, not on the soldiers on the road, but at the command headquarters and bulk of the remaining Khanate army.

Jochiin called a subordinate. "Standby. They'll be here in twenty minutes." He hung up and looked her over. "You stand too straight, talk too slow, and sit too still."

Tam's eyes narrowed—Khair's face wasn't meant to play poker.

"Batu would be upset if his daughter was gone, and the rest of the 'verse would fear us less. You'll pretend to be sick and be confined to your quarters, but whenever Batu tries to holo you, you'll keep up appearances. And if you try anything, I'll put Khair's body in a doctube. She'll rest, but you? You'll be conscious, unable to move, barely breathing, for years."

Tam's stomach dropped.

But it wasn't a terrible deal. With Tam in Khair's body, UOD had an advantage. But if Tam was confined to Khair's room, whereas Khair was still one of Taivan's most trusted officers, it was better for them to pull Tam out again. Though it galled that Jochiin had found her out so quickly.

But not nearly as much as even now, looking at him coach artillery commanders and prepare missiles, she had to fight Khair's urge to help him. It would be as effortless as helping Zion with the dishes.

"When she went back into the *Bankhar* after the crash, it was for you." Tam's inflection sounded more like Khair's, though she hadn't tried.

He looked up from his maps, but his eyes darkened when he saw her, back still straight. "Then you took too much from her. Whenever she questioned Chuluun's orders, he'd threaten Batu. She would have done anything for him."

And proved it.

"Did you love her?" The body couldn't help but ask.

He looked her in the eye, opened his mouth, and returned to the news. "I'm done with you, Chip. Go."

Tam went straight to Khair's room, locked herself in and turned on the news, trying to purge Jochiin Taivan from her mind.

***

July 28, 532 DH

Chip isn't my name, but it'll do.

For the sake of preserving knowledge, I'll continue this narrative. I'm biased against the Khanate, but I'll mitigate that. I'm working with foreign sensory organs, in an unfamiliar setting, so I'll gather corollary research to understand my observations[1].

It's highly probable the Khanate has secured the only obstacle in their way to Coloma. Through the spy Aidan Riley, Jochiin Taivan convinced Kolpol authorities to attack his force in mass. Taivan had sent one-third of his force at Kolpol, and concealed Albion land-based missiles within his ships. When the Kolpol fleet and

---

1. My mind inhabits Khair's body and my own. Both bodies have the same thoughts yet I can move one body without the other. Either my consciousness is splitting, or Khair is still there. I hope she is; I didn't want this. No one deserves it, no one has the right to inflict it.

vanguard attacked, he decimated it with his missiles, and the third of his force attacked, seizing a quarter of the city.

They could have fought on, but they were in chaos. The soldiers didn't know they'd been guarding dummy missiles, and their own jammers hampered communications, moreover, ace pilot Jun Jiao's ship was seen flying toward Kolpol, which had lost a good portion of its air support. They surrendered.

July 29,

Taivan hasn't moved against Coloma. His forces use Kolpol as a base to subdue the Asan countryside. Like Khair, I can't discern the military purpose behind attacking these towns. Asa is no threat to his flanks, or anything else. He isn't indulging himself. He never compromises his mental faculties or coddles himself, although he trains from 0530 to 0700, so he's most vulnerable then. Maybe he's weakening Coloma's resolve, or he doesn't think his troops are ready yet.

His uncle, Armariin Chuluun, showcased his conquest to recruit others. Maybe that's his plan. Or he's in love with war.

July 30^2,

Taivan invited me to his quarters for dinner. I had been in a 12x12 room for a few days, so even with Khair's treadmill and virtual reality games, I accepted, specifying my diplomatic intentions since Khair is clearly infatuated with him.

He was flipping through old Coloma news when I entered—not politics, but their singing shows and sports highlights. I offered him UOD's money to leave, and he reminded me I didn't have that authority. When I offered to contact the proper authorities, he laughed. He rebuffed further negotiation with glib humor, niche historical insults, and what I assume was flirtation, but it was difficult to tell.

---

2. My superiors are attempting to extricate my mind. My own body won't last much longer. If it dies, I may retain this body, or my untethered mind may die as well. I don't know what will happen to my host, and I see her pre-Mercy Mission memories in my dreams. I've no estimate on how long either of us will last, so I'll not yet bore you with final words.

I won't want to wander into classified territory here, but I asked why he was doing this if not money or power. He said he'd already told Khair, so I should know. Then he changed the channel and for the first time in this body, I had a sensation that was mine alone; I went cold.

He showed my home. A little mountain town with nothing to do but hunt or hoop, freezing most of the year though the sun always shines, where I always felt too big and too small. Poets say home can be anywhere with loved ones, but that's not true. Home is the familiar, the comprehensible. It hasn't changed, but I didn't recognize anyone, and it wouldn't recognize me, regardless of what body I was in.

He offered me a chance to return if I helped Sophie bring Khair back, then he changed the channel back to the present day and the war.

I was caught flat-footed, so it took me a moment to see the threat, my home and this destruction he could cause. I stumbled out.

Khair wondered if this man had a true self. I've seen it. She should count herself lucky she has not.

July 31[3],

The Khanate's raids on the countryside continue. Coloma forces have not yet been lured out.

Khair,

I've done my best to treat your body with dignity. I've exercised us and eaten a measured diet, waited three days before I showered. Your gums bled when I brushed your teeth and I've tended the callouses on your hands, although they reopened when I trained.

I understand why you've been so faithful to such faithless men. As suspected, it's partially a survival tactic. But you have a greater imagination than I, a greater

---

3. I'm unable to control my own body, and I see Khair's past in fragmented hallucinations in my waking hours. I don't want to die in the wrong body. This brain is more frightened than my own. But death is nothing more than when a child faces a needle to be inoculated against some disease they cannot fully comprehend.

Thankfully, I'm an organ donor.

capacity to hope. My empathy has never been tied to the individual but to their way of understanding the world. I've been incapable of pity because I've seen nothing valuable in Taivan's perspective. This is perhaps a flaw, but the greater flaw is not being sure in my judgement and thus being incapable of improvement.

Anyway, if you read this, I'm likely dead ~~or insane~~, my words destined for the flame. I've no objection. I only ask you to remember your helplessness and pity those in your power.

August 1,

I may not be able to use objective language, but there's a time to flip tables.

Taivan insisted on personally mopping up the streets after a skirmish. He allowed me to accompany him to keep up the charade that Khair was still a great general at his disposal.

The village was, as Taivan should've known, utterly worthless strategically. He was there because the dawn lighting would look good on a poster. When I noted there were more important targets than random villages, he ordered me to help the medics. I obliged.

I knew he offered people what they wanted on his terms, and still I was taken in.

As I helped wounded civilians, Taivan bent beside a girl of about six, and spoke with her. I grabbed a scalpel.

The girl stabbed his armored chest. He yanked out the knife and stabbed her. He called for a doctube, but that's no credit to him; he was a grown man scared of a child he'd orphaned. I concealed the scalpel and ran toward him and the girl (she was already dead) as if to save her.

Taivan grabbed me so it appeared to be an embrace, pinning my arms. I tried to stab him, but he did some trick with his leg and I tripped over the girl's body and sliced my hand.

I attacked him still, but someone shot at us. It was a town like home (historically inaccurate, edit later) where every potbellied old man thought himself a budding hero but still feared his mother so they would've fought to the last after that.

Jiao and her squadron swept down, firing at everything that moved.

Taivan told her to 'abort, friendly fire.'

Jiao cut back, flying between sides, firing between peoples so no one could cross the gap or poke their head up to shoot. Taivan rose, the only one standing, looking like a hero, and let the people go.

Even Jiao didn't trust him and escorted them away, only landing when they'd fled beyond the horizon. They probably froze to death.

I stabbed what should've been his femoral artery but forgot about his prosthetic, and he was dressed for the cold with no sign of it. He kneed me in the head.

How many hours have I trained? And this body is stronger than mine, though slower, three inches taller so the limbs feel gangly, my style wrong. But I wasn't just beat, it was easy. Yes, I'm forty and he's in his prime, but I had a knife and he had nothing. I've killed men his age before. But I had my squad then.

And my sense. If I had controlled myself, if I'd waited, maybe I could've rid us of that plague. But even if I had, since Sargon of Sumer and the birth of civilization, people like him have had their way. I could kill him a thousand times and there'd always be another.

Is it only vanity to try? An effort to write my name in humanity's shared consciousness, as deluded as Taivan—worse, deluding myself?

Maybe my efforts are self-interested, but so is eating and sleeping and putting on an oxygen mask before helping your neighbor with theirs. Altruism isn't disguised self-hate, putting everyone above yourself because they're other. It's joy in helping others. Love that would prefer to suffer pain than to inflict it. Friendless here, I have no options but to be selfish or rely on reasoned principle.

Duty should be enough. But it's hard to shed real blood and suffer real pain for an intangible concept.

I digress. Jiao landed near Taivan.

"We need to talk," she said. (I've watched this tape repeatedly to see what I should've done, dialogue is precise.)

Taivan dropped the bloody knife. "Talk."

Jiao turned her translator off. I don't know what she said. But Taivan kept his on and said, "I'll continue to respond proportionately."

Jiao flipped her translator back on. "Proportionately? Is your strength equal to a seven-year-old, then?" She held her pistol. "Somehow, you're all the family and friend I have, Jochiin Taivan. But—"

She wasn't done, but Batu caught her attention, waving, standing by a gaggle of kids he had distracted from their classmate's death.

"We've done enough," Taivan said. "We're ready to face Coloma now."

Jiao had looked from me—Khair—to Sophie leaning over an injured man's chest to check his breathing and better eavesdrop, to the Khanate. "It was never about being a good pilot. I was pathetic."

I looked for that scalpel, but I was still groggy.

He bit his lip, reaching for his translator, but covered it, cracking his knuckles. "I hold you in as high esteem now as ever."

Jiao looked away. "You can play to an audience, or keep your best pilot; I'll be in your room when you finish cleaning up."

Sophie approached Taivan, kept her distance. "I could try to bring the girl back."

The words of a woman desperate to survive or some Faustus selling herself to the devil? Is anyone capable of that?

Taivan scowled at Sophie, more so when she didn't react. "When she starts to rot, bury her."

I expect clips of it in the news, everything cropped but mighty General Taivan, slayer of children, standing firm amid gunfire though it's his admiral shooting.

August 2,

I'm cut off from my body, so I have no back-up[4]. Khair, I couldn't protect your body, I will try to redeem your name.

---

4. The images of 7701's former life seem triggered by Batu, Jiao, or Jochiin. I don't believe she's fighting for her body, but rather this is the last activity of a dying mind. As to why 7701 had this reaction and the two previous subjects I've overseen didn't, I am likely at fault; we had blocked information, so I transmitted my own. Yet 7701 grew some principles, and the others did not.

Now that it's just about over, I can apologize. I can't say I understand or approve of most of what you've done, but I know what it's like to have no good choices, no recourse but to pray to the Judge that sits on the mercy seat. Clearly, I have no advice. Life is miserably hard and we can do nothing but endure it.

So much for my faith, but the end comes and it will be sight.

I've requested Sophie's medical attention for my head injury, claiming it was worse than it was. I hoped to enlist Sophie's aid, but Taivan came with her. Sophie prodded at me with medically unnecessary but cathartic force, and when she checked my vitals, left a note in my hand.

It says she knows I'm UOD, and she'll send trustworthy nurses to see if we can turn Taivan's forces from Coloma. She didn't seem inclined to hurt him, merely to bring her people home.

***

August 3,

We're rolling toward Coloma. Their forces have attempted to stop us on the road. Jochiin stays away from these incursions, only occasionally acting as Jiao's gunner. Now, they wi—

Khair's body collapsed, pen still in hand.

The pen twitched.

Khair's body woke again, jerked out her chair and stumbled back over it, only slowing down when she realized she was alone. She righted the chair with trembling fingers.

*Welcome back the proper captain of this ship *bows to glorious applause and Chip's ugly weeping**

I'm lost.

Part III

It seems as if you've been gone long enough.
  Death should've slipped off now like a loose cuff
  and if the grave himself misses you, tough.

  I expect to hear your voice and suspect
  I always will, paying my last respects
  when I look for you, my mind derelict.

  There's got to be some better way to say
  I miss you, some pathos to make Heaven stay
  his sunny gaze, turn aside his long rays.

  You didn't want to go. Would you return?
  If you did, eternity's light would burn
  all you tried to hold. Yet I, useless, yearn

  for this necromance abomination
  as if I could provide you salvation.

"Necromancy" Tamika Moore, 531 DH

Home, If You Can Call It That

COLOMA CITY STRETCHED OUT beneath Khair like a rousing tiger. The finest gunsmiths in the universe had built the city's aerial defenses, but gunsmiths weren't engineers or generals. Leadership held a loose rein, little cohesion in the defense, though even some houses had cannons.

It wasn't impenetrable. But there was sufficient deterrent for anyone who was less fond of pyrrhic victories than Pyrrhus of Epicurus.

Khair sat in her swivel chair and stared out the window, desecrated journal on her lap. She'd barely been gone one week. 'Gone' wasn't the right word—she'd been there, pounding Chip's mind as her body tried to kill Taivan, shrinking as Sophie slapped Chip around, watching Batu treat the enemy as his daughter.

Her own memories had flashed before Chip. She'd felt their pulse, their heat, but they lay buried in dark water, only a few meters away but lost in a medium she wasn't meant for.

Occasionally she'd drifted in Chip's current and been pulled out into her body. Laid there, a machine breathing for her, nodes on her chest keeping her heart beating, limbs cold and numb. The doctors might've been robots for their charity, though they tended their own soldier. She couldn't move there, either.

She hadn't heard from Chip since she'd been freed. And she had been freed after Taivan maneuvered so that her own mind was more valuable to UOD than their imprisoned agent's; she had been powerless to escape. But Chip's presence remained, a blanket of suffocating otherness.

Khair didn't warrant an explanation. How it'd happened, what it meant, if it could be prevented. If they'd kill her or let her suffer it again. Any details would tell her of UOD's capacities and limitations beyond those palpable in her flesh.

The physical world was supposed to be hers, but it smelled of laundered clothes, steamed vegetables and microwaved fish, someone else's shampoo on her pillow.

The bed was the worst. When she collapsed in it, it was warm. She wrapped herself in quilts and reached for her stuffed wolf with the Khanate banner over its eye, but it was banished to a corner.

Her posters of the Altai mountains, Manchurian steppe, Milky Way, covered her risqué posters. Her weights were reorganized. Most of her manga lay untouched, dusty, but the historical ones were leafed through, with a coded note as a bookmark.

She should burn it.

Since being in Chip's body her tongue lay wrong, trying to speak another language. Her hair felt too short, the fade strangely light. She avoided her reflection but there was no escaping that her temperature ran cooler, her torso was longer, her skin lighter. Her own self and it was wrong now.

Someone knocked.

She flinched.

"Tell UOD that if they return Khair," Taivan said. "I won't attack their Coloma allies."

"Taivan?"

He swung the door open so hard it shook on its hinges and studied her, hand falling from his pistol. "Welcome home, baghatur."

He spoke her language without a translator mediating, voice so rich and kind she blinked back tears. She'd expected a lifetime of apathetic silence. "Chip's still here. You can't trust me, I..." she tried to smile, and it nearly broke her face.

He shut the door and crossed the floor, kneeled by her chair and clasped her hand. "Sophie's working on regeneration, she might be able to build you from scratch, without Chip. Though without these memories."

No.

"You said you could get Chip out of my head, get me my memories. That was a lie, wasn't it?"

"Yes." He released her. "I didn't know how the program had changed you then; I lied a lot. But if we capture a UOD scientist, maybe they can figure something out."

She pointed to Coloma outside the window. "That's not UOD. Unless they're hiding in an underground bunker to rival Dìxià Chéng."

"Coloma has something like that. I've no idea how many soldiers, rations, or—"

"Don't change the subject." He raised an eyebrow, but she didn't let him protest. "When are we going to stop beating up farmers and fight UOD?"

"ZAX arms UOD mercenaries, Coloma is a crucial ZAX station. So ZAX is sending faster than light ships to save Coloma, and we need those ships." Taivan stood, steadying himself with the back of her chair, his thumb against her shoulder. "This was necessary. And we've been far more lenient than we would've been in UOD's service."

"'In UOD's service?' Aidan's seen a time we help those goons?"

"Something like that."

Even piloting her body again, her fate was beyond her. "You have permission to massage my shoulders."

Taivan obliged. "Do you remember anything about Chip we can use?"

"Besides you threatening her home so she'll be extra awful? No." Khair winced as he worked at a knot by her neck. "She may be dying."

"She'll try to steal your body."

"Self-preservation isn't high on her to-do list."

"Her superiors will order it."

Khair batted his hands away and leaned so far back in her chair she hit her head against the window. "Can Sophie help?"

"Not yet, but maybe she could do something for Chip."

"Whoop di doo. And I follow it makes taking my body unnecessary, it's just irritating. Side note. Sophie was working with Chip to stop you but she didn't want to kill you."

"Sophie told me, she was keeping Chip busy."

Khair laughed and came alive then. Though mostly from fear of reprisal, slimy and dark, worms wriggling in a sealed can waiting for the hook.

Taivan glanced at the door. "I have to brief Jiao in twenty minutes, but you can come, or I can call Batu. Or do you want to be alone?"

Not that. She needed a lifeline even if it turned to a puppeteer's strings. "Call me someone pretty whose loyalty I can buy for a few hours."

"You have our loyalty." Taivan opened a comm link. "Aidan earned a break; I'll send him here so you can watch he doesn't shoot a rifle with his feet or something. He might steal Whiskey for you."

"I'm not a babysitter," Aidan said over Taivan's comm.

"No, you're the babysat. You two can oversee logistics."

Aidan grumbled what might've been agreement.

"Not him," Khair said. "Last time I saw him he was trying to paint something from the Kamasutra, and when I commented—without malice—that it looked nothing like it was supposed to, he flicked paint in my face and said 'behold, anything can be art if it's sad enough.'"

Taivan grinned. "You recognize the Kamasutra?"

"Nope. Aidan described it in painstaking detail."

"Skipping the part about gross emotional intimacy," Aidan said. "Would you prefer Krishna blabbing about just war theory or some reincarnation nonsense?"

"How many times have you died and been reborn?" Taivan said.

"I remember my past selves, so it's no reincarnation. I'm just old." He yawned. "It's the only beautiful lie. But neither good nor evil deeds affect my next life, and the chasm between me and everyone else in this universe is uncrossable."

Taivan rolled his eyes as if he was the immortal hearing things for the thousandth time. "At least he didn't claim to be god."

"By definition—"

"You remember other versions of yourself between timelines," Khair said. "What else do you retain?"

The comm went quiet. Then Aidan snorted. "Your grudges. Sometimes your loves. The real question is why Taivan, whose usual lineup is Arrian, Musashi, and Clausewitz, knows the Kamasutra."

Taivan winked at Khair. "I don't hire my companions."

"Don't boast, she'll try to hire you," Aidan said.

"Is that really the worst that could happen?" Khair said.

"No, that'd be turning a joke into a lecture. If you want to be treated like an adult, function through a minor inconvenience."

"Minor—"

Someone peeked open the door. Sophie crept in, smiling so broadly Khair would cross the street if she saw her in public. "Aidan's back?"

Sophie didn't realize Khair was back, or notice Taivan.

Taivan nodded to Khair. She sighed. "Yes. He has access to Taivan's cup, if you can get us something to put in it."

Sophie's smile died. "That's premature."

"Is it?" She'd never heard Chip's real voice, didn't know the cadence or tone, but with her current snappishness there was no acting involved.

"Aidan," Sophie said. "What do you say? With my collar, there's not much I can do."

"Wonderful," Khair said, bored. "I'll go kill the most powerful man on the planet with no plan, because hey, I'll be dead, and it'll be someone else's problem."

"Khair?" Sophie stepped back, raising her hands. "Taivan knew—"

"What did I know?" Taivan said, voice cold.

"That I was working for you. You heard me, general, I didn't plan violence against you. Is Aidan safe?"

"I'm with them," Aidan said.

"With us, you mean." But she bit her lip to keep from crying. "I'll be in my lab."

"There's something wrong with the Mercy Mission program," Taivan said to Sophie. "Keep Chip alive in her own body."

"I'll try, but I don't know what technology UOD has, or the length of the time lag between them, or how it happened. Is there a backup plan?"

Khair groaned. "Yeah, I have a fantastic funeral."

"You didn't get back on your own?" Sophie said. "Then their scientists are on it. Rest and we'll treat your symptoms, medicate Chip through you."

Khair settled into bed, hugging the khanate wolf stuffy. "I dream with her half the time. Go, I'll find a way."

She slept much longer than she intended, nearly two days. Her strength grew. Her mind solidified. And on the other side Chip did the same at a different rate, her own person. No memories were shared, no images. Feelings, tone of voice, words always came too easily, so they fought over how it happened.

Chip thought she'd poured too much of herself into Khair. Ghosts hid in Chip's words. People she labored to save but had killed, and felt the death she inflicted.

Chip was wrong. She couldn't help but to question, fight, teach. Her past subjects might not have been able to keep up like Khair, but she would've thrown herself into them, nonetheless. No, it'd started with the war, a hint when Sophie's ring exploded and worsening when Chip was forced to the front again.

But when Khair asked her about it, there was genuine denial.

UOD had blocked Chip's memories, too.

Family Dinner Diplomacy

If KHAIR THOUGHT CHIP would have more compassion after being in her body, after losing some of her memories, she was sorely mistaken. Emphasis on sore. Chip was healthy besides fatigue but her sense of wrongness permeated Khair's mind and she lashed out like a dying star, destroying everything around her.

Probably Khair should have some compassion after being in Chip's body, after losing all her memories. But she was busy trying to avoid electrocution. And waving a pan at the smoke alarm so her cooking didn't set it off, while Taivan and the Rileys ate a late dinner, and Batu listened to people complain per his ministerial duty.

"What's the latest reporting?" Taivan asked Aidan.

Jiao should've been his second in command but she was off flying wherever she could avoid Taivan since he'd stabbed that girl.

"No change," Aidan said. "We can't crack their codes, but they can't breach our siege."

"Any sign of ZAX?"

"Not yet."

Taivan nodded. "What of our soldiers, Albion's condition?"

"Naguib says Albion's better off with fewer mouths to feed," Sophie said. "We've got combat wounds, cold injuries, and some idiot engineers got burned. Overall, we're operating at 95% strength."

"A fuel shortage delayed our northern supply line, but it's operating again." Khair had gotten logistics back from Aidan, who preferred snooping and gossip, otherwise known as intel. Ensuring their supplies were properly transported, stored, and rationed so she could burn these burgers wouldn't give Chip an excuse to barbecue her.

Jiao barged in, helmet in hand, loose hair pasted to her forehead. "I contacted Coloma's eastern rivals. They'll lend us ships but they want to talk to you, Taivan, make sure it's a good investment."

He stood. "Any fit for interstellar travel?"

"No, three tankers, six landers, and two dozen dogfighters with able pilots."

"Good work. Catch up on the situation here, then rest." He left.

Khair pulled out a seat for Jiao and flipped a burger on her plate. Jiao pushed it away.

"You're a missed meal from the hospital, so your refined palate is gonna have to stoop." Khair meant she was back and wouldn't abandon them again.

Jiao let her hair down and untangled it. "Aidan, what's going on?"

"Nothing new." He pretended he hadn't been staring at her mussing her long hair and brought her zucchini dumplings. "But IGH-3 is streaming an exhibit of their early exploration collection, you can fly some vessels. There's one simulation where you blow up."

"Any faster than light?"

"To look at, but not to practice on. They have funny ideas about mercenaries getting free practice. You have piloted at light speed?"

"Where are we going anyway?" Khair said. "Does UOD have a base where all their leaders are conveniently located?"

Chip shocked her and once it stopped hurting, shocked her again.

"No, Chuluun only had three vessels capable of it," Jiao said to Aidan, downing a biscuit. "Did you make these? They're amazing."

"I didn't have time for the sauce, but this should make up for it." He poured her blackberry wine.

"When's the exhibit?"

Aidan tipped his glass to her and sipped; Jiao lifted the glass but didn't drink. "Right after the lost civilizations exhibit, with artifacts and models of Harrapan, Cahokian, Minoan sites. And newer, extraTerran locations."

Jiao arranged the dumplings. "Jungang ju?"

Her home planet, decimated by Chuluun.

He nodded.

"Well. I think a Gu Kaizhi wing would work better with—" she stopped, looking as if she was experiencing emotions for the first time and wanted to unsubscribe. "How?"

"Scavenged, or bought off scavengers," Aidan said. "The hub's seven light years off, slow, I could take back your people's things. Though Jungang ju's in Khanate hands so I'd have to take that, too."

"We're Khanate," Khair said.

"Thank you. Truly." Jiao ignored Taivan's incoming call. "But I can't exile you, or open another front. Sophie, you've not had further issues?"

"No, thank you." The same reverent tone Sophie reserved for Taivan.

"Good. Message me if anything changes."

Khair took Jiao's seat and squeezed BBQ sauce on her untouched hamburger.

"So," Sophie said to Aidan. "Since when do you do nice things for other people?"

"Since I've found someone with good taste." He poured Jiao's wine into his cup. "Mostly."

Sophie snorted. "Here I was thinking that was why you sold me out to Taivan. Pour me a drink."

Aidan gave her one finger's worth.

Khair held out her cup, but Chip buzzed her. She looked for desserts in the fridge, found only shortbread with the appearance and taste of C4.

"You could've warned me, helped me escape to Io or Titan," Sophie said to Aidan.

"We'll need you."

"You'd let them kill me otherwise? Keep pouring, and I'll pretend it's an apology."

He filled her cup. "You'd kill me for Albion, I'd let a version of you die for the multiverse. But you're always necessary."

"Just say you love me while I can still hear it." She took out a bottle of painkillers. "I feel you staring, Khair, and yes, it's because someone poked their dirty thumbs in my skull. Stop gawking."

Khair broke the cookie in two and tossed the smaller half to Sophie but it hit her and bounced into her drink.

"What does that help?" Sophie fished for the cookie, couldn't find it, and drained the glass.

"That's desecration," Aidan said.

"Nothing this gross is holy." Sophie gestured with a soggy cookie. "And don't pretend to be cultured, vandalizing museums doesn't count."

Batu said she had siblings. Would they have been so annoying together? **Chip, let me look them up. They're dead, what could they hurt?**

The point is to make you a different person.

So, say no. Tell me I have to abandon my dead family.

Care for your living family.

"I switched my work into the Andromeda Fine Arts Center and no one complained," Aidan said.

"They had lax security, so what? You could do something with your mind—"

"I am. The enemy will use any tool you make, any discovery. Not my paintings. And my mind's no more public domain than your body."

Sophie held her glass out for a refill. "When everyone you love is dead and you're trapped in endless eons, you'll have no one. Make yourself suitable company."

"Tough," Khair said to distract Chip from her sudden tension. "Speaking of impossible tasks, how's the whole memory—" She slapped the table, shocked.

"Don't posture." Sophie clenched her hands beneath the table but there was no tremor in her voice. "Brain surgery can be so terribly tricky."

"You're not touching my brain," Khair said.

You'd benefit too, you stupid cow. And don't I have some credit? I offered my life for Jiao, unless you've forgotten.

Warm relief as Chip did remember, but that didn't stop her from grasping around the strange, fresh gaps in her head, aching like a lost tooth.

Taivan entered with Batu. "We're meeting with President Buck Davids."

Good, you can give him your numbers and positions.

Batu, carrying a picnic basket, bowed to Taivan, who nodded awkwardly. "I overheard Chief Keshig Riley say he needed a meeting with Buck—wasn't eavesdropping—but he seemed busy. So, I called and asked for a tour before or after the meeting, whatever's easier."

"When does Davids expect you? Does he only expect you?" Taivan said.

"Don't know, I just asked for a tour." Which to a soldier meant reconnaissance, but Batu meant sampling food-trucks. "He said anyone was welcome, and I said I'd try to bring my daughter."

"Maybe someone less valuable would like that opportunity." Khair looked to Sophie.

"It's me, isn't it?" Sophie said after no one spoke. "Much as I enjoy being paraded, he doesn't respect Albion, you won't win any points."

"Fine," Khair said. "But there better be good food."

Within the hour, she was at the city gates looking for the man who'd help her betray her friends.

The Wrong Way to Love

If Khair had a choice between living in Coloma City or living in a landfill of sharp glass, open wires, and human feces, she'd probably pick Coloma. But at least she'd have the landfill all to herself.

"It's so big," Batu said. "Big buildings, big screens, big streets, big ships, all the people."

The city had no age or rhythm; horses and bikes and rickshaws shared moving sidewalks, buildings of hand-hewn stone displayed digital signs, a fifty-lane street merged to ten. No matter how wide the curb she ended up jostled into the street.

Everyone here knocks into me, not letting me hit back is probably offensive.

Chip ignored her. A quick smackdown gave her a reference point, silence left her groping in the dark.

She didn't trust this place. The buildings were new growth, cranes towered, drills echoed. There was no cohesion in the monolithic jumble, no way to ground herself when the buildings were the same height and the signs changed constantly.

"Where are we meeting Davids?" Khair asked.

Batu disappeared up the stairs awaiting public transit. Trains cut across the skyline like aqueducts, the shelter beneath claimed by the homeless and equipped with outdoor latrines, showers, and fire pits. It didn't erase the smell, but the streets were mostly clean.

The cab was stuffed to saturation: three people sat on one lap. Batu nestled inside, happily wielding his elbows. She followed.

The train lurched forward, and she jolted back into an old man in a cheap suit too comfortable with her pressed against his chest. She screwed her boot into his foot as she straightened.

"Batu, this is important. We need to get to... wherever we're going."

The train screeched to a stop and people pushed in, so much mass that pushing out was like fighting through a shield wall. Khair led with her shoulder and pulled Batu out with her.

"That was fun," Batu said. "What next?"

"Find Davids."

"We should eat first." He wandered into the street to get a better look at the signs.

"Get back!"

A honking motorcycle cut between them.

She retreated to the sidewalk, jamming her elbow into a young woman for rolling a suitcase into her heel. Khair gritted her teeth and waited, but nothing happened. There was such a mass of people Chip must not see everything, especially with so few hovering copcams.

"In a second." He stepped backward, a full meter into the street. "Do you want soup or—"

"Dad!"

He stopped moving, attention snapped to her, smile lighting his face.

So, she saw his grimace for a spilt second when a taxi hit him. Time slowed, let her feel every frame, yet raced so quickly there was nothing she could do.

Batu bounced off the hood and rolled down, his pants caught on the solar panel so the car dragged him until they ripped. The cabby didn't stop and the car behind tailgated so closely it ran over Batu the moment he fell from the cab.

He didn't move when a third car swerved too late, its low bumper pushing him into the ground. Blood poured from his head, gravel in the grooves of his scars, tread marks on his shattered arm.

UOD's blood revulsion mastered her, and she gagged, turned away—and saw a truck careening toward Batu, driver laying on the horn.

She rushed into the street. Batu tried to push her away, slowed her. She grabbed his arm and dragged him toward safety but his open back left chunks of tissue—organs? it looked like a half-bloomed bud—behind. She dove out of the way.

The truck stopped.

The driver hopped out. Good. Someone in his dungheap had to pay and—"I'll direct traffic. Lay the pieces on the cleanest part of his shirt, wrap his head if you can. We can carry him to a doctube three blocks down."

"He won't get in one, he needs a hospital, now. And I need your truck."

The driver shook his head. He was fat with a weathered face and thinning hair, a brace on his knee, but he somehow blocked her punch. "Guess I'll get his guts off the ground, and you direct traffic."

Chip did nothing. Was she jotting notes for a future frying? The line between them was still taut, but silent.

"Give me the truck!" Their med-evac choppers would be on standby for the war effort.

He started to answer. But when she raised her fists, he rubbed his pastry-sticky hands on his pants, scooped Batu up with organs on his shirt, and laid him on the passenger seat. He tried to step away, but she blocked his path.

"Take us to the hospital," she said.

"Just use the 'tube, he'll understand. I can't lose my job over this."

"Better than losing your head."

"Lady, I got fifty kilos on you and my good friend sanity." She cocked her fist, but he didn't move. "Though the doctube doesn't have a psych ward, so hospital it is."

Khair crouched in front of Batu as he lay slumped in the passenger seat. If there was an accident she would make sure he didn't go through the windshield; she wouldn't lay a tight seatbelt over his bruised and ripped torso.

The truck navigated well by virtue of being able to crunch everything else on the road, forcing everyone out of the way. The driver stopped at a light where six roads intersected.

"What're you doing?" Khair said.

He gestured to the people in the crosswalk.

She leaned against the horn. The throng didn't hurry. If anything, their saunter slowed to a meander, and a straggler stopped in the middle searching the street signs.

"Tuya?" Batu said, held her hand as he called her mother's name. Though the truck was still, the outdated engine wheezed, making the chairs bounce, and blood zigzagged down the ripped upholstery of the maroon seats. "It'll be okay."

Said the one hallucinating and farting as some organ failed. Khair pressed the horn until the pedestrian turned around, flipped them off and moseyed back the way he came. The lights changed, letting someone other than them go.

She tapped the dash, willing the lights to change.

The driver fiddled with the radio, stalling on upbeat brass horns before she glared and he changed it.

"Witnesses say that displaced persons from Kolpol are bunkering—"

She changed the channel. Batu gasped and held his chest, his eyes settling on her, but she couldn't bear to look at him.

"Can you provide for your loved ones after you're gone?—"

She turned the radio off. "Hurry up."

The driver pointed to the cars crossing ahead. "What do—"

She punched his throat, slammed his head against the steering wheel, and sat on his lap, feet barely reaching the pedals from his lap.

Cars zipped by. But none were big enough to stop her truck, so she pushed a pedal. They didn't move. She floored the other one, and they jerked into the intersection.

She tried to weave through traffic but the trailer swayed. Speed reduced wobbling, so she rammed forward, brushing a work van into another lane. She clipped another trailer and drove on, skidding around pedestrians and knocking into a car that her truck pushed until it slipped into the other lane.

This would be easier if she knew where she was going.

And the driver was unconscious. She shook him, taking her eyes off the road and foot off the pedal. A car bounced off the back. She started again and drove in two lanes so she could turn wherever she needed to.

People screamed but leaped on the curb, clearing her path. The cars that insisted on blocking her changed their mind as she got closer. She followed signs for the hospital, past a policeman who jumped into his car, radioing for backup.

Hospital parking was a kilometer away in an underground cavern with far too many sharp turns. She couldn't park Batu across a road given how some people drove, so she parked at the front door and raced inside.

"I need help!" No one moved, all gawking at the dented truck outside. "Today, people, I know my translator's on." She pulled Batu from the truck, making sure she carried all of him, shooed away a pregnant woman, and laid him across five chairs.

No one moved.

"Is this the deaf ward? Two cars hit him, kinda three, and he can't use the doctube. I'm an Andromeda Khanate baghatur and we took over half this planet; I have power and money or whatever to get you to listen."

Baghaturs did not have power or money and the translators suggested 'knight' or 'hero.' Not good. How many heroes would kill you if you didn't cooperate?

Batu squeezed her hand. "This chair isn't comfortable." His voice barely registered over the stalled engine and the sirens on the news.

She snatched her hand back. "You heard that? We need pillows, stat!"

"This is a maternity ward." The nurse who said this looked two years pregnant.

"Wow, isn't that great? Think of all the helpless babies I can take hostage. You help people, do your job."

Khair had expected the pregnant nurse to be sympathetic, but she leaned back, held her bump, and looked at Khair as if planning a brain transplant with dull spoons.

"Tuya," Batu wheezed. "Hold my hand."

It was more order than request. She obeyed.

If she hadn't knocked out the driver, they'd be at the correct doctor. Or if she'd grabbed Batu when he first stepped out instead of cowering, he wouldn't lay in a hospital with busted ribs, mashed organs, and no pants.

She raised her hands. "He'll die without treatment, and this wasn't his fault. Also, there's a helpful truck driver with a concussion who deserves some prize—guess I'm not the greatest character witness, but it's true."

Nurses gathered up Batu, strapped him down so they could take him from her.

She waited alone, and finally watched the news, where a hundred cars piled up in three different places.

"Must have set a record," Khair said, with as much bravado as she could muster.

No one seemed particularly impressed.

Forty or fifty people must die every day on those roads. And if she hit a car and the driver died, that was on her, but if they hit someone and they hit someone, by the third or fourth collision she couldn't be blamed for the driver's inferior reflexes. Right?

The news interviewed a widow, who refused to believe her husband had died.

"That wasn't supposed to happen," Khair said. "He was dying. I couldn't just...."

How were people supposed to accept death?

In the truck, the cars below had just seemed like machines, inhuman obstacles. Finally, she saw other people.

It was no grand revelation, no rummaging around newly discovered dig sites, or piecing together neighborhood gossip. The truth was right there, but she had gouged out her eyes.

It didn't seem real.

She sat with her hands on her head, waiting for the police, while women congregated in the corners clutching newborns or cupping their stomachs, and a dozen nurses circled her.

Aren't you going to shock me? I won't complain.

Her mouth dried. What was going on?

Scold me at least? Tell me—

"Kerait Batuyin Tuya?" someone said to her.

She would have ignored him, but 'Kerait' had been a large Terran Mongolian tribe, the name reclaimed in space after the Soviet purge, 'Batuyin' was her patronymic, and... that was her. Kerait Batuyin Tuya.

Named for her mother and those UOD freaks had still—wait. She'd taken the name; she'd cast off her family. Why? They were dead. What could they possibly have done?

Nothing. They had just been weak.

"Close enough," Khair said.

The speaker was trying to discover how poorly he could dress and still be attractive; he wore a toga, a cowboy hat, and a baby carrier with a toddler.

"I'm Buck Davids. Come with me, please."

Kerait Batuyin Tuya or Khair or whoever she was supposed to be followed Davids and his kid outside, expecting to be tackled or shot.

She wasn't.

"Your father's in surgery."

The baby kept smiling and reached toward her. Khair crossed her arms and ignored him. "What're his chances?"

"Too early to tell. It was just bad luck. I assure you, we had no intentions against him." Davids was in his mid-thirties, hair cropped and clean shaven, skin dark, lips naturally downturned. His clothing was too loose to tell if his thin frame was athletic or sickly, his wide shoulders suggesting the former, but he constantly sniffled. "That stunt is what my boy would do if he could, not an adult general who won thirty battles. The Mercy Mission program works?"

"Not well enough, apparently."

His boy started to cry. "Let's get him somewhere quieter." He walked across the parking lot and waited. Where were his police, security?

Smoke drifted from down the road.

"Taivan won't pay for me, but if you frame it as reparations, Jun Jiao might." She had nothing to give but dumbbells, posters, and her stuffed wolf.

"I'm not after money."

"They might need it."

"And you're providing charity? The poor Albions needed a change of leadership, and young Riley couldn't stand to have her eyes?"

Khair said nothing.

Davids let his boy chew his finger. "If you want to start making things right, let me give Riley a new set of eyes. A small consolation but—"

"No, I've been warned: the only thing ZAX does better than weapons is creepy spytech."

Davids smiled thinly and rapped a knuckle against the air, which turned millions of clear pebble-sized panels, becoming a sleek chopper. "It has its uses."

There was no one inside, no visible weapons, so she stepped in. The doors swung down. She swirled as they locked, but the boy clapped. Davids charted a course as they rose.

They swooped around skyscrapers fitted with rail guns, steeples with cannons, arches with mortars, entire sectors of the city devoted to weapons manufacturing.

Was this all for them?

The city wall had defense missiles that could intercept most shells, the outside land had rings of barbed wire and trenches to stop vehicles, minefields to deter infantry. Their chopper flew dangerously low. There must be an invisible aerial defense above them. A dome would explain why the skyscrapers were clustered by height.

"Why build the universe's least child-friendly amusement park?" It wouldn't save them; guns couldn't feed people in a siege or stave off illness.

"It was a contest we were uniquely situated to win." He looked away, finger to his ear, and nodded. "Rodrigo Schwartz, the driver, came out of the doctube healthy. The Williamson sisters died on the operating table."

He said it like he expected her to bring them back. "Please don't tell me."

She had to stop running from reality at some point, but clearly today was not that day.

"I can forward the names of next of kin to your ship, if you were serious about helping the families with funerary expenses."

Maybe today had to be the day. "Just no pictures."

They landed in a garden hedged between marble municipal buildings. A dozen soldiers with Storm C2229 shotguns—short range but enough stopping power to stop a bear through a cement wall—waited below. A blond woman in a pantsuit with a pistol took the baby and started to scold Davids, but he kissed his child and walked away.

She followed, swallowing back the last hour and forcing herself to only exist now. "Everyone is dressed normally but you. Why the Caligula impression?"

He stepped onto a hologram platform.

Sophie appeared in Taivan's chair, her punctured eyes unobstructed. No blood, yet the sunken pink flesh set in unscarred fresh skin made Khair's stomach ferment.

Sophie managed a crooked grin. "Bucky."

He glared at Khair. "Ms. Riley. I can negotiate sanctuary if—"

"My people are here."

"I see." He stiffened and started to take it back, but Sophie only shrugged and he pressed on. "Where's General Jochiin?"

"Busy. I can act in his stead." She swirled a flask. "ZAX won't reach you in time and even if they come after we've taken Coloma, your city will be crippled for generations and you'll be dead. A professional courtesy, Buck. Give him whatever he needs and let him move on."

"Tell him he can collect his lackey anytime he wants, as long as he does it in person."

The People's Champion

KHAIR PACED THE HOTEL room she was locked in, waiting for Chip to scramble her brain. It had been hours, but the crash still dominated the news, interviewing witnesses and widowers. Rodrigo Schwartz dodged reporters as his boss berated him over a headset.

The only word on Batu was that he was the same man whose adopted daughter Jun Jiao, lost heir to the greatest empire the universe had ever seen, had been willing to sacrifice herself for. Had Batu officially adopted Jiao?

Regardless, the story compared the death toll in Coloma to the destruction in Jungang ju to whip up the populace. No self-respecting journalist missed the chance to post Jiao's picture—mainly one where she was about sixteen, with a bloody lip and slipping dress strap. For all that they bemoaned Jiao's fate and worse, her purported Stockholm syndrome, they had no trouble showing her half naked, or mangled corpses from her home.

Apparently Khair wasn't the only one who sat high up in a truck and forgot there were people in the cars below.

No one even asked if Batu, 'a minor soldier with no diplomatic experience,' still lived. Khair was 'the lone Khanate operative' conducting a 'probably unsanctioned attack of no strategic value.'

She massaged her temples.

Was this Chip's new technique, battering her with anticipation? Had something jammed the transmission like in Albion?

She shadowboxed for as long as her dehydrated body could manage, fruitlessly searched for food, and threw the remote out the window when she couldn't figure out how to turn off the news.

Someone knocked. "Room service or death squad?"

Davids entered, looked around the mess with a deepening frown, and righted the couch. "I asked the news not to report on your father's condition."

If he'd only asked, they could say no. "What I know doesn't affect him, and I don't think you'd hurt him."

"No." He sat on the floor across from her. "What do you want?"

"Dinner."

"Crab cakes and chowder will be up shortly. I meant with life. Not many people get a second chance. You must want something beyond this afternoon's fiasco."

"I've done this feely chat with Sophie. Then she decided to kill me. I decided against it, and we came to an accord." Khair waved her thumbs below her eyes. "Besides. I'm a lackey. Why negotiate with me?"

The food arrived, but the servers didn't enter. Davids spread the picnic himself. She studied him. Loose clothing still, probably body armor beneath, no apparent weapon. He leaned against the couch, ignoring the knife he'd supplied her.

"Is there someone else I talk to?" Davids said. "Jun Jiao, perhaps?"

"Cause she's the good one? That just means when you contact her, Taivan will know everything you say." She was blabbing, but she hadn't talked for hours.

"A strange definition of goodness. Wouldn't it be better to realize your mistakes and do better?" He spoke as if educating his toddler.

"Could you abandon your people as irredeemable, Mr. President? Whatever our mistakes, we'll be the ones to fix them."

He drank, though he couldn't see her as he raised the glass, and did so slowly, ignoring her as he dabbed his lip with a silk napkin. "I don't think my translator is working properly; 'mistake' is a strange word for an entire campaign. Especially one so methodical as yours."

She twirled the knife. If Davids had a weapon, he didn't reach for it. She was tempted to toss it at him to check his security, but that seemed a good way to die, so she stuck it in the carpet.

"I'll listen to your flattery all night, over breakfast too, for a pretty guy like you."
He coughed, and she pressed on. "But my food is cooling, so get to the point."

"Must there be a point? You may be here for a while, but if you'd prefer
solitude, I won't impose."

She'd rather be dead.

"I get it. You don't like to be called pretty. Handsome, then." No reaction. She
was only flirting to get him off-kilter. Why was she looking for approval? "Can
we start over?"

He laughed, a surprisingly undignified bark. "Not at all, but I'll pretend."

"You have numbers on us, technology, yet that didn't matter at Kolpol. You
want an insider."

"We also have more food, medical supplies, allies, and manners, but yes."

"Are you waging war with cutlery, then?" She wanted to hear him laugh again.
She didn't. "Sophie's the obvious choice, but she's closely watched. Aidan's
weird. But I've endured his rants—he made a slideshow with paintings on one
side and the deserved punishment on the other—so I'm the closest thing he has
to a friend. He's as gung-ho as Taivan."

"What if I offered Jochiin's safety to Jun?" Davids said.

'Jun' was the proper address for Jiao, but Taivan was Taivan. He'd be mortified
Davids hadn't researched their culture given how many all-nighters he'd spent
learning to write convincing fraudulent orders. And to rule well when he won.

"Still fixated on Jiao?" Khair shrugged. "Taivan can't be beaten, only killed; she
knows that."

"How does he maintain her loyalty? Or yours."

Davids' education was lagging and solely pragmatic, but he was serious enough
to do it himself and go to the source. Few allies? Or more curious, even concerned,
than he let on.

"Inertia." Taivan had been the only one to notice when Chip replaced her.
He sought her opinion, confessed to her his shortcomings, made sure she was
okay. How could she turn away? "You're not scary and you've ditched the kindly
father act. What do you rule by?" She gestured to the food, which smelled
delicious. "Bread and circuses? Unless my translator's malfunctioning, the rest
of the universe says 'bribery.'"

He grinned, not a reward like Taivan, to show he wasn't threatened. "Who says I rule at all? I guide our ship for a time, then someone else will, but the ship moves by itself."

"Let me guess. The ship is 'the will of the people' or 'a constitution' or some other nonsense."

"Not even Jochiin can act without his mechanic's approval."

"You say that 'cause you're safe. What are they gonna do, revolt and get slaughtered, run away and freeze?"

"He does rule by fear, then."

This all sounded too much like something Chip would say. "But you're above the law of club and fang? Why do you think your people pay taxes or obey laws?"

"Depends on the person. And you're vastly distorting the scope comparing a local three percent sales tax with an invader's conscription. What about your father, would he—"

She laughed. "If Taivan got cold, Batu would set himself on fire."

"Why?"

"Were you ever a soldier?" Probably not, too at ease with an enemy, not attempting to lower his tenor, in no great hurry, but he had an officer's polite interest and put himself in danger without hesitation.

"Farmer. Don't wait for me, I ate."

"Soldiers love whoever brings them home."

Taivan didn't care about Irmeg. But he'd keep them safe together, and that was home enough.

"You consider yourself a soldier though you haven't done anything this last campaign?"

Davids was making her sell herself. So she ignored him and ate.

The chowder was almost too hot to drink, so creamy and buttery it was worth burning her mouth. The crab crumbled off the patty and came with a tangy sauce she licked off her fingers. "Didn't know there was an ocean here."

"We made one. We also had to synthesize photosynthesis to farm. Albion thought of it first but wouldn't venture from their caves."

Coloma could control the weather with the dome but they kept it clear and let rain seep through. If Sophie had that tech, she would've optimized sleep schedules and proper nutrients from the sun. Davids was a true believer in his own people.

He must absolutely hate her.

"We'll take care of the Albions," Khair said. "And your people, after."

"You can't. And your master won't."

She wiped sauce from her chin. "You have any alcohol here?"

"To further lower your inhibitions?" He tilted his head, leaning into a message on his comm.

"They're low enough, don't worry," she said to cover her eavesdropping. She didn't hear what happened.

"Your people are coming tomorrow. I'd like to show you the city tonight."

"Are the 2229 shotguns coming with us?"

"C2231s—an upgrade—and no."

Davids led the way outside. At night, the city was no calmer and barely darker with the moons' reddish light, but they ventured from the main district to a sidewalk where if she stumbled, she wouldn't be trampled.

Evergreens divided the street, wintry shrubs blocked the sidewalk and road, and wheat grew on the roofs. The houses' electronic facades hid their face and shop doors swung at her approach and reluctantly closed again, looking like giant pincers.

A train passed, another thirty stuffed cabs. How many people were here? It didn't look like there was enough housing, yet there were relatively few homeless people. Other apartments might hide behind illusions, but there was little room off the streets and the dome created an upper barrier.

Taivan had said there was an underground city, and there must be. But there may be a twin city, like in the ancient Mediterranean, some place to flee if the main city was taken. Or maybe she was putting too much stock in Davids' toga. But unless he lost a dare, what was up with that?

"So, if my people are picking me up tomorrow, and you're trying to leverage my father," Khair said. "Either I only have to last a day, or you're keeping him."

"He gets a say in his location."

"While he's higher than your aerial defenses, and will do whatever you suggest? He came in peace and he hasn't breached it. That was me."

Advertisements spun on the sidewalk and called her by name selling Mustang sidearms, soliciting her for combat sports for an over-forty league, and asking her to help a gangly woman that looked like a bargain-brand Jiao through postgraduate studies.

She cleaned her boots on Jiao's doppelgänger. "Why are you showing me this? I hate your city."

Batu would love it. For all the twinkling lights, complicated tech, and cheap curios, there were tangible things. A petting zoo attached to a barbecue and leather store, a craftsman spreading pungent oils over buckskin while bystanders watched with racks of ribs. Mechanics tinkered on a tractor's nuclear generator. Craftsman shaped violins while kids wandered in and battered on drums.

"You've seen less than one percent of it." He bought two Coloma Kicks from a street vendor. "You can't hold or govern this city. Even if you destroy it, you've gained nothing but a powerful enemy in ZAX corporation."

The drink was vodka with lime and ginger sipped through a hollowed hot pepper straw. She drank to get it down before deciding she liked it. "Taivan won't care."

"He can't beat ZAX. He'd have to use Terran guns we can't turn off, with limited ammunition, less lethal rounds, and shorter range. Your army is conscripted. And he's already lost an actual army."

Maybe drinking wasn't the greatest idea, because Davids made sense. But Taivan had lost that army saving her, because his soldiers were willing to stay behind and die so he lived. Because he'd fooled them, or because he was worth following?

"What do you want with me?"

Davids kept walking.

The streets grew crowded again, malls and taverns cropping up, each with its own music so that epic orchestra played over electronic folk.

"Walk away," Davids said.

"That's it?"

He nodded.

She finished the drink and studied the hot pepper, wondering if it'd soaked up enough vodka to be worth eating. "I must've been something if you're that scared of me."

If she stayed with Taivan she'd end up fried by Chip or stabbed by Sophie or shot by Jiao. Or they'd burn this city.

But she had nowhere to go, no resources, no talents, no family to fall back on. Batu could be dead, but even if he was in perfect health, he couldn't help her and she'd no intention of watching him decay and die. She'd give him money, and that had to be enough.

Her life was half done and there was nothing to show for it. Taivan had a chance to change the universe, time itself; if she stayed, so would she.

"You wouldn't take me?" She looked at him through the nibbled straw.

Davids adjusted his sleeve. "We could find a consulting position."

"Ha. Now I know what you look like when you lie. Let's go back, it's cold."

He took her back the same way, moving quicker than before. Navigation was more difficult the second time, her confidence swelling beyond her ability, the same building flashing a different front.

When they attacked, they'd have to rely on their sensors. Their eyes were useless here. They'd be surveilled not only by copcams, but by whatever corporate tech let the advertisers analyze her.

Davids brought her to her quarters, waiting outside to lock it.

She lingered in the doorway. "Listen to Sophie and help us. She's a high-ranking minister and hasn't been hurt since she surrendered."

But Sophie was young enough to move on, with a craft outside of governing. Would Taivan want an overthrown president? Probably not, but he needed farmers.

"When we migrated here," Davids said. "We expected to grow out of a democracy, so we looked to the most successful republics in history: the first Martian expedition, Rome, Indian confederacies, the United States—my ancestral home. It was late. We got drunk and had a sheet and hat, and ended up in a meeting dressed like that. Rather than admit our mistake, we took it as a new tradition."

He was a pioneer, a gambler. Not great news. "Sensible."

"It was meant to remind us we were fallible, to adapt, and stay humble. But that'd been my great-great-great granddaddy's hat, and to me, it was a reminder of a man who spent his last days battling a tyranny he knew he couldn't beat, and his granddads before him who fought for a land centuries before it cared for them. I will never wear a collar, Ms. Batuyin, nor leave a world where my son wears it in my place."

Chip's Confession // File Not Found

WAKE UP.

Khair sat on the edge of her bed, facing out so she wouldn't vomit on it when the shocks started.

Eighty-one people died in your accident. Normally Chip's emotions were dull and dry, but her anger was wet now—ungraspable, undulating, all-pervasive. *Give me one reason not to kill you.*

She'd planned for this, but that had been with her awake brain, before heat leached from her fingers. **I like Davids.**

Aw, poor Taivan. I should've been specific: give me a good reason not to kill you.

I can be the diplomat you wanted. Taivan won't win without losses he can't afford, and I must care about Davids 'cause I don't want him to die.

You cared about Batu. That didn't help anyone, including him.

She slid to the floor so she couldn't fall, checked the bed frame wasn't metal before she leaned against it.

'Caring' isn't enough. It's superficial and transient without moral responsibility.

Was this a test? Were Chip's memories buried deep enough to keep their minds separate or had the carnage dug them up? No, the gorge between them was uncrossable and widening.

It's an improvement. I can—

Is it? You don't love him, else you'd get him away from this. You've only deluded yourself and become more dangerous.

Khair wrapped a blanket around her shoulders. ***There was blood. You guys programmed a reaction to it. I can't think clearly.***

Chip thought, no emotion coloring the silence. *I'll look into that. But that's a smaller issue; we're all subject to our brain chemistry.*

"So fix me!"

She reached up and claimed a pillow with the trepidation of a soldier poking her head from a trench, and laid flat on the ground. No pain yet. Had to remember what it felt like.

That wasn't good enough. She had to get out of this, this meat and slime that barely fit. No, she was her body, Chip was a guest, she had control here, no different than pushing up the barbell on the last rep with shaking arms.

She couldn't feel her arms. Her heart galloped, numbness freezing out from her center.

I can only justify sparing you because you accepted your guilt for Jiao at the trial, but you were stalling.

She must have done some other good thing, but what?

Still, we act for a myriad of reasons, so intention isn't nearly as important as the action itself.

Khair tried to control her breathing. ***Are you changing the room's temperature?***

The room had dumped itself into the Gobi Desert.

Is this boring you?

She shook her head, throat constricting too much to answer. Had Davids released a poison gas? No, he would need to pass it through the proper channels, and that took time. Maybe Taivan decided not to leave a hostage. But he would make it quick. And Chip would pass the sentence with gratuitous detail.

What was killing her so inefficiently?

Help.

Her head was imploding.

What? Oh. That's a panic attack. I can't fix it.

All this spine shattering, teeth cracking pain was self-inflicted bullshit, yet she couldn't stop it. ***Maybe don't torture me.***

Chip considered it. *Go to bed.*

She didn't move, would keep one place safe. ***Please get it over with.*** Tears ran down her face. Water. That would make it worse, wouldn't it? She cried harder. ***I won't get better. I don't know how, and even if I did, I can't do it.***

Chip said nothing.

No pity for the sinner who distorted her soul? No scorn as demons drag me offstage as the crowd cheers? Say something, fucker. Do something.

How can I, when I'm as guilty as you?

Khair froze, waiting for Chip to drive her out to scavenge for some sense of self while blithely dusting off her cobwebs.

Worse.

Khair wiped her eyes. ***If there's such job dissatisfaction, maybe the role of rebelling paragon needs filling?***

Chip laughed.

Oh.

No wonder Chip had hated her for being complicit. Chip was either a mole working for her enemies, or had betrayed her own organization.

Then we're on the same side! Taivan wants to destroy United Oversight for Democracy, so do you. We—

I will not ally with that man.

Maybe, but—

Someone may be listening. Shut up and sleep so you can pretend to be productive tomorrow.

She laid motionless on the floor for hours, but when she woke, she was no worse off except a tingling where she laid on her arm. Breakfast had grown cold, but the omelet was mostly edible.

Chip, if you're in a better mood, we can talk?

Don't kill anyone and we have nothing to talk about.

The door was locked, so she spent the morning pushing the couch around for exercise before she realized she was marking up the floor. She flopped on it and slept.

When she woke, she couldn't see a clock or make out where the wimpy sun hid. She was tying her belt on a hook in the ceiling to do pull-ups when Davids walked in.

"Good aft—" He saw her standing on a chair beside a belt loop. "Should I call someone?"

She stepped down, cheeks heating. "Just working out. Y'know, gotta stay in shape to beat up big locals trying to help."

Davids nodded slowly. He wore a tailored suit, though he still had his cowboy hat and that throwin' hay bales' strength. "Did you think about my offer?"

Since she'd spent the night begging for her life, that was a hard no. But she didn't need to. "If I say I'm undecided, will you give me free stuff?"

"This isn't a planet that allows for freeloaders."

She sighed. "If I beat you in a pull-up contest, could I get some assurances?" A presidency didn't fall into a farmer's lap, he eked that out, and ambition didn't fade because he'd made it.

"Your father will be taken care of. But if your people don't come for you, I don't know what will happen."

You can get me out of this, right? I'm no use in a cage. Although, she didn't know if she was more of a pennystock or interstellar shipline type investment.

"So, what I'm hearing is you don't think you can beat me in a pull-up contest." Khair stretched to flex.

Tightlipped, Davids removed his hat and jacket. "If you win, you can leave once Jochiin arrives. Or I'll try to get you probation and community service in our defense if he doesn't come."

"Not only are you physically deficient, but you struggle to exercise any power at all."

"When I win, you'll supply us a list of his ships and guns. And if Jochiin doesn't come, you're on your own."

You'll give him that list, regardless.

Davids grabbed the belt. "I have to ask: you do know what's at stake? You might spend your life in a labor camp."

If he wanted, she'd end up there anyway, but till now it hadn't occurred to her that he might double cross her. Even if Coloma was what? UOD's weapon supplier's manufacturers, UOD's second cousin. "I don't have anything on the calendar."

He pulled himself up for the first rep, movement so mesmerisingly fluid she almost forgot to count. They'd be here a while. He didn't rush, so he'd no worries about his grip strength, movements in a rhythm he must've done for years. He slowed around fifteen and his arms shook by twenty, but he got his chin over the belt loop half a dozen more times.

"Twenty-six." He coughed and blew his nose to cover his panting. "Full range of motion, no leg-swinging shenanigans."

"Heavens no, we are civilized folks, no kinky shenanigans here."

I'm considering a mercy killing.

Is that a joke? Woah, look how friendly we are. Unfortunately for you, you're too boring for my taste.

I'm considering suicide.

Davids was strong, but this world was low-gravity; it was never a fair contest. She reached twenty-seven, did an extra in case she miscounted, and quit. No point making him hate her.

He collected his hat, veins swelling in his forearms. "You went easy."

She shook out her arms. "You should've demanded a bench press." Doubtful, though he was bigger, his eyes had a sickly yellow tint and he was never without his handkerchief.

"Then I'd have to bring in equipment and explain how foolish I was being."

"You're a politician, it's expected."

"Is that what you expect from Jochiin?"

She retrieved her belt. "A talking contest, I yield."

He opened the door and led her down a side staircase in an empty hall, not even an outdated poster for her to bother. "It doesn't concern you that you have no argument for him?"

She pointed to her head. "None I'm allowed to say. How's my father?"

Davids walked her through abandoned halls to a garden. The trees weren't tall, fresh growth dependent on added topsoil, sprinklers, and LED lights, but there were hundreds of them. The air smelled wetter, fuller. Beetles and birds and rabbits and squirrels played, their chirps familiar enough from white noise machines but the real thing had no pattern, life playing over itself in dissonant chords.

"Have you ever seen anything like it?" Davids asked.

No. She hadn't known a leaf's underside was paler than the top or that leaves had a waxy sheen, that the venous pattern varied. The leaves seemed in a permanent autumnal gold though spring buds bloomed around the hedges. Acorns littered musty leaves, patchy and unique even in death. There were no weeds, but she wouldn't have minded.

How much of this would they destroy?

"I would've limited our population to keep it all like this," Davids said. "There's less wealth disparity in the farms, so a republic has a better chance. But my people are generous. If you convince Jochiin to march past, we'll take in the Asan refugees, you and your father, Sophie, even Admiral Jun. Whoever prefers peace."

The Asans were soldiers now.

"I'll try."

Aidan entered through the garden's gate. Not an illusion to get her talking. The grass crushed beneath his feet, tree branch shadows on his chest. He was unharmed, wearing his Albion kilt and vest, an axe strapped to his back, five years shaved off with his beard.

"I wasn't sure Aidan was still here," Khair said.

"Where would he go?" Davids said.

"A different multiverse or another time. No one tells me anything; I don't even know why ZAX is so into Coloma. It's not like you're their only manufacturers."

"We're their last stop in Andromeda, and lots of us have family ties from when the corporation was in Montana."

"You're not interested in the whole time travel spiel?"

"Someone's teasing you." There was no doubt in his voice.

"Cause if you don't understand it, it couldn't possibly be real."

"Because if it were true, there'd be anomalies that aren't present here."

"They were in Albion."

Guards confiscated Aidan's axe and scanned his clothes. They collected shuriken, an atlatl, C4 hidden in a pack of gum, a miniature flame thrower, and a pistol with bronze knuckles on the handle.

"Jochiin's lying to create a common enemy." Davids watched the growing pile of weapons without concern.

"He has you," Khair said.

Aidan finally passed inspection in checkered boxers. The wall and trees blocked the wind, but it was barely above freezing and he didn't shiver. "I would've brought my attack dolphins, but they get flight sick."

Davids offered his hand to Aidan. "You did seem underwhelmed for the occasion."

Aidan shook. "Just underdressed."

For a moment, neither spoke, Aidan patient under scrutiny. Davids was broader, taller, dressed, but Aidan, expressionless, seemed to mind not at all. He looked ten years younger than Davids, but there was no way to know how long he had travelled the multiverse, and though his people had been conquered, he hadn't been.

Davids adjusted his hat. "I can't return Ms. Batuyin to anyone but Jochiin, but you're welcome to stay."

Aidan looked to her. "You're not hurt. Have you told them anything?"

"No."

Davids motioned for a guard to return Aidan's clothes, finally de-weaponized. "We have warmer clothes and—"

"I'm not a prisoner or a beggar. I convinced Naguib to turn and Taivan rewards his allies. I've nothing to fear from him."

"Is that his best sales pitch?"

"Listen to the futures I've seen and find out." Aidan took his clothes back, but didn't put them on.

"I don't need to be saved from fates that don't exist; tell Jochiin I'll hold him accountable in this world."

"I won't leave until you listen. Westley—"

Davids held up his hand. "Careful."

"You'll lose custody this week." Aidan searched his clothes. "The judge will deliberate between three and five minutes, thank you for your public service but tell you that averaging a seventy-three hour work week makes it impossible to be the primary caretaker. That day in court would've been the last time you saw him, but there's nothing that stops you from seeing him now."

"You're trying to save your sister, that's—"

"She dies. I can't. That part's always the same. Don't put a bug in my clothes, or I'll walk around naked."

"I'm sorry, Aidan. But if Jochiin wants anything from me, we speak directly, or over the hologram if security is an issue."

"Give it a week. Remember, three to five minutes."

What Rules Us

KHAIR JUMPED AN INVISIBLE rope on one leg. "Did you get it? I said—"

"I got it." Aidan laid on the hotel couch, legs draped over the armrests, eyes closed.

She pushed his leg over and sat beside him. "What if your prophecy was wrong? Do you have cards or manga or anything?"

They had been locked in Khair's room, and a cot was brought up beside the couch. Aidan had pushed her to the cot.

"Just a headache."

"Does switching timestreams hurt? Can it even be considered time travel at all, if you're going through different streams?"

Aidan tossed her his notebook, a page earmarked that said "FAQ." She batted it aside in midair, which Chip buzzed her for, but it was worth it when he opened an eye.

"In case it didn't cross your puerile brain, letting you see this is a significant act of trust."

It hadn't. She snuck a peek and saw 'streams flow at different rates' before Aidan snatched it back and said: "Especially since you're usually dead by now."

"How?"

He opened to a chart—he'd written in the Jungang ju dialect, pointed to a box, and allowed her translator access: 'Don't ask about your future. It'll change, and there are no good options.'

Some people supposed we lived in the best of all possible worlds, and this during a century of endless war, while absolutist kings ruled. All those miseries, and that was the best we could aspire for.

I'm glad you and Aidan never talk; he'd have you hanging yourself. Wait, actually...

Chip must be lonely to admit longing for the original time apart from her side's meddling. Play buddy-buddy with the baddy in her head, and she might earn a looser noose.

I'll pretend I didn't hear that. But Chip didn't shock her, not even a hum on the lowered voltage. How much was an act to keep her cover? Maybe the person who knew her best didn't really think she deserved to suffer.

"Why do you speak Jiao's language?" Khair asked Aidan.

"It amused me to learn it."

"Enough amusement. You're a fossil compared to Jiao. Add someone else to your collection."

He smoothed the page's edge.

"Oh, the silent treatment. Don't you get tired of your taciturn act?"

"An act, is it? It must be; there's no other life than the one you, a barely house broken infant, endure. These unwarranted assumptions kill you."

Her face heated. "You still die."

"Of course." He said it like a father permitting his child a second piece of cake. "Chance kills Sophie. Nothing else can. Batu dies in sacrifice or stupidity, if there's a difference. Jiao and Taivan are assassinated or die in battle and either way, fight till they flatline. Who cares? It's inevitable. But which masterpiece Emmanuel N'Dour paints to end this cultural malaise, which puppy Sophie picks for Whiskey II, that changes, we can change it. That matters."

"So, the multiverse is ruled by variance and your amusement."

No, he serves self-determination and beauty—which is far more dangerous. Beauty actually exists, has laws of its own, and a magnetic pull toward tragedy.

"No, I rule myself by variance and amusement. You should try it. Detach yourself from Taivan and the rest. He'll like you better for it, and you won't even care."

"If you believe that, you must sample allegiances as often as appetizers."

"In that, I was terribly consistent."

"'Was?'"

Aidan stood and stretched. "For all your concern about Jiao, do you see why that mistrial hurt her? The slander and miscarriage of justice, of course, but mostly being forced to stand with you. It's no insult; my hands are as sullied as yours, but I'll never be forced to drink bleach. Her personhood was reduced and poured into the Khanate's. It's worse than death."

"The crowd found her innocent."

"The crowd found her interesting enough to forgive. But Jiao doesn't believe in grace. Why should she? Neither do I. And UOD dehumanized the one person I loved without reservation."

"Yourself?" It couldn't be Sophie. He didn't value her as much as his revenge. "Being against them isn't the same as being for us."

"Taivan understands. And he knows that as long as I can paint, I'm on his side. Anything we do beyond reacting to stimuli, any creative or stupid, self-determined act, defies them."

"But considering that you probably know more than anyone ever, and you're with us, we must be doing something good?"

Hint hint.

"Or maybe I want to die spectacularly, or maybe we win." Aidan smiled. "Or maybe I am sneaking off with Jiao."

The door slammed open and Davids stormed in, tripped and recovered over the thresh hold. "What did you do to the judge?"

"Ask your guards," Aidan said. "I haven't left the room or communicated with anyone but you."

Davids slipped off his suit coat, loosened his tie and rolled up his sleeves, his chest ballooning for each shallow breath.

"Fight, fight, fight, fight," Khair whispered, half to show Davids how foolish he was being.

"I'll find your comms system. You've accomplished nothing."

Aidan sat on the couch and draped his legs over the coffee table. "Westley—"

"Don't say his name," Davids said.

"He has a good, long life in six of seven versions."

"If you threaten him, I will kill you."

Khair stepped between them, hands out in a placating gesture from which she could strike. "Go visit your son."

Davids glared past her with the venom of a pit viper, taking a good three seconds to remember she existed. "We'll discover how you meddled with our courts. Batuyin, if you tire of fighting families—"

"How's my father then?"

"Better off!" Davids lowered his voice. "Don't fool yourself. You're camped outside our city waiting for us to hand it over because you demand it. Slink off and go home."

"If Westley sickens," Aidan tore the 'Time Travel FAQ' page from his notebook and offered it to Davids. "The Khanate has the antibodies he needs."

Davids looked to her. "I'll bring you your father when you bring me to Taivan."

"Done. But have Aidan stay here."

"He'll find no Minister Naguib here."

"Aidan's the only one to time travel."

"I know of five others," Aidan said.

"Who? And why are you so special?" Khair said. "Aidan is valuable to Taivan, so if you go to his camp, keep him here until you return safely."

"Unlike the Khanate," Davids said. "We don't revolve around one man."

"Then I'm sure you won't mind dying," Khair said.

He retrieved his jacket. "If you have nothing worth dying for, I pity you. Your father's in the hall."

She hopped out before Davids changed his mind, but when she saw Batu, she shied back. He was too friendly with his guards, but it wasn't that. She'd scooped his organs from the pavement, but though he needed a cane, he stood, and his smile wrinkled his burns.

The guards grabbed their pistols when they saw her. Batu stepped toward her, extended one arm, leaning on the cane.

She embraced him. "I'm so sorry."

He held her with both arms, his arm shaking as he held the cane across her back, cradling her head against his chest and leaning into her to keep his footing.

"We're going home." She released him as Davids and Aidan strode by in awkward silence. "He's letting us go."

"To Irmeg?"

"Not yet." She took Batu's left hand, shooing back a guard who would've helped. "What was it like?"

"Cold, like here. Lake was frozen most of the year, but good fishing, good skating."

Outside, Davids prepared his chopper, Aidan his jet.

Batu picked a fallen auburn leaf, sighed as he buckled up. "You have a great city, Mr. Davids. You and your son are very lucky."

Davids scratched his throat and said nothing more on the flight to the Khanate camp.

The *Sphinx* and other ships had remained cloaked with their soldiers quartered inside since they'd arrived, but the fleet was visible now, and soldiers played a ball game with no rules.

They were puny beside the city.

Davids stepped outside the chopper without checking for traps. "Albion had a larger fleet, plus the ships at Kolpol."

Taivan reclined on a couch in Coloma banqueting fashion, beside a feast of silver platters on a blanket. He wore jeans and a fur-lined jacket but kept the Albion-esque scarf and his jade crown. His sword had been stabbed in the sand beside his head. Jiao stood beside him with a pre-ZAX rifle that couldn't be controlled.

Taivan stood. "Batu, welcome back. Soph, bring him out of the cold, make sure he was well treated."

Davids wrinkled his nose as Sophie, in a low-cut dress emphasizing the collar with a transparent veil to keep dirt from her eyes, scuttled around the couch over uneven terrain. Batu led her to the *Sphinx* by hand, chattering about how impressive Coloma was.

"You're here sooner than anticipated," Taivan said. "How did Aidan convince you?"

"You have until nightfall to leave."

"There'll be a storm tonight limiting your scanners, and by tomorrow, we could be anywhere."

Davids spat out phlegm and dabbed his mouth with a damp handkerchief, folded it in squares. "We'll occupy Albion until your soldiers desert to retrieve it."

He would need parliamentary approval before attacking Albion. She had been denied access to the news since Aidan arrived, but she'd had a balcony and there'd been no sign of change in the streets below.

"Gallant Scipio attacking Carthage to save Rome." Taivan gestured for Davids to sit, and remained standing when he refused. "The moment you attack Albion, I'll drop everything to save their home, confirming I'm on their side."

"Not if you can't keep it," Davids said.

"I won't. We'll arrive tragically late and witness the explosion, leaving them nothing to return to. Nothing but me."

Jiao hugged her rifle. Aidan picked dirt from under his nails.

"I don't believe you and if I did, I'd never negotiate with you," Davids said.

What can I do?

"You're here to negotiate; I wanted supper," Taivan said. "Khair, dig in. There's shepherd's pie, shawarma, rice pudding, apple cake—"

"Congratulations, we're as well supplied." Davids put a finger in his ear to boost his comm's signal and walked away.

She ran after him.

"Ms. Batuyin, I don't have time for..." He gestured toward her.

"Ouch. Well, you don't have permission for war and your people aren't ready. Maybe you'll die for freedom, but do you think a seventeen-year-old making googly eyes at his sweetheart will feel the same? And sure, seventeen-year-olds were the ones at Iwo Jima and Europa. But they shouldn't have to be."

"I don't disagree." Davids turned to his ship. "Get Jochiin to feel the same and we can have a productive conversation."

"Surrender your armory," Taivan called.

But that wasn't what Taivan was after. He was after ZAX, and through them, UOD. Davids didn't believe UOD could time travel, but maybe he'd turn on ZAX.

"You'll meet our guns soon enough," David said.

"War isn't about guns." Taivan said. "It's skill and guts. Jiao, can you shoot his pinky at this distance?"

Jiao nodded, tightlipped, but didn't move her rifle.

Davids swirled and shot Taivan.

Jiao put two rounds in his chest.

Under New Management

AIDAN WHOOPED AS DAVIDS hit the ground.

Taivan stayed down. Jiao set her rifle aside and plugged the wound with his scarf. He'd worn an armored vest, but that was scant protection against Davids' ZAX round. Jiao hushed his floundering orders and pushed him down as he tried to stand, but he raised a weak fist for his men.

"Khair, get a doctube," Jiao said. "Aidan, lock Sophie in her room."

Davids hadn't moved, his breath a wet rasp, but he didn't bleed and his sidearm lay beside his hand.

"Khair, the doctube, now!"

"There are thousands of other soldiers, JJ." Khair reached for Taivan's sword. *Don't.*

Khair left it and approached Davids slowly. "Wore a vest, huh?"

He reached for his pistol. She dove for it, landing on his wounded chest, pinning his arm, but he'd already grabbed it.

Chip shocked her. Davids yelped too, but pushed her limp body off him.

She raised her hands as best she could. "Don't kill the hostage." But with all the guns pointing at them, it was more like a last stand. "I'm gonna move to shield you."

He stood with her, hunched over, but kept his distance.

"Step closer," Khair said. "If you're that far off when they get authorization to shoot, you're dead."

"You move to me. Hands interlocked behind your head."

She complied. "If Taivan's dead, we'll move out, but it'll take time. I'll play nice. Just give us a few days' grace."

He grabbed her collar and pulled her closer, but he was taller. Even with her basically on his toes, he was exposed.

Bullets grazed overhead.

A cannon bellowed, and his chopper exploded.

Both of them cringed and covered their heads, debris scattering in the dirt and punching their shins. She collapsed. Bloody white tubes stuck out of her leg. Shots volleyed, the far ones popping, closer ones whistling by.

At least the rifles were seven hundred meters out with a strong wind, designed for a different gravity.

Davids, bulletproof vest tattered, lifted his pistol and aimed at his own chin.

She ripped burning metal from his leg. He screamed. She grabbed his wrist, twisted his thumb. He squeezed the trigger, shooting between their shoulders.

"I'm trying to save you, com'on!"

He punched her stomach, but she didn't let go. "Fine job."

She didn't have a comeback. The pain had started out like a mosquito bite, but it grew till it was the only thing she could process.

A second chopper's wings approached, swirling the wrecked one's smoke and dust, obscuring them. But she couldn't see it.

Let him go.

Sure boss, just make me bulletproof.

Wind rushed, the invisible chopper only meters away. This was how people got decapitated.

She rolled on top of Davids, the pistol pinned to the ground and pointed away from them, her ruined legs digging into his. She pressed her forearm into Davids' throat, pounded his wrist against the ground until he dropped the gun, and shoved it out of reach.

The chopper became visible as it landed—so close the skid lay between her legs. It was unmanned, Davids not trading lives for his own.

Khanate soldiers raced toward them, bullets ricocheting off the armored chopper, close enough to ring her ears.

"Hold your fire!" She covered both their heads, expecting a bullet to plow through her wrists into her head. To Davids: "I'll get evidence for UOD's time-travel and you will listen."

She heaved Davids into the chopper. As his weight hit the floor, the door shut and it rose, disappearing immediately.

She started to stand—knew she shouldn't, but her burning legs demanded she find some place she didn't hurt—but Sophie pushed her down.

Khair groaned. "No, not you."

"Stop moving, you're dirtying your wounds."

"I want a doctor who can see." Sophie ordered soldiers to put her on a gurney and strapped her hands down. "Or a doctor I didn't blind." Sophie found her knee and ran her hand down along the junkyard that was her shin. Khair whimpered. "Tranquilizer?"

"Thought you'd never ask."

"Wait." Jiao wiped her hands with a spotted towel. "Keep her conscious. I have questions."

Can you take the edge off?

Does an 'atta girl' count?

I hate you.

An expulsion of air that might be Chip's snort or chuckle. No way of knowing if it'd earned a raised eyebrow or quirked lip or steepled fingers. If Chip would hurt her for it later.

All that burning metal in your legs, and it's fear of me spiking your vitals?

She latched onto the distraction. **Apparently.**

I've been authorized to read the record of that hostile takeover. Chip turned off the voice automation. Her real voice wasn't much different, just muddied by inflection, the similarity a strange comfort. *If I could, I'd let you go. Maybe kill you in battle, but not like this. I'll stop you from hurting anyone, but otherwise, think or say or do as you'd like.*

She sucked in a deep breath. Was this a trap? **Then, from the bottom of my heart, you're a heartless bitch.**

Keep up appearances, I could be audited; if I shock you lightly three times, someone's coming.

If this is a joke, I don't get it. Please tell me you're serious.

The gurney bumped over dirt. Khair pressed her nails into the sheet, glanced at her legs, but her head swam.

Usually.

Okay, okay. I haven't thought this far. Khair couldn't celebrate over the shrill, immobilizing pain. *If we start breaking down again, take this body completely and tell Taivan who you are, help him where your interests align.*

I don't want it. Her voice was so measured it might as well be computerized.

Why? I'm way stronger and hotter than you. Sure, you're alright—

Her bed rolled up a ramp, its thin ridge lines vibrating the bed and shifting the shrapnel in her leg. She rattled off curses.

Just remember the three-pulse signal.

They reached the *Sphinx's* floor, and smooth tiles. One of the wheels didn't turn right, jolting on a four-beat count, and the sharp turns almost flipped her out.

This would be a great time to pass out, but no, Sophie pushed her to the end of the hall, down another. They left the main corridors.

"How long will Taivan use the doctube?" Khair asked. Nothing else would help against a ZAX round.

Sophie shooed away a janitor and pulled a curtain shut. "Three days, if he lives."

Sophie unsealed a wheeled countertop surgeon kit by the gurney and found a scalpel on its raised grid. She covered Khair's mouth and plugged her nose.

For a moment, Khair let her, sure it was some strange new procedure. But Sophie pressed down so hard her head ached. Khair bit her, but she laid her full weight on Khair's knee and tapped the scalpel to her thigh.

"You know you'll die if I nick your femoral artery?"

Her hands were strapped down so she could only muffle 'yes.'

Sophie released her nose and traced the scalpel around her knee. "How do I deactivate this collar?"

"If you kill me—"

"Jiao's in charge. She won't care."

"How would I know about this technojumble? You're the scientist—"

The scalpel pierced her thigh. "You got away with killing a hundred people in that car wreck."

"It's not the same equipment!"

Either let me kill her or help me take her leash off.

There's no signal from her necklace.

"Chip can fix you. Untie me and lean forward."

Sophie pushed the scalpel a centimeter deeper, twisting as she loosened the binds. "If you kill me, you won't survive it."

Khair snapped the chain off.

Sophie shrieked and jumped, swiping the scalpel like a sword. "It was fake?" Sophie opened a shelf to a bag of shots.

Khair groaned. "Really, that's—"

"It's morphine."

"Yes, please."

Jiao finished giving orders and entered alone, glancing at the broken necklace and Sophie's neck. "Are there any guided missiles left in Albion?"

"No," Sophie said. "Unless they were brought from the Asa region."

Jiao tore the shred of necklace from Khair, checked its dummy mechanics, and threw it in the trash. Sophie winced at the clang.

"Do you have anything easily weaponized?" Jiao sanded the edge off her voice but couldn't blunt it. "Something we can control—I don't want unguided bombs killing civilians."

"Typical nuclear reactors, but there's no controlling that," Sophie said. "Biochemical hazards? We could try to tailor it somehow, but once we release it, it'll mutate and then.... It's a city full of citizens, there's no getting around it."

"Send me the biochem credentials." Jiao glanced at a message on her wrist-con, paled. "And turn in your wrist-con."

"What? I need my translator. My political allies are all dead. I'm only talking to friends, extended family—"

"It's only until Taivan recovers."

"If." Sophie leaned against the protesting wheeled desk, running her thumb along the ridges on the far side Jiao couldn't see. "Is your loyalty to the Khanate or Taivan? Because now, our best defense is to turn over his corpse and—"

Jiao held up a finger to shush her. "I don't want to kill you."

Sophie found the scalpel, but Khair pulled the wheeled desk out from under her. She fell. Jiao, polite enough to pretend nothing happened, never noticed the knife.

"How is she?" Jiao asked.

Sophie stood, using Khair's bed as a crutch, shaking it. "Depends on how large the shrapnel is."

"Go to your quarters."

Sophie dosed Khair with morphine. "Now you're still in my debt."

"Sophie," Jiao said. "Lock your door and don't open for anyone but me or Aidan."

She nodded, half a bow, and left.

"You helped Davids escape," Jiao said. "Did you know he would shoot Taivan?"

That was the dumbest thing she'd ever heard, and that included Sophie suggesting Whiskey might want a cat friend. "No, that message set him off. What was it?"

Jiao set her jaw. "His son contracted a rare disease from Irmeg."

"Did we do it on purpose?"

"I don't know." She drummed her pistol. "We have cloaked ships circling the city, waiting to strike. If I don't, we're target practice."

"Unless I go back in. I'm from Irmeg, I'll have antibodies."

"Perhaps."

"Test my blood."

"If your blood can protect his son, they'll take it and you'll have no leverage."

"Unless you fire at the walls occasionally. Don't look at me like that. I'm not saying grill civilians, just distract them."

Coloma gardens passed over Khair's eyes. The hated, crowded streets. Farmers pushing their tractor out of the mud at dawn, professors ordering bitter caffeine, old folks gossiping as they walked through simulation rooms, weathermen fixing the dome.

Stop getting my reality all twisted.

It's not your reality; that's live footage, real people, that is reality.

You're forty years old, use your big girl words.

"We can't do that," Jiao said. "Our firepower won't impress them. When we strike, it has to be fast and precise, followed immediately by an invasion. Even then, I don't like our odds. Especially if their civilians fight, and they're armed."

"So, we've no options but giving my blood for free?"

"You and Sophie escape in this chaos, and offer a wealth of information on our defenses that'll take a few days to process."

Everybody's Got a Tragic Backstory

KHAIR'S AUTOPILOTED JET DOCKED outside Coloma's wall, so they had no vehicle except her wheelchair. It was only temporary, so she didn't mind the chair; it was the only way to get around without more pain. Except people infantilized her even more than usual, and tried to move her like she was a toy left out in the middle of the floor.

"I can't do this," Khair said to Sophie as she rolled into the city. The shrapnel was out and her legs were in compressed painkiller sleeves— the worst invention since telemarketers, alarm clocks, or Agent Orange. Her legs were so numb it looped back around to being painful. But it meant the doctube was occupied, Taivan still alive. "I'm a bad liar."

"It's easy." Sophie kept her hand on the back of Khair's chair for guidance. They moved slowly, but the roads were smooth. "Say things like 'this is a great plan, Jiao,' 'don't worry, Sophie and Khair, you're not expendable,' and 'we're totally on your side now, Bucky.'"

"But I make this face." She cocked her head, widened her eyes, opened her mouth halfway.

"I'm sure that's appropriately hideous, but," Sophie waved to her sunglasses. "Just tell people what they want to hear and mix in as much truth as you can."

Lie to yourself about lying. Annoyance slipped through, but Chip snorted and it dissipated. *Nothing is so difficult as not deceiving oneself.*

I had a lot of help there. But maybe Chip wasn't only talking about her. **What am I supposed to do?**

She stopped her chair ten paces from twelve soldiers with C2231s blocking the road. Coloma's projected wooden gate had shut with such a complete seal not even dust got through; the invisible dome stopped projectiles and jammed unwanted communication. There was nowhere to go.

Help them surround Jiao with overwhelming force. She'll surrender to save her men.

It was one thing for Jiao to swoop in providing aid and bask in people's adoration. It was another to yield her fleet and her life, especially after all that happened the last time her forces were overrun.

Some of us haven't taken the thirty pieces of silver yet.

Chip's pain felt like biting an undercooked potato with a rotten tooth, but she wrenched it out without hesitation. *You turned yourself over to UOD with a bomb vest under your shirt to save your people, chickened out, and submitted to this mess.*

What? Taivan said I sacrificed myself.

Humiliation blew over her, such a mild breeze it would leave a ship stranded; she had never been brave and had no reason to start.

Does that sound like you? Never speak of that again, others may hear.

The city square was cleared as far as she could see over the shrubs on the neon buildings, traffic a distant growl. Cement barriers blocked the street entrances. A net lay above to catch flysuits. And a dozen red dots marked her chest.

"That's close enough." Westley's mom, commanding the soldiers, said.

"Hey, Cassia." Sophie only had one red circle on her knee. "Tell your president-lover I'm free, and I want my nation back."

"You won't find it here," Cassia said. "Stop moving, Khair."

She stopped playing with a beetle on her wheel.

Sophie kicked Khair's wheelchair forward, isolating them both, and raised her hands. "Search us. We've got nothing but our clothes and information."

"And your brother," Cassia said. "You'd save yourself and leave him?"

Sophie lowered her hands. "His birth father had mental health issues, and he's been through a considerate amount of trauma. He's sick, and Taivan feeds his delusions to control him."

Okay, that sounded more plausible than time travel.

"Ship's clear." Davids entered Coloma behind them, in a business suit with a shotgun, standing without a crutch or cane. "I'll take it from here, captain."

"You don't get a doctube next time," Cassia said. "Don't be stupid. Sir." She stepped back and hit a button on her wrist.

The illusion faded away. Khair and Sophie were alone with Davids in a spherical room with padded walls, no bed, no toilet, and no entrance. She still wore a dozen red dots.

Are those guns a trick of the light?

I don't know, there are no cameras.

You didn't know it was an illusion.

Aidan had said she always died making unwarranted assumptions. Here, where multiple angles and secondary confirmation were no guarantor of truth, she couldn't take anything for granted.

No, but that expensive tech's an outlier, and I'll piece your prison together based off outside footage.

"So, this Cassia," Khair said. "Doesn't seem too professional with the whole—"

Davids handed Sophie a needle, tube, and clear bag. "Take her blood."

"That's a big bag," Khair said.

"You'll fill it three times and leave." Davids looked to Sophie. "He holds your people hostage. You can't expect me to believe you."

Sophie drew a plastic cylinder from her bra. "Here's their ship's blueprints."

"I won't risk a data breach; we know your ships already."

"They have assorted craft from all over Asa. And before you shot Taivan, he sent word to the other surviving jinong."

A jinong was the heir-apparent, there should've only been one. Chuluun must've died before he narrowed the selection, or expected candidates to eliminate the others.

"Hoelun and Timur are coming, maybe others," Sophie said. "They have another hundred thousand marines, five destroyers, and a Dreadnought. Jiao's supposed to retain command, but it'll descend into," she waved her hand and said "bad shit" as Davids said "blood tanistry."

Khair wheeled back and forth to see if the lasers followed her. They did.

"Is he dead?" Davids asked.

"Jiao won't say," Sophie said.

"ZAX records show Hoelun and Timur are lightyears away."

"That's a lot of certainty in a company selling tech that deceives the 'verse." Khair rolled along the wall, feeling the padded panels for guns.

"We're prepared for Hoelun and Timur," Davids said. "I'm more concerned about unconventional warfare."

"I've not seen biowarfare capabilities," Sophie said. "But I haven't had full facility access. I doubt Taivan would use it. It's difficult to control and with everything that happened to him, of course he's a control freak."

He wasn't. But Davids, loose-handed in governing yet always in the center of the storm, was. So he crossed his arms and sighed. "I'll bite. What happened to him? How can I use it, and what are your sources?"

"Batu talks too much. Apparently, it was common knowledge." Sophie had been using him? "Taivan's the oldest of nine, mom died young, dad was a layabout. I looked into kidnapping his siblings, but they're lightyears away. His dad tried to keep him from his uncle, so he was among the masses during the early rising, fighting starvation, bandits, and Irmeg's natural surliness."

"Most of Chuluun's old troops come from conquered nations. That doesn't help."

Sophie adjusted her dress, hiding a scowl. "It means he's a survivor and a loner, not a soldier with a chain of command."

A fat leap. Though it wasn't exactly usual for an officer to massage their subordinate's shoulders on command, as Taivan had.

"Once Chuluun conquered Irmeg, he summoned his family to help. Taivan was about twelve. Considering Chuluun's proclivities, there's no question how Taivan earned so many favors at his age, especially since his extensive training is a typical male trauma response."

Khair must have known, known and did nothing.

"The boy grew up," Davids said. "And I can't offer asylum from the dead."

"Wounds linger. Especially now, he'll be in pain; send him a peace offering, some oppyin, say it's a traditional gift. He won't take it at first, but frustrate him a while, he will."

Taivan hurt himself through overtraining his healing leg and sleep deprivation, nothing else.

Davids' nose flared. "Your idea is to keep him here and fund him through valuable medicine?"

"Maybe he'll become an entrepreneur." Khair bungled that word so much the translator gave up.

He pointedly ignored her.

"We both know oppyin's more than medicine." Sophie lowered her voice. "It's smoggy enough here to give you that cough. But what shrinks your pupils? Long hours, insatiable gambling, not as strong as you were. Perhaps nausea, headaches, erectile dysfunction?"

"Not at all. Thank you for your concern." He fought a sniffle and sneezed instead.

"I'm not looking for blackmail."

"You wouldn't find it."

"But people don't need evidence, just an entertaining spectacle." Sophie raised a hand as if he'd protest, but he didn't. "Take plausible pictures, pass them around, and his people—my people—will destroy him."

"If I trust you enough to hold back my forces."

"You lose nothing by waiting," Khair said. "ZAX brings more firepower than the jinong."

Davids turned to her. Her heart beat faster, lasers still over her chest. "And you? You're not here to save my son."

She made the stupid face. "I wanted a Coloma Kick? Not really, though I'd totally take one. But we can be on the same side. You saved my father, I'll save your son, and with your tech and Taivan's generalship, we can save the galaxy from the time clowns screwing with my head."

"Even if I believed in your 'time clowns,' they've not given us cause for war."

"Their existence is cause enough. If they control time, they control reality and we'll never be free. How can you arm them?"

Davids swiped at the wall, and the lasers disappeared. "They have no more bearing on my freewill than any other weapon that can end my life. Now, if you—"

"Let Aidan speak to your people," Khair said. "You might not consider it proof, but let them decide, and fight UOD if you won't."

"Allow a besieging army to recruit my people?"

She groaned. "That's not—what evidence do you need? Any footage could be doctored, any prophecy avoided, and sooner or later Taivan will wake up or Jiao will get antsy."

"Enough," Sophie said. "Her brain's pulp. She's latched onto this to pretend away the unsurmountable differences between you and Taivan."

"I'm capable of my own judgement." Davids scratched his new stubble. "You're right, Ms. Batuyin, there's no plausible argument unless I experienced time-travel firsthand, and even then, it's likely a simulation. But I can get a doctube for your legs."

"Definitely."

"Wait," Sophie said. "This isn't for free. I want to see again."

Davids said nothing.

"You're staring? Think I must be Taivan's toy if I'd ignore my own bans on your tech and let you connect to my brain? But I know why you take oppyin. Because if you don't, there'll be a call, some crisis only you can fix, and if you're finally home, you won't return. So, you can't go home. You work when you should sleep and find a way to be at your best, whatever it takes, all for your people. Though you're always alone."

Khair's face heated when she discovered Sophie still had working tear ducts.

"Let me see my parent's picture before I forget their faces, look through a microscope, fix my hair in a mirror, wander the street like a normal seventeen-year-old with nothing better to do. Let me see Taivan's corpse and make sure it stays dead."

"There's a long waitlist, but I'll see what I can do." Davids hit a button on his wrist-con that made their prison pod unfold and sink into the street. Cassia, the guards, and the chopper waited. "Ms. Batuyin, may I?"

She nodded, and he pushed her wheelchair to his chopper. "Batu is my father. I'm Khair."

"Can I trust Riley?"

"Can you trust anyone? I mean, we're all out for ourselves, and in her case, Albion, but who aligns with—"

"So no."

Khair shrugged. "I wouldn't, but I really only trust Whiskey."

He sighed. "Vodka has been quite reliable as of late."

Noble Lies and Other Transparent Excuses

"DID YOU KNOW?" DAVIDS asked Khair as she stepped out of the doctube, her legs limp as overcooked noodles.

"What? Probably not." Her doctube had been wheeled into a gray room barely bigger than a closet, and the door was locked.

Davids flicked up a screen.

Taivan stood sweating, scarred, and bare chested except for bandages, in front of sooty walls. Smoke veiled the halls, red lights circled in the background. He leaned against a buck head cane sword, but he'd run a comb through his hair and washed off the doctube goop.

She pinched gunk out of her hair, flecks splattering on Davids' polished shoes.

"Zacatecas Xavier Technology, this is Jochiin Taivan of the Andromeda Khanate. At 0537, on the 15th day of the 8th month, President Davids used a human bomb in an attempt to assassinate myself and my staff."

Had everyone survived?

"Clearly, he did not succeed. He's violated your warfare regulations, forfeiting your protection. If you stand down, I'll have no further issue with you."

Taivan was attacking Coloma to draw out ZAX's faster than light ships; this was to confuse Coloma and buy Jiao time while he recovered.

"You used a human bomb?" Khair said. "Run to Canis Major or the Milky Way, separate yourself and Coloma in his mind."

"I did not. And the only person of yours I've had an opportunity to plant a bomb in—"

"Batu." She almost looked over her shoulder to confirm it with her father. Davids nodded.

"There's no body. It could be—"

"He attached DNA evidence." Davids straightened his shirt, looking down before he could feign sadness. "I'm sorry."

She couldn't breathe. Batu would never have expected it, would never have hurt anyone except to protect her or Taivan or the others, could never have defended himself.

Davids took her arm. "Here, sit."

She shoved him and stumbled away.

He hadn't been old. Sixty something, seventy? He had seemed frail compared to the other keshig, but he'd been spry days after being run over as many times as a railroad. Life thrilled him still. Even if it hadn't, it was better than what, an endless, dreamless, paralyzing sleep?

Tell me this isn't true.

"You're trying to get me to turn traitor," Khair said.

I'm sorry.

Davids kept his distance. "Sophie's investigating. She'll call to verify."

"Oh, did she pinky promise not to conjure evidence this time?

You have every reason to lie. You're lying to your handlers. Why wouldn't you lie to me?

Listen to Sophie. But don't watch the video.

She paced. Maybe Davids had set up a dummy comm system and video. Maybe that wasn't the simplest solution, but Ockham's Razor was a trend rather than a hard rule, and even if Davids had been honest and Taivan hadn't and—

Go on, tell me how I deserve to suffer the deaths of a bazillion family members. But what did Batu deserve?

Her eyes burned, but she didn't have the decency to cry. How could she? She barely knew him. He'd dedicated his life to stirring up the ashes of their dead family, but they were snuffed out with him. And all those people she had killed in the car crash, those ruined lives had bought Batu what? A week?

"Does your son have enough blood?" Khair said.

Davids hesitated. "We believe so."

"If Sophie returns, don't trust her, but help her see." She marched to the door before realizing she didn't have a ship and couldn't fly. "Take me to Taivan."

He relayed the order into his earpiece, unlocked the door, and shooed away the guard. "If he sees you coming, he'll shoot you out of the sky. Consider—"

"Yesterday, we could consider anything. Now Batu is dead."

Take a day.

She walked fast, pulling Davids along, though he guided her, hand on her elbow. ***The one time I'm brave and it's not good enough.***

Chip's organs felt like mush and Khair hated her for it—she had no right to care and multiply Khair's pain. *Take some time, improve your courage by making it a conscious choice.*

Cassia tried to stop Davids, but he kept walking, told her to reschedule, and hooked his arm around Khair's elbow.

Does it matter why I save humanity? As if one deed could wipe out all the rest. Fucking joke.

Not for them.

Batu had loved Taivan. No, not just loved—believed in. And Taivan had decided to spend his life on a feint Batu wouldn't fully understand.

Davids walked her past the gardens overflowing their beds and the fountains with legions of dead legends—Cincinnatus and Washington, Brutus and Tubman. All stony and impervious, faces unconcerned, stronger than their diet and moderate gravity would've allowed, framed against a cold sky.

Batu wouldn't get a statue. Didn't even have a body to model one after. He should be laid out on Irmeg and consumed by animals, aiding other creatures in his final act. But he was a stain on the wall.

Still, his matter and energy would be conserved. A different life may grow from the parts.

Why did some amoeba get to live when her dad was dead?

She stopped at Tubman's statue, leaning on Davids, and looked up to the taller woman. Even after her war was won, she had suffered. This was easier.

One moment and it was over. But this woman from centuries ago seemed almost divine, her sacrifice and courage simply expected.

Davids slipped his arm free. "Do you need a moment?"

Khair shook her head, yet her feet wouldn't move. "If you actually liked her, you'd build her in forty meters of stainless steel, preferably on a horse. It's what the cool kids have."

He raised an eyebrow. "She was a hero to heroes." And Chip. "First American woman to lead an armed force, saved 700 people in one day, even in chronic pain."

At least thirteen trips back to slave-states, with no reward but being reviled where she was supposed to be free.

Thirteen impossible acts of courage? Khair just needed one.

And it was too much. What did it matter when she couldn't save him?

Khair sucked in air. "How can people be that good? Do all that for strangers, people she couldn't possibly love?"

He couldn't answer.

She smiled thinly. "Probably because she got hit in the head as a child." She nodded to Brutus. "Isn't he normally the bad guy?"

"He killed a man he loved like a father for the republic."

He didn't look like a righteous man, with a weak jaw and empty eyes. "Or he resented ol' pop's power."

"Perhaps. But it was a reminder for us: sic semper tyrannis."

"Didn't they say that about Lincoln?"

Davids smiled weakly. "I don't think Jochiin Taivan would have much use for Honest Abe."

"Just to see if he was as good a wrestler as people said." She exhaled softly, savoring the flowery air, misty with the nearby bubbling fountain. "I don't want to kill him, and I don't want to die."

Davids said nothing.

"But I would like one of those puppies." She tapped her nose, slightly crooked. "Make me look good?"

He started to say something about commissioning committees, but ate it and brought her to the chopper. "I've programmed the coordinates. Here's the gun. If you turn it on while you're out of range, they'll shoot you down."

"I'm doing this in person."

"And this button will bring you back."

"In case I chicken out, like last time I tried to sacrifice myself." When she gave UOD her mind to spare her body.

He held out his hand. She wasn't sure how hard to squeeze and her hand was clammy, so she hugged him instead. He stiffened and she let go. "No, bad idea, one of many. Going now."

"I can stay on the radio if you need."

She did need it. "There's enough flashing lights for me to worry about."

Khair poked a button and the door shut behind her with a soft click as the chopper rose, leaving the lush garden for the tundra beyond. Her foot bounced, ever quickening, and she couldn't stop it.

The ride seemed slow motion, the traffic frozen, wind dead so that the evergreens stood as stiff sentinels, the people colorful dots against cracked concrete.

"I should've asked about the stereo."

I could hum. Chip tried to say it lightly, but awkwardness shed off.

And it made her think of Batu. Which was stupid. Every idiot who couldn't remember the words hummed, but only Batu would hum as their shuttle broke up in the atmosphere. He'd seemed happy then, and she hated him for it.

She hadn't thought he'd had a good life. But maybe he had.

Coloma City was too dazzling, too aromatic, too fast and crammed up close, but it was beautiful at night, at a distance. Vivid lights showed off the details engraved on the arches too subtle to see by day, shows played in parks while bundled families watched and ate and heckled together.

If she pressed that button, not a meter away, she could return.

'And may there be no sadness of farewell,

when I embark;

For tho' from out our borne of Time and Place—

Khair snorted a laugh. **Clearly, they took your memories of actual danger.**

Fear is grief, and I know that well enough. Besides, this isn't the time to discuss me.

Why not? You're the one with a future.

She blinked faster, growled at her wet lashes, spat to the side to show a little water didn't matter. Though it stirred old taboos and she tried to wipe it clean.

Do you have a family, Chip? Living parents, a hot guy I can steal, munchkins of your own?

Her loneliness ebbed through Khair, a weak eddy swelling to a frothing roar at its loudest as it swept out and faded. *Yes.*

But you're not happy together?

Coloma's domed roof opened and spat her chopper out. The city seemed frail from here, though her guns could tear through any Khanate ship.

We're happy. Just not together, but it doesn't matter. They know that... I couldn't love them so much; except I loved honor more.

It was the thrashing of a drowning woman. Chip didn't have a country, didn't have a family, her honor was a leaking lifeboat. People like them didn't get an overarching moral principle. They were liars and cowards who continued on because they were smart enough to rationalize themselves.

No longer.

Chip tried to let it pass, tried to let Khair think what she willed, but protests sunk through. *I've broken the letter of my oaths; I can still be faithful to the spirit. I—*

It's just me, Chip. I don't judge.

She shrank in her own mind. *Thank you.*

Might as well have one friend. Khair breathed into her hands to warm them, ignoring the water flowing freely now. ***Why didn't I have anyone but Batu? No lovers, no friends, not even the brat I kidnapped, my anda just betrayed me.***

She was so weak. Decades lay before her if she let Taivan get away with it. As if Batu was nothing. She hadn't loved him in life, but she could love him in death. If there was an afterlife, she wouldn't find him; he'd looked after her long enough.

Do you want me to be honest, or do you want me to be kind?

She laughed. ***I wanted—***

"Khair, this is Jiao. Do you copy?"

"Go away, kiddo. The adults were talking."

"Land and dismount." There was something wrong with the signal, Jiao sounded nasally.

"Take me to Taivan."

Long pause, so Khair slapped the dashboard until a warning sign lit up and Jiao returned. "We need to talk."

Her resolve would jelly. "We'll talk when Taivan brings back Batu."

"Batu volunteered."

Heat rushed her head. She'd been a kid listening to the magician's jokes while his hands worked below the table. "So not only did Taivan kill him, he convinced him his life was worthless?"

"No, it," Jiao's voice cut out. "I'll explain."

The chopper landed in front of the *Sphinx*. One step down. Now came the hard part.

Where's the happy gibberish?

'Love lives beyond

the tomb, the earth, which fades—

Actually, shut up. Having Chip obey her almost made it worth it.

Jiao waited outside, seemingly alone. Khair looked for the reflection of a sniper's scope in a ship's window. Why? No point getting antsy on a suicide mission.

Khair stayed in the warm chopper, showed her palms but didn't raise her hands, in as close to a fighting stance as she dared. "Bring me to Taivan."

Jiao didn't have her rifle, only a long, serrated knife. Her eyes were red. After Khair hopped to the dirt, glancing around because somehow this seemed a prank and Batu was laughing around the corner, Jiao extended the knife's handle.

"Hold me accountable."

Khair walked past her. "Come out, Taivan, you pig sucking corpse. Always picking on the weak, but we're an even match. Face me!"

Jiao still offered the knife. "Listen—"

"Because he convinced you to die for him, too? No."

"He's in the doctube."

She slammed Jiao against the chopper and pinned the knife to her throat, though the blade was in Jiao's hand. "Has he been out yet?"

"For the video." Jiao was so quiet Khair only heard her because the war had scared the countryside into an unnatural silence.

"But not the murder?"

Jiao tried to look her in the eye, but her head drooped.

She smashed her palm into the chopper beside Jiao's head. "So, when you say 'hold me accountable', you mean you murdered him?"

Jiao sniffled and tried to speak. She croaked.

Khair tossed her to the dirt, and though she wanted to stomp in Jiao's ribs, she couldn't look at her. "Why?"

She fumbled for words, stopping every few breaths to collect herself so she never got anything out.

"Go on, sob. Just tell me why you killed my father!"

Jiao laid out a round disk and a clear blue hologram of Batu appeared.

Daughters

THE PICTURE WAS FROZEN, Batu leaning back in strained contortion as someone coached him, his last words not his own. What was the point of watching someone else's excuses?

Khair threw the disk against Jiao's chest. The hologram fell face first into the dirt and disappeared.

"Let's go inside. You're not dressed for this weather." Though Jiao didn't have the energy to stand, she gave orders just fine.

Khair shook, but she wasn't cold. When she went in, Jiao would show her what Batu had said, Taivan's plan, the power of approaching ZAX ships, and she'd understand. Agree it wasn't so bad her father was dead.

And why shouldn't she, when she'd never been a daughter to him, even now more concerned about her grief than any unpleasantness Batu had soldiered?

"You're not coming to my quarters; I'll go to yours."

Jiao stood facing the ship, away from Khair.

Chip, take the day off.

She hesitated, the unease of hard words, not indecision. *That ship has nuclear weapons within range of a hostile city filled with civilians.*

Khair shoved Jiao toward the ship. ***I forgot, you're all buddy-buddy when I do what you want. Afterwards, I'm on my own.***

Excuses bubbled to a hot boil, but Chip turned down the heat. *I'll be quiet if you don't do anything drastic.*

Don't talk about a trial.

Taivan had been the law. Now there was none.

Jiao brought her through a lower exit, avoiding cameras. It smelled of grease and fresh laundry; the engine whirred soft and smooth, soldiers pressed themselves against the wall to let them pass.

If Jiao had hidden soldiers in this labyrinth of plaster walls and squeaking floors, she'd die. There was no cover, no concealment.

"Consider the trap sprung," Khair said.

The walls were barren plaster blocks, a colorless bulletin listing unfinished tasks. Jiao had pinned new rules but used Taivan's name—twenty bulleted and sub-bulleted points detailing the treatment of civilians, prisoners, subordinates, superiors, and equipment.

Nothing about murdering ministers to discredit the enemy.

"Hey, I'm talking to you." Khair grabbed Jiao's shoulder.

Jiao spun her arm, snapping off Khair's hand. "Quiet. Our soldiers don't need a spectacle."

If she wanted to observe proprieties, she could start by respecting Batu, her elder. "'Our soldiers?' You're not Khanate." She tapped Jiao's memorandum. "You're so much better, remember?"

Jiao walked away and unlocked, locked, and unlocked an industrial strength lock on a door in a dead-end hall.

"No keshig to protect you? Either you want to die, or you're under delusions people like you."

Jiao entered, turned off the alarm, and removed her boots. Khair stomped dirt on the vinyl floor, ignoring a welcome mat, but stopped when she saw the portrait of a stern, greying woman staring at her.

"Hold the dogs." Khair said politely to the picture and crossed her arms.

Jiao's quarters had a kitchen and mock cockpit, the bed lofted for more space, but clutter shrank it. Not in Khair's 'I can totally find this later' way. Weeds of organization had sprung in the corners but weren't allowed to overrun the room.

"Did you barge into a stranger's room?"

Jiao's cockpit was so clean she could lick the floor. Here, the compost and trash compactor were filled, their recycled energy masking the smell. Dirty laundry spilled out beside books of pressed flowers, an unnecessary number of cardio machines faced a smattering of angry abstract paintings, with oily rags scattered among makeup removal wipes.

"I didn't expect anyone." Jiao waited, light on her feet, hands clasped behind her back.

"Get me a drink." Khair turned from the imposing woman, only to see a repeating film of a little boy. He cried with a scepter, slept in a flower bed, squeezed a long-suffering puppy, all in front of a seven-storied wooden palace dwarfed by mountains.

Jiao heated water. She hadn't meant tea, but she'd never seen Jiao drink.

A screen altered its angle and showed the Andromeda galaxy. "Sorry to interrupt, Jun Jiao," the pronunciation was slightly different than what everyone said, and Khair couldn't replicate it. "There is breaking news."

Had Davids tired of waiting?

"Zeng Dai has qualified for the Shenzhou Kite Finals!"

Khair snorted. "It's not a sport unless you hit someone."

The screen showed an open, crowded field. People were happy there. Watching mythological animals fly alongside cartoon characters and caricatures of people whose unamused but perfectly captured faces were shown at the bottom. Boisterous announcers made a measly flick of the wrist to keep the kite flying sound like, well, the flick of a wrist for a walk-off grand slam. Old couples made smoochy eyes. Musicians surfed a young crowd with more enthusiasm than strength.

The mountains in the background had the same steep angles and permafrost line where the boy played, but the palace was gone.

Khair's face heated, and she made sure Jiao didn't notice her studying the room. Most of the baubles were from Albion: a bracelet of dappled marble, a snuffbox of fragrant resin, etched and painted stone sarcophagi, sculptures of smooth bog wood. Things mined from a specific quarry or carved from a distinct tree that could be mimicked but never remade.

Jiao's heirlooms had burned in the *Bankhar's* crash. Everything that survived was public domain, fenced off and mocked by clucking historians and bored students.

Khair's fury didn't abate in the slightest, but her stomach ached for two.

Someone knocked.

"Sorry," Khair said. "Jiao's about to have a really bad day and can't answer."

"I'm here for you, Khair," Sophie said. "You should arrange his funeral. And we're getting low on supplies. That's your responsibility."

Khair flicked the door's veneer to clear. Sophie appeared alone, but she could have soldiers hidden by light refractors. "Go away."

"I can give you a sedative or oppyin, a joint, whatever you need."

She needed her father. "I need vengeance."

"Sophie." Jiao's voice was soft, but she kept her back to the glass door. "Aidan controls the army until Taivan wakes. You'll be safe."

Sophie leaned her hand against the door and lowered her voice. "Look at me, Jiao."

She didn't turn, pretending to be terribly busy warming her hands over the stovetop.

"Half your life, you've been beaten and humiliated. But you found a way to survive, to change the world around you for the better. Are you going to lie down and die defeated?"

"You're talking to yourself," Jiao said.

"And what young monarch have you been saving when you protect me? It doesn't matter. Let me in, I'll take you somewhere safe. You owe me a chance to win my money back."

Jiao looked over her shoulder and started to speak, but Khair stepped between her and the door. She turned back around.

Even without eyes, Sophie glared at Khair. "Let her live. The Khanate follows her."

"Albion followed you once."

Sophie slapped the door. "In peace, yes, but I couldn't hold them. Listen. Without her, we'll have to surrender to Davids and his mob rule. Everyone you know will die in chains."

"I can beat Davids," Khair said. She was talking about a war, but it seemed no more than their pull-up contest, like he'd survive the loss unscathed.

"And how many of our people will survive that victory?" Sophie lowered her voice. "Khair, please."

"Please, what? Forget my father?"

"Jiao," Sophie said. "Don't be selfish. There's no justice in letting us bear your crimes."

Jiao's hands hovered closer to the flame. "Taivan will wake soon."

"You can't know that. When it comes down to it, you lost one soldier."

"He was more than that," Jiao said.

"Open the door, or I'll turn off the power for this entire—"

Jiao turned on her comm. "Aidan, there's a disturbance outside my room. Please clear it."

Sophie laughed. "Whatever absolution you're looking for, you're not gonna find it. You can't suffer enough to bring him back, and whatever Khair does next won't be justice."

"No?" Khair paced in front of the door. "Cause you haven't devised it on a spreadsheet, made it all regulated and pretty, gotten it peer-reviewed? I'm sure Batu's death was."

"So, it was painless. If UOD followed your vindictive—"

"They should have." It would've been cleansing, merciful, and it was deserved.

"Aidan be here in three minutes, Sophie," Jiao said.

"You deserve each other." Her shoes squeaked as she left.

They were left alone, accompanied by specters and the whistle of steam. The table was buried under schematics and dated machinery, so Khair sat on the floor.

"You were all in on it," Khair said, half a question. "Sophie's biotech, Aidan the director, making sure his ashes got on a pale enough wall."

Jiao set out a porcelain tea set, wiped it, and Khair figured she was about to drink dust, but Jiao's motions had slowed in some rite that massaged the tension from her shoulders. When she'd relaxed, she sped slightly, silent except for the soft clank of the grinding pestle, and poured with her left hand over her heart.

Khair huffed. Only Jiao could make her feel like a peasant while confessing to murder. "Where's the milk?"

Jiao drank and watched her not drink, her forehead wrinkling. "I could get some."

Khair didn't like leafy water, anyway. She waited for Jiao to make some excuse she could whack down her throat, or reveal some science-magic to bring Batu back.

But Jiao scowled at the floor.

"Was it vengeance?" Khair nodded to the repeating photos of her beautiful, dead baby brother laid out in a crib where her people now played. "Was it my fault?"

Jiao turned the picture around and froze there, arms dangling. "I did it."

She drank the scalding tea, the oolong earthy and unnervingly calming.

Batu had treated Jiao like a daughter. She'd pleaded for his life, offered herself in his stead when he was captured. What had happened? "Were you jealous I was spending time with him?"

"No."

"And? Tell me something."

"I was glad to see him happy, even with you. He talked about your family for the first time—"

"About why you killed him!"

Jiao glowered. "The fleet was in danger. They were buzzing around us, and there was a defense ready if I gave the word. So I did. And their jets were recalled immediately."

For the Khanate, then, with PRGC survivors scattered among them. For Taivan and his dream—of what? No United Oversight for Democracy, but if they had a time-machine and were as bad as he said, why hadn't their victories been undone?

Khair invaded the fridge, but there was nothing but kimchi, potato pancakes, and chickpea salad. "You're a vegetarian? Won't eat precious crickets, but—"

"I told you what you need to know. Kill me or leave."

She shook the kimchi to see if there was anything good among the vegetables before putting it back. "You've told me nothing."

"I gave you the holo."

"Believe it or not, I don't want to see my father blow up."

Jiao leaned against the wall. "I showed him videos, so he knew what it was like. Kept showing them, wrote out a waiver, laid everything out. He still didn't change his mind. I reminded him that Taivan planted the bomb in his head after years of service. But he didn't change his mind."

Khair searched the cabinets for food—she should've lost her appetite, but she was ravenous—and found nothing but trinkets and pictures. She flipped it shut and something shattered inside. "You gave him that choice; to him, it was like giving an order."

"Don't steal his sacrifice. He knew he didn't have to, and he did it, anyway." Jiao cracked her knuckles, fingers quivering. "Afterward, I thought 'I could have volunteered,' but it never occurred to me before. There was so much else." She swallowed. "Or maybe I thought I was more valuable. Or I didn't want to die."

Khair turned on cold water, spun it in the cup, dumped it down the sink. "Me neither."

This room was suffocating, but there was nowhere to go. And Jiao's mother watched her, her face nothing like her daughter's but the expression identical: mouth in a neutral line, head tilted a few degrees, grave eyes seeing through her. Khair dipped her head to the picture. "I'm sorry."

Jiao tried to step back, but she was already against the wall. "Please don't."

She nodded and walked toward the door.

"The day Chuluun stormed the palace, you broke my wrist and told Batu to fix me. He gave me medicine, food, space, and for years he was the only one who dared be kind to me."

Khair couldn't answer.

"I learned to fly so I could kill Chuluun. Batu got me lessons. A few years later, Taivan caught me hijacking a ship, he could've done anything to me. He asked for a ride. I obliged; thought I could kill him, too. But he had plans beyond Chuluun and I listened long enough to land safely. He brought me on as his pilot, and I met his crew, normal people. Hated them for it, but I stayed, so here I am: abandoning my family and playing chauffeur to their murderers."

She shrugged, the movement exhausting her. "After you saved my life, you left me, a kid, to whatever thug passed by."

Khair gritted her teeth so hard her jaw hurt.

"But I'm still your responsibility. So end me."

"No." If for no other reason but that she was all the way across the room.

THE LITTLE TIME ALLOTTED US

"You're no real daughter to him."

Khair stiffened, then laughed. Jiao looked up to her though they were the same height, small fists curled at her side. With everything the girl had suffered, she'd never been the cause of her misery. The poor bitch. She had never learned the crime was the sentence.

Jiao burned red as Khair laughed, but she wasn't the punchline; Batu was. If he hadn't been kind to his enemies, he wouldn't have been murdered by his friends.

"I wasn't," Khair said. "But I was starting to. Might have been with more time."

Jiao finally looked Khair in the eye, eyes glazed, and spread her arms.

Khair crossed the room in three bounds, not sure what she'd do until she'd wrapped Jiao in her arms and hit her back against the wall, crushing her ribs. Jiao struggled to breathe.

She could've ended it, might've done the kid that one favor, except Jiao gripped her shirt, maybe for support, maybe to keep from fighting back, but whatever it was, needing her. Then, barely loosening her grip, Khair buried her head on Jiao's shoulder and cried.

Jiao held her. They stayed like that, Jiao supporting her, hunched over and shaking with effort, Khair halfway kneeling, breathing only because Jiao's heart thumped against her chest and showed her how to live.

"Sorry to interrupt, Jun Jiao, there is one breaking news story for you."

"This better not be another kite," Khair growled, not releasing her.

"Jochiin Taivan is waking up now."

Worst of All Possible Worlds

"I NEED TO GET to Davids." Taivan stepped from the doctube naked. He hopped to his wrist-con and summoned his prosthetic without checking the faded scars on his chest.

Jiao looked away; Khair didn't. He was safe. Movements stiff, but otherwise, lounging in the 'tube seemed the best rest he'd gotten in weeks.

His prosthetic was so clean fingerprints could be traced but he dusted it anyway, applied a gel liner, and fit the sleeve over his calf. He skimmed a summary of everything that had happened since he entered the 'tube at a speed even Chip could admire before looking for his clothes.

"Coloma must be clamoring to surrender now." Taivan flicked through supplementary reports and Coloma news. "But if they realize ZAX is still coming—"

"No," Khair said. "When did you put a bomb in Batu's head? Who else has one? Don't light a match, Jiao, you might get a nasty surprise."

Jiao looked up until her eyes stopped watering.

Khair lowered her voice. "He gave everything for your cause, Taivan, for you. Do you deserve it? Or were you just another battered kid he sheltered?"

Taivan buttoned his shirt without looking at her. "You didn't watch the video. Batu—"

"I don't care. We're not attacking Coloma; you're not benefitting from his death. I believed you back in Albion when you talked about your soldiers. I thought their deaths—their lives—meant something. Congratulations. That was the last time you fooled me."

He looked to Jiao. "You'd rather Batu died for nothing?"

She gave half a nod.

"Do you hear me?" Khair said.

"You told me to care for the living. So let me. Time's running out, and I need to speak to Davids." Taivan walked around the lab, each step less sure than the last, and stopped after one lap by a bag of oppyin.

Khair tossed the oppyin in a cabinet, but it bounced out. "I've got to be there. I saved his son. If there's any trust, it's between us."

"Good." Taivan threw the oppyin in the trash, his bad leg shaking as he bent over. "Jiao, you'll have the fleet."

Jiao shook her head.

"There's no one else I trust." His leg spasmed, and he griped the counter to keep steady.

"That's on you."

Taivan sat. "Batu?"

She didn't answer.

"He went out on his terms. Enkhiin Batu be remembered alongside Chanakya and Yelu Chucai in the new, better world we make."

Chucai had been a captured scholar, nothing like Batu, except they both pleaded for the people to a more powerful man that often ignored them. The other... ***Do you know those men?***

No.

"How is this better?" Khair said. "You tell Jiao we fight for a just world and a home for what's left of the Khanate. You tell me it's for glory. What do you tell Aidan? This better world will be as twisted as the last."

"They're not mutually exclusive."

"But you have to prioritize and I don't trust you to choose."

"I'll take that from Jiao, not you," Taivan said. "Don't pretend this is about some ideal. It's about your father."

"People change," Jiao said softly. "Let me go."

"Where?" Taivan's brow furrowed. "You'd be captured by pirates, warlords, vengeful governments."

"If I stay, I'll lose more than my life."

Taivan snorted, turned his back. "Somehow, you're all the family and friend I have, Jun Jiao."

Khair had figured as much, but it stung all the same.

He's echoing her. I had your body.

She'd heard, but time had divided into with and after Batu, and everything with him happened to someone else. Why had Jiao said that when she had Batu?

You're defending him?

Just stating a fact.

But the little relief in Khair's stomach reverberated in Chip's.

"Take time to mourn," Taivan said to Jiao. "Or rule Albion, Jungang ju eventually. Give the word, I'll take on the old powers and lay Earth itself at your feet. But don't run to death."

"Then imprison me again; I can't be your admiral." Her thin shoulders were set, eyes hard, but her reedy voice betrayed her.

Taivan plopped a disc on the table. "Like Aidan, I've seen futures, alternate worlds. I don't know how, if UOD was targeting me or if I was just shuffled by accident. Watch."

An endless, dense city of mildewed cardboard houses and littered streets. Soldiers encased in armor patrolled with rifles at the low ready, dragging people outside as they clung to homes that collapsed on them. After soldiers hauled away their prey, neighbors yanked off the soon-to-be orphans to mine radioactive materials and searched for bread for their children with the reward money.

Screens in every plaza told of United Oversight for Democracy's benevolence, how if the people beat out their tune and reported on troublesome neighbors, they'd get enough points to live in an obviously CGI'ed mansion.

Aidan Riley sat in a palace, slippered feet on a leather couch. He lounged beneath a frescoed ceiling, surrounded by jade encrusted walls, an orchestral stage on his right, on his left a museum of entertainment devices—hunting falcons, scuba gear, pac-man, but he played with a yo-yo.

He wore silk pajamas and ate cinnamon rolls, so the apocalypse was working out for someone.

"If the west is acting up, increase raids in the area." He broke the yo-yo against the floor, but a flamboyantly ugly servant replaced it before he noticed. "Better yet, raise taxes on everyone else and give them the excess."

Khair stood twenty meters from Aidan with a squad at her back, stuck in a pantsuit so ironed it should've been singed. She'd tattooed an (admittedly cool) dragon over the left side of her face and had no weapon except a whip with a gold gilded hilt. "Seems like a lot of work for not a lot of men. When are we getting reinforcements?"

"When we meet the quotas. Keep them fighting each other until then."

"I don't know, Boss Man, they're pretty wired, my guys are—"

"Do you think there's any shortage of thugs here?"

"Absolutely ready to crack skulls. We mopped up that uprising, took a leader alive."

Teenaged Taivan dragged Jiao inside, her legs broken behind her. "Sir, this is—"

Khair waved him to silence. "You're here to look pretty, pup. Your strident voice ruins it."

Taivan threw Jiao on her face. He wore a crisp white and red uniform a size too small, only an ensign's stripe on his arm, with two legs and fidgety hands.

"She's small," Aidan said. "Show her face."

Jiao bit Taivan as he grabbed her chin, but Khair seized Jiao's hair and yanked up her head. Her eyes were gone and shallow scratches littered her face, but great pains were taken to keep her pretty.

Aidan leaned forward, suddenly stiff. "Khair, for a joke to be funny, it has to have an edge of seriousness."

"I recorded everything. Watch the film."

"I will. Find someone to nail outside the palace. Your choice."

"Anyone you have in mind, some magistrate that's getting uppity?"

"Initiative for once! Too bad it's wasted on politicking. No."

"You sure? Naguib's a little woman too, but she—"

"I need public opposition. Just grab some gross drunk no one will miss, or better yet, someone respectable with a family to weep at their feet."

Jiao spat. "You're going to—"

Khair kicked Jiao's jaw, the crack of bone echoing through the hall. "What do I do with this?"

"I'm sure I don't care, as long as you do it elsewhere." He paused. "If she asks to die, let her."

Taivan grabbed Jiao's collar with the trepidation of a man grabbing fire, pat her broken jaw when she didn't fight. "Can I keep it?" He dragged her toward the door.

"You've not done anything to deserve a prize, and I can keep you entertained. Throw her on the heap."

His head bobbed in a nod as he struggled to carry Jiao out the door. Khair held the door open for him, smacked his ass as he left, bowed to Aidan, and shut the door behind them.

The hologram stopped.

The room seemed less real than the vision, the colors dimmer than the palace, their engine's roll out of place.

That was her better dressed and way better paid, Jiao too, and Aidan's evil twin. But how was that Taivan?

"We're not responsible for our counterparts," Taivan said as Jiao turned from Khair, rubbing her cheek. "But that's what happens if we balk, or decide we can't pay the price."

"That was Gürragchaa there, Genepil, our crew," Jiao said.

His jaw tightened. "They were as good as they were allowed to be, better."

"Batu would never do that," Khair said.

Taivan said nothing

"That's Coloma," Jiao said. "So why are we here, fighting UOD, bringing them here, destroying the planet like you've seen?"

"Because I'm not that neutered boy. Aidan's on our side. That's not Khair anymore. And we're all with you, Jiao; you're not fighting alone."

"No?" Jiao sat on the counter. "That's my eyes gouged out like Sophie's, Aidan's same pajamas and—" she swung her feet. "I can't endure that."

Taivan leaned beside her and offered his hand. She ignored it.

"There's no escaping this," Taivan said. "In every future Aidan sees, UOD hovers over us as our enemy or employer. If we run, they'll pick us off."

"And we fight every time. Maybe we're creating that monster."

Taivan blanched. "Are you serious? Our ships, terraformed planets, the net—our entire civilization—depends on their tech. Sure, if we don't fight, they'll play the benevolent masters, for as long as it's convenient. Then they'll break your legs to put you on your knees. I thought we were done being other people's toys?"

"That's enough," Khair said.

"No, it's not. We all die, so what? But if you let them control you, you're nothing but their machine, never lived at all." Taivan slowed, composed himself. "There's my priority, Khair: to destroy them and live, no better than a cornered beast."

Jiao's eyes reddened, and she rocked slightly.

Taivan looked to her.

That video was real, wasn't it?

She half hoped it wasn't, didn't want to be like that, didn't want Davids to see it.

It doesn't seem doctored from here. I'll look into it.

She inhaled. "I've destroyed worlds. I'd like to save some. Jiao, even if we don't fight, Davids will once he sees their true face. We need to fight together."

"Even with Coloma, it's not enough." Jiao touched her knuckles to Taivan's.

"Probably not. What else can we do?" He kissed her hand.

She stood. "Make a treaty, or buy them off, use poison or... whatever it takes, even if no one remembers your name."

"Aidan's seen those versions; they end with you in his place."

Jiao left, said: "I'll stay with you," over her shoulder before shutting the door with extra care.

"That was a lie," Khair said. No matter what happened, there were some impossibilities.

"Just a desperate planet, and Jiao was a decent ruler with few good choices." He pinged Sophie and ordered a fitting for a more permanent prosthetic as his leg healed. "Do I have a tell?"

"Answer me something first."

"Yes, great baghatur." He was only half mocking.

"How long did you live over there? Was I really that terrible to you or was I preforming for Aidan?"

"That's two questions and only one pertains to you."

"But you trust me." She said it as a question, but he didn't deny it. "You don't have one, you just say outlandish things. Half the time, they're true. Though you get away with more than I catch."

He itched his stump. "I thought you'd ask about Batu."

"Would you tell me?"

"Chip might hurt you for it."

She didn't hesitate. "Go on."

"I put the bomb in his head when I had to sedate him to let you fly to UOD because I wanted to win something in his death if he chased you when he woke. The human bomb bluff wasn't supposed to be him, but no one else was ready. Jiao didn't know about it till I was in the 'tube and she had access to my files."

Heat trickled up her spine. "You're only concerned for her sake."

"She—and you—are the only ones suffering."

She snorted, eyes burning. "You didn't care about him?"

"Evidently not." He stretched his leg. "Batu treated me like a man when everyone else saw a boy, so when I wrote the letter to Chuluun, I brought it to him for suggestions. He followed me ever since."

The universe was so much lesser now. "And how I treated you?"

"What does it matter?" Taivan spoke slowly, jaw tight, measuring his words not so that they'd sound right, but so he could understand. "Those worlds are gone."

"I—I've been unreliable, I've got a spy in my head and can't be trusted near a motor. But..." Khair wanted him to keep confiding in her, to have someone. "But I want to be useful."

"Of course you are. I can't hand out positions to my favorites."

Except with Batu.

Someone knocked. "Come in," Taivan said, as Khair said "Wait."

Sophie stepped in with a long briefcase.

"Why can't you use another doc?" Khair said. "She can't be an expert in everything. You're messing with her."

Sophie scowled and walked around them.

"I like working with competent people."

"Wow, that narrows it down to 98% of doctors."

"Sophie." Taivan said. The kid straightened the briefcase across the counter and turned to him. "You can recommend a specialist knowing that if they betray my confidence, it'll reflect poorly on you, or you can stay and be properly compensated."

"I am an expert in everything, and I'll stay."

"Good," he looked to her. "Rest, I'll call you when we're ready to call Davids."

Reluctant Converts

DAVIDS EYES NARROWED WHEN he saw her standing besides Taivan. "Zero for two on the heroic sacrifice, then."

He wasn't alone, sitting in an office with three secretaries working on the side, their chatter inaudible over the holo feed.

She waved the disc. "You need to see this."

"I won't yield my nation over the hologram of a hologram."

Let me speak through you, I can corroborate.

Her heart skipped. This was the first time Chip had volunteered to help her.

You're sure you can find yourself again?

The spitting acid in Chip's stomach was enough of an answer, but she didn't flee it, walked deeper into the sparks and let them provide their momentary illumination. *I don't always know who I am or who I'm supposed to be, but I know how to look.*

Wonderful. Be quick, and don't make me look stupid.

Chip's invasions before had been like stomping on a hose, cutting off the flow of her thoughts, of her.

This was an expansion.

The world wasn't filtered through Chip shaded glasses, no, her peripheral vision widened, opened up more vantage points though none were as sharp as before, perceiving more and more aware of the gaps in her perception.

She couldn't move, yet could hear and smell her surroundings, feel the chilled, colossal shadow of Chip's presence. Her head ached like it was used as a dance floor.

"This is Sergeant First Class Tamika Moore, born thirty-six years before the creation of the Ito Arc Dilator. It allows us to bend universes until two discrete points touch and so travel through the multiverse, and with it, cross time as universes age differently," Chip—Moore—said through Khair.

Moore. A real name for a person who needed food and sleep and missed her family. The consonants easily pronounced but the vowels unfamiliar, curt but not harsh, just from a different world.

"What've they done to you?" Davids said, not unkindly.

The timbre of Khair's voice was the same, but Moore spoke slower and projected better, took Khair's hands from her pockets and clasped them behind her back.

I didn't agree to all that, Moore.

Irritation flickered at her name, a reprieve from the hooks of her focus. *I don't have total control.*

Boo hoo. Figure it out.

"I've broken my nondisclosure agreement telling you this," Moore-in-Khair said, letting her nausea gallop since Khair shared it. "But the nation I pledged to has whimpered out, infiltrated by United Oversight for Democracy."

That's not what I should've said. Khair's mind guided the rivers of Moore's thought, the contents Moore's but the path, with its bends and drops and rushes, was Khair's.

Who thought that?

"Even if I believed your information, I wouldn't trust a traitor," Davids said.

"They called Washington the same." But it was flat as a sales pitch read off a teleprompter. Moore wiped Khair's palms. The action broke the spell, and Khair retreated to her own corner, where the bandaged grief over Batu held her unraveling nerves together.

"Washington never broke a nondisclosure agreement," Davids said.

"My contract was sold to UOD without my consent. I signed the NDA because they made it clear I would serve as an agent, or an experiment. The only voluntary oath I swore was to the United States. As proof of my intentions, I'm sending coordinates of the approaching ZAX fleet with UOD representatives onboard."

Are they really there? He's checking. She might've let Moore quash whatever withered weed of credibility she had.

It's highly probable.

'Highly probable' isn't 'yes.'

It's the best I can do in war.

"I can find my own ships," Davids said. "Please, Khair, I understand your need to justify recent events, but there comes a time you can only accept the past and do better."

"Do you preach that to your UOD clients before or after their massacres?" Then emotion washed from her face as Moore took over, no more at ease, but a better actress. "Can proof sway you, or do you need to see it?"

Davids massaged his temple. "There's medicine for this, and no shame in taking it."

"I'm not crazy!" Khair said before Moore could speak. "You know UOD's in my head, you said so when we met."

"I knew they had experiments, but they're little more than a charity. Clearly their scientists weren't up to the task."

"A charity?" That could have been either of them. Khair took over. "What charity hides its dealings, or needs warships?" She tapped her head. "Are they on the side of liberty, Buck?"

"No. But there are other goods in the 'verse, and people are free to choose them." He nodded to Taivan. "And they have a good reason for warships."

"So do we," Khair said. "Agree to go see who UOD really is."

He opened his arms. "Fine."

Nothing happened.

"Uh, Sergeant?" Khair said.

Davids lowered his hands. "See? That's—"

Aidan popped beside him, wearing a kimono and holding a glass of red wine. "I was taking a break from this timeline. What now?"

Davids retreated. "So, you have a new light refractor. Congratulations. I'm more interested in how he passed our defenses."

"Take him through time with you," Taivan said. "If you've figured out how."

"It's a working theory." Aidan waved toward the secretaries. "Leave."

"Absolutely not," Davids said. "My people stay, and you'll tell me exactly what you're—"

Aidan flicked a dagger from his sleeve and knocked the hilt across Davids' forehead in the same motion.

For someone who groaned every time he left the coach, he had an immortal's speed.

Davids stumbled, hands raised in a boxing position, but Aidan kicked out his knee and hit his head again as he fell. He caught Davids in a headlock and spun around to the secretaries, a knife at Davids' neck.

"Turn off the holo and leave."

One of the secretaries raised a finger. "Don't—"

Aidan tightened his grip on Davids' neck. "That was an order, not a recommendation. A recommendation goes like 'that dress makes you look eight months pregnant, so unless you happen to be nine months pregnant, reconsider.' An order goes like this—"

The secretary called security.

"If you don't leave by the time I finish this sentence, I'll liquify your organs and pour the boiling mixture down your tongueless—"

They fled.

Aidan choked Davids till he was unconscious and turned off the hologram.

"What're you doing?" Khair said.

Moore, what's he doing?

"Taking Davids with me, one way or the other."

I can't see.

"How? Could you take an army with you?" Taivan said. "Why can't you—"

Aidan winced, audio transmitting without video. "I'll be back soon. If not, I'm better off somewhere: lounging on a beach, hiding in a cabin, or dead."

He turned the hologram back on, wandered behind Davids' desk where his shoes stuck out. Davids twitched, and the shoes disappeared.

Who controls this time manipulation? You, Aidan? Is he one of you?

"UOD can do something similar on a more powerful, less accurate scale," Moore-in-Khair said.

Great, close the door gently on your way out.

Khair had expected the tension in Moore's mind to ease now that she had undeniably committed treason. Whatever doubts she had in Taivan and Khair were meaningless now. But the woman struggled like she was being eaten by rats, nibbled away bit by bit.

Taivan stared at the hologram, cursing Aidan, but finally shrugged. "I owe you, Moore, that went far better than—"

Davids and Aidan poofed back on top of Davids' desk, Davids huddled in a ball waving a revolver while Aidan, sunburnt and in overalls without an undershirt, pried open a coconut.

Davids stood, wobbly, and tried to throw up, but there was nothing left. "That was a wonderful simulation. My compliments on the—"

Aidan stabbed him with a syringe.

They disappeared and returned in an instant, bundled like they'd been exploring the Arctic, Aidan drinking cocoa with marshmallows while Davids swirled with a harpoon over his head.

Davids's shaking hands tried to work his comms. "Cassia? Cassia!" He swirled to them. "Khair, you can't—"

Gone. Back lounging in swimsuits and sunglasses, grinning widely until they exploded and returned wrestling a rolling gator. A flash and Davids choked Aidan while Aidan tried to keep a remote away from him, then boom. Aidan slumped in Davids' arms and blood pumped from his chest, Davids sputtering, an impression of a noose around his neck.

Aidan disappeared again, Davids left holding air.

He slowly untied to rope and dropped it, eyes distant when he looked back up. "You don't have to—"

He turned off the camera.

Coloma's gates opened.

Between Masters

KHAIR AND TAIVAN WAITED outside Coloma while Jiao held the fleet. Her head ached, and every time Moore so much as sipped water, the sound surged through her head like the roaring ocean.

"He's not our ally yet," Taivan said. "And when he is, we'll have to deal with the republic's machinations."

She grunted acknowledgment and massaged her temple.

Davids' empty chopper landed in front of them. Taivan hesitated. "There's no evidence he's losing control of the city, but did he confide any doubts with you?"

"It was mostly 'don't touch that,' 'you need crazy pills,' and 'you're better than that, Ms. Batuyin.'" The last word caught in her mouth.

Taivan stepped into the chopper and glanced at the gift she held. "You don't need his approval, baghatur."

The propellors rushed, and she didn't try to speak over it. They flew to the edge of Coloma and landed at a personal residence. The house was just a hobbit hole dug in the hills, but in the open pastures, the red barn could compete with Mughal palaces. It doubled as a fortress, twin towers overlooking both flanks, four domed granaries, and the small tinted windows were a sniper's dream.

A stained stump sat beside the chicken coop.

Soldiers picked apples or drank moonshine. No guns, but they had axes and competed to chop wood, carved squash with their children.

Why would anyone leave this place? The soil was bouncy, dark, moist. Rows of golden wheat and tall corn crisscrossed the plains, water towers and windmills interspersed between. Trees laden with fruits she'd never seen grew without rods or mulch, though none were thicker than her. Horned, wooly cows grazed in distant meadows. Food would come easy now.

Davids sat hunched by a fire, clutching a hot cider, watching a skinny pig turn on a spite. "ZAX ordered us to stop negotiations with you and lower our shields so they can manage defenses."

"That's UOD," Taivan said. "We have no demands, only help us take the war to them."

Davids said nothing.

Khair handed him a gift wrapped in sky-blue paper.

He accepted it like it was an adder, glanced at Taivan, shook it, and held it up to his ear.

"Rude," Khair said.

Davids gently pried off the paper, threw it in the fire, and left the gift in the box. "It's an expensive old knife. Are we severing diplomatic ties? Are you threatening me? Is this a bribe?"

"It's an authentic Roman gladius." Taivan had told her a gift would go badly and so she didn't let him see it, but he looked jealous until he laughed. "To go with the toga."

Davids, wearing washed out jeans and a dark purple button-down, did not laugh.

"You went off with Aidan for who knows how long," Khair said. "I thought you might want something of his. Aidan and I went to an animal shelter, adopted dogs, made sled teams, and my team won, so I won it from him. Then we left the dogs in Sophie's room."

Davids examined the sword, green and brown age marks making it seem part of a branch. "Thank you." He shut the box.

"What happened?" Khair said. "How long was it?"

He looked to Taivan. "I destroyed you. And years later, they... your uncle was a child kicking shins in comparison. But my people won't believe it." He drank. "Can't blame them. They'll say I'm caving and vote me out. The militia answers to congress, not me. And even if I could get them to join you, I've seen the footage from Asa, the refugees in the street."

Taivan blew into his hands. "Your Washington didn't have the south's support initially, did he? He didn't have enough men there, so he said, and pulled back into the wilderness. Let the British demand food and lodging, let the southerners see British guns. The south joined their brothers, then." He shrugged. "No one's ignoble if they save you in the end."

Davids turned the pig over.

Always revolutionary history with him. Whatever world they made—if they got a chance to—would have little resemblance to this. Even if it wasn't hers, she wished it was, wished it could stay like this. But their presence would destroy it.

"You can't justify yourself with the end; you don't know it, it doesn't exist," Davids said. "Even if it did, that girl you stabbed wouldn't see it."

"With my scientists, she might." Taivan squeezed Khair's shoulder and left to flip tractor tires with the youngest soldiers.

Davids offered her his drink.

She took it and sat beside him, stretching toward the fire.

Already, Taivan earned backslaps and swapped insults. Davids shook his head. "It was disturbingly satisfying to watch him die. He had the gall to do that well. Better than I did, anyway."

Khair swallowed the cider so she didn't spit on him. "What?"

"Didn't die, technically. Just found death's asymptote. Does your Sergeant know if Aidan's alive?"

Talk later, I'll faint now. "She'll find out, or try to."

He shivered.

Khair handed him back his cider with one sip left. "If that's your clever trick to have me lend you my coat, you'll be quite disappointed."

"I could sit closer to the fire."

"There's only so close you can get to a fire. I'm much more amenable."

He flicked a twig at the fire and moved a few centimeters closer to both her and the fire. "How have you forgiven him?"

There was no point implicating Jiao, the only legitimate one in his eyes. And Taivan had put the bomb there. Jiao was responsible, but so was he and Aidan and Sophie, so was she for accepting it.

"I want to mount his head on my wall. But," her mouth dried as she watched him act the callow boy so the general could recruit an army. "I need him."

Not for protection, Moore could kill her anytime. But he was her best chance at hitting UOD, and she couldn't bear to be that woman in Aidan's throne room.

"He's your first love, isn't he?" Davids asked. "It passes."

Khair gasped as Moore's heart broke. Longing rolled over her like battering thunder. No light, only noise. Moore couldn't move, sitting in a room of people she'd betrayed, but inside she gagged and choked, clawed at the walls of her mind.

Davids grabbed her arm. "Khair? Sergeant Moore, this is unnecessary."

Khair squeezed the grass and rested her head against the cool dirt. *You can cry yourself to sleep after work like the rest of us. Get it together, comrade.*

Moore snarled back.

"Sergeant, the intelligence from Ms. Batuyin is worth an occasional indiscretion."

There's never an obligation to be obedient to orders, which it would be pernicious to obey. So said your long-winded saint, remember?

My heart has left its dwelling-place and can return no more.

She quoted a poet who'd died abandoned in an insane asylum.

Khair gazed to the sapphire sky, spotless except for a shimmer of the dome shield at the edge of the horizon. She let Moore hear toddlers quarrel and parents scold, wind brushing through chimes, dogs barking at lowing cows, soldiers teasing. Breathed in smoke, pine, honey, grass, barbecue. She murmured thanks to Davids, his hand on her shoulder, and lay her head on his lap.

"It's passing," he said, more command than fact.

Moore held on to her pain as proof of loyalty, but breathed easier as Davids massaged Khair's shoulder. She managed half a smile. He was so careful where he lay his hands.

By the time clouds formed and darkened, though Moore's heart burned and the world seemed a muddy, formless clay, she found a way to continue.

Davids had to know. He has to lead, not Taivan; I can't promise any more help. Moore's breathing still skittered. *I should have found another way.*

"The sad thing is." Khair sat, hoping she hadn't drooled on Davids' jeans. "This is still the best party I've ever attended."

Davids stood and stoked the fire, putting distance between them. "Are you yourself?"

"Good old Hyde chasing away Jekyll. Anyway, we were saying something about you joining us."

"Don't you need a doctor?"

"Drugs don't solve everything, Mr. President."

Take a sick day tomorrow.

I've never done that when I have a subject. It'd look suspicious. And they would put someone else on your case.

Shit.

He brushed strands of her hair from his pants. "How frequently does that happen?"

"About as frequently as Asa pulls moons made entirely of pastry into its orbit. Never happened. That's my very clever cue that I'm hungry."

"The pig's not ready."

"Then back to business. Wait. Is that rude in your culture?"

"Skipping small talk, no. Asking 'is that rude in your culture' in a diminutive tone is not a great sign in any culture."

She wasn't sure what the d word meant, so she said: "Sorry I'm not pansophical." That might not be a word. "You were saying UOD is terrible."

"I was saying you don't owe Taivan anything and there could be other ways to beat them."

"How?"

Davids said nothing.

"You told me of your people. Let me tell you of mine," Khair said. "Alan, the mother of my people, noticed her five sons preparing to fight each other after her husband died. She gave them each an arrow, told them to break it. They did. Then she bound five arrows together and told them to break it. But they couldn't. We must hang together, or we will surely hang separately, no?"

"Yes." Davids swatted away sparks. "But ZAX is a long-time ally, and if I tell my people UOD is about to attack, UOD will drop its veneer of civility." She started to protest, but he cut in. "Either way, I'm throwing in with a tyrant, but at least UOD will likely win."

His soldiers whooped, a circle formed, bets placed, half cheering for Taivan. "I could stay with UOD, reform them from the inside."

Khair snorted. "Jiao thought something like that with us, right until she killed my father."

"What?" His stick caught fire, and he swatted it against the wood until the burning piece broke off. "I'm sorry. But Jochiin burned through Asa. He threatened to bomb Albion when it was his. UOD is worse in other universes, but here he is."

"Sure, we're not a bunch of pacifist monk goody goodies. But UOD would never picnic with you as equals."

"That's because I shot him in the chest."

She laughed. "It was a remarkable bargaining point, but no. We don't want to hurt you."

"You don't. Khair," he laid his hand on her knee. "They killed your father to frame me. If you were me, with no allegiance to anyone but your people, who would you join?"

She didn't speak, but that might be because his hand warmed her knee.

"So, we're at an impasse, and—"

"Taivan." It felt like treason, but there was nothing more Batu-like than throwing herself behind the Khanate. She nodded to the crowd, the fight over, impossible to tell who had won, but their adoration obvious. "The one who would fight beside me, who would sacrifice for me, who listens to me. And you, Mr. Bound-To-The-Will-Of-His-People, would choose him too."

He removed his hand. "I can't attack ZAX ships—and those are technically ZAX ships—without declaring war, and I need congressional approval. I'll never get it."

"But if they're coming with destroyers, it's an invasion of airspace."

"Absolutely, as your camp has been. And they still have too much firepower."

"You guys designed those guns; didn't you design your dome to withstand it?"

"It can't hold forever. Though with an election in months, no one'll want to say we can't win. You'd have to turn your ships to face the outside—exposing the weaker side of your shields."

He said it like it was impossible, but Coloma had never been their goal.

"We can manage that."

He raised his cider. "To foolish people and unscrupulous politicians."

"Liberty and death."

Official Record

IN A DAY, COLOMA shook as ZAX ships breached the atmosphere, their giant hovering ships so loud that windows broke across the city. Within hours, citizens demanded something be done.

In two days, the Coloma City Senate had voted.

In three days, President Buck Davids had declared war.

On the fourth, bombs rained.

Besieged

Yellow blasts melted against Coloma's shields. Fissures of light shivered down the dome and fizzled out in the grounded rods outside the city. The streets were silent. Buildings projected a flat gray, with bogus heat and energy signatures.

"The shields have two days left," Davids said.

Coloma's guns had been popping ZAX destroyer hulls like bubblewrap, but their jets extinguished the flames as the giant ships patched themselves and shielded their smaller vessels.

"The underground has another month," Davids said. "But the damage to the arable land will be severe."

Khair, Taivan, and Sophie sat at a round table on the capital building's greenhouse roof, with Davids and his cabinet. Jiao led the dogfight above.

From here it looked like rugby, lines of ships forming and spiraling out as they punched through and reformed, spinning and hurdling from chasing missiles.

The cloud of smoke from exploded dogfighters was smaller than the smokestack jettisoned from a scratch on the destroyers. There was no way to tell whose ship exploded or what class it'd been, hot metal hailing and dissolving on the shield.

No way to tell who was winning, either.

"Stuff everyone underground," Khair said. "Throw down the shield like it failed. Then when they land, we can raise it again, dividing their forces."

Moore shocked her, little more than a tickle, and only after she had finished. UOD would watch this battle. So, they competed to keep their cover, to keep their feelings docile and avoid a feedback loop. Seven destroyers looming overhead didn't help. All battles could be deadly, but this was on a scale neither had seen:

each destroyer was the size of a town and the Dreadnought was big as a city. They stuffed the horizon and snuffed out the sun.

Taivan grounded Khair. And not just because his knee nudged her thigh whenever a floundering jet exploded above her. He watched a three-dimensional view of the battle, rotated perspectives and adjusted the magnification, compared current enemy movement with past tactics and relayed opportunities to Jiao. Nothing was too vast when it fit in his hand.

Coloma ministers gawked and glared. Their generals took notes. Taivan wore a headset and took no more notice than a bear sharing a cave with rabbits.

"They'd level everything above ground and kill our waiting ambush," Davids said.

"If you sortie out from—"

"Or we can surrender these mercenaries," a secretary of something trivial waved at them.

Taivan snorted a laugh, covering his microphone.

"That's enough," Davids said.

"Go on." Taivan said, voice beige neutral, not looking up from the model. "Enlighten us with your martial prowess."

"The only way out," the minister, so old he belonged in a museum or better yet, a mausoleum, said to Davids. "Is for you to step down in favor of someone who hasn't yearned for war since they took office."

"We knew this day would come," Davids said. "ZAX's requests have swayed toward demands for years. But our alliance was profitable, and we were safe, so we let them shove us around and thanked them for the privilege."

Above, a wedge of friendly fighters split and encircled a destroyer's battered command center, ropes of fire entangling it.

"They were lightyears away," the minister said. "Whatever the formal agreement, we controlled our daily affairs."

Enemy jets chased Jiao's, driving them off and spouting water and metal patch at the destroyer's wounds. But it was too little too late.

"That's not enough," Davids said. "Even if we governed ourselves, their sword hovered over our heads. How could we be content with only the freedom granted to us when we've built this city with our own hands?"

For the first time, he got some nods.

The destroyer's officers parachuted out in neon, off-limits life pods. Its bridge collapsed, shattering against its own hull in a grating roar that echoed above the constant din of fire, and the ship tipped toward the shield.

The minister slow clapped. "Bravo. If you wanted to kill yourself, you should've stuck with oppyin and let the rest of us live."

The destroyer made one last attempt to right itself before the front buckled under the weight of the bridge. Ten thousand life-pods shot into the sky, bursting against debris or hit by inadvertent fire.

"They're no cameras here, Bharat, don't pander," Davids said. "If you want to instigate a vote of no-confidence, go to the senate."

The destroyer, its descent seemingly controlled though parts fell off and fire crept through its halls, sunk into Coloma's shield. The sky shuttered. Its clear visage tinted gray, flashed transparent again. The destroyer dissolved centimeter by centimeter, steam shot off, pieces flung off or spat back. Black ivies bloomed across the bending shield.

A hundred thousand tons of glowing warped steel collapsed into Coloma's inhabited streets. The rush of oxygen through the dome added to the flame. Explosions splashed across the streets, unheard beside the burning destroyer.

Block walls rose among the streets, cordoning off the damage. Home guard helicopters swooped in, rescuing survivors from burning buildings or collapsed basements.

"Shit." In those densely packed houses, there wouldn't be many survivors.

"Riley," Davids said. "If I provide transport and rations, could you spare space in Albion?"

"If your people are self-sustaining for a long stay, yes." Sophie wore sunglasses now that they were pretending the last weeks hadn't happened.

The shield turned gray, broken edges grew to cover the hole. It remained opaque. Explosions rumbled and cannons kicked out of sight, air thickening and sticking in Khair's throat while the shield trembled.

"The shield will hold for a day," Davids said.

Bharat pushed his chair back and headed toward the door, taking ministers with him. "I'll see you at the senate."

"We have another weapon," Sophie said. "We've been altering it for the past week, but it should be ready."

Taivan didn't move above the table but kicked Khair's foot; he hadn't authorized disclosing anything so soon. Khair was supposed to speak for Taivan since the ministers were skeptical of anything he said, and because he was busy showing off.

Moore was no help either. The sergeant was a soldier, not a marine or sailor. When Khair asked for advice (trying and failing to be discrete), she said 'cross the T or something'—literally, 'or something' was her plan.

So, at this point, anything other than surrender or kamikaze sounded great.

"We outfitted our automations with guns." Sophie barely concealed a baby-faced grin. "They might not be efficient weapons, but they're unorthodox and unmanned, so there's no downside."

Davids pinched the bridge of his nose. "Your coliseum toys?"

"It's not like we used them against real animals, or people." Sophie kicked her under the table, and she didn't contradict it. "And, yes. But is there any way in the 'verse their commanders are prepared to deal with giant serpopards?"

"It'd keep them busy for our real attack," Khair said.

"Which would be?" Davids asked.

"Commandeering their Dreadnought."

Every ship UOD brought could travel faster than light, but the Dreadnought was the most powerful.

"There's a quarter of a million soldiers on that ship," Davids said. "You'd never take it."

Above them, the Dreadnought's broad wings seemed too short for its circular body, its tail poised above it like a scorpion's, the command deck a strip of tinted glass flanked by turrets. It carried countless missiles and guns, but one shot from the massive hull cannon would destroy a fully shielded destroyer and bankrupt a nation.

Taivan pulled his headset off. "With the automaton distraction, your techcrews could jam their screens long enough for us to land thousands of breachers. And most of the crew are on guns or keeping it in the air, not physical security."

"That's far too risky," Davids said. "I have to have sufficient manpower for a ground defense."

"We'll do it," Taivan said. Meaning the Dreadnought would be theirs. To Sophie. "How long until the weapon's ready?"

"Naguib's transporting them. They'll be ready tonight."

"I'll have my people inside and ready to defend themselves if it fails," Davids said. "We'll need a representative on that Dreadnought to make sure no one gets any ideas."

"Let me guess," Khair said. "That representative is yourself."

He nodded.

Taivan turned on his mic. "Jiao, keep your force topside, but I need to brief you immediately."

The Dzud

IT WAS HOURS UNTIL the assault. Khair had done everything she could do, so nothing distracted her from the fact that she could be dead in two hours. Technically, that was always true, but that wasn't reassuring.

She walked Whiskey in a courtyard a few blocks from the flight-line, three trees and a rickety gazebo making up the garden. These scraggy trees would've seemed majestic to her days ago, but now she let Whiskey water them.

The translucent roof let in sunlight but not the battle overhead.

"You're personally leading the assault?" Davids sat across from Taivan in the gazebo.

Khair ducked behind the tree, though her arms were thicker than its branches.

"Yes." Taivan didn't look up from cleaning his rifle.

"You do remember battle is no respecter of rank?"

"I remember Cyrus the Great, dead at seventy on the battlefield." David snorted at 'the Great.' "The Lion of Thermopylae, and my uncle the Khan. Mr. President."

"And if you die, what guarantee do I have that the Khanate won't turn against us?"

"'The Khanate' is Khair giving blood to save your son, and Jiao shooting your vest instead of your head. You get along fine." Taivan set his rifle down. "You're risking yourself as well. If you die aiding us, I'll respect Coloma's sovereignty."

"I'll be on your ship; if I'm dead, so are you."

"There are other dangers."

Don't worry, I won't let him hurt Davids.

"Save the threats for when you're not in my power," Davids said. "What do you want?"

Taivan leaned back, a veiny arm draped over the bench. "A pledge you'll aid Jiao's Khanate if I die."

"I, personally, will assist Jiao in surviving the battle. She's legally complicit in your crimes. She'll spend time making amends, but I can make it sound like an honorary position to spare her pride."

Whiskey nipped Khair for not paying enough attention to him. She scratched his ears.

"That's not good enough," Taivan said. "Aidan will return to this time-stream eventually and you have no weapon against him. If I'm dead, he'll take vengeance not only for Jiao, but the Khanate, especially Khair—I don't care what she did before the reboot or in the crash. Whatever the law says, as a man, you owe her."

Khair's mouth dried.

"You don't help her by protecting her from her own actions." Davids stood. "But she'll have the best lawyer in the state. Let's just make sure there is a state."

Whiskey finished squatting and kicked up dirt, giving her away. She pretended to be terribly occupied cleaning up the mess, though she hadn't brought a doggy bag. Davids nodded to her as he left.

Khair joined Taivan. "You're our best commander. You shouldn't go."

Taivan sighed. "At least you don't want me dead."

She'd thought he'd protected her because he cared for her, but maybe he just owed her. "I could tie you up and throw you in your room."

"No, you couldn't."

"I'd like to try." She turned to find a place to snack or scream before battle.

"Anda," Taivan said. Brother-by-pact, brother-in-battle. If it was true, he'd killed his father—whatever he said, he meant it couldn't all be for nothing. "I never expected to have Coloma's help, not without losses. We have it because of you."

It was such a small thing to celebrate now. "If we die, it'll still be worth it, right? Worse ways to live." Though she couldn't think of any. Maybe living as a zoo exhibit or being born in one of those prison colonies, like Australia.

"Then we've only left everyone worse off than they were a few months ago. This will only mean anything in victory. We can win." He ran a function check on the rifle.

"Rather stupid plan if we couldn't."

"It was always going to be poor odds, but they're decent here."

"We'll throw a party on the other side, with all the barbecue and cheesecake a person should never eat."

He grinned faintly. "That'd be premature."

"Then I'll try not to taunt chance. In the meantime, look less like you're planning your own funeral; everyone takes their cues from you."

"What else could I want?" He mimicked an old man's accent. "My greatest pleasure is to defeat my enemy, see his loved ones in tears, something about pillaging."

Whiskey's ears drooped.

"I don't need that mask," Khair said. "I knew you from when you were a boy and all you wanted to be was an inventor? Big game hunter?"

"Policeman." He grinned. "Or a polar bear. I've got to go brief."

"Guess I've got to listen."

Taivan briefed the commanders, briefed them again once the plan had filtered down to the lowest level and bubbled up with inconsistencies. After the final meeting, there were no more questions. Just redundant gear checks of unnecessary or substituted equipment, and personnel accountability of soldiers who'd sat on the same cement patch since dawn.

Then the comm checks, atomic clock synchronization. A ten-minute countdown while officers with washed boots warned everyone to be brave with trembling hands, shouting to be heard over violent music.

Ten minutes.

Their ship held two dozen soldiers with Terran rifles, flysuits, helmets with rebreathers and comms, electromag boots to counteract gravity tricks. They clasped overhead handles, though the ship hadn't moved. Khair waited in the cockpit with Taivan, Davids, and Jiao, no marking on their ship, the *Dzud*—a Mongolian storm—to set them apart.

Nine minutes.

Taivan leafed through his notes, highlighting and crossing out parenthetical details no one else remembered. His rifle was slung across his back. Their old Hartfords were unwieldy, heavier and with less stopping power than the ZAX rifles. But they weren't controlled by fingerprints that got dirty and sweaty and stopped working every two seconds, and ZAX couldn't turn them off.

Still nine.

Jiao slipped on oily, fingerless gloves, pat her wheel three times, and ran a rag over immaculate instruments. She adjusted her seat, settled in the same position she'd started in, and placed a silver bankhar dog on the dashboard.

Still nine.

Davids sat across from Khair, grinning like he'd found his ex in a public meltdown, an antique rifle on his lap. He patted it. "The rifle that won the war."

"Which one?"

He studied it, wooden frame, skinny barrel, simple buttstock, and offered it to her. "Doesn't matter now."

She hesitated, making sure Moore would allow her to hold it. "So, when you don't know something, it doesn't matter, but when I don't know something, it's 'Khair, you know that's an explosive, right?'"

He laughed, though it wasn't funny, so handsome there, at ease while the rest of the world lay in dread.

Then somehow, less than a minute left.

She returned the weapon, took her own. Moore couldn't let her use a gun, but she could pose as a diplomat since they were bound for the Dreadnaught's bridge. She carried their flag, the metal staff a club.

The enemy had guns and body armor.

How much leash would Moore give her? Chip had spared her life but Chip was barely human and had no life outside of Khair. Moore had her own fight. Chip was all rules, Moore principles. Chip felt nothing. Moore had lost everything she loved.

Chip would hurt her. Moore, who knew? It was war, and she was expendable.

Jiao ignited the engines on Sophie's signal, her automations entering the area of operations. Taivan manned the guns, standing on an elevated platform in the center of the cockpit, wearing tinted glasses that let him see above the *Dzud's* roof or below the floor, with sensors on his hands to shoot.

Their ship rose above the dome.

The night turned red. Crooked, elongated projectiles filled the air like confused rainbows. Pink streaks left gray powder in the air. Missiles rained, but Jiao was already flipping them from the inundation.

Khair's strapped in boots kept her from falling, but she squeezed the bar above her head and shut her eyes. Waited a second after they'd stopped spinning to open them again.

Their ships had splintered into dozens of arrowhead formations, ships curling away for evasive maneuvers and veering back into the protection of the group's firepower.

Except there was little protection there. The enemy's jets hovered around their destroyers to protect the sensitive areas and put out fires, so with their jets safe, the destroyers had no reason to dilute their fire. Seven destroyers staggered their shots to compensate for their slow reloads.

There was no way through this.

How did Jiao see through it? The cockpit was reinforced glass, but still scratched, stained. Their speed made them weightless, flattened objects in front of them and stretched things beside them, cut out any delay between Jiao's command and the ship's compliance.

Taivan whirled and punched air, his cannons clearing their way, but the *Dzud* quaked as nearby explosions turned their course and shrapnel bombarded their shields.

She should've stayed in Coloma, caught a sudden case of common sense. She flexed her fingers, bit her nails.

The sphinx's mammoth paw swiped at the Dreadnought. The Dreadnought turned its cannons to the sphinx and tilted, its hangar doors grinding open. Dogfighters poured out. They cleared the hangar in the exact same diagonal slant and dropped as one.

"They're drones," Khair said.

Davids motioned quiet.

The drones moved as clusters, half a dozen operating under the same function at a time. There was no person controlling it, someone had predicted the defender's pattern and programmed accordingly.

Did you snitch?

Dread steamrolled her stomach. Maybe Moore's guilt had bested her, or she had to keep her cover. No, there were other possibilities. She had to wait, wait on Moore like she waited to burn, or to get impaled, or free fall. Exploding would be best. That wasn't best, none of this was best. Why was she on this ship?

The light of the Dreadnought's loading cannons overpowered the moons.

Something clipped their wing. Jiao flicked on 'prepare to evacuate,' but no one moved. Staying in a crashing vehicle was less deadly than diving into that crossfire.

The sphinx, its crown removed to lighten it, its human face placid, pounced toward the Dreadnought. Cannons screeched, plunged a syringe through her ears, forced her to sit on the bench beside Davids, ears ringing after the blinding shot fired and her sight dribbled back.

The sphinx should be destroyed. But it survived, smoke bellowing from the space between them where some traceless automation and savior had died.

The sphinx shrugged off jet's fire and nose-dove away from the Dreadnought, aimed at a destroyer. The Dreadnought loosed its cannon. It bleached the sky, and the sound shook their ship.

The sphinx remained; the destroyer was gone.

So many dead. Enemies. She had no pity for the poor suckers she might've bought a drink for on Irmeg, no lightening the weight in her gut at the minuscule increase of their chances. This was outside her, beyond the glass. Irrelevant.

Jiao spun them, tightening the line of their travel beyond what an unguided missile could follow. The guided missiles were no more difficult to lose; they sought heat, and the sky was aflame.

A four-drone squadron flew at them. Jiao dove but pulled up, the fire of a dogfight below an uncrossable border.

"They're creeping closer," Jiao said.

"Got them." Taivan kept the enemy off their tail with jabs, hooked a finishing cross. The same blow worked twice on the drone's identical pattern, but a burning Coloma vessel smashed into that formation and detonated.

Junk metal rained. Dodging debris was futile, it was about knowing which missiles would slow the craft, damage it, or destroy it, a multimillion-dollar ship now a billiard ball.

Khair couldn't read the instructions popping on dimmed screens and Jiao ignored them, the machine silent as it diverted power to the area shield most needed in that nanosecond, hairline fractures dinging through the craft and echoing through the cabin. In the back, their squad kept a silent vigil. She leaned into her hands to cover her mouth.

Batu, it must be easier on the other side. Please, let it be easier.

The sphinx herded a destroyer toward a hill and a serpopard leapt from it. The serpent's neck wrapped around it, its paws embraced it, and destroyer and beast plummeted, exploding on impact.

She couldn't bear to sit, didn't dare move. Out of the ten thousand soldiers on that destroyer, only the pilot could have prevented that. One person messed up, thousands died. And here on the *Dzud*, there was nothing for her to do but will death away.

She tapped the bench, impossible to notice under the ping of shrapnel and pounding explosions, but her one contribution—silence—slipped.

Help me do something.

Three short shocks for no reason whatsoever. *Busy.* Chip had turned on the computerized voice.

No, you're not, cause I—

Mercy Mission Designation 7701. This is Colonel Strudel. The three-shock signal they were watched, she'd forgotten. *How do you read me?*

If he was doing a radio check, maybe he'd go away if she ignored him? She jumped off the metal seat, but metal clasps held her boots to the ground.

And she wouldn't get out anytime soon. For all the ships and people lost, the Dreadnought was as distant as when the battle started, rising above the fray. But Taivan wouldn't call it off. He had nothing else. If he failed, he'd die in the attempt.

That was probably for the best. They wouldn't become the monsters he'd seen in that other world, even if that was how they would be remembered.

Yet even if she was gone, she didn't want to imagine a world without Taivan or Jiao or Davids.

Taivan's hands hadn't slowed, the quick circles of his strikes almost a dance, almost summoning magic. Looking at him, she'd believe they were winning.

Davids put his hand on her knee, stilling her bouncing leg. Freezing her entirely, really. And since the cockpit was dim, everyone otherwise occupied, she grabbed his shirt and leaned closer until he recoiled.

She released him. "I—"

Jiao tensed, and the ship jerked. Taivan leaned too far on his magnetized boot and, as his hands dropped to catch his fall, a wall of mangled steel raced to meet them.

Jiao yanked them to the left. Gauges clunked; screens flashed warning they were going into auto-command while Jiao fought to regain control.

I've killed us. No need to worry, no need to fight. The worst would happen and there was nothing to do.

She seized under the shock lash, muscles freezing so she couldn't scream. Davids jumped, shocked through the bench.

You do read me.

Not to brag, but I'm illiterate. She'd laugh if Davids wasn't looking at her so betrayed. Dead people couldn't read.

"Davids, shut her up." Jiao grit out the words, leaning over her instruments as if to communicate via osmosis.

Davids offered his hand, but she didn't take it, wouldn't hurt him again.

We've noticed a marked change in your behavior. How often have you been shocked?

There were no consequences. She could say 'can't talk now but leave a message at the explosion,' or 'every time your mom gets frisky' and what would he do, kill her twice?

I haven't kept track, sir.

He was investigating Moore too, and Moore would keep fighting UOD after their death.

Have you been promised a reward?

She had Moore's answers ready. That character shaped fate or that each action was its own reward. And it was true. But she couldn't say it when a third of their fleet had died.

The Griffins and serpopards and phoenixes were destroyed, only the sphinx remained. The soldiers in the back of the *Dzud* awaited death with only jokes and prayers.

No.

A destroyer lumbered toward them, blocking their way to the Dreadnought. The sphinx cut between them, wings over them, robbing it of its mobility. Its newly installed armor might withstand the destroyer's guns, but it had forgotten the Dreadnought overtop.

The *Dzud* blasted from the sphinx's explosion. Their guided parachute deployed, and Jiao wrapped it around them as a shield. The Dreadnought had a slow reload; it was out of the fight for two minutes. They just had to slip by the destroyer.

But its guns were prepared and their shield couldn't absorb that hit.

Have you formed any bond with your handler?

The destroyer's cannons glowed, a bluish gray seeping into a dark purple and softening to a dull yellow like a sunrise, like beginnings yet to come.

Jiao opened the door for the soldiers to escape with their flysuits, but stayed at the helm instructing over the intercom. Davids' hand clasped hers. Taivan, standing again, calf bleeding where it turned to metal, kept fighting. And the soldiers in the back, strangers all, stayed.

No.

Can you explain your behavior, or are you simply taking the path of least resistance with our agent, as you'd done with Chuluun?

She couldn't see anything but the light of the cannons. But she heard Jiao's control panel beep, Taivan's guns fire, felt Buck's breath as he whispered something she never heard as the missile launched and the sky split.

Must be.

Something bumped, but there was no pain except a tingling in her ears and sore bones. The cannon's light was a stubborn beast, but when it finally retreated, it was replaced with stadium lights inside an enemy hangar bay.

The Nautilus

"Not bad," Taivan said to Jiao.

Jiao slowed her panting and looked at him as if he spat on her baby.

"Wait till the Dreadnought fires, then take us to them." He leaned against the copilot's chair, ignoring the blood streaming into his boots as his bent prosthetic fixed itself.

Their ship had docked illegally, nothing pinned it to the hangar. A machine gun rambled against their shield. It must be unmanned, the volleys too rhythmic and in too tight a grouping to be human, but red lights flashed. A counter-boarding party would be on them soon.

Jiao tapped the scanners. Half their fleet and all of Sophie's automatons were gone. The enemy had five destroyers and the Dreadnought still.

Their jet formations were broken, too outnumbered to flank or lay down suppressive fire, each captain alone. Some spent their lives and crews charging the Dreadnought's bridge to win it themselves, but were blasted before they got close. Others loped around the dome, waiting for permission to flee. The best retreated.

"It's poor odds." Jiao flicked the screen, and it went dark.

"You made it this far," Taivan said. "One more push and we're through."

"Even if we landed, we have twenty-eight people to a quarter of a million."

Taivan's hair was a sweaty woven mat, his biceps swollen and face flushed, but behind his darkened gunner's glasses he was unfazed, lips a straight line. "We'll reach the bridge, negotiate from there."

"They'll gas us out." Jiao looked around the ship. "I'm sorry."

Translation: they wouldn't crawl a meter closer to that Dreadnought.

"This ship's a command ferry, only has about five hundred men," Khair said. Though, next to twenty-eight, that still equaled way too fricking much. "And it has faster than light capacity, like we need."

Taivan glared at the hangar as if trying to shoot lasers from his eyes. "Pull up a map."

Jiao poked the screen to life but a band of white cut across it, the words 'Unauthorized Access' emblazoned across.

"There's another option." Davids opened his jacket, an explosive vest beneath. Huh, maybe that was why he didn't want to kiss, can't smooch on a bed of bombs. "We'll take out half their command team."

"And all of our own," Khair said.

The lines on the screen widened and showed the ferry's bridge. That room seemed a cavern, automatic guns pinned in the corners, vents where gas could be poured in, holes in the ceiling that were either ugly light fixtures or murder holes. Their armor was a metal shell flexible around the joints with no apparent weaknesses except it was yellow. Easy to spot, and gross.

The captain's eyes widened when he saw who he faced. "Uh—er—I am Captain Wang, and you are welcome on the *DPO Nautilus*. Welcome to surrender."

Never heard of him.

"Stand-up comedy's tomorrow night," Khair said.

Davids stepped in front of the camera, red lines on his vest glowing. "I offer the same courtesy. Surrender this vessel, and you and your crew will be unharmed."

The man laughed. It sounded like a hiccup, but his baggy eyes crinkled and his thin lips cracked open. "Jochiin would stop you."

Taivan said nothing.

"Come out without grav-boots, comms, or weapons. If you return our property—"

Taivan grabbed Khair's flag and smashed the camera. He tossed it back.

"What property?" Jiao said.

"Coordinates to the ship with the location of the time-machine," Taivan said. "It's heavily guarded. That's why we needed the Dreadnought."

Outside the *Dzud*, lights turned off. The guns stopped firing, total darkness projected, deafening sound shrieked. Jiao filtered it off, leaving them in silence.

Taivan offered the gunner's gloves and glasses to Jiao.

She grabbed her bayoneted rifle from the cabinet. "This is a land battle now. We need someone who understands ground tactics to cover us."

Taivan looked to Khair. "I need to be out there."

Moore buzzed her three times; they were still watched. "Can't we try talking to them again?"

Taivan aimed his pistol at her face.

No one protested.

Khair swallowed, looked past his finger in the trigger well to his flat eyes. Why did he have to put her at his mercy? Wasn't taking Batu enough? "Me too, anda?"

"Remember what you saw, the future that awaits," Taivan said. "Help stop it. Your masters may kill you, but you'll be spared the atrocities they intend."

He wasn't talking to her. She held out her hand for the gunner's controls. "We're not done, Taivan."

He gave her the gloves and glasses, less than five kilograms, but it controlled warheads. "I know. Davids, lock the vest away in case you're shot."

"The controller is set to my warm fingerprint. Nothing else can detonate it."

Khair slipped on the gunner's sensors to her hand and put on the glasses. Moore shocked her. She stiffened as her nerves burned and her muscles melted. The voltage was up again.

"Are you okay?" Taivan asked.

Khair nodded, opened her eyes. The gunner's glasses worked as natural eyes, squinting to see farther and able to adjust focus, with a 360 view of the hangar. She had access to machine guns and missiles, their platforms multi-jointed to bend shots around corners.

Khair flicked the controls from cannons to machine guns so as not to destroy the *Nautilus*.

Taivan put on a grin and opened the door to the back, where two dozen soldiers waited. "Let's take this ship."

Ma'am, she had to grovel. Strudel was still around. ***Order me to stand down and sacrifice my comrades to spare myself, and I will.***

But how could Moore say that?

Taivan opened the *Dzud's* door, batting away an incoming flash and gas grenade into the enemy ranks. One tried to throw it back, but it went off in his hand, so bright Khair watching through goggles turned away.

Green gas pumped out. Everyone wore rebreathers, but it burned the centimeters of exposed skin between uniform and boots or gloves, added a green haze to the sky that seeped in where the helmet connected to armor.

Khair punched air and the *Dzud's* gun fired into the widely spaced line of enemy soldiers. The enemy's Napoleonic tactics got a lot of flak, the line easy to flank, easy to spot. But it was perfect here without room to flank, when all the firepower was needed at the front, when they spread out so a single volley couldn't wipe them out.

When there were so bloody many of them.

The ZAX guns had ridiculous 'blast a hole through your armor and kill your buddy behind you' power. But Taivan charged their ranks. Khair fired in front of him. He rammed through their lines, muddying the sides, so every shot risked friendly fire.

Numbers and weight mattered. Her soldiers may have punched into the center and branched out like a malignant tumor, but ZAX retreated at the edges, searching for safer ground to fire from. Khair fired on their outskirts, forcing them back. But up close they had the advantage—they could rotate men and stay fresh, legionaries reborn.

Taivan ripped the rebreather from a man's helmet. He spun and kicked out a woman's leg as she charged with bayonet, hit the rifle-butt into her face, swirled and pulled the trigger. Enemies charged him in waves, but his soldiers were drawn to him, the fight coalescing around him.

The automated machine guns swiveled toward him, but Khair shot them.

Enemy soldiers gathered in the halls, armed with shields and riot guns—pain rays that totally incapacitated but weren't lethal. They were an easy target between those narrow walls and never got close.

The *Nautilus'* gravity turned off. Soldiers shot at each other's grav-boots, but it was a small target and few landed.

"On the count of three," Taivan said over the comms. "Everyone turn off their boots. Khair, kill everything on the ground."

Heat drummed against her head, her fingers weakening. "You can't say 'neutralize' or 'incapacitate'?"

Taivan ducked a blow, stumbled as someone was thrown against him, kept his balance by stabbing his bayonet into the attacker's foot and leaning for a second against the cane. He yanked it out and slashed up the leg.

"Three."

He spun the injured man around him as a shield, threw him, and shot the woman trapped beneath.

"Two."

Khair's goggles turned off and the battle outside disappeared.

What?

"Taivan, wait!" If they turned off their boots, they'd have little control of their movements and no cover. They'd be dead in seconds.

"One."

"Abort, weapons off-line!"

Soldiers rushed into the *Dzud*. Khair reached for the flag on the pilot's chair, but a shield smashed her into the instruments. Its edge pressed into her stomach, bashed her again into the lumpy panel. Her blood splattered against clear, hardened plastic. She choked on broken teeth.

If she had to get squashed, she could at least get smooshed by an elephant, or wrapped in a rug and trampled by horses.

She tried to spit her teeth at them, but they ricocheted off the shield and hit her face.

"We need that gun," Taivan said.

Khair tried to hit with her knee, elbow, but her limbs were pinned out to the side, no angle to hook a blow, no leverage for power.

The shield raised slightly to hit her down again, but she kicked herself off the desk, propelling them both to the ground. They swarmed her. She grabbed the chair and used it as a battering ram, smashing into the shield, buying space to grab the flag-spear.

Finally, she was in the fight. Or would be if she wasn't facing a firing squad of riot-control pain guns.

She raised her hands apologetically and tried her most winsome smile, though blood snaked down her chin. "I'm sure we're all nice peo—" The prongs imbedded in her armor. Nothing? "I'll take reinforcements anytime, Taivan."

She charged.

Khair fought. In this crowded room where their bulky shields hampered their movements and their guns couldn't touch her, it was easy. The weapon in her hand moved with a mind of its own, the flag flickering, distracting, covering her movements, while the spear found targets her eye couldn't see.

Pain remained, her face and torso aching, runny blood gushing from her nose and bubbling from her mouth, her broken teeth poking her tongue, electricity hitting her—isolated to a side, directing her where the next blow was coming from—but it didn't matter. There was no fear, just impulse and movement, a pure, free game where she was everyone's equal.

How had she avoided this for so long? Fists bloody and feet light, breath unsteady and blood roaring, this was her natural habitat.

Stop playing.

The glasses flickered back, showed their squad cut in half, Taivan's prosthetic ripped off, Jiao with handprints on her neck. Where was Davids?

Khair focused past the glasses into the cockpit, slashed her spear, gaining space. "Taivan, lift, now!"

He echoed the order and their forces floated. Khair punched air, shooting everything on the ground outside while dancing around the six soldiers left standing in the cockpit, fighting two battles.

She'd only win one.

She concentrated outside, her immediate surroundings hazy, shooting as quickly as she could, the punches enough to trigger the gun but too weak for the surrounding fight, wasting her energy. Her feet slowed, hemmed in as she searched for an angle outside and retreated to the bloodied pilot's table.

The spear was too long to use backed into the corner. Each blow was tentative, careful she didn't stab into a wall and get stuck.

Khair should warn Taivan she couldn't provide cover much longer, but she didn't have the air. Her heel banged against the table. No more room.

She threw the spear into someone's chest. "I'm finished, Taivan." So much more to say, but it'd only distract him. "Can't surrender, eh?"

The remaining guards charged, their shields interlocked, too wide to avoid. She hopped on the desk, punched air and killed more enemy outside, tried to leap over the shield wall. A shield hit her leg, and she careened to the ground, landing on her knee. A shield smashed her back.

She screamed as vertebrae cracked.

Khair pushed her arms forward as his weight pressed into her spine, her vision shifting so she saw only the battle outside. The pain was so incomprehensibly great it ceased to exist. So, she swam on the ground, her shots echoing outside.

Then, blasting inside.

Davids fired; his old rifle pierced shields designed for faster projectiles. Two charged him, but slow as his weapon was, it still shot faster than they ran. The last one raised the shield to smash her skull, but fell dead on top of her.

"Yippee," she said, offering him her hand. Davids crossed the floor cautiously, rifle pointed at the enemy, kicking their weapons from them. He took her hand and tried to pull her up.

Her legs wouldn't move.

How the Battle of Coloma Ends

KHAIR GRABBED DAVIDS' ARM so frantically she nearly pulled him down.

When the shield bashed her back, it'd hurt so much she couldn't be paralyzed. And she could shoot the guns with her hands, could raise her eyebrows or quirk her ears, still felt her legs. But they wouldn't obey.

"You're safe." Davids explosive vest blinked.

"Wonderful. Let's sit down for a candlelight dinner. I can't move my fucking legs!"

Davids tried to help her sit, but she slapped his hands away.

"Do some zappy magic, get the neurons firing."

I can't do that.

"Khair, they still need support."

Outside, Taivan floated in zero-gravity, his blood rising with him, firing down, standing on a corpse he maneuvered one-legged like a surfboard to shield himself and control his movements. Jiao had turned her grav-boots on once she'd reached the ship's roof and shot from a sniper's position on the *Dzud's* roof. They had eight soldiers left, scattered across the hangar.

Connect me to their captain.

Why?

To negotiate. Where's the bridge?

Vertical 30 degrees, horizontal 170, 1.76 klicks away.

Captain Wang appeared on the cracked screen, and when he saw her with her face turned inside out, laughed. "Not your day, is it?"

She fired a missile at the bridge. It hit protective compartment walls and wilted before it reached him, but it shook the ship and started the sprinklers.

"It's about to be."

"Those missiles will destroy this ship. If you were willing to do that, Davids would've already."

"Davids is a good guy. I'm not."

"That's—"

She fired again.

The ship tilted. Foam fire suppressors sprayed, hardening on systems and making them temporarily unusable.

Two more shots, and you'll down the ship.

Then I've got one more shot.

No. One more shot and the ship will—

She cocked her fist. "I ain't running out of missiles anytime soon."

"So, destroy it," Wang said. "You still won't have it."

She could do it. Kill herself and end this pain. Kill Jiao and Taivan for what they did to Batu, because it was the only mercy she could give them. Kill Davids so he'd never live in chains, because he was willing to make that sacrifice. But if only they could meet the end in a final stand worthy of their names instead of in an unplanned blip.

What did that matter? She just wanted to embrace Taivan and tell her anda she was with him to the end, to nod to Jiao and hope Jiao understood she would've done anything to fix the past. To—

You'll kill everyone because you got a boo-boo? They'll be an operation, maybe some pins—

Just die and leave me alone already.

She nearly pushed Davids away, hid her face, and cried. But she could still shoot.

Outside, enemy soldiers turned off their grav-boots and rose to Jiao's level. There were too many for her to shoot. Jiao rolled off the ship and activated her boots, buying a few seconds, but she didn't have long.

Taivan couldn't help, one man on his back with arms across his neck, a woman using both arms to pin his one, a third aiming at him.

They only had six others alive.

Khair fired at the bridge.

The ferry sank.

Gravity slammed back, throwing Taivan thirty feet down. She didn't see how he landed. The bay opened and everything not tethered by grav-boots or docking clasps swept outside—including the *Dzud*. Davids jumped over her to the controls and wrestled them back in, hovering them between debris and their soldiers.

The *Nautilus* tilted back upright, and the bay gate closed behind them. The sprinklers stopped. Patching foam piled across broken sections of the walls and floor in inverted gray pyramids; misting cold water hardened a second layer of gel while everyone lay still.

The lights turned off, then all systems restarted.

Taivan lay on two twisted bodies, broken ribs making his breath sound like leaves crinkling in an autumnal breeze. Jiao struggled to her feet, head bleeding, while a man pinned beneath a shattered wing aimed a pistol at her.

Davids landed the ship on him.

He helped Khair sit. "The Dreadnought must've seen that. They might know the ship is compromised."

The *Nautilus* was too valuable to destroy lightly, but perhaps not valuable enough to spare them.

"We have to get to the bridge," she said.

But she couldn't.

The pain drifting at the edge of her consciousness solidified, so dense it was a black hole pulling all her thought to it. Her useless legs ached, her sliced back screamed, her busted nose and ripped gums swelled.

"Doctube?"

Davids shook his head.

She slapped the floor, eased off the wall, and let herself rest against the cool steel. "Wheelchair?" Cause a half-burned hull of a ship was sure to be ramp accessible.

"Haven't seen one." He glanced around, then drew a capped syringe from a pocket on his vest. Oppyin. That explained why he'd been calm as trout in hunting season earlier. His jaw stiffened. "It's the only way I can do what's necessary."

"I thought Sophie was yanking you around. Your ministers—"

He started to put it away. "My people won't believe you, and I could get a prescription if—"

"Buck. I'm not trying to hurt you, I just... there're no side effects?"

"Of course there are."

"So why?" His life wasn't perfect, but it was a whole lot better than most people's.

He snorted. "Who says there's a reason? But if anyone needs it, you do."

You can't have it. You have a predilection toward addiction, and abuse often begins with legitimate need.

She groaned. What did it matter if she was in pain, if she was going to lie here and do nothing while everyone else fought?

Guide Davids. Moore's voice softened when she shook her head and let her eyes close. *You only have to try a little longer.*

We lost.

It will be a difficult negotiation. Khair almost laughed. Moore still thought she could keep her cover? The only way she could've done that was to kill Khair. *Would it be easier if I spoke through you?*

It would. ***Don't.***

"Stay quiet, I'll be back if I can." Davids left the needle behind. He found Jiao helping Taivan up, but Taivan would only slow them. Jiao gently released him. They had five other survivors.

Davids led, Jiao at his shoulder.

"Thirty soldiers ahead." Khair looked through the gunner's glasses, though Moore added her cameras when needed. "Turn left, then right." The giant hole from her missile had cleared most of the way, which left no concealment. "Sharper right, backtrack, the cameras there are dead, over."

Davids spun them back into Moore's line of sight as ZAX started shooting down that hall. He tackled Jiao, saving them both, but two soldiers behind them were killed in one shot.

What can I do?

Bullets tore up the wall behind Jiao, Davids, and the other survivors. Too much metal in the air for them to fire back, no option but sheltering in coils of sparking wires while enemy reinforcements flanked them.

Khair switched from missiles to machine guns and gave cover by wagging a weary finger until she ran out of bullets. The remaining ZAX mercenaries started shooting again.

"Khair," Davids said over the comms. "There's nothing I can do but detonate."

Jiao laid beside him, behind a chintzy piece of metal, trigger squeeze and breathing unaffected by this announcement.

"Tell me when you and Taivan get out. Hurry." The line crackled. "I wrote a letter. It's on my desk at the farm. Tell Cassia it's for Westley, over."

'Over' meant 'I'd done talking. Please say something brilliant to save us all.'

She tried to ask Moore for a better option, but though she formulated the words, she didn't have the strength to send the message. All she had left was the missile. One more shot to down the ship and let gravity decide the rest.

Taivan stumbled onto the *Dzud*. "Why aren't you firing?"

She motioned an explosion.

"Khair, do you read me?" Davids said. "If I don't hear you, I'll blow the ship."

"Negative," Taivan said. "Hold on, out."

'Out' meant 'the discussion's over.'

A bullet struck beside Davids' head, his ear bleeding. He kept firing, but ran out of bullets. He crawled toward a dead woman's magazine, but a bullet grazed his shoulder. Half his upper arm was blown away. He lost so much blood, he could only whimper before he lost consciousness.

Jiao grabbed his foot and pulled him to her without leaving cover, trying to use her belt as a tourniquet, but the wound was so close to the shoulder joint she struggled to wrap it high enough on the arm to stop the bleeding.

Jiao's last surviving comrade's brain splattered across her face. The enemy advanced, undeterred, stood over her, cocked a pistol at her head. Her rifle lay beside her, untouched. She tied off the tourniquet and raised her hands.

He shot Jiao in the head.

That was fine. They'd wait till Aidan returned to this dimension, probably wearing swim trunks and eating ice-cream, and he'd bring Jiao back from wherever he wandered off to.

Jiao would be fine.

Khair would not be. She'd rather someone use her entrails as a bungee cord, or stab a hook through her stomach and use her as piranha bait. Or listen to Jiao lecture—it wasn't funny. Nothing was funny. Or sad, really. Davids' oppyin lay beside her, but she didn't need it.

Davids. He was still alive, but that was worse because he was dying unconscious and she couldn't comfort him.

She fell to her side—Taivan had been shaking her.

"Pistol's riot control, you hear? It'll hurt her when she moves, but she's not dead. And this ferry will have a doctube for Davids, we can still take this ship."

She laughed. "Can't move."

They had four people left: two couldn't walk, one couldn't move, and the other was unconscious.

"Is pain stopping you?" Taivan found the oppyin syringe.

"Back's broke."

He inhaled deeply, winced at his broken ribs, and rolled up his sleeve.

"You can't take this ship alone."

"Probably not." He easily found a vein.

She hit the floor. "We got a weapon."

Taivan put the unused needle on the counter and flicked the *Dzud* to life. "Autopilot, take me to," he looked to her.

"Vertical 30 degrees, horizontal 170, 1.76 klicks," Khair said.

"At twenty kilometers an hour." Fast enough they'd smash through any resistance without hurting the ship.

The *Dzud's* wings rent through the walls, triggering alarms again, but sprinklers couldn't stop them. Soldiers shot at them, but their bullets bounced off the *Dzud's* shield back at them.

"What're we gonna do once we get there?" Khair asked.

"Can the washing hoses be operated from here?" Taivan asked, switching on a dozen auto-pilot systems.

"Yes," the *Dzud* replied, its blank voice the same as Chip's.

Enemy soldiers chased them, lagging behind.

Now's the time to ask about prisoner transport, hostage negotiations.

Khair didn't bother. They could take prisoners while their soldiers lived, now they couldn't; any rebellion would overwhelm them.

Moore buzzed her three times.

Since Davids and Jiao were shot, pain hadn't bothered her. ***At this point, they're either stupid or they know.***

You're low priority, whereas I had a sterling reputation before your case. Cooperate.

She wasn't gonna try to save these people when the time it'd take to restrain prisoners could be used saving Jiao and Davids. Wasn't gonna act like she cared to cast Taivan as the monster, as if it was a crime to win.

Nah.

"Take the oppyin," Taivan said to her.

She shook her head.

He squeezed her shoulder, his hand heavy. "I'm sorry."

Taivan turned on the jet-powered industrial hose on the ZAX soldiers outside the cockpit. She sizzled on the ground, unable to flail, breath wheezing in through gaps of her broken teeth. So close to Taivan that if she stretched out her arm, she could hold him, feel something besides pain, but she curled her fist, and focused on his cologne.

She couldn't see the crushed spines within dented armor, or skin stripped from bones, but she heard them try to breach the ark.

It didn't last long.

The current stopped, but aftershocks pulsed through her, and Moore's mind flipped like a circus freak to justify Khair's pain and the bad deaths outside.

Save the self-loathing, I hurt enough.

Taivan used the Khanate flag as a cane and ventured outside. He returned riding a doctube, blood on the flag shaft. "Put it on life seeking mode, get to Jiao and Davids. I'll get us out of here."

The Dreadnought was overhead.

"And Coloma?"

Shouldn't have asked. She could see in the slump of his shoulders that when they'd lost the fleet, they lost the city. It was never mission essential. But it meant losing their aura of invincibility. Buck's home. Batu's resting place.

"Jiao will be in pain for years," Taivan said. "Tell her—actually, don't say anything."

She gave a thumbs up, all the speech she was capable of, too weak to haul herself into the 'tube. He helped, wheezing.

Khair landed the 'tube beside Davids without crushing him, the extent of her piloting skills. Then she was stuck. She pulled herself over the side and flopped on the ground.

This was not going to work.

Jiao cranked her head to look at Khair. "We won?"

"Taivan's at the helm."

Davids' arm still dripped blood, his skin cool and sweaty and turning blue around his nails, pulse and breath skipping with no more pattern than the wind on a stormy day. She tapped his cheek, smacked harder. He didn't wake.

"Republics are dumb. Democracies are much fairer and would never take away anyone's rights."

He didn't stir.

"Monarchies are much more efficient and obviously the point of government is to do as much stuff as possible."

Still nothing.

Jiao hooked her arms under Davids' and hoisted him into the 'tube. She slumped beside it, frozen but for quiet tears.

Tell me something to help her.

Moore's mind was empty.

"I'm sorry," Khair said, knowing it wasn't enough.

The Price of Losing

TAIVAN LANDED THE CLOAKED ferry outside Albion. He hadn't left the helm once in the twelve hours it took to lose their pursuers.

Khair had gotten her nose reset and her teeth filled. Creepy robot prongs operated on her spine to fix her legs. She was conscious for all of it. Her head was so heavy, she couldn't lift it from the pillow. But once she stumbled through those first steps, it was worth it.

After surgery, she wasn't allowed anything stronger than fish oil until Moore tired of her crying. Her first sensibly drugged act was to drag Taivan from the controls long enough to get his ribs set and leg restitched.

Davids wasn't much better. He had replenished his blood and had his shoulder reconstructed with cadaver bone, then holed up in his room with his oppyin stash and bomb vest. Now that ZAX occupied Coloma, he was barred from his son and his city.

Nothing could help Jiao. Sometimes she needed a wheelchair, sometimes a cane, sometimes she managed without assistance. Hopefully, she let someone help her, because Khair tried and wasn't allowed to.

Moore too had a mood sour as lemon flavored vinegar. Something had happened with Strudel, but she wouldn't discuss it.

Khair should be commiserating; they'd lost 94% of their force to death or Coloma's capture, and 99% of their will to fight. But Taivan prepped their captured command ferry to reach the *DPO Hopper,* the cruiser with the time machine's location on the other side of the galaxy, still trying to break UOD's hold. She had helped until he sent over Batu's things, just one cardboard box with a blue bow, and she forgot everything else.

She reverently ripped the tape. On top was an unsigned childish calligraphy sketch, a red envelop with Jiao's cramped, thin signature, and a crocheted beanie hat in joyful orange stained with barbecue sauce. Why had he kept it? It must have been from her mother or siblings.

She kicked the box into a closet, lay on her bed buttressed with pillows, and pulled the beanie over her ears. She started sniffling, so she found her stash of beef jerky and worked a new gaming system with a screen as big as her old room.

Taivan knocked, already entering. "Will Davids detonate the vest if we storm his room?"

"You should've warned me you were coming, and we could do the proper hospitality." Khair flipped the race away and brought up supply scenarios to get their ferry to the *Hopper*. She'd lightened their ship for a fast getaway since they had no other option; attacking a cruiser from a ferry was like shooting arrows at a tank.

"We could put a sedative in his food." The bags under Taivan's eyes could serve as airbags. "But, he—"

"He doesn't trust you with the vest. That doesn't mean he'll use it." She rummaged through her fridge, found him something with water and electrolytes.

"I have more dangerous weapons." He checked the drink's sugar content, frowned, and chugged it.

"He knows, but he doesn't want to be responsible for any more loss."

Taivan browsed through her proposed plans and starred her favorite.

"Go hunt with him or something," Khair said. "He knows UOD weaponry and ships better than us, and you need someone talking sense to you now that Jiao has other concerns."

"Don't sideline her. She can endure anything but that."

She sent him the chosen plan and waste management automatically took its place. "Why do you love her so much?"

Taivan scrolled through her assignments: maintaining the water electrolysis for breathable oxygen and hydrogen fuel, covertly finding repair parts for the ferry, and supplying cheap entertainment to keep everyone sane. "Why do you care?"

"You pointed a gun at my face and threatened me as leverage against a woman who tried to kill you and stole my body. You'd never do that to Jiao. How much blood do I have to give for a Jochiin Taivan deluxe loyalty package?"

"I saved you by the best means at my disposal." He gestured to the room: a library of war documentaries, a jacuzzi, fridge filled with desserts she couldn't pronounce. "What else do you want? I've offered you a planet once. Now, the best I can give is Albion."

"I'll think about it."

"Think fast. We'll leave when we're repaired." He tossed her drink in the trash. "If you go, take Davids."

That was too much, acting like she was no different from a man who had shot him weeks ago. "I'm not Davids. I'm not a rival or an enemy, and I never have been."

"No?" He pulled up his pant leg. "I wake in the middle of the night biting back screams. If I'd been faster maybe—doesn't matter now."

There was no point apologizing. "Moore offered to return my memories if I killed you. Taking a leg was the closest I could come."

"Close enough."

"What would you have done? A day old, someone electrocuting you, and you were free if you killed a stranger?"

He looked her in the eye and she felt herself shrink, though she kept her chin up. "Whatever I did, I wouldn't do it halfway."

"I'll remember that for next time, anda."

They disembarked in Albion. Sophie and Naguib provided a repair team and five hundred of the best soldiers left. That was all their vessel could take.

The command ferry had enough doctubes for them to sleep during the trip and not waste their years. But it was a twenty-year journey and someone trustworthy had to stay awake to monitor the auto-pilot. It'd be torture for Jiao, Davids had Westley to consider, and Sophie had Aidan, though he didn't really count.

Taivan told her they'd settle it that night. That gave her time to do something useful, like be a dutiful daughter and listen to her father's last words on the holo. But she was sick of death. So she took Sophie to downtown Albion, mostly to pet Whiskey. There was little question where they'd end up.

You were always a violent drunk, you'll hurt someone.

Khair settled into a plush booth and ordered a vodka, Whiskey whining in protest.

This is my last night before it's night night for twenty years, unless I'm sentenced to decades of drudgery.

Don't risk years of work for one night.

Khair drank. Or tried to, but Moore zapped her and she spat it on Sophie. She threw the cup at the wall.

You told me I could live as I wanted if I didn't hurt anyone. She didn't care how petulant she sounded. **You promised.**

Moore's stomach soured, but her computerized-mask was firmly in place. *I had other vows first. You knew Strudel watched and still—*

Fuck you, Tamika Moore. Sell your soul for your revolution instead of your regime. The only difference is you'll die a traitor.

"So, either you've started a new religion where you sacrifice your drink to the wall spirits." Sophie dabbed blue vodka from her white shirt. "Or your buddy decided you're the designated driver."

Khair pet Whiskey, ordered a root beer float, and blew bubbles through the straw as angrily as possible. The tavern smelled like liquor and syrupy biscuits. Rugby and jet racing dominated the screens, bagpipes and lutes played outside. Well, two out of three wasn't bad. "I should stay here."

"You can't." Sophie got a refill. "You bring trouble. My people don't need that."

Khair would be queen. She could arrange the defenses.

Outside the window, engineered beasts played among the neighborhood kids. It was a good place for freaks. But after she'd gotten used to the noise and lights of Coloma, it'd felt not homey or safe, but suitable. Really, she'd take anywhere but where she was going.

"Taivan offered me Albion," Khair said.

Sophie switched the closest screen from rugby to rowing, as repetitive and interesting as an assembly line. Granted, rowing was something Sophie could do. "Don't accept."

"Or what? You stabbed me already, it didn't take."

"Currently, I hate you the least. Troubling enough, all things considered, so don't make me kill you."

At this point, being hated the least was equivalent to a rain drenched, rose filled declaration of love, so she shrugged. "Only if you elaborate on why I'm your favorite."

Sophie grinned. "Because you're so easy to manipulate."

"If your devious machinations bring me here, I won't complain." Khair sucked the melted ice cream at the bottom. "That's a joke, right? You're not screwing with my head?"

"Whatever helps you sleep better." Sophie finished the drink. "About that favor you owe me. Have Taivan let me stay. Naguib can be his minister. I just want to be home, even under house arrest."

Khair's face heated. "You ask that after exiling me?"

"I can't exile you from a place you've never belonged."

"He'll say no."

"Just try." She spun her cup. "I'd let you stay if you didn't have a spy in your head."

"Yeah, yeah, ten out of ten manipulating right there." But tension leached from her stiff back and she relaxed into the booth, watching the muscled rowers. "Where are they, anyway? Davids mentioned a sea."

"Hardly. They made a lake with waves, but these guys are on a rowing machine in a gym in front of a green-screen."

It was still pretty, water rippling beneath the oars, a butterfly parading among flowered lily pads.

"There's gotta be something better than this," Khair said. "Someplace like that."

"No, there doesn't. Everyone pretends they're better and better off than they are."

The rowers mesmerized her. Even if there was no reason to, they worked in harmony. "It's not pretend for them. They made things better."

"Looks the same to me."

Khair pushed the dregs of the shake around. "I should volunteer to stay awake. We need Taivan, and I guess I give a shit about you people."

"You got all that from gawking?"

"You'd understand if you saw their forearms."

Sophie flipped her off, flagged down the waiter, and ordered another drink. "Taivan won't let you. You'd be sixty. What could you do?"

Wouldn't be terrible to have twenty years of ease. Lonely, but no more than now, caring about everyone far more than they cared for her. But Sophie was right. Besides war, what did she have going for her?

Jiao fell into the booth beside Sophie and draped her arm around her, so abrupt Whiskey growled. She laughed and bopped his nose.

"Hello?" Sophie asked. "Whiskey, bite them."

"Good puppy." Jiao pet Sophie's head and kissed the dog. She snapped her fingers at a waiter while Khair picked her jaw up from where it'd fallen so hard it landed in the basement. "I want something nice for everyone. Your choice. I won't know the difference. Also, a dog bone. Not the bones of a dog, rawhide. And I'll tip well since you're cute, and money doesn't matter 'cause I inherited an empire, except it got looted."

The young man, admittedly cute but not totally-forget-how-to-mimic-a human-being cute, bowed slightly and left quickly.

"So, did it hurt when aliens abducted Jiao and replaced her with this clown?" Khair said.

Jiao slapped the table and cackled.

"I'll treat it like a system's upgrade. This one downloaded a sense of humor."

The waiter returned with three strawberry daiquiris and a soup bone, and extricated himself after Jiao's seventh pick up line. Khair reached for her drink, but Moore buzzed her, so she gave it to Whiskey. Which left her the meatless bone. Nope, Whiskey finished spilling the daiquiri and ate that, too.

"Easy." Sophie untangled herself and reached for Jiao's drink, but she hugged it to her chest. "I've pumped enough stomachs to know you don't need that."

"Or you can not do that and then I'll die."

"Shut up," Khair said.

Jiao splashed the icy drink in her face, the only bit she got to taste. "You're not responsive—responsible—for me. You wanted to be my mom, tough since you killed her, and my dad and my brother. Then I killed your dad, so here we are, drinking together like we don't hate each other."

Khair blinked. What would Batu think of his daughters? "JJ. Can't we..." she shrugged and wiped strawberry chunks from her cheek. They were past forgiveness. And there was no point denying it: she did hate Jiao, if only a little, the hot worms of hate eating her stomach indistinguishable from respect and pity and love.

Sophie tried to crawl out from under the table, but there wasn't enough room.

"They'd be so ashamed of us," Jiao said.

"Let's walk back to our quarters," Khair said.

"Why didn't you just kill me?" Jiao said. "Never asked you for anything else."

Sophie tried to call someone, but they didn't pick up. "Hassan? Call back when you can. Please."

Khair took Jiao's arm. "Let's go."

"Get off me."

"Unless I'm killing you, right?"

"You'd use a gun, obviously."

Sophie put in headphones.

Khair massaged her temple. "How about we go back to my place where there're pictures of cute men like that waiter?"

"No, I want to go to my room." Jiao eyed her suspiciously. "You won't touch me, not even to help me walk?"

"No."

She patted her pockets and teared up. "I forgot my wallet. How'm I supposed to tip him? He won't like me."

Khair left a generous tip.

Jiao faltered on the sticky steps out to the street and Khair instinctively reached for her, but she threw herself against the railing to avoid it.

"I'm sorry, I forgot."

Meters away, smoking teens giggled at Jiao, and beyond them, old women wagged their heads.

"My clothes are too heavy," Jiao said softly. "Changed three times, all too heavy. I should wear my navy dress to the trial when Sophie lets me finish it. Even if Batu agreed, there're rules beyond us, beyond survival. Doesn't matter what happens to me now. I can't be a pilot anymore."

Khair's jaw quivered.

"I'll stay up while everyone sleeps, heal," Jiao said. "Or figure how to be useful. If nothing else, it's twenty years of penance. Not enough—" She vomited on her shoes so violently she could barely hold herself up. Khair let her sink to the hard stone ground.

Jiao spat and wiped her mouth. "Wanna go home."

Khair crouched beside her. "Taivan will let you—"

Jiao pointed to Albion's high, dark ceiling. "Mom was a Buddhist; dad was a Christian. If dad's right, she's in hell, and I will be too. If she's right, he's some animal and I will be too."

Was there a theological term for 'that sucks?'

"I think I'm a Christian now, cause they can drink. But orange looks nice on me, so I could be a Buddhist monk." It really didn't. "A pacifist. Wouldn't be any good at it, though. Wouldn't have to worry about being good as a Christian, but I'd end up eating meat, and that's disgusting. And Buddhist monks invented kung-fu."

"Paul and Angulimala marvel at your wisdom." A Christian and a Buddhist, both reformed killers, and Jiao's eyes brightened. "But let's save the major life choices to another time."

"After I go to bed."

It was the only sensible thing she said all night, blabbing about universal truths and redemption of sins. Khair tucked her in with a bucket and apple juice.

She almost walked into Davids as she locked the door behind her. "Let me guess, you want to sacrifice yourself and waste twenty years cause it's terrifying, so we're all pretending we won't mind."

Davids stepped from the yellow rose he'd laid outside Jiao's door, a note attached to the stem. That was decent, especially since Jiao was shot saving his life. "It wouldn't be a sacrifice for me. I could talk to my son."

"Or nap. Then when you see him again, you'd still be able to pin him in wrestling. Stop being all scared and noble."

Jiao knocked on the door. "I have to pee."

"There's a bathroom in your room." She sighed. "It really is hard having our only brain cell."

He scratched his neck. "I also wanted to thank you for not saying anything about what I offered you earlier. I know it's over the news—looks worse than it is—but still." ZAX, as UOD's front, had used his addiction to accuse him of corruption and incompetence.

"You're lucky none of your political enemies asked, cause I would've sold it for a dumpling."

"Doesn't matter now." He scraped his boot against a smudge on the floor, rubbing it clean. "Now that I'm not running a country, I don't have an excuse for it."

"You don't have to be cheerful. Sometimes life sucks. Doesn't mean you have to do this and race out of it, because apparently the afterlife is worse."

"If I don't, the only impression my son will have of me is an absent failure."

"We're going to fly faster than light to fight people who invented a time-machine. You can leave him a holo."

Which Westley probably wouldn't watch.

"Thank you for your concern." He turned to leave.

"Davids." She took his hand gently enough he could pull free. He did, but didn't flee. "Sorry about that mess on the *Dzud*." Mostly, she wanted to bring it up. "I thought we were gonna die, and you were kind to me. Shouldn't have acted like an idiot."

He nodded. "It's not a problem."

Not flustered at all? Then totally not interested. "Friends, then?"

She must've handed off that brain cell.

"Sure."

But whoever had picked it up, it wasn't him.

"Actually, no," Khair said. "What's wrong with me? Am I too much like a kid? Am I too old? Is it that I have to ask both those questions? You seemed into me sometimes. Maybe I had the whole dangerous mystery thing going, but now I've saved your life a few times, so you figure I'm safe or something."

He shifted his weight. "Yes."

"You might as well answer 'licorice' or 'persnickety' because that's equally vague."

Jiao knocked. "Argue quieter. Also, Khair, tell him to wear that cowboy hat more, very exotic."

"Fine. Is there anything he should tell me?" Yes, she was fishing for compliments.

"Fix your voice. You sound like an irate duck."

"At least I can swear properly."

"Quack quack."

Davids covered his mouth and coughed.

"Go watch a kite. Anyway," she looked to Davids.

"It's not exactly fair, but you asked for the truth." Going formal, great. At least the 'Ms. Batuyin' thing had been kinda hot. "You look like someone who was an enemy for years."

Huh.

For years her face was plastered under Chuluun's beside burned out towns. She'd proved herself to him—must have—but that was the measured, limited trust of allies facing a greater enemy. It wouldn't dampen his ingrained revulsion.

"Can you pretend I have an evil twin?" She sounded choked, which was indeed worse than a duck.

His face softened, but his voice was firm. "I know you've changed, but I can't see you like that. And you are about two months old."

She looked away and saw the rose. "You and Jiao?" Jiao had shot him, but hey, anyone but her, apparently.

"It's not your concern."

"No? She killed Batu to frame you. You would force her into some parole little better than slavery and I should be fine with that? Com'on. I thought you were the good guy."

"Grow up." He picked up the rose and showed the note: I'm sorry. Not "my condolences"—he'd done something. "It wouldn't have been slavery."

"And that riot-control pistol you guys make isn't torture."

He had the decency to hesitate. "They customized it."

"I don't care. If you hurt her, I'll kill you."

Moore shocked her. Khair fell to one knee and Davids jumped back, hands rising to defend himself.

Moore had upped the voltage again. Not as high as in the beginning, but high enough her heart skipped. Rage sang. With Moore beyond her, she imagined crushing Davids' skull and letting his brain squeeze out his ears.

He dusted off his suit from some hidden indignity, as Jiao did every time she came within two meters of Khair.

"This is why," Davids said. "I shouldn't have to explain a one-night stand to keep you from threatening me. And you, Moore. How can you expect your ward to grow as you regress?"

Oh, I've stopped regressing. But you'll wish I hadn't.

What had UOD done to Moore after she and Taivan had taken the ferry's bridge?

"We're both idiots, and we're sorry. Or should be, anyway." She faked a smile very poorly and left to kidnap Whiskey. Her wrist panel blinked, Taivan calling her. Why not? What else could the boss say to make things worse?

He managed.

The Last Legitimate Power in the 'Verse

TAIVAN SAT ALONE IN his room. It looked like a jail cell with a mini-fridge and woodstove, without pictures or posters.

She stood in the hall, hands up, spinning Batu's beanie on her finger. "Don't worry, Moore hasn't made any more appealing offers."

"I don't worry. Come in."

The host and guest should exchange small gifts, he shouldn't wear a sleeveless t-shirt, she shouldn't wear hand-warming gloves, and he motioned for her to sit on the left, the host's side. There was no room for the old world's rules between these unpainted steel walls and laminated floors.

"You're disappointed," Taivan said. "The conqueror of Temujin's line, and he won't even offer a snuffbox to his guests."

Given Temujin's descendants were slaughtered in the wars of succession down to one boy by the time Queen Manduhai the Wise saved and married him, it was unlikely Taivan had that lineage. Even if he had, clan names were outlawed during the Soviet occupation, everyone's family history lost. But it was a good story, repeated enough no one would doubt it.

Not that their foreign soldiers would care. Even Batu hadn't. It was just her scrounging for any history or extended family.

Taivan tossed her his pillow, and she sat on it since he didn't have two chairs. "Why do you keep the Borijin name when you don't care for our history?"

He joined her on the floor. "It's my name; it's my history."

She waved at him. "Millenia of evolution and human civilization, and here we find our pinnacle."

"What do you want me to do? Ride a horse to battle, dance around entrails and ask the skygod if it's okay to wage war?"

"That's not all we are!" She'd been on the verge of tears all night, but she fought still. "Batu is dead. My family is dead, and I never knew them. Moore won't let me learn, but even if she did, it wouldn't be enough. And you, the only one left who shares my history but you only ever scoff at us, like our story ended when the ink of *The Secret History* dried."

He stretched out his bad leg, changed a setting on the prosthetic. "Jiao's the personification of our sins. How could I enjoy my heritage when we destroyed hers? And I'm supposed to lead Albion. Would it be any easier for them to die under our nine-tailed banner?"

The old conqueror's problem: to rule the people, they had to learn them and adopt their ways. Manduhai had avoided it by uniting her people but never stretching outside her territory. What would she think of this nominal empire spread through the stars?

"I would have been happy in PRGC," Taivan said. "If Chuluun had been born fifty years earlier, they could have put him down. They might've challenged UOD with their own tech, instead of whatever it is we're doing." He snorted. "Or maybe it would just be them instead of me destroying everything."

He had said he wanted to be a cop, but he'd skipped the PRGC part. "You really just wanted to enforce someone else's law?"

He shrugged. "Things were different then."

Or he had been different.

"I wish I could have seen it how you did," Khair said. "Forgot we were PRGC citizens first. But you wore a wolf and deer on your armor, that's a medieval Mongolian rallying cry. What happened?"

"Chuluun died."

His abuser couldn't hurt him, he'd been freed from the past she brought up so often.

"Oh. I'll just talk to Aidan when he comes back. He'd love to critique the Tuuli or whatever." She stood. "I'll try not to bring it up again. You and the others are my country now."

She walked out.

"I do miss Imger sometimes," Taivan said. "I only ever had to look out for my family, and I could always hunt something or find scrap metal. We were poor, but at least I didn't have to shoot my half-brother for stealing my fish, eh?"

As Temujin had.

She re-entered, slowly sat.

"Spent fewer hours working then, played dembee and called it math class. Da had us read together since we didn't test into PRGC's programs, didn't have time to study. My siblings are all grown now, and I'd only endanger them going back."

He stretched, socks dangerously close to her legs. "Why do people revere their ancestors?"

"They loved dead granny?" It wasn't the right answer, but it was the sensible one.

"Or they don't trust the living or want someone to remember them in turn."

Khair didn't know her siblings' names and even if she had, her children—assuming she could convince someone she wasn't a monster—or grandchildren would forget her sibling's names. But there was Batu's hat. She didn't even know who made it, but she wore their skill and carried their kindness.

Taivan lowered his voice and leaned closer. "Do you still love him? Chuluun."

She couldn't even picture his face. "If he was here, maybe. But no."

"I killed him." He tapped his thumbs. "Planned it since he killed the other generals, but I couldn't do it alone. So, I told UOD where he was. Jiao knew—I contacted them with her systems. We ate dinner together—didn't dare feast, since we couldn't look like we were celebrating—and waited for the news."

"But they killed more than Chuluun."

He nodded.

How old had the abused boy been when he'd finally hit back, when the mantle of empire first warmed his shoulders? Who else had he purged? "I'm surprised you didn't give them my coordinates."

"Never considered it." He waited for a response with a stony face that didn't suit him. "You took it better than I thought."

"I'm glad it was you. Both of you. And his legacy won't be ours." She didn't know Chuluun to mourn whatever part of him had been decent, if there'd been any. But Taivan let her know him.

"I killed more of our people on that day than he ever did. That's when I decided to use the time-machine."

Her stomach throbbed, and she didn't answer, Moore's heart clenching.

"As a boy, instead of fighting off giant bats and hog badgers, watching my da starve giving us his meals, watching my uncle on the news, I'd hop in a jet, praise Chuluun until he turned his back, and cut off his head. I'd corral the factions together. We'd never hurt Jiao's people, never need UOD, and when Batu sacrificed himself, I decided I'd help you get sober so he could stay home."

He laughed. "I was a child."

Of course, Taivan, who wouldn't leave the *Nautilus'* bridge despite three broken ribs, would try to remake history. She'd just assumed he'd start in the present.

And that she was more than an afterthought.

What else could she do for him, and Buck, and Jiao, even Moore? They were the empire builders and breakers. She was their guard dog, growling at their enemies and looking to them with wagging tail, hoping they'd scratch her ears.

"I'm staying here."

Taivan threw a log in the stove, turning his back on her. No chance to read him until he faced her again, his face cold and stolid though heat flashed in his eyes. "I won't use it; I know what happens now. I won't trade it for the unknown."

"Congratulations, I'll hit a punching bag till it breaks or I do, then drown in fried dough."

He poked the fire. "I wouldn't have shot you. And if I'd been in your position, I probably would have killed me, and I vaguely remember you thinking you could fix my leg. I shouldn't have brought it up. There's no debt."

"Enough of the flattery, please. I'm overwhelmed."

"You're very valuable, both to me personally and to the Khanate. Happy?"

"No." Value was for objects. "Let the time freaks do what they gotta. We're people. We were always gonna suffer and die. Does it matter how?"

"Yes."

He said it more simply than gently. Yes, their lives mattered. Yes, their actions mattered, even if they changed nothing. Yes, she mattered.

"That's why I love you." He didn't react, which was better than throwing her out, so she hurried past, not able to explain how. "I'm tired of watching you and Davids and Jiao and Sophie get hurt. There's... there's gotta be something more than this."

She'd keep saying it until someone agreed.

"There's not." He'd traversed galaxies, multiverses even, and there was no doubt in his voice. "Not until we make it."

Maybe he was only pretending to be better than he was. But she believed that illusion, could make it real by her action if she chose. If she could trust him. Well, she did trust him. He would do whatever was necessary, whether it was killing Chuluun or putting a bomb in Batu's head.

"There are two things you need to know before you decide to leave," Taivan said. "Aidan's back. He'll meet us tonight. From the future he's seen, we only get the coordinates if you and Moore are with us."

Moore's unease cut off instantly, the filter between them dammed up.

"Secondly, I'll tell only one more lie."

She snorted. "You love all your minions equally, but it's Sophie or Davids stuck doing twenty? And I'm only spared because I'm useless at everything but fighting?"

He sat across from her, closer than before. "Self-pity is unbecoming, baghatur."

"Did you forget the part where I'm half a flattened microbe from starting a career as an Albion bartender?" That seemed more fitting than a queen.

"And? I can't read your mind."

It'd be more fun to stomp out and slam the door behind her, but she had to see him in a few hours. "You were talking about your grand new world, and I wasn't in it."

He cocked his head. "Technically, I was correcting wrongs, and with you sober and not beholden to Chuluun, there was nothing to fix."

Oh.

"We could use the machine."

He shook his head. "I've met UOD scientists. They're not much different from Sophie, certainly better intentioned than I was, and look what they've done. We can't use that machine."

"I could be better. Batu must live in at least one universe. Or my whole family…" But there were trillions of other people in the 'verse, people who would get lost in the shuffle. "It's not fair. We can't use it, and it's not fair."

He looked through his fridge, not much but vegetables and beef, gave her a protein shake with not nearly enough sugar. "I'm sorry."

She'd thought she'd given up on the pestilence of hope.

"Let Sophie stay here." It was one debt she could repay. "She'll accept house-arrest, she's trying to stay safe, and I think she's got a sweetheart, Hassan something."

"We keep disappointing you." His wrist-con showed Albion's streets. "This is Sophie's palace and this, inside, is where the ministers meet. Hassan Naguib is Minister Naguib's son."

"So, they spent a lot of time together, that doesn't mean—"

He brought up a picture of the younger Naguib, the man ten years older and a hundred kilometers out of Sophie's league. "An impossible crush. That doesn't mean she's betrayed us. It was a matriarchy, right? He probably wasn't involved in politics."

Sophie had told her she was easy to manipulate and here she was, preceding over the court of fools defending her.

"Fortunately for me, the matriarchy is over. I don't know what she wants with Hassan, but I can't risk it."

Khair played with the chunky shake. "We'll have to raise the abysmal state of morale cheaply, do impersonations of the people we don't like or something."

"I'd pass out coffee and cigs, but my supply guy's a bit of a dullard." He said it with a grin, but things were tight without Coloma's resources.

"Whoa, a shortage in a recently conquered nation? Shocker."

"Albion will survive. Coloma's ZAX now, and even if they don't like it, there are advantages to empire." He snorted. "The strength to fight us off, for one. But

I do need one favor. I've written everyone's name down and thrown them in a shoe—"

"Yuck."

"If we do it on the net, it'll look rigged. Whoever's name is pulled will stay awake. You'll choose and pick the cold slip. That's me."

"What? Why?"

"It's one thing I can accomplish for us."

She crossed her arms. "This isn't a 'let Khair dupe them' thing, cause if it's someone else's name—"

"Then tell them."

His shoulders were set, his eyes hard, no tremble in his hands. Alexander the Great's teacher had taught that standing firm against fear wasn't enough for courage. There must be some pleasure in it. Dim pride lit Taivan's face; he couldn't be dissuaded.

But she still saw him as half a kid, hands up to fight the universe, though he couldn't see through a swollen eye and wobbled on his feet.

She sighed. "You won't like being alone, having no one to perform for."

"I know."

He guessed; it wasn't the same. She flung herself at him in an embrace. "Thank you." He gave a muffled grunt of acknowledgement, and she rewarded him by releasing him. "I'll let you get back to your fancy scheming."

"There's nothing else now."

She stayed. For a time, she asked him about the *Hopper* and debated new names for the *Nautilus* (*Nothing to See Here, Cookie Delivery,* or *Lord of Silence*) eventually settling on *Osiris*. She talked herself out, until he admitted how often he thought of Irmeg, though he never called it home. He spoke of the scenic valley where his mother's remains laid, how his little sister had been hurt in an illicit logging accident but they didn't dare take her to the hospital, when they'd finally bought a sewing machine and it'd been confiscated for taxes the next week.

But he missed it somehow. Irmeg, yes, but PRGC too, the home of his youth, the gluttonous empire he helped destroy, the last legitimate power in the 'verse. Not for what it was, but for what it should have been.

They made a better world together. Didn't need words so much anymore, but there was no wrong answer, no penalty crouching at the door.

Night came too quickly. She and Taivan weren't first to their own meeting; Aidan waited in the conference room. He actually looked older, a haggard twenty-two, with the haircut of a man three times older, reading the news to orient himself.

"Judging by the mullet, the future's not great," Khair said.

"It's not."

Jiao arrived in a wheelchair and sunglasses that didn't hide her hangover, Davids in faded jeans and his straw hat. Sophie, green makeup only accentuating how close she was to tears, entered behind Whiskey. Whiskey dragged her into Aidan, Aidan not looking up until he lay on the floor with a shepherd on his chest.

"Oh, you're still alive?"

Sophie hit and embraced him. The dog weaseled in between, thumping them with his tail.

"What's that 'still alive' thing?" Sophie said. "Is that for me or the dog?"

"The dog."

"Your voice gets lower when you lie."

"That was a different time. Maybe now my voice gets lower when I have boring conversations."

"Yes, brother." Sophie answered in a robot voice, moving her arms in a stiff arc. "That seems an adequate explanation. Thank you for clarifying with your usual precision."

"We can have this conversation later, if you must have it."

"I'm not waiting. Remember when we played Mercy? I would bend your thumb to the breaking point, but you would never yield. I wouldn't break you, so you won. I'm not a stranger, Aidan. You took everything else, so if you're gone now, tell me."

He held out a small box. "It's a model of a particle Ito found in the cell. It never made any official reports, and no else knows, but I have it and stole Ito's notes. It might help explain how people travel."

She grabbed it like he might change his mind.

"Just don't get your hopes up. I don't know which memories you have, which you I'm talking to."

"I took Albion from your shoulders." Her voice broke. "You have to know I love you."

"You can't love what you don't know."

"I know enough."

Aidan's cheeks reddened as everyone else pretended to be fascinated by Whiskey growling at Davids' fur-lined boots. "You deserve better."

"I know that, too."

Aidan nodded to Taivan.

"First order of business," Taivan said. "Dinner."

He pressed for room service. They had everything from roasted goat with onions and potatoes stuffed inside—a delicacy Taivan had talked about earlier and she'd wished to try—to fluorescent seaweed, lobster macaroni dripping with cheese, spicy rice that cleared her sinuses. Nothing alcoholic.

"So, we're really not going to like this news?" Sophie said. "I've been thinking, I'm the youngest, and Aidan says I'll die soon—"

"Shush and eat," Taivan said.

No one rushed. Whiskey deemed Khair the weakest and laid his head on her lap, looking up with baleful brown eyes.

"Aidan will stay awake," Taivan said. "But there's no guarantee he'll be there the entire time, so he's an alternate."

He laid out their names in bold and sloppy handwriting, threw them into a thankfully washed sneaker, and passed it to her. "Do the honors."

Sophie leaned back, eyes closed. Jiao hunched forward, concentration lines on her forehead. Davids laid his hand across the back of his chair, mimicking relaxation as if he'd never seen it, while Aidan piled mac and cheese on his burger.

Taivan massaged a knot in his left hamstring and flicked vegetables at the disappointed dog.

She didn't have to pick his name. He'd chosen her as his confidant. After he'd spent twenty years with Aidan, she wouldn't be. She'd be alone again. Besides, maybe he was sacrificing his time for his people, but maybe he didn't truly trust any of them still.

He'd trusted her to do this.

Just to cheat.

But she'd agreed. Maybe not aloud, but she'd let him trust her.

"Taivan." She messed up, said his name before she'd fully opened the slip.

He exhaled slowly, and Sophie pat his shoulder in a spooked, placating gesture, not seeing his ghost of a smile.

***

In only a few days, they had prepared everything they could, and Khair stood in their ferry, trying to convince herself to get into the doctube.

Khair was halfway up a rollercoaster, jerking higher on some shaky, possibly rotten wooden frame, too high up with no way off. She sat at the edge of the doctube while soldiers slept around her. What did their fluctuating gauges mean?

"Here's your lines, Moore: 'Don't be stupid, Khair, we won't steal your memories again for absolutely no reason whatsoever.'"

At this point, she wouldn't mind General Pastry answering.

Someone knocked, and Taivan entered.

"Do you have a plan to get the map?" Khair said. "Or do I have to ask again in twenty years?" By the time they reached the *Hopper*, the *Osiris* would be flagged and their faces were notorious.

"We'll forge authentications, pose as security audit," Taivan said. "Aidan will try it out in a few timelines."

"We don't have their uniforms."

"We're not going against ZAX suppliers or security. This is UOD themselves. They wear civvies."

Moore didn't respond, didn't try to keep her cover. Was she alive? How would she change in these decades?

"You gonna ask me to stay awake?"

"Wish I could." He sat beside her. "Sacrifice looks different for all of us today."

She sighed. "But wait, there's more. Let me guess: Jiao won't be better when we wake up?"

"No, it's linked to consciousness and movement. Sophie'll work on it. She really does want to stay up and Aidan hasn't seen any scenario where she lives long, so I'm letting her."

Her stomach clenched, but she nodded. Losing him to Aidan, an immortal time-traveler, wasn't so bad, but to a kid who'd tried to kill her, her sorta drinking buddy?

Can't you say 'love only increases with practice' or some nonsense? Scold me for acting like a toddler who found out her mom's pregnant?

"Are you really being nice staying awake, or do you just not trust her to do it alone?" Khair asked.

"Yes."

Then she just studied her friend. Felt like she was handing him to the grave, though he'd only be a few years older than her. She handed him Batu's hat. "Hold on to it for me. And if I don't remember anything, tell me—" she shrugged. "Give it to Jiao."

He took it.

"You're not allowed to see me as a child when I wake up. I'm doing this for you. I trust you."

He stood and offered her his hand, helping her into the 'tube. "I trust you, too."

"And not just cause I've nowhere else to go?" She kept talking so he wouldn't shut the door, though his hand held hers below the glass. "Cause if I wasn't Albion's queen, I'd be security. Do you see what they do all day? Smoke with their buddies and help old ladies catch their train to collect gossip. It would be wonderful."

"I'd call in threats just to keep it interesting." He hit the button, and the door started to shut.

She released his hand but kept her eyes open, fighting against the numbness in her eyes, the dryness in her throat. "That's why we'll always get along."

Part IV

It tastes like old cough syrup the first time
    you realize you could be wrong. You try to stay
    strong but that gulp of scruples, tribal crime,

    scratches at the back of your throat. Swallow
    hard, but that new knowledge or found falsehood
    opened a cut that at first seems shallow

    yet you feel it with every sour morsel.
    So, you put yourself on a diet, eat soft
    foods, your digestion too weak for forceful

    fare. But it doesn't satisfy. Hungry,
    starving, you guzzle poison, call it sweet,
    though that fuel roils, you still store it dumbly.

    Yet you know. You must taste the difference.
    Keep me from my saccharine ignorance.

"Lines on Easter" Tamika Moore, 532 DH

The First Casualty in Twenty Years

"I ABSOLUTELY HATE HIM." Khair jumped out of the doctube, joints cracking like popcorn cooked by fireworks. An automated system had freed her, not even a personal 'hey, did the rogue frenemy soldier in your head take over yet?'

A hundred soldiers shook off goop, globs melting on the floor. It was in her ears, between her toes, up her nose. Ew, how often did their systems recycle it and where did their waste go?

Some questions were best left unanswered.

But 'where were her friends?' wasn't one of them. Her soldiers parted for her. They weren't excited about being awake after twenty years; it seemed like waking from a deep nap that left the impression of the bed on the arm, with no outside connection to prove otherwise.

As she circled the room's perimeter, the shower bay opened, cheap toiletries waiting on floors reeking of bleach. The door to the rest of the ship stayed closed.

"If I didn't know better, I'd think he was up to something," she said to whoever was closest.

They gave her the standard 'yes ma'am, whatever you say ma'am, screw off ma'am.'

The shower water was lukewarm. Her skin was paler, hair only a few centimeters longer than her usual fade, skinnier body not as responsive as before.

Twenty years for this?

You retire yet, Sergeant?

No answer.

Khair sighed and sat on her doctube, legs dangling. They were vulnerable here. A hundred soldiers, four similar chambers nearby, with sealed doors and no windows. There was nothing in the room except the doctubes extending from the walls, recessive lights, cold tile floors, and an off-line comm system.

What happened to the comms? They were pulled out of the wall, the line cut. Pirates would've jettisoned the 'tubes or kept them under for ransom. The only people that might've touched the comms were Taivan, Aidan, and Sophie. Sure, Sophie had reason to mutiny, but she was with Aidan, and Aidan was with Taivan.

Aidan had betrayed his sister, could see the future to play a long game, and was a despot in at least one future.

Couldn't think like that. Not when there was absolutely nothing she could do. But what was the other option, pretend malicious, tech savvy mice had eaten through the one wire she needed?

Well, she had doctubes. They had a max speed nearly a hundred kilometers per hour and weighed a ton. Eventually, it'd beat through that door.

'Oh no, Khair, be precise, 100kph x 1000 kilos equals some amount of force I don't know without the conversion factor and the noise would alert enemies, but sure, break things.'

Wait. If Moore had retired or transferred, she would've given a heads up to ensure Khair didn't snitch. What if she had died? What would happen to Khair? Maybe she'd been in a 'tube, too? Or if Moore was being investigated, UOD might let her continue and incriminate herself.

How much of her mind could they read?

"Can anyone fix this comm?" Khair asked.

Given that they had no supplies, and the wires were cut, the answer was no.

She did pushups, moving to pretend she wasn't trapped. Then she lay flopped on a grimy floor while her soldiers decided they should also do pushups, which gave her secondhand embarrassment for their horrendous form.

UOD couldn't read her mind. If they did, they had enough to arrest Moore and kill her, unless she was allowed to live as their window into Taivan's operations. But then, wouldn't they have replaced Moore?

It was safest to assume UOD had access to everything she saw and all cameras in the vicinity.

Even if it was still only Moore in her head, would Moore help? She had aided Davids and Coloma, but there were no nearby civilians here, and she hated Taivan.

Khair did more pushups, shook the soreness from her arms, and tried to rip the doctube from its berth. Couldn't do it. A kid beside her pushed a button and the 'tube floated free.

If this ship was taken, she'd need all five hundred soldiers.

If this ship was taken, Taivan was dead.

She marched around the door like she circled an enemy. The metal sounded thick when she knocked, no window, its handle a bar, its lock a heavy magnet. It'd be easier to jar that magnet loose than bend a hole in the metal door.

She squeezed shampoo at the cameras in the corner of the room.

"Anyone smart knows how to make an electrogizmo battery, one of those spiny wire tricks?" She'd watched Albion classes doing science experiments in a park, so now she was fully qualified to make a baking soda volcano.

"If you want an electromagnet, you'd need an electric current." The speaker had a caterpillar on his face some might call a mustache, with a nose almost fat enough to hide it.

"Can't you get that from electrolytes in citrus like that lemony soap?"

"That's water and alcohol." Said his stentorian-voiced companion, her problem being a lack of a nose, which did not distract from the wispy mustache.

"Oh, it's a group project now. Great." Khair needed them. She just couldn't care. If Moore was gone and someone else watched her, she'd have better odds squaring up against a bear than beating UOD.

Even if Taivan controlled the ship, she'd have to leave her team. They didn't have enough resources for some triple agent thing, and she couldn't guard her mind constantly.

"Can you get us out, or can I break something?"

No answers. Guess that happened when she played whack-the-initiative.

She pushed the doctube in front of the door while her soldiers waited for her to tell them how everything was not in fact a forgot-to-turn-the-oven-off level debacle.

"I don't know why we're locked in here, but we'll find out." They shifted at the 'we.' "You don't have weapons or anything, but really, it's just the weapons and the armor we'll miss. If we gotta fight, we will. Otherwise, we'll raid the chow hall."

Even that didn't earn a cheer.

She called over the mustache twins and had them program the 'tube.

Normal room clearing procedure had everyone form a line outside the door, but with a hundred soldiers that was stupid. She arranged them in three columns, the most that could fit through the door, and told them not to trip over each other. Rush into the next room and keep moving, grab anything that could be a weapon.

Their only defense was to charge, rest on numbers and courage.

The doctube rammed the door. The sound pounded through the room, hopefully muffled on the other side. The door didn't budge. They pulled the 'tube back farther to ensure it reached maximum velocity, which caused a barely perceivable dent.

Her pulse should race, shouldn't it? She could be walking into an ambush again, first in line, as soon as she was shot, she'd be trampled. But what else could she do?

Send others first. Though they might not move, so she'd have to stand in line to die.

The doctube hit the door, and its front compressed slightly. Okay, now 'what else could she do' wasn't a rhetorical question. Maybe she could stack two or three doctubes?

She had the sappers—sappers, ha, with hospital gowns for armor they weren't exactly Ptolemy's legions—stand aside, then jiggled the handle and simultaneously smashed her shoulder into the door. Unsurprisingly, that did not work.

"Are there emergency releases?" Khair said. "If I set something on fire, will the smoke trigger the door?"

"Yes, but it'd mean we had died of smoke inhalation," Bad Mustache 1 said.

Back to the doctube, then. Five minutes later and they were still at it, while the other soldiers sat on the ground, wincing at the sound.

She was about to do pull-ups on the shower rods until she thought of something when Taivan opened the door for a woman in a crisp suit.

Who was hit by a 1000 kg coffin at 100 kph and died before she saw danger.

Reasonable People

KHAIR SCRATCHED HER NECK as blood dripped down the walls and slid down Taivan's chin. Chips of bone had sprayed across the room like cookie dough flung off a mixer.

She gagged.

Like, poor lady but it wasn't a bad way to go, especially if it meant she didn't have to look at that sad, broken skull whose concave break sorta looked like a frowny face and—it sounded like Batu hit by a car in Coloma, before she caused the accident.

Why was she like this?

At least she'd didn't hurl till others did and the smell got to her.

Forty-three-year-old Taivan wiped flecks of wet flesh from his square jaw and spoke into his comm: "Change of plans, wake them all."

Khair spat out chunks of vomit. "Who was she?"

"Our UOD liaison, supposed to verify us and our ship before letting us board the *Hopper*." His voice hadn't changed. He spoke a little softer, a little slower, but the same bass, somehow wry and earnest.

"Ah, the *Hopper*. So are we fighting a rabbit or grasshopper, cause I don't want to kill a cute bunny." Didn't want to kill anything, with this stench of guts and half-digested food between them.

"The *Hopper* doesn't have guns, but it's accompanied by two Dreadnoughts and seven destroyers."

So, she had just murdered their best of boarding that ship and finding the time machine's coordinates. "I'm sorry."

He'd woken her with no one and no clue again, but that'd be a private discussion in a soundproof room. And she was sorry. She'd never know that woman as an enemy, never see the worlds and lives her machines ruined. Just another person she'd killed without thought.

Khair's eyes clouded.

Taivan folded his coat over the body and walked past her to their soldiers. "Welcome back. Your planet is safe, a ZAX colony, although Albion is ruled primarily by Minister Naguib and mostly unchanged. Once we accomplish this mission with the *Hopper,* you can contact your families."

Meaning stealth would no longer be an issue.

"Until then, we have news and transmissions from home." When he spoke, he had little wrinkles in the corner of his eyes. He was handsome still, a hair taller in the lessened gravity, though he'd never be accused of being tall, broader but not as lean—not stout, if anything, a healthier weight. His hair was shorter and salted; he might've fixed that but, no, he had twenty years of preparation, and it showed.

"We'll catch you up on food, vaccines, and med-checks, then you're off the clock as long as you stay in your duty uniform and keep your tools ready."

As soldiers raced to the chow hall, Taivan directed her toward their conference room. His walk was off.

"If you have any side-affects," Taivan said to her, now that they were alone. "Sophie has medicine for headaches and anti-nausea."

She had plenty of nausea, but none of it related to the doctube. "What can she give you?"

"I'm good, just a little overkill in the gym."

"You seem better." His shoulders weren't hunched in an Atlas impression, and he wore the Khanate warrior's thumb ring.

He raised an eyebrow and kept walking. He hadn't decorated, outdated memorandums and memes graffitiing the halls. "Dangerous ground. You mean to say I wasn't perfect?"

"That's why I'm here, isn't it? To not let you point at a horse and call it a deer." As Chancellor Zhao Goa prepared for a coup, he brought a deer before the emperor and called it a horse. The young emperor asked if he was mistaken, and Gao asked his fellow officials. Those who agreed with Gao had lived.

"Then I'd have to cut you down."

The years had sanded off the edges, time to see what blade it forged. "Or abandon me in a locked room with no communication."

He slowed. "Albion mechanics missed a damaged wire in the safety check and we didn't have a replacement. It was a fire hazard. You were only supposed to be awake for a minute before we showed up; the inspection took longer than expected."

"Hm."

"It was bad luck; no reasonable person would hold you responsible. If anything, I—"

"Com'on, Taivan. Have you seen such a mythical beast as a reasonable person?" There was no sound but their squeaking boots. "How did you stand peace?"

"I'll tell you when I find it. All we heard was news of war, and there was nothing to do but stay the course. Can't complain though, it's not like we suffered."

"Maybe not. How were things with Sophie and Aidan?"

He stopped outside the conference room, Sophie and Davids arguing inside. "Aidan and I always get along. Sophie argued at me and I ignored her the first year. Then I figured out everything I could without more intelligence and got bored, so we married because she wanted to plan a ceremony. Worst three days of my life. Then she planned the divorce, which was far more celebratory."

"Congratulations?"

He pushed the door in and smirked. "None of that happened."

"What—"

He entered before she could punish him.

There was no feast, but there was expresso, milk tea, and chocolate-covered coffee beans. Three walls had been painted with scenes of the peasant rebellion at the start of *Romance of the Three Kingdoms,* the normally villainous rebels painted with their faces. But the project was abandoned, the last wall mere splotches of paint. Glowing lanterns and beads hung from the ceiling, green and gold tinsel draped around otherwise spartan chairs.

Sophie sat in the captain's chair, presumably responsible for the basket in front of everyone's spot. Jiao and Davids hadn't opened their present, so Khair only snuck a peek. It was dark.

"Eva Dufort, the UOD liaison, was killed," Taivan said.

"That better be a bad joke. She was decent, actually understood cosmic inflation and the horizon problem, unlike you lot." Sophie's freckles had faded, and she'd almost learned to put on makeup without looking like a ghoul, but there were blonde highlights in her red hair so she must still be blind. "Was it an accident?"

"Yes," Taivan said. "But I doubt they'll see it like that."

Khair hugged the basket to her chest.

"Now we need another way onto the *Hopper*."

As if Dufort's life meant nothing, while Moore's dead polymaths asked what was stupider than killing someone over their ruler's quarrel despite no personal animosity. Standing by and letting the other guy's ruler take over the multiverse, obviously. But how come the casualties were normal people and not the rulers responsible? Although, in this case, she was responsible.

Khair raised her hand.

"And we can't sneak anyone into Dufort's coffin and invade like Ragnar Shaggypants."

She lowered her hand. "Then I'll take a bathroom break or make some other convenient escape before I ruin everything."

"We need everyone, baghatur."

"I'm not talking about any mission stuff until I figure out what's going on with my chip, and if everyone's okay. Davids, still handsome, no signs of oppyin—" His nose flared. "I mean, how's Westley? Maybe we can go on a camping trip very far away from important meetings."

"Back to busin—" Taivan said.

"I want to see a picture of Westley," Sophie said.

Davids pulled him up, though Sophie grinned at her own joke. The baby Khair had seen weeks ago was a grown man now, with his mother's sapphire eyes and his father's midnight hair, too thin, with a smoldering anger that was all his own.

"He's beautiful," Khair said.

Davids turned off the picture. "Seriously!"

"I'm not into him. He's just pretty. Aidan, you like art, back me up."

Aidan brought up other pictures, Westley Davids studying UOD's approved curriculum, bragging about a cramped apartment as soldiers patrolled in the background. "He is pretty, and I am into him."

Davids snorted. "No, you're not, you geriatric—"

Aidan passed to family pictures with Westley's mother and another man.

Davids stopped talking.

"At least your ex seems desperate," Aidan said. "One ear is bigger than the other, his—"

"Enough," Jiao said.

Aidan flipped past, which brought up Wes and his other dad playing soccer in an alley, playing poker and betting canned beans, playing guitar. Aidan turned it off. "He uses nylon strings. How good can he be?"

Sophie plopped her basket over Aidan's head.

"It's what I wanted," Davids said softly. "A good life for my son. Taivan, can we trade with the *Hopper*? This ferry, with its doctubes, and Dufort's body."

"It's not remotely close to the coordinates' value," Taivan said.

No one else spoke. Clearly, Davids had said all he wanted to about it.

"How long do you need to find the coordinates?" Khair asked.

"Depends on their cybersecurity, but probably at least half an hour," Taivan said.

Khair opened her basket. A mocktini, bread with raisins and cherries, apple tarts, baklava, and pancakes with creamy filling. Batu's orange hat at the bottom. She grabbed it as if it might disappear, reverently scratched at the flecked sauce stain. She nodded thanks to Taivan and ate a pancake.

"What are you doing?" Taivan said.

"Enjoying myself while I can. Sophie, this is awesome. When did you learn to cook?"

"When people wrote down recipes, and I became literate. The men made the bread."

"Wonderful," Khair said. "I would've preferred they learned cartography, but hey. How can you get into their computers? None of us are hackers."

"Dufort had half the access code," Taivan said.

"And the other half?"

When he didn't answer, Khair poured mocktini in her espresso.

"What were you thinking?" Jiao said.

Though it'd only been a day for Jiao, she seemed the most changed. Even Sophie, an adult now, dressed similarly, had the same expressions, the same color scheme and sweet tooth.

But Jiao slumped in her chair, head barely visible over the basket. Her voice was strained, and the translator didn't pick up all her mutterings.

"I made allies," Taivan said. "Hoelun, Timur, and Dogface will join us." Chuluun had nicknamed them years ago, but none had reclaimed their name. "Once we get the coordinates, we'll be able to seize it."

"How long will they wait?" Khair asked.

"They're not waiting, they're recruiting," Taivan said.

"What stops them from selling out and killing us?" Jiao said. "There's not a Duke Xiang among them." Xiang allowed his enemies to regroup after crossing a river and promptly lost the battle; he'd died praising his own honor.

"Open your basket," Sophie said.

Davids pushed it toward Jiao when she didn't move, but she gave him such a withering glance he hid his hands below the table. Jiao's movements were sure, but pain carved through her face. She looked to Sophie, not touching the contents.

"I made it. You'll maintain motor functions at all times, you can fly. Unless it doesn't work," Sophie's voice trailed off, and she added loudly: "I tased myself, and it worked."

"So, it doesn't prevent pain. It forces her to work through it?" Khair said.

Everyone but Jiao glared at her.

"It's perfect," Jiao said. "Taivan, tell them you'll auction that code if they don't buy it back."

Taivan called. "I have half of your computer's access code. If anything happens to my ship or crew, it'll be uploaded to the net. If you don't buy it back, I'll broadcast it to the entire 'verse."

"That's not necessary," a professionally dressed man said, frantically typing a message to his boss and signaling his coworker. "We—"

Taivan hung up.

Jiao activated her comm. "This is Admiral Jun. I piggybacked General Taivan's signal and heard him demand you buy your code back, correct?"

"Correct." This speaker dauntlessly struggled to stay awake—the other guy must have run to his superiors.

"He's put malicious code on it. Once you use it, your firewall will disintegrate."

The lackey put them on mute.

"Jun," the new man's voice was vaguely familiar, exuding condescension in a single word. "You can't expect us to trust Jochiin's lapdog."

Jiao, who had apparently missed her calling in customer service, didn't change her tone. "I've given my name and business. Who are you?"

"Someone about to call your bluff and blow you out of the sky. We suspect you've already murdered Dufort and if not, she's only a grade five."

Khair mouthed 'Captain Cinnamon Roll.' Jiao rolled her eyes and pointed to Khair's basket of pastry. She sent them a message. *That's Colonel Croissant? Strudel? Sergeant Moore's commander.*

Moore was stationed here.

The Remix Nobody Wanted

MOORE, WE'RE CLOSE. K HAIR meant to tell her to hold on, but with UOD listening, she made it sound like a threat.

Taivan researched Strudel. After passing flaky dough pockets, he discovered Dana Strudel had been a colonel in the United States Army on Earth back when Ito was president before transferring to United Oversight for Democracy. He'd reportedly died that year. But this wasn't a descendent—his speech cadence and verbiage matched exactly. He had stepped through time—through another 'verse and back again, not knowing where he would land.

What power could match that?

"Strudel," Jiao said. "I'll separate the malware from the password, you'll get both a zero-day hack and—"

"You're not touching our computers."

Khair probed around for Tamika Moore, expecting a shock, but there was no reaction.

She found an image of the woman tinkering in her head.

Khair had been in Moore's body, but never seen her. Her uniform was squared away except for grass stains barely visible against the camouflage, coils twisted in a severe bun, with a soldier's build. Smile forced, teeth too white, eyes older than her stated age, a birthmark on her chin but otherwise nondescript.

So stupid normal.

"I can hand it over," Jiao said. "But I don't trust our networks to send it. Let Taivan board, I'll go with him, split us and I'll make the trade."

Moore had been transferred to UOD as their power eclipsed their
nation's—not officially, but evident in the allocation of resources and shielding
legislature, power leached from elected bodies and law to bureaucracy and
memorandums. Her trail ended after she'd been sent to UOD's space station.

"He doesn't board this ship," Strudel said.

Khair delved into public records. Nothing. Moore didn't even get an obituary.
The only sign of her was a doting pre-canned graduation letter to her son in a
museum of early space pioneers, but it wasn't dated.

"That's nonnegotiable." Jiao's hand twitched. Davids offered her the brace,
but she ignored it. "He doesn't trust me anymore. If I go alone, he'll shoot me
down."

A long pause, long enough for Khair to flip through Moore's personal
life according to the museum. Born in Montana (America, but it looked like
the steppe) five hundred years ago, enlisted after high school though she had
scholarships—they were about to go to war, married some string-bean mechanic,
had three gremlins. She'd been thirty-six when she disappeared, her kids between
eight and twelve. The youngest died generations ago.

"If Jochiin enters the ship," Strudel said. "Mercy Mission 7701 must
accompany you."

They thought they could control her. ***Moore, if you're alive, start —***

She tried to scream as her muscles froze before the pain even started. The
voltage was higher than ever—the metal in her head seemed to vibrate and
overheat.

What the fuck did I tell you about giving me orders?

Sophie helped Khair ease to the ground. Moore had made her stop cussing; her
cursing meant something. But she couldn't think.

"7701," Strudel said. "Is Jochiin with you and Jun?"

Taivan tiptoed toward the door.

Khair wheezed, so out of breath, Taivan had time to sneak out. "No."

Sophie checked Khair's pulse. Sophie's comm pinged, Davids asking how to
help. She sent back medication for arrhythmia, muscle relaxants, and a ventilator.

She expected this to last awhile.

"Let me rephrase," Strudel said. "What does Jun intend?"

Khair stared at one tile on the wall as the room spun. "Maybe to end her pain. Please—"

"I can do my own negotiations," Jiao said. "Colonel, I'll bring your abomination with me."

Khair blinked.

"But I want assurances. You—"

"Jochiin will upload the access code if attacked, that's guarantor enough. What else do you want? Don't look for medical assistance. You'll only find that in Davids' oppyin."

"Shut up," Khair said.

Strudel waited, apparently, for her to start sizzling. But Sophie was loosening her jacket, making sure she could breathe, and Moore let it go.

"Pledge Taivan's safety; I don't want to owe him anything." Now that it was only Aidan left at the table, Jiao reached for her brace. "And I want a jet with three times my weight in gold."

"Out of everything you've seen, what's finally made you flee?"

"Now it's three times your weight, Colonel." The brace slipped and fell to the ground. Jiao looked at it as if it lay across Andromeda.

"Agreed. There's an alternative if you can bring me Jochiin Taivan and Aidan Riley."

"I don't make the cut?" Sophie flipped them off with a gentle smile to Khair, but she couldn't return it.

If they wanted Aidan, they knew about his time-traveling abilities, otherwise Sophie was more dangerous.

"You've seen us erase parts of human consciousness. We can also transfer it," Strudel said. "Your body will suffer, but you don't have to. We have bodies in doctubes here, criminals all. You could take your pick."

"We're criminals," Khair said when Jiao didn't look properly revolted.

She got shocked, but since Sophie refused to let go of her hand, there wasn't enough voltage to hurt anything but her dignity and her jabbering heart.

Congratulations, killer of free speech.

Apparently not, but we can try again.

We? The 'we' could be her and Moore, but then the 'you'—Khair—had been in a different category. Moore wasn't alone.

"I can't give you Aidan. He'll be at the helm," Jiao said. "But I'll give you Taivan."

"Whoa, whoa, whoa," Khair said. "No one asked what I want. I know your chippy bird in my head is a person who thinks they're clever cause they know words with a few syllables—*polysyllabic*—"Like 'addendum' and 'queue.'" *That's one syllable.* "If you want me to cooperate, I get to see that bitch face to face and tear her face off."

Pain hit, and as she blacked out, she realized maybe she did need to work on her vocabulary.

***

She woke, heart pounding, a mask blowing steam into her face, two abnormally strong adhesives on her exposed side and chest. A woman with dyed hair and half a dozen earrings hovered over her.

She tried to push her away, which turned into holding her arm at a joint, for support or snapping, whichever was needed. "Who are you and who am I?"

Man is Born Free...

DON'T PANIC. IF YOU start hurting people, I'll shock you again.

"There's something in my head." None of her words escaped the mask on her face. "Who else hears the angry robot?"

She ripped the mask off, though the warm air was the only vaguely comfortable thing going on, and howled when the doctor yanked off resuscitating stickies.

But I don't want to hurt you. Did the voice change? It almost sounded like a person.

"Guys, I'm right here," she said. "Not to be old, but can't we just talk to each other? Who are you people? I can't— oh shit."

She couldn't remember anything.

There were four people. A man in his mid-thirties, somehow classy in jeans and leather boots, a revolver on his hip, with broad shoulders but sunken eyes. A wiry man in his twenties sporting a red beard and full sleeve tattoos, eyes ancient and mischievous. A young hottie with a spidery brace and a Mustang dragoon. Like wow, even wearing modest pajamas she was—all of them, really—were beautiful.

People were good. Not as strong as ants or as durable as turtles, but people had their expressive faces and unique clothes and she was tearing up now because she was like these people. She was good.

You can be. But not everything is as it appears: listen to me and verify later, we don't have a lot of time.

"Stay still." Said the doctor with pale green makeup, jingling bracelets, and scars where her eyes should be. Well, not everyone could be a winner. How was she a doctor, anyway? Cause if the doc messed up and put a robot in her head, she was gonna sue and comfort herself on a pile of money.

"Are you a cyborg?" She asked the woman with the brace, a metal arm on each of her limbs from her arm to her fingers.

"No." Cyborg drew an orange hat from a box.

"Would've been neat, but okay—at least you have metal knuckles." She punched air to demonstrate, aiming at the doctor. "And you. What did you do to me? I don't like you, witchy." Wait, she needed her. "Much. At first. But now you're not too bad."

Why would you say that? I thought you were trying to be good.

I didn't say I'd try anything, but maybe I'll try eating fish-eyes or squid. Is that yummy?

"I'm not a witch, but I've made advances in necromancy," the doctor said. "Though our enemies beat me to it."

"I get sucked off into the timeweb," the tattooed man said.

"And I'm Princess Khutulun. We're all special." She knew that name, but nothing about it. Maybe she was? Then she would order them to massage her feet, draw her a hot bath, and haul this weirdo out of her head.

Don't assume yet. Wait, watch. You don't have much data to extrapolate from or use to interpret sensory information.

You're boring.

"What's that voice in your head saying?" Classy man didn't sound concerned, but his hand rested on his lap by his gun. "It's not your friend. Why don't you lie down and rest—"

She groaned. "I'm not tired, just very sore and sorta weak, and hungry for fish eyes."

Beautiful Cyborg looked at the tattooed man. He sighed. "It's trying to teach you how to learn, isn't it? Don't bother. People used to be disgustingly democratic, thought truth was like light through a prism and everyone got to see a shade. No. If you stand on a planet, it looks stable, though it's moving thousands of kilometers an hour—we have to get above ourselves and the world or we know nothing. We can't."

Cyborg raised an eyebrow.

Tattooed man shrugged. "But fret not. Knowledge represents what is, the definite, uncertainty means possibility. So, sample whatever nonsense your friend tells you, as long as you don't let any idea consume you."

"Aidan, Buck, Sophie," Cyborg said. "Give us the room, please." Her tone was stoic, but there were undercurrents of emotion there, slippery fish too quick to catch.

Cyborg stood beneath streamers and banners and lanterns. Yellow glitter stuck to her brace, ignoring the gin and scones on the table.

"What do you think of this?" Cyborg waved to the wall.

Thousands of people in yellow turbans rallied beneath steep mountains, red and purple rocks stippled across the sides, snow tumbling from the peaks but not reaching the plain. It was a parched land, but the world under the vast, clean sky was a part of her. More than her, less than her. She couldn't survive there, and neither could the crowd.

It called to her nonetheless.

She had been painted in the crowd, with Aidan, Buck, Cyborg. They were all dressed for war, swords in one hand, lunch in the other, but they laughed. She stood in the middle of them. One of them. There was a man beside her, his picture inviting, so she caressed his cheek, expecting the paper to be warm and soft. "You look happy here, somehow."

Cyborg kneaded the ugly hat.

"Have you been happy? Doesn't seem anyone is, but maybe you're all too grown-up." She was kidding, mostly.

"It's better to accept circumstances and limitations, hungering only to do good without being satisfied." She stuttered. "We've done things, Khair. Now we should never be happy."

Khair. What a stupid, common name. "What sort of 'we'?"

"You thought of me—Jun Jiao—as a daughter or younger sister."

Awkward. "Liar."

Only family could look that pissed, nothing but a shift in her not-daughter's jaw, light in her face, a cold fire in her eyes. That phrase, light and fire, was familiar—not something she'd said, something far older, as permanent as those mountains. But it was nothing to her now. "Then fix your thoughts."

"Fine, JJ. Who am I and why did my memory fly away?"

Jiao sat beside her on the floor, leaning against a chair. "What do you remember?"

"Words." Khair had no personal history, and universal history was only vague contours: isolated individuals or kingdoms, the story connecting basic facts evaporated. "Numbers." But calculation was iffy. "I can read people's expressions, name them, but it's distant."

She swallowed. "So, I'm stupid and psychotic."

What do you know morally?

Residue that only streaked, no matter how many times they tried to clean it.

What'll you give me for it?

Nothing, then.

Or maybe I don't owe you anything. People had been pretty until they started making demands, but now there was no drive but survival—hers and her loved ones. Except that was no one.

Jiao reached for her leg, so sudden Khair flinched.

"What happened?"

Jiao squeezed her pant leg. "It'll pass."

"No, you need a doct—"

"They can't help." She closed her eyes and whispered something about torturous beans with a cadence only mostly mangled in translation.

Khair waited for it to pass. The lights swayed while laughing people walked by with squeaky shoes and Jiao grit her teeth so hard the veins in her neck showed. Her eyes fluttered twice before they opened.

Khair started to ask a question she hadn't quite settled on when Jiao spoke. "In two hours," her voice was soft, but sure, "we'll board an enemy ship and use their computers to steal a map. You have to be levelheaded by then."

"Why can't you steal oppyin or jade or something cool?"

That's the wrong question.

"How much is the map worth?"

She jumped, pain flaring from her spine to her fingers. **Why are you hurting me? I thought you wanted to be friends. You'll feel better if we are.**

"Don't speak until I'm done." Jiao hesitantly took her hand and told her the plan, if it could be called a plan.

"No thanks."

Jiao blinked. "What?"

"You haven't told me who I am or who you are and I'm supposed to go die with you? I just got here. You got to live for a long time already. It's not fair."

Give me Jiao's ship and gold, and I'll give you her and the rest.

She's like your sister.

Don't kill her, just capture her.

Jiao lay down a small recording disc. "It's your father's last moments before he sacrificed his life for the cause." Her throat bobbed. "I killed him for us. If it fails—"

Khair ripped her hand from Jiao's and backhanded her. "You killed our dad?"

She ignored her bruising cheek. "You should watch his last moments. He kept your family's memory alive—"

"Did you kill them too?"

"No!" She kept on, stammering, gave up, and held out the disgustingly orange hat.

"Convincing."

Jiao looked her in the eye for the first time. "You killed my family, half my entire planet. Jun Sung, Tan Jia, Jun—"

"Shut up." She massaged her head. "I get it now. Everything's bad. Has this been amusing enough for all you sickos? Can I just live now?"

"Of course you can't."

"Oh, I'm sorry, I didn't know beating yourself up would raise the dead."

"They're worth remembering." Jiao's voice was so tightly leashed it could snap if Khair tugged it a little more. Then they'd see who Jiao really was. "Are they worth more dead than you alive?"

"I made a deal saying you'd come." Jiao said, voice shaky with an attempt at imperialism. "I'll give you anything you want to join us for one job."

"'Anything?' Begging's a good look for you, add a low-cut maid—"

Jiao smacked her. She pulled her hand back immediately, color draining. "I won't apologize, you—"

Khair tackled her. The intruder didn't have time to stop her; there was no way to shock her without hurting Jiao.

Jiao had learned some tricks and the sectional joints of the brace pinched, but in this life and any other, Khair could fight. She pinned Jiao, knee across her stomach and the gun's holster, elbow across her neck, fist poised.

The fight was over. But it was still fun, Jiao's pulse throbbing beneath her forearm, her sweat sealing them. She leaned into her arm, Jiao's eyes widening and whitening, grasping at her face, but she batted the weakening hand aside.

Whatever mercy you show, you'll receive in kind.

"Why don't you say hello to my father?"

But Khair eased up, waited for Jiao to hit back and make it interesting.

Jiao twisted her thumb. She leaned back long enough for Jiao to throw the chair at her. She covered her head, laughing for joy at the game.

Jiao struck her palm against Khair's ribs, wriggled free and grabbed Khair's arm, tried to lock and break the elbow. Already enough pressure to hurt. Khair punched her, and she dropped. Khair kept contact so she didn't get shocked, pinning her again.

The blood bubbling from Jiao's nose turned her stomach. It didn't slow her.

Jiao grabbed her collar, but she kept striking. Jiao had finally clutched Khair's neck when she howled and curled in on herself, tapping out against an invisible opponent that didn't care.

That better not be contagious.

Jiao was too preoccupied trying to breathe to fight and Khair had obviously won so she slid off her, but didn't release her wrist.

"Shh, you're okay. I won't hurt you anymore," Khair said. "Give me a life-pod off to a major trade route for pickup."

Space isn't a crowded highway, you'd starve, everyone thinking you were worthless space junk. Which isn't far off presently.

"I won't be your hostage." Jiao plugged her bleeding nose. She had never reached for her gun. "Do one job and you're free and well paid; fight us and you're alone in space on a hostile vessel."

My partner took a bathroom break, and he talks to everyone on the way. I've got twenty minutes. It sped up, human voice no more modulated than the computer mask. *I had to shock you, severely, to maintain cover. This was an unexpected side-effect. I'm sorry.*

Really sorry? Guess it's okay I'm three brain cells from a zucchini.

I'll make it up to you.

Her memories played in her mind's eye, the earliest first, while she stood outside of time and watched them, feeling everything she once had.

...Yet Everywhere He Is In Chains

IT WAS LIKE FLYING out of thick clouds and seeing the world again. If there was a giant storm tossing the plane around and obscuring the ground in silvery fog, and she had an aisle seat, and the plane was on fire.

Khair couldn't move; Jiao spoke, but the words were scrambled.

She saw the past on closed eyelids. First the chaos of otherness—things like her she couldn't control, things unlike her she didn't understand—a manifold of smells and sensations in flux. Toddling around and finding warmth and hunger and exhaustion. And learning. How the moon shone in the evening, how to work the recycler, how to share candy and end up with the bigger half.

She had parents, of course, with normal, strained, happy lives. Enkhiin Batu and Ganyin Tuya. Two younger brothers and a youngest sister, Bataar, Tolui, Altani.

They'd wrestled together, though Tolui hadn't had the temperament for fighting. Milked yak and herded goats, searched caves for aluminum to sell for rocket fuel, though little Altani was a good cook and stayed home. Bataar had been closest to her age, so much smarter, so ready to be a man at thirteen, to contribute to the family.

Khair watched, but her presence wasn't even wind or shadow, a spectator viewing from an outsider's angle her past self hadn't seen. A reconstruction. Done by the intruder or her own imagination?

Bataar would've been a miner, Tolui a teacher, Altani a mother and handy-woman. Khair was supposed to be a veterinarian like her mother, but only because her parents saw how she admired soldiers bound for off-world wars.

Tuya and Bataar and Tolui and Altani stopped showing up.

One day, seventeen-year-old Khair threw dice with Bataar as he talked about a girl he was afraid to talk to and when she helpfully demonstrated all the ways he could be rejected, Tuya sent her out to help Batu fix the generator before the blizzard. Then she and Batu sat in a diner, Batu's face bandaged so he didn't see her poison her liver.

And for years she sat there while Batu struggled to provide and tried to apprentice or marry her into security, while she gave him nothing but contempt. Why had he kept trying?

Then came Chuluun.

He'd blasted through the People's Republic of Greater China's garrison on Irmeg while she'd slobbered on a counter. His men came looking for PRGC collaborators. Khair pointed to Kija and Nari, the old couple running her diner, and they were dragged off. Chuluun's recruiters offered her a job and how could she say no to free food and travel, a chance to do something, to be part of something, a chance to make someone else understand the pain of losing someone, to die?

But Batu joined with her.

They had machines to de-tox but the cleansing nearly killed her—though she had to piece that together through shreds of infantilizing impressions. And then she was off to become a soldier, already a brawler, but learned to take and give orders, to navigate land and space, treat combat wounds and work the comms for med-evac.

And she was good at it.

In theory, death was a relief. But she saw too many people spitting out last grunts on foreign fields to believe that was the answer, so death must be avoided at all costs. Any terrain trick, unsanctioned gear upgrades, awkward interpretations of orders, studying the best generals, watching PRGC propaganda, anything to stay alive.

When Chuluun had charged over an enemy parapet to get his hounded men to follow and no one had, she'd realized the land was too flat and desolate to flee. So, she'd sworn to shoot anyone who retreated, proved it, and followed him.

She was the first one up the walls—alive, she'd used her lieutenant's corpse as a shield—and fought to that raging mountain of a man. Whatever else Chuluun had been, there were bulls smaller and more timid. And with no hope but victory, she'd matched him. When it was over, he had her kneel, praised her prowess, laughed at the pumping human heart she held, and christened her 'Khair.'

Kerait Batuyin Tuya hadn't protested when her family heritage was erased. Batu had been left with the baggage and saw it propagandized. She'd ignored him when he asked about it. But she'd wept in private the first time he used it.

So many times, Batu tried to ask about it, asked her to come home or at least home to her name. But he saw she was sober, hoped this would give her purpose, help her heal.

It did. Chuluun inducted her into his inner circle, and if he had his eccentric tastes and ensnaring temper, well, the universe had always suffered under tyrants, so why not the tyrant she sparred and dined with?

But she cringed when she saw families crushed under houses or starved in fields. Cringed and crossed the street and forgot once she walked past. Yet she had to believe in something, so she believed in her men and getting their lazy, ingenious dumbasses home.

Years past, and her place drifted to the side. The PRGC officers Chuluun defeated and recruited spent their youth studying politics and history. But they wanted glory. She never fought unless she maneuvered so that the battle practically won itself. Chuluun elevated her, but never trusted her—she was too skilled, too ambivalent toward his politics. She was on the periphery when they took PRGC's last stronghold.

Their best troops stormed the military bases and the factories where the partisans camped. She seized the palace as Chuluun's honor guard. The palace would be left intact, a wooden facade intricately painted with greens and blues, figurines carved in the rafters, with thousands of untested safety features. The people weren't to be spared.

She hadn't blinked when she'd gotten that order. Not even an order, Chuluun mentioned 'no quarter' in the same sentence he'd asked whether canned or powdered vegetables provided more nutrients.

It'd been a hard week, and she'd seen her boys die, but she'd understood that; her people had fought PRGC the same way once. No, she was tired, couldn't imagine reining in her soldiers after all their labor and blood.

Chuluun hadn't been interested in their deaths, hadn't televised it or displayed their corpses. He cleared his new house like someone laying out mousetraps. If she'd spared the royal family efficiently, he wouldn't have cared, might've approved if it kept bullets from spoiling the wallpaper.

But she hadn't.

Bullets popped across the hall, but she and Chuluun gained the throne room unscathed. There the People's Republic died as it should, utterly wasted, spending everything in a final stand that showed it had been worth fighting for.

As Chuluun ascended to the throne, Khair a step behind, a girl jumped from behind the chair, steak knife slashing like a cub's claw. Khair knocked Chuluun aside, took the scratch on her forearm, and raised her pistol.

Khair gritted her teeth as Jiao shook her outside time, impotent as her other self pointed a familiar Mustang Dragoon 2587.

Jiao hadn't just been a princess; she'd been a tween kid. Her yellow dress was short at the ankles as she'd grown too fast for royal tailors, hair in loose pigtails, a polka dot purse overflowing with food and blankets slung over her shoulder. Every emotion her little mind ever processed was plastered on her face, but when Khair pointed the gun, it dissipated.

"No," Chuluun said. "Let their bravest warrior have her day."

Khair had grabbed Jiao's hand and flipped her so hard it'd knocked her wind out, twisted her wrist till it snapped. Jiao screamed and hit with her other hand. Khair let the harmless blow land and squeezed her broken wrist.

"And still, their only soldier with any heart." Chuluun kneeled beside Jiao. "I'll make the pain up to you, little one."

Somewhere else, Khair wept. She should've stayed on Irmeg and drunk herself into an early death.

No. She should've stayed with Batu, worked in the mine to give him a few peaceful years. She might have died of lung cancer after a short, dull life, with no friends and precious little family, but she would have done one, little, nameless, unremembered act of kindness. Not enough to redeem herself, not enough to bring Batu relief. But in an uncaring universe filled with evil people and their victims, she would've fulfilled a purpose, same as a worm that did nothing but eat dirt and die.

She couldn't even manage that.

In the palace, Batu saved her. He entered the throne room with his battered squad, Jiao seizing with fear at his barely human face despite the monster beside her. Batu saw Chuluun caressing a girl's chin, and his finger fell into the trigger well.

Khair shoved Jiao toward Batu. "The Conqueror says I've defeated their best warrior. Aren't you proud, father? Take her to my quarters and tend her arm. I don't want to hear her whine."

She unloaded the Mustang with her back turned and faced the kid. "Jia, isn't it, princess?" Her mother's name. "Your people are broken today. You're their leader now. If you set a good example, you'll be safe and one day you might get a chance to use this."

She handed Jiao the pistol and Jiao immediately aimed it at her face and pulled the trigger.

She and Chuluun laughed. She pat Jiao's head, an affront in the culture Jiao would be immersed in. "Don't die too soon, kiddo, I'd like to fight you for real some time. Keep the gun clean till then."

Chuluun waited till Batu and Jiao left. "You took the greatest prize without my permission."

He hadn't seen how Batu nearly killed him.

"She'd kill you, Boss."

Chuluun had snorted. "Worse ways to die. Don't test me again, Tuya," her old name, the name he had no loyalty to. "Or you'll find out."

So, she didn't.

When she saw Jiao harassed, she mocked the offender for choosing such frail opponents, but that was the extent of her intervention.

Taivan roared onto the scene and her past self had grudgingly loved him on sight, finally did something decent as she followed the precocious teen into battle to make sure he lived. The punk ended up saving her.

She knew then she wanted to go home, to have kids, love again, get a job where she could have a bad day without people dying. But Chuluun was generous, so she put it off. And what else could she do? Pretend she hadn't seen pits of discarded shoes? Guilt refused to let her do better.

And besides, there was no one she loved but Batu and Taivan, though she didn't love him enough to interfere with Chuluun's demands. Chuluun favored him, and Taivan didn't yield to anyone, so if he allowed it, it was weird, but—

She never believed it. But she was always busy, convinced herself she'd fix it after she ensured her soldiers had enough blankets, and drilled enough to keep out of trouble.

Could she have saved Chuluun? He hadn't kept it a secret, like he hadn't known it was wrong, and he'd been such a perfectionist he would've done anything to improve himself. Whatever else he'd been, he'd given her a life. Could she have saved his if she'd been loyal enough to confront him?

Probably not. But Taivan wouldn't have suffered alone.

Eventually, adult Taivan asked her to sign a petition requesting a more pragmatic style of war—code for an end to the atrocities so peace was possible. She'd made herself a distant assignment and when she returned, the other generals besides Taivan and Chuluun's brothers were dead.

All the while, she'd known it was wrong. Whether by innate law, the memory of her own grief, her parent's better example, she had known. So, she'd drunk to forget and pushed away Batu when he'd held her hair back.

He had spent his life caring for her and Jiao, no thought to his own comfort or advancement. How many years had he wasted?

She'd been wasted when Chuluun died.

Taivan had met her in practical armor instead of a white mourning dress, finally wearing what he willed. "You have one of the best Khanate armies and you can't use it properly."

He was twenty-two, a prodigy, and hadn't talked to her since she'd refused to sign his petition. But she'd kept her fleet near his. He didn't lose, and she didn't have much dirty work with him. Jiao captained his flagship.

"It's yours, then." She was hungover and more concerned with why the walls of her cruiser's best bar changed colors overnight and whether this corresponded to the paint under her nails.

"I need more than that," Taivan said. "Dogface is gathering soldiers too, and he'll draw large sections. I need you to be the warrior who charged a city alone to save my uncle."

"I had my men."

"Who would've fled without you."

There was something irritatingly ardent and genuine about him. "Or I could see what UOD would pay for your head."

"If you want money, invest. But if you want purpose, lead your army under me—"

"Like that part."

His jaw tensed, but old her hadn't noticed. "And I'll give you a planet."

She'd laughed. "Nah. Just give me a steady pay." She'd considered asking something for Batu, but she couldn't think of a single thing the old man would like except a foot massager and a hat with earmuffs. He did favor orange for some reason.

Taivan raised an eyebrow. "You don't want to ask what we'll be doing?"

"I've been with you long enough, Buddy Boy—Boss Man, now. I trust you not to screw me over." She'd winked and thought herself very clever. But then she realized he had very good reason to do just that, considering how he had clearly not been as fond of Chuluun as she'd pretended. "Or I would, anyhow, if you would swear an anda oath with me."

If he had done so without hesitation, she would have been wary, but it took him a moment and he shifted slightly. "I will."

For two years they'd been on the run, but somehow it was good fun, or seemed so now that she was safe. She had tried to tease Jiao and the woman nearly shot her every time, no matter how many times she saved Jiao's life until she saved Taivan's. Jiao had sent her tea.

But one of Taivan's generals had betrayed him and UOD closed in. They'd called with demands, including either she or a few officers now dead submit to the Mercy Mission. She'd agreed, hugged Taivan, saluted Jiao, and put on a bomb vest.

Major Strudel had sent the demands but was too important to be there, Staff Sergeant Moore waiting in the enemy cruiser instead.

"Kneel and put your hands on your head." Moore had a squad at her back, her pistol holstered and untouched.

Khair had worked with plenty of stiff, PRGC old guard, but still this woman annoyed her, her entire life not worth ten words.

She had smirked, hands shaking. She hadn't planned on getting here, expected to think of something or accidentally blow up. Hadn't considered how much her head would hurt, how her intestines would curl. How she'd miss the wastes of Irmeg.

"Squad, retreat to Bravo-3 hall." Moore casually rested her hand on her riot control pistol. "I see the vest, Batuyin. If you detonate it, my nation won't mourn. And you didn't survive nearly two decades of war to kill yourself for no strategic benefit."

Khair had wanted to, if only to beat Moore, but this woman who hadn't flinched at a bomb didn't lose if it detonated.

"Guess this means the deal's off." Khair was a few years older than Moore, ten centimeters taller, but she sounded younger, smaller.

"It doesn't have to be. Spare my life, I'll spare yours."

She'd snorted, watched in a small window as the *AKS Bankhar* shrunk into the void. "Yet only one of us will go on with our memories."

Moore had unclipped the holster. "Only one of us murdered across the galaxy."

Khair had raised her hands, sank to her knees. "Promise you won't remind me."

Moore had made no such promises.

***

After Khair was handcuffed and the vest disabled and removed, the images stayed with Moore, Moore's emotions roiling through Khair though hidden behind a proper military bearing.

Moore's memories?

Mercy Mission 7701, formerly Tuya Batuyin of the Kerait, also known as Khair, was sedated and her vitals were recorded. While inhuman amounts of alcohol were purged, tattoos removed, hair buzzed, lasers restored her vision, and she received much needed dental work, Tamika Moore watched from behind a glass wondering how she'd ended up here.

Khair reddened as her past self was handled like a zoo animal, stripped and examined, measured, showered with a hose, scars smoothed, and tied in that hospital dress. All recorded. Her old self, drugged so she could barely stand, bumbled and fought and flirt, unaware and not particularly concerned.

Tam considered the ordeal vulgar, particularly how familiarly they handled the prisoner, a woman who'd killed with her bare hands. They'd done this often.

This was cruel and unusual punishment instituted by a social body with no oversight, no transparency, and no claim over the people it punished. How did she fix this?

Definitely Moore's thoughts.

"What's the status, sergeant?" the major asked. His hair receded and his belly bulged, natural in a civilian his age, but an officer should set a better example.

"Everything's on schedule, sir."

"So relax. It's New Year's Eve. The soldiers shouldn't see leadership so homesick."

"It's not that, sir. I was just thinking that Sergeant Juarez is newly promoted. This could be a good trial run for him."

Shame on her. If this had to be done, she should conduct this evil, free her men of that burden. Though perhaps willingly doing evil was worse than if Juarez, who believed it right, did it.

"Not high enough profile, eh? Batuyin's an old fool." Batuyin could kill him, even in present condition. "But she was a general once. We can use her—after we've finished the leftover cookies and eggnog."

"I'll meet you there, sir, if I have time." She regretted it as she said it, basically dismissing her officer, but he was already chasing those cookies.

Tam had two of these missions already and had killed both within a week. It didn't feel right to kill from safety. But she had warned both women more than necessary and killed them only to save civilians.

Her mind believed it, but her body remembered every moribund sensation.

It'd been suicide by cop and she'd driven them to it. Felt their fear, a vast, deafening, constant waterfall, and their misting relief as consciousness ended. Rosa Aguilar and Nicole Vampatella. She didn't mourn them. But she understood her victims, and she remembered them long after anyone else did.

On paper, Batuyin was worse than either woman. The last hour hadn't endeared her; she talked incessantly with a voice that drowned out thought, had broken a nurse's nose for giving her a shot, and seemed genuinely surprised that was a problem. But Batuyin had agreed to this. Perhaps that would make a difference.

Or this whole thing, playing with time, playing with minds, playing god, was a sham to grasp at power.

Tam had gone through the authorized whistleblower channels and her complaints were ignored. How long was she supposed to wait? Especially now when she was centuries away and could see that her country had been hollowed out.

She'd sworn to uphold the Constitution and to obey the officers appointed over her. So, what happened when her officers flouted the Constitution? Was it not hers to interpret? Yet she was a citizen, not merely a soldier.

Maybe she was homesick, and eggnog and cookies would cure this. But it hadn't last year, or the year before.

Batuyin broke her thumb to free her shackled hand and grabbed for surgeon's scissors, leaning so far, she flipped her gurney. Tam rapped on the glass and yelled for the doctors to retreat, bursting in with her pistol drawn.

Batuyin ignored her until the gun hovered between her eyes.

Tam stayed out of arm's reach. "The worst is over. Wait five minutes and you won't have to worry about any of this."

Probably her own future. How else could the Mercy Mission stay relatively unknown unless they retired their own people that way? She'd be a worse person for it, but happier.

Batuyin was so high she'd left the atmosphere, ignoring the bone piercing her hand. "I'm cold, why am I in this ugly dress, didn't I have tattoos, I—"

She had a nearly overwhelming urge to cover the woman's mouth, but despite everyone's selective forgetfulness, she wasn't allowed to touch a prisoner except for consensual medical procedures. "Shut up and calm down, or you'll hurt yourself."

"Ohhhh," Batuyin looked up at her with the same trusting eyes as her Labrador Retriever. "Why don't I like you? You have a pretty gun and a calming voice and you're kinda cute in a dom—"

Tam roughly righted the gurney and Batuyin yelped as she was flipped upright, which wiped the grin off the nurses' faces.

"Stay with me," Batuyin said. "Pretty sure I'll hurt someone otherwise, don't need to give you more reason to kill me."

Tam pulled up a chair. Any excuse to skip the party was a good one, even if karaoke provided wonderful blackmail. "Someone fix her hand."

Batuyin grinned. "Ha. You could've killed me a few times. You like me—one whole person likes me, that's not too shabby."

This was a woman who had won thirty-three pitched battles without losing one, and would've been venerated if she'd retired a year ago.

"I hate you." She wasn't sure if she did, so she tested it out loud. It wasn't true. "Which is why I'll be decent to you if you; I want to be better than you."

As she said it, she realized what that meant and her throat closed.

Batuyin had sat by for years as a faction of her People's Republic had swelled out of control and subjugated the rest. She would not do the same.

***

Khair sucked in air, coming up to the surface after being sucked into a riptide. Memories kept barraging her, her own as Jiao landed them safely and Taivan took Albion and failed Coloma, as Batu saved them for the final time.

And Moore's, as she prepared to go public with UOD's dealings and turn herself in, but was recruited by a revolutionary from what was left of the United States. As Moore was questioned after allowing Khair to live despite the Coloma traffic incident and demoted, outright handcuffed and polygraphed after the battle on the *Nautilus*, but Strudel asked the wrong questions.

Water washed over her. Khair kneeled in the office once more, sputtering as Jiao turned the icy sprinkler off. Taivan and the others gathered around.

Taivan crouched beside her. "Khair—"

"Tuya. My name is Tuya."

He cocked his head and waited.

"I remember everything. I can't go back to Chuluun's name."

He hesitated, but Jiao cut in. "You have to be Khair for now—we're boarding the *Hopper*."

Conservation

"IF YOU HEAR ME and think this entire time-line is a bust, say check." Aidan's voice carried through an undetectable transmitter tied in with their translator that connected them to each other and the *Osiris*.

"Check." Jiao moved slowly to join Tuya and Taivan in the little transport ship that would carry them to the *Hopper*.

"A little louder," Tuya said. She repeated the name to herself, trying to remember. It meant something about light, a Buddhist name. That was why her devout mother had been so adamant Tuya avoid the army despite the money she might have sent back.

Now she understood Jiao's shame.

What had it meant for Batu to defy his wife's memory and enlist to protect his daughter? Though her mom would've done the same had she lived.

The old name didn't fit. Or wouldn't have, except a tuya was when a volcano erupted through a glacier or thick sleet, which only happened in places like Irmeg or Mongolia. Volcanoes, glaciers, home. That fit well enough.

"Don't draw attention to yourself," Taivan said to Aidan.

Tuya paced their boarding craft, barely used to her body or this time. It was one thing to know time was the internal sensation necessary for perception. It was another to live years in minutes.

Another self had subsumed her. The green miasma between distant stars, the dimmed chilled windows, Aidan's tenor, the tight fur over Taivan's shoulders, Jiao's lavender perfume, all populated in files she could barely access.

"This shouldn't take long, Tuya," Taivan said. He never hesitated over her name, but he said it too often.

"How long did it take you to adjust after time-travelling?"

"I was sixteen; I never did."

"Explains why you were such a bossy kid."

The journey between ships seemed ridiculously slow. Tuya hadn't looked at Jiao since her memories had returned, and even Taivan... she teared up. She thought she'd understood what she'd done to them. Even now, she'd seen so little of their suffering. What had her soldiers and her old master done when her back was turned?

"Anda," she said, needing that bond's protection.

Taivan looked to her, his eyes so similar to the boy he'd been, though his face was longer, hair sprinkled with grey, no longer in the lithe build of youth. "Baghatur." He leaned in to whisper, hand on her shoulder, thumb by her neck. "I forgive you."

"How?" The word slipped out.

He kissed her forehead, his lips burning. "I need forgiveness."

She bowed, knees so watery she had little choice in the matter, and her eyes caught Jiao's as she straightened. She looked away.

"It's nice to build a new life at first," Aidan said on her link alone. "It doesn't last."

"It will," she whispered. Neither Jiao nor Taivan commented, as she often spoke aloud to Moore.

"Appearances change, but the essence never does. To be conscious is to be deluded by desires and to suffer in otiose striving toward them."

She did feel more like Khair than Tuya, mocked by someone else's voice in her head, her stomach filled with hornets as they approached Moore and UOD. "Desires delude, I'll buy that. But doesn't suffering?"

"There's no difference."

"Then why don't you choose the delusion and be happy?"

"Because I don't seek happiness anymore, Khair." He spoke her language flawlessly, and the old name sounded natural. "That's the only way to find it. And you never will until you realize there's no difference between you and those selves you pretend to be."

Their ship docked to the *Hopper* with a silent lurch; Jiao stumbled, and Tuya caught her. Jiao straightened without fighting.

The door opened.

"Let her go, Khair. We have to pretend to be civilized." Taivan exaggerated his regional accent, layered on aristocratic disdain, and topped it with a booming projection to create something admirably monstrous.

Her scowl didn't need to be faked as Taivan shoved her out first and draped his arm around Jiao's shoulder. The entrance pod was empty, no guns or cameras, not even a bench. The door to the rest of the ship was shut without a window.

Taivan released Jiao and dusted off her shoulder. "Any movement on your end?"

"No," Aidan said. "Don't ask, I'll tell you."

"Why, busy with—what is it now, calligraphy, reggae, expressionism?" Taivan said.

"Death metal," Aidan said. "I imagine it'll be thematically relevant soon. Strudel's thirty seconds away. Pretend I'm not here."

They looked like the stray, rabid dogs UOD was expecting. Taivan wore his jade crown, a sword-cane, a tie-dyed ermine fur over a black jumpsuit, and sunglasses. Jiao overshot reasonable in a fitted suit jacket, tie, and a knee-length skirt, with oily pilot gloves and a purse of scrap cloth. Tuya was at least comfortable in Batu's beanie, sweatpants, and a cropped t-shirt.

They didn't wear armor, and except for Taivan's cane and Jiao's perilously tall heels, no weapons.

The gate to the main hallway opened slowly, Strudel and Moore on the other side. They must've traveled in doctubes too, Strudel a military forty—late thirties going on fifty—Moore still Tuya's peer.

Her face heated. The staticky connection between them remained, but she didn't dare speak to it, might spill her heart to Sergeant Juarez, Moore's understudy who believed in the Mercy Mission program.

Moore didn't look at her, studying Taivan too closely.

Even if Moore was an unflappable bastard, seeing her made it easier to read the emotions they shared. Echoes of family lost and life wasted, a painful loyalty that should be left to rust. If she trusted the link between them, she'd tell Moore she was wrong, Jiao and Aidan too. Like matter conserved, they could break down the elements of their lives and rearrange it so that though they changed and evolved, nothing was wasted.

Strudel coughed, so he didn't laugh at them. "Jochiin. You've gotten old, my boy." Strudel had shaved his head to hide his baldness and had as many chins as wrinkles.

Taivan scratched his thick hair. "Who are you again?"

"Khair, stop staring at Moore," Aidan said.

How could she? She'd lived in Moore's memories, in her body. Had seen Moore risk everything to keep her alive, had stood with Moore as her own body was abused and dehumanized. And Moore wouldn't look at her. Sure, she had to play it cool, but couldn't she acknowledge her as a person of interest, a person at all?

"You'll forgive me if I don't trust you after Omega Centauri," Strudel said. She had been there at Chuluun's largest slaughter, so had fifteen-year-old Taivan. "We can talk business after you and your servants are searched and decontaminated."

"There are no servants here," Jiao said.

Taivan grinned easily and waved her down, a flippancy learned when potential allies brought up his years with Chuluun. "Easy, love, if we let him live you can claim him, though I can't imagine he has many uses. Do you cook?"

Strudel matched smarmy smiles. "Split up male and female for the de-con. It won't be more than ten minutes."

Taivan shrugged. "I'll ruin your cyber defense if you look at me or mine incorrectly."

"Don't worry, Mr. Jochiin, some of our families raised us right."

Taivan's smile dropped, but he didn't move. With her memories, she knew he was thinking of his father working himself to death to provide for his children, not Chuluun's abuse—Chuluun wasn't family. Then he snickered. "Yours must be so disappointed."

Strudel waved Taivan in front and to the left at a fork. Tuya stood with Moore and Jiao, braggadocio echoing down the thin hall.

"Do you have the code and malware?" Moore asked when Taivan was out of sight, not giving Jiao a chance to posture or size her up. Her voice was slightly lower in person, echoed off the walls, with traces of a guttural accent.

Jiao looked down the hall, scanned the walls with her wrist-con. It found a platoon in a nearby room, pockets of sleeping gas in the ceiling and lead in the walls to conceal electronic signatures. Jiao circled Moore, the shorter, broader woman allowing it.

Finally, with Jiao distracted, Moore looked at Tuya and gave her a slight nod. Her expression didn't change, but there was a soldier's respect for danger in her stance.

If Moore had been interrogated for helping her but was still on the case, this must be a test for her. Maybe it would help if Tuya hit her? She grinned and Moore crossed her hands by her belt, where she must hide a pistol under her jacket.

"Do you have the gold and ship?" Jiao said.

Moore brushed past Tuya and opened the hangar beside their docked ship, a chest of gold inside the room but outside the attached jet. Jiao couldn't lift it alone.

"We'll load and undock the ship once you've fulfilled your end," Moore said.

Jiao raised an eyebrow. "That ship has only a nominal shield and outdated cloaking. I'll be shot by a bored kid in a trainer, if radiation doesn't seep in first."

"You're hardly providing a service; you're returning what you stole."

"Doesn't seem reason to kill her," Tuya said.

"If our systems are compromised, people will die," Moore said. "The only reason you're alive is because we have to confirm your information."

"So, what'll you do afterwards?" Tuya said.

"You'll take 7701," Moore said to Jiao. "And we'll support your claim over the Khanate."

They planned on taking out Taivan. Aidan warned him.

"I won't be your vassal," Jiao said. "Threaten if you want, as you said, your people will die if I compromise your system."

Moore glanced at Tuya. "Everyone has a master, whatever their personal inclination."

Seemed like Moore's rebel command had no interest in collaborating; seemed Moore would prefer they did.

Jiao allowed herself a smile. "And you'll never be mine."

"I can't get you a better ship, or an escort," Moore said. "If you venture out alone, you'll be pirated within the week. Stay as a contracted pilot, we—"

"Don't pretend to care. It doesn't suit you." Jiao reached inside her jacket for the envelope, and Moore stepped toward her.

Tuya blocked Moore's path and Moore's attention snapped to her.

Jiao raised the envelope slowly and handed it over. "I switched it with a blank copy so Taivan thinks he has it." She'd learned to lie as a prisoner, Batu setting the example, telling the others she was properly punished for her pride.

Moore checked it, re-sealed and pocketed it, called for her goons to load the gold. That was it, no verification? They needed more time to get the map.

"How soon until I'm cleared to leave?" Jiao asked.

"We're halfway through the pre-flight check and you can make your own observations."

Something wasn't right. If UOD planned on nabbing Taivan, why let one of the galaxy's best pilots go with buckets of gold? And if they thought Jiao was their in-road into the Khanate, why give her a death trap of a ship?

Moore was dressed to fight: in pants, flat shoes, suit jacket loose enough to punch and buttoned to conceal a pistol.

"I will." Jiao stood aside as UOD mercenaries loaded the gold. She took a bar from the pile, checking its weight, biceps flexing as she strained to curl it.

Tuya smirked and looked aside. Moore tried not to smile and ironed out her expression when Tuya caught her.

"Their escort destroyers are drifting closer," Aidan said. "Find out if they're trying to shoot or board."

"Part of your consciousness is in her," Jiao said to Moore, nodding to Tuya. "Could you put my mind in a different body without this pain? I'll give you Aidan Riley in exchange."

Moore straightened. "That might be arranged."

"That's code for 'I'm an overpaid lackey, I've no idea,'" Tuya said. "Call and check."

"As soon as you send the map," Aidan said. "I can escape, but then you're—"

"Silence, 7701," Jiao said over Aidan. "I'd like to see my potential hosts."

Moore clasped her wrist in front of her. "It's untested technology. You could negotiate a safer, surer prize."

The six UOD soldiers finished loading the gold but stayed within the hangar, between them and the ship.

"What're you offering?" Jiao said.

Moore scratched scuffs from the floor. "The lives of your crew."

Collision

"THEY'RE SURROUNDING US BUT haven't fired or attempted to board," Aidan said. "We can't evade for long."

"You don't have any leverage," Moore said, unable to hear Aidan. "We've got our codes, your general, and your ferry is hopelessly out-manned. Surrender Riley and we won't fire on your ship."

"I'm not being taken alive," Aidan said. "Taivan's off-line, but he wasn't in distress when he lost contact."

Tuya and Jiao faced six soldiers armed with riot-control rifles. No way of knowing who Moore would fight for, but if she was part of this trap, there was no trusting her. And none of this mattered without the map.

"I'll creep toward you as if ramming the *Hopper* for leverage," Aidan said. "Call me off if you make progress."

"No way, bad idea," Tuya said to Moore and Aidan.

"That's not my ship anymore," Jiao said.

"Those are five hundred of your soldiers," Moore said.

"I'm neither Albion nor Khanate."

If Tuya attacked the UOD, she and Jiao—who could barely curl twelve kilograms—would face six soldiers. But there were no cameras in the hangar bay. If she fought there, UOD wouldn't see and Moore might join them.

"Let's check your ship," Tuya said to Jiao.

"You have ten minutes till collision," Aidan said.

Jiao retreated into the hangar. The mercenaries stepped aside and let her corner herself, entered after. Tuya and Moore followed. The room was so crammed that when fighting started, no one would shoot until people started dropping and clearing space.

Moore turned around to take a call.

"How do you feel?" Tuya whispered to Jiao.

Jiao rapped the gold bar against the wall, short for a club, but it'd do. "I've had worse days."

Translation: pretty shabby.

Moore turned around. "Call Riley off or we'll blow him up."

"You can destroy that ship," Jiao said. "But it would take minutes and all that time it would get closer. The debris would irreparably damage your fleet, and you'd be left stranded with Hoelun and Timur prowling."

"You'd lose far more than we would."

"But we don't have a choice," Jiao said. "You do. Call your destroyers off and Aidan will stand down."

"Taivan captured Strudel, but he's besieged in the control room," Aidan said. "Taivan's shot."

Tuya grabbed the gold from Jiao and held it in front of her to absorb the only shot UOD got off. She smashed the bar into the closest man's ear. He spun into the man beside him, unconscious, but the soldiers behind her spread out, gaining space to shoot.

"He was being dramatic, it's a graze," Aidan said.

Too late now, Tuya closed the guns, smashing jaws with the bar, throwing elbows, punches, open hand strikes.

"Hold fire!" Moore flipped her holster's strap open but hadn't drawn.

Tuya glanced behind her and saw two pistols—actual guns, not riot control—aimed at her head. She raised her hands.

Jiao attacked Moore before she could draw her pistol. Moore ducked and punched back. Jiao, still bruised from the beating Tuya had given her early and unsteady on her heels, almost fell, but Moore didn't chase.

"Stand down, Admiral," Moore said.

Jiao wouldn't win. She was younger, longer, but Moore had seen how easily Tuya beat her through sheer force an hour ago. But Jiao couldn't back down; if she was captured, they lost Taivan's advantage in capturing Strudel.

Tuya gathered all her guilt, everything her pacifist mother might have thought, how her guileless siblings would have seen her, what her old neighbors would have said as they wondered what happened to the sweet diner owners she had betrayed. It was a hot, infected brand over her heart. And she forced it all through the connection between her and Moore, purging the wound. But Moore shed it with a pleading prayer and cornered Jiao.

Tuya recalled every aspect of Moore getting shot: ribs breaking, bone stabbing muscle, friends dying beside her, bullets popping inches from her head—memories taken by UOD—and gave them back.

Moore's fists lowered for half a second, eyes blank.

Jiao took advantage.

She hit Moore's eye and kicked her knee. Moore silenced her emotions though she was still half blind and reeling from the kick, but not before Jiao grabbed her belt and shoulder and started throwing her over her hip.

Moore swept out one of Jiao's legs. Jiao reset but Moore found her footing, wrapped her hand in Jiao's tie, and smashed her against the wall. Jiao gasped for breath and Moore kept hitting her.

Tuya sent all her aching fear and ghosts, but it didn't help. Moore punched Jiao's side till a rib audibly cracked and stepped back, rubbing her own blood from her knuckles.

Jiao slumped. But she straightened and raised her fists, though she struggled to breathe. Moore dipped her head in salute and stepped toward her.

"Wait!" Tuya said.

Moore shoved Jiao back against the wall. "Stay—"

Jiao inhaled softly, gathering her reserves, and spun into a low kick. Moore stepped over. Jiao turned into a back kick on her other leg, connected with Moore's hurt knee, and slapped her palm against Moore's ear. Moore reeled, but when Jiao closed the distance, she embraced her and threw her to the ground, landing on top.

"Easy!" Tuya raised her hands. "Jiao, she's got you, it's fine, Aidan's coming."

Moore kneeled on Jiao's chest, Jiao flailing, silently crying at the weight on her broken rib.

"Sarn't, we got your commander. Let our girl breathe."

Moore let Jiao up and sat behind her, one arm wrapped around Jiao's throat and the other hand holding her right wrist. But Jiao was a lefty.

Jiao steadied her breathing and kicked off her heels. Moore tightened her grip. "Enough. Tell Riley to stand down."

Jiao drew a knife from her brace and stabbed Moore.

Moore released her. Jiao left the knife in and drew a second, pressed the blade against her throat.

"Step outside and lock the door," Jiao said, voice thick with pain.

The mercenaries didn't move, guns aimed, fingers on triggers.

Tuya kept her hands up and stepped between them with caricatured slowness. "Get a doctube ready."

Moore nodded at that, eyes glazed.

The mercenaries obeyed. Tuya locked the door behind them, but they gathered outside and called for reinforcements with shotguns and door-cannons. There was no first aid kit here, nothing useful, and Jiao's ship couldn't detach without authentication.

"Should I change course?" Aidan said.

"No, keep steady," Jiao said. "How long until collision?"

"Eight and a half minutes. Taivan's gone dark. I doubt he has that long."

Jiao forced Moore upright and leaned her against the wall. Moore shivered though sweat raced down her forehead, grasping for the knife in her stomach until Jiao seized her wrists. "Leave that. Give me the coordinates for the Arc Dilator and I'll have Aidan change course. We'll trade Taivan for Strudel, and both get our commander back."

Moore said nothing, wheezing in steady time.

Tuya crouched in front of her.

"Go on," Moore said. "Fitting."

Tuya cut away Moore's shirt around the wound so the shirt wouldn't infect it, to make sure the bleeding was stopped up with the knife, to feel her and make sure they were two separate people. This body was five hundred years old; she was reverent with it. Moore didn't look at the knife, pinning Tuya with her gaze, but she tensed as the blade sawed through the cloth above her heart.

"I wish I had water, but I don't, so hang on." Tuya wiped sweat from her brow.

Jiao found a canteen in her purse. Tuya offered it, but Moore couldn't lift her arms. She held it to her lips, but Moore ignored it until Tuya gently hit her cheek and helped her drink.

"Cute. Move faster," Aidan said. "And no one should drink after they've been stabbed."

"Any painkillers?" Tuya asked Jiao.

Jiao raised an eyebrow and braced her broken rib.

"Finish it," Moore said.

"I'm not taking your orders currently, thanks. You helped us recruit Davids. Why do you think you're better than him?" She raised Moore's drooping chin, forcing her to look her in the eye. "We can destroy it if you let us."

Moore gathered her slipping strength. "Sergeant First Class Tamika Moore, 2856855952."

"They demoted you, genius. Look around: there are no cameras, they can't hear through the door. Do you know where the map is, or do we have to keep killing people? Cause that's the only way we'll leave, unless we all blow up."

"In seven and a half minutes," Aidan said.

"Staff Sergeant Tam—"

"You're gonna die, Tamika," Tuya said. "Maybe not today, but soon. And you'll leave a lot undone. Your revolution might succeed, but for every problem you fix, you'll create two more. But if you tell us, maybe we can do this one good thing together."

Moore closed her eyes. "He worked with us. We're paying him—"

"Who?" Tuya gently hit her.

"Resting my eyes," she said.

"Rest later. You got seven minutes." Tuya turned to Jiao. "We need a doctube."

"We can't open that door."

Moore said nothing, her eyes closed.

"This 'not dead' thing isn't convincing." Tuya splashed water on her face. "You've been lying for so long. Don't you want to tell the whole truth? What are the coordinates, Tammy?"

Moore snorted, blood seeping from her side. *Tammy? Go back to hitting me.*

***You're in shock, send me some of your pain and survive long enough to
reach the doctube.***

"No, Tuya," Moore said, barely audible. Her eyes flickered open for a moment,
and a faint warmth—friendship? pride?—fluttered through. Tuya should resent
it. Tomorrow she might.

A safety clicked off. "Move." Jiao held a riot gun to Moore. "You have ten
seconds to give me the coordinates, and then you're going to be in pain for a very
long time."

"Or she'd take someone else's body," Tuya said, not moving.

"Looked into it," Jiao said. "There's been no successful record of it. Stand
aside."

"She tortured me. I got dibs on the interrogation, JJ."

"You're—"

"It's been ten seconds." Moore rasped, eyes still closed. "You've lost credibility,
and I don't know, anyway."

Jiao pressed the barrel against Moore's forehead. "I'll—"

Tuya took Jiao's shoulder and gently turned her around, careful not to hurt
her ribs. "This isn't what Batu died for."

Jiao shoved her away and aimed again.

The rifle shook. The longer Jiao waited, the heavier it grew, till she tapped the
barrel against her forehead and flipped the safety on.

"Aidan," Tuya said. "Any news on Taivan?"

"He's trying to threaten his way into their systems, still alive. But in six minutes,
that'll change."

"It's not too late to change trajectory," Tuya said.

Jiao handed her the rifle. "Aidan, stop advancing. Taivan's got us leverage." She
turned to Moore. "I'll still kill you if necessary."

But Moore didn't respond because she was too busy being dead.

Ends are Always Incomplete

Jiao froze. "I didn't—I needed to get free."

"I know," Tuya said.

I couldn't save your sergeant; she was brave, I'm sorry.

Moore lay dead against the wall, the long knife bloody to the hilt, a few centimeters of blade loose. Jiao tried to close her eyes, but one was stuck half open. She took back the knife. Blood rushed out, pooled in shirt creases and dumped on the floor in repeating spurts like leaves heavy with rain. Moore's body leached to gray.

Tuya's chip buzzed, but it was no more than the irritation of flickering lights. She crouched by Moore.

"So strange, to outlive you." Tuya kissed Moore's still warm cheek and quoted her countrymen's 'Peace on Earth.' "There is hunting in the heavens—sleep safe till tomorrow."

Outside, forty mercenaries argued about how to set up a battering-ram cannon fastest. Jiao tried to start the jet, but it was barred to the *Hopper*.

"Aidan, how's Taivan?" Jiao said.

"Making a break-through on the coordinates. If he beams them to me, I'll reach the machine."

"What about us?" Tuya asked. Not just for her, but Jiao and Taivan.

"I don't know, but since this is the only time we've reached the *Hopper*, I'm not risking it."

They could go down fighting, but there was no gain killing a few mercenaries.

The line between Tuya and Moore hummed so loud it hurt, not static, but some language so foreign she couldn't imagine a person sounding like that.

Tuya braced herself against the wall and checked that Moore's corpse hadn't moved. ***Moore, there's probably a time difference between us, but your body is dead. Rest easy.***

Happiness floated through her gut. Like she shot a buzzer beater, all the mistakes of the game forgotten as the ball left her fingers at perfect arc, suspended in time as she floated midair, only waiting for the team to celebrate.

Moore's feeling/memory/vision/self, but it didn't overpower Tuya. Was she imagining it, all this time together warping her so that she couldn't live alone, whole?

Taste and see; drink and thirst no more.

She stilled. It was close enough to Moore's voice that it could be Moore, but it wasn't the same. Who programed this? ***So, you finally figured you need to make philosophy for the people and not the other way around. Are you cognizant? Or is Juarez getting a laugh right now?*** She would never get an answer. ***Damn you! Why can't I be happy that I'm free?***

Taste and see—

Shut up!

"Aidan," Tuya said. "Is Sophie still into necromancy? Cause there's a dead woman in my head and her corpse is here."

How much of Moore remained in Tuya's head? She had those weeks Moore had shown her, and Moore's knowledge, facts inked with her commentary so her interests and secrets remained.

Moore would be antsy about raising the dead, but if she was running repeats in Tuya's head, she wasn't all dead. And if they failed? She'd be a stuck with a mostly dead woman in her head.

Aidan sighed. "Why send more people to a sinking ship?"

Not just people, his sister.

"We need Taivan," Jiao said.

"Not anymore," Aidan said. "He recruited Hoelun and Timur's armies and sent me the map's coordinates. Jiao, I don't have enough firepower to help, but if you charge the mercenaries, you won't be captured."

"Understood." Jiao flipped her knife, but didn't spare the soldiers a glance.

Tuya turned off her comm. "Can you reach Sophie?"

Jiao opened a radio panel on the jet and played with wires. "*Osiris* medbay, this is Admiral Jun. Is Dr. Riley there?"

They found her.

"Sophie," Jiao said. "You've got a chance to raise the dead, if your brother will let you try."

"Aidan," Tuya said. "Could you get the coordinates tattooed?"

"My body's new each time and in other 'verses I don't have an army."

"Memorize them."

"They're 4096 digits long."

"Then upload them to the net!"

Aidan said nothing. It wasn't about the coordinates; he just wanted the army.

"I'm not boarding that ship without an exit plan," Sophie said.

Jiao switched channels. "Davids, do you read me?"

"Yes," Davids said. "Aidan locked down the ship."

"Can you capture the bridge?" Jiao said.

"Yes—"

"No," Aidan said, cutting Davids' line out. "But if you're going to be so reckless and ruin everything anyway, I'll let her over once you get their agreement."

"Strudel will let us go if Sophie brings back Moore," Taivan said over the comm. "And Jiao takes a chip—he wants to duplicate Moore in another chip. Jiao, you can say no, but I need an answer fast."

"'Duplicate Moore?'" Tuya said. "What kind of copy and paste are we talking about? Why?"

"If I were him," Taivan said. "I'd take my best, most loyal soldier, duplicate them, and put their mind in the body of everyone I captured. If anyone finds out, placate them with eternal life."

"Then we don't do it," Jiao said. "Even if we don't get another deal."

"They're so close, I don't think another few years would make a difference. And if we live, we have a chance to destroy their time-machine."

"What else do they have?" Tuya said.

UOD's mercenaries cheered as the cannon-ram revved up.

"Get Sophie to take the chip instead of Jiao," Aidan said. "Odds are, she'll be dead soon and we won't have to deal with a second spy."

Taivan hesitated. By now, he'd spent longer with Sophie than Jiao. "I'll check."

"No," Jiao said.

"Even if it severs the riot-control," Taivan said. "When it severs your consciousness, it won't end your pain, they'll shock you whenever—"

"I won't discuss it," Jiao said.

"This is death, Jiao." Taivan sniffled. "Forgive me this, but at your age—"

"I was a year older." Her voice was gentler than Tuya had ever heard.

"Almost your age. I looked ahead and knew I'd never be happy. But I have. And you deserve happiness so much more. Live a little longer, and you will be. Not all the time, not some perfect euphoria, but a contentment you can feed off of for years." He steeled his voice. "Aidan's right, I've done my part. I'll do it."

"Please don't." Jiao blinked back tears. "I don't want this, but," her eyes watered and she couldn't hold it back. "Don't die for me."

"It would be no burden."

Tuya swallowed. What was she supposed to hope here?

"You'd be too dangerous."

Background whispers played over the radios as Taivan hogged the comm. "I love you. You'll always have a place with us."

Jiao smiled, wiped her eyes. "I'm glad I didn't kill you."

He laughed and beeped out.

"Sophie will be over soon," Aidan said. "Don't let anyone in until then." When no one spoke, he signed off.

Jiao sat across from Moore's corpse, struggling to fit her knife back in its sheath.

Tuya couldn't look at Jiao. She lay Moore out of her sticky blood, smoothed down hair that slipped from her bun, and shut her jaw before her face froze with her mouth agape.

"You won't try to talk me down?" Jiao leaned against the wall, pale and limp as if she'd given birth.

Tuya wiped her bloody hands on Moore's shirt. "You know what you're doing, right?"

Jiao stilled her pattering foot and tried to straighten her awry tie. "I'll be dead. It's the rest of you that have to suffer it."

"You don't have to downplay it."

"Yes, I do." The tie was tightened to her throat and just as twisted as before. "May I?"

Jiao nodded.

Tuya loosened the knot slowly so not to shake Jiao and hurt her ribs. Jiao bore it with closed eyes.

"Am I wasting my life?"

Tuya's stomach churned, but she measured both sides, looped the knot in a slender triangle, and adjusted Jiao's collar. "I don't know."

"It doesn't absolve me, but it's not a real choice." Jiao smoothed the pressed lines of her shirt. "I don't want this, but here I am and I can't do anything else. But I uh—maybe I shouldn't be plaintiff and defendant both—maybe I'm shirking my duty but I don't care, I don't have to anymore. Even if it's all I can do. I'm dying, and all I can do is talk, as if that ever fixed anything? I'm possessed already!"

Sophie arrived, Taivan and Strudel accompanying.

Jiao rested her head against the wall, breath ragged though she tried to steady it. "Don't tell me about my family. I—I don't think I could take it."

Tuya flinched.

"Sorry," Jiao said.

Taivan briefly looked in the window, then led the mercenaries away, allowing Sophie, a UOD doctor, and a cart of medical equipment to reach the door. Here was their chance to fight, but she didn't raise Jiao's hopes.

"I thought Taivan would see me." Jiao's hand crept closer to Tuya's, pinkie stretched out. Tuya hooked her pinkie around it.

"I wanted to..." Jiao coughed until she could speak levelly, hand against her rib. "Tell him that no matter who I become, I was always loyal, always his sister, his shield. Because I know he would have served the Republic if he ever had a choice. And he did right by me."

Sophie entered with a UOD scientist. "Ignore the irrelevant observer. I've got great drugs; you won't feel a thing."

She tripped on Moore's legs, kicked them out of her way. Tuya swallowed and let it go.

Sophie crouched beside the body, swept her hand down the torso, and stuck a gloved finger in the wound. "You bested Tuya's buddy here once. You'll manage again."

Jiao glanced to the window, but Taivan couldn't come. Tuya's throat dried. She'd have to let UOD in her head to reach Moore-in-the-chip. She could use him, too.

Sophie felt around Moore's ears. "This'll do." She took off her gloves and held Jiao's hand. "I heard I was next on the list. I'll pay you back somehow."

Tuya was about to let herself cry when Jiao looked back at her. "About Batu. I die like he did now, Tuya; I hope it brings you peace."

Tuya. The name apart from all she had done—Jiao had outlived Khair, at least. "He'd still love you."

Jiao swallowed and turned to Sophie. "Make sure Taivan speaks to me first. I don't want their people to influence me."

"We have to examine you before we let you go," the UOD doctor said.

Jiao pressed flat her tie. "Goodbye, then."

Chicken Pot Pie and Tea Cake

KHAIR—NO, SHE WAS TUYA again, with memories and a family and a life outside of Chuluun and her own worst impulses—woke with one hand cuffed to her gurney. The room was dark. She kicked at the motion-sensors, giving her thirty seconds of light.

Her head ached like it'd been used for batting practice and the gurney was chilly against her bare stomach, but better her crop top than a hospital gown. The only intrusion was a cotton ball taped to the base of her skull.

Jiao lay unconscious on a second gurney, her head shaved and bandaged, a healing sleeve around her torso, breathing evenly. Her brace lay against the wall.

"Aidan, is our comm up?"

Apparently not.

Tuya pushed against the wall, sliding the wheeled gurney, and tested the door. It was locked.

If Sophie wasn't here, she was probably with Moore in surgery. But where was Taivan?

The quarters were at a reasonable temperature, gravity a little less than standard, two potted flowers freshening the heavily oxygenated air. The walls blinked through natural hues, accompanied by a classical score synchronized to Jiao's heart monitor.

Moore, did you make it?

No response. Tuya kicked her gurney to Jiao and checked her vitals, though the numbers meant nothing to her. They couldn't be bad, since no one rushed in to save their experiment.

The door squeaked open.

Moore limped in using a wheeled IV bag as a cane, wearing nothing but underwear and her wrist-con, stitches bleeding. Like Jiao, her head was shaved and bandaged. Her eyes glowed a draconic yellow, the rigor mortis in her face not totally reversed, skin still dulled to ash.

"Batuyin." She sounded like a toad. "My memories are filtered through you. I don't exist. But I still have that buzzer, so don't play around. Who am I?"

Tuya was too stunned to speak until Moore reached for her wrist-con. "A rational, creating animal? A being constituted by care of the truth?" Though Moore had sealed any emotion from her face, her shoulders curled in and she leaned on her back foot. Tuya sighed. "The image of God?"

Moore laughed, brittle, massaged self-inflicted scars on her wrist.

Tuya shrugged. "A five-hundred-year-old sergeant with a death wish that can easily be accommodated."

"I've looked up my file, but I won't tell you what I know, so you can't lie." She paced, dragging the IV over her foot without reaction. "People aren't meant to live past their death and see how little their life meant."

"Am I supposed to say something comforting? You said to establish a source of truth—"

"Investigate my surroundings, find people I can trust, which," she waved to Tuya. "Not a great start."

"Maybe you shouldn't have been such an asshole."

"Yes." Moore rubbed her head. "You're the reason I'm still alive, so thank you. Although I could be in heaven, or some version of me, so—"

"So sure of your own righteousness?"

Moore leaned against the gurney. "Not my own, never. Tell me everything you know about me and I'll get you a chicken pot pie or something. It's meat in bread, you'd like it."

It did sound good. How much of her did this Moore know?

Tuya told her everything: the name of her husband and kids, her high school, how she'd been promoted and demoted and recruited by insurrectionists, about Rosa Aguilar and Nicole Vampatella—how their deaths were so miserable she was willing to risk her cover to keep Tuya alive.

Moore listened in enthralled silence for the entire two minutes. "That's it?"

"You weren't exactly forthcoming."

"Trusting you got me killed. There's—"

"You never trusted me," Tuya said. "You were zapping me till the day you died."

She shrugged. "Didn't say I liked you."

"Fuck you."

Moore wheeled back on her. "First of all, I've stated my priorities. Secondly, you would've remained a shell of yourself or perhaps your pitiable truest self without my—"

"Thirdly." Tuya stepped closer, Moore tensing. "You're always searching for truth because your life is a lie. You fight tyrants by lording your power over me. And all your talk of me doing better, when you do what? The exact same stupid thing."

"Yes." Moore measured the distance between them but didn't retreat. "How foolish that I can't ethically destroy the bounds of time and universes, or constrain one of humanity's worse criminals whose mind I'm forced to inhabit."

"So, you are convinced of your own righteousness."

"I'm a whitewashed tomb. My good deeds are filthy rags. As I lay dying, I forgot the resurrection and thanked God for delivering me from evil. But I'm back, and you're stuck with me."

When Tuya didn't answer, Moore held her gaze a moment too long and looked away. "You treat this like a friendship when it's a business transaction and we're both the commodity. Get a dog if you need a friend. Use your head in the meantime."

For a moment, she was too angry to speak. But Moore didn't storm out or give orders, just stood there, barefoot and bleeding. "You think you'll kill me, don't you? Don't distance yourself. Life is much longer than death. Besides, I've died before, haven't really minded."

Moore crossed her arms. "Probably my influence. You were desperate to live before."

Probably.

"I flipped a switch and now there's nothing wrong with you," Moore said. "But I'm not sane."

"Obvious News Network called demanding their headline back."

It wasn't Moore's violence, Chuluun would've passed any psychological test, and her unease in battle was healthy. But no one could hold that many competing views of reality or themselves.

"The Army kicked me out when they realized it. UOD knew about it. I think that's why they wanted me, thought I was easier to control, or maybe I wouldn't miss anyone or some nonsense. It's not an excuse. I'm just saying all my studying, praying, it won't fix me."

'We're all subject to our brain chemistry,' Moore had told her once.

"You're more than a soldier to UOD now. Bargain for medicine."

"They took my memories and you want me to voluntarily let them drug me?" Moore tried for calm but only reached repressed. "Perhaps it's paranoia, but it's still my best analysis."

She waited for a contradiction.

"I'm sorry."

Moore grinned faintly. "Naturally. But I don't like hurting you. It should bother me more than it does, and that bothers me."

Tuya, or at least Khair, had imagined Moore coming to her with only enough memories to beg for forgiveness. There was nothing satisfying in it. It was hard to be kind when life was meaningless.

"While you were trapped in my body, you journaled," Tuya said. "I'll forward it to you, help you relearn yourself, but you have to read my part too, how you hurt me."

"Thank you." Moore sagged against the wall. "I'll get you that pie. Right now, scientists are tinkering with my memories on Jiao's chip. They might invent or change memories there, then inject them in me, and this truncated version of myself won't know the difference. But I've written this."

She flashed a sealed envelope. "Each morning, I'll say '0503 1306 2807.'" Her children's birthdays. "If I don't say that, read this to me; I've written in rewards for you."

"I have demands."

"Two pies?"

"Don't take Jiao's memories." Could she have bargained for a shock-free existence?

"They're only blocked. I could bring them back now, same as yours. But how could I hide that?"

"You were a Soviet linguist. Why would they expect your explanation on neurology?"

"Russian," Moore said. "Soviet isn't a language."

"Welcome to the future, where no one cares about the problems of the twenty-first century." It was the wrong thing to say, Moore blinking, blinking, and staring as if there was nothing behind her eyes. "Back on subject—"

"When you were so taken by Taivan twenty years ago, I thought of a novel where a woman falls for the much younger Tea Cake, and laughed since Tea Cake goes mad and she shoots him. People looked at me funny and I started to explain, but no one had heard of it."

"That's because Taivan's more of a Beefcake."

"It's only been a few centuries," Moore said. "And already, the champions of my day are remembered little better than someone graffitiing their name to say they were here, they existed."

She sounded so dazed Tuya stepped closer in case she fell. "We lived. Our inventions are obsolete, our stories are unfashionable, our theories proved wrong, but we lived."

"We do."

She didn't seem to hear, didn't move when Tuya clutched her feverish arm above the wrist-con. "I wonder if UOD could do some good. But no, an eternity of this life would be hell. Better to die. Better the tree of knowledge than of life."

She would've kept on, but Tuya squeezed her wrist until pain cut her off. "In *Their Eyes Were Watching God*, Tea Cake wasn't as bad as everyone thought, and only went mad protecting Janie from a rabid dog. I listened to Aidan's quincentennial edition. Not everything is forgotten. Let the people of Jungang ju last a little longer with Jiao."

"They won't. You think peasants live since we translated cuneiform and read their shopping lists, or that my old classmates have any real substance dependent on my mind?"

"Then we last as long as we're needed." Tuya's thumb traced circles on Moore's wrist, closer to the wrist-con. "And when every part of us has served its purpose—even our memory—it rests with everything that formed it, everything we've loved."

"I died. And that wasn't what I saw."

Tuya couldn't wrestle off Moore's wrist-con. The UOD-issued machine was fused to her skin. "All I know is that I love Jiao, and I've wronged her in every way. I will harrow hell to get her back, understand? Take back my memories and give her hers, say it happened in the transfer if you need to, just save her."

Moore glanced down to Tuya's hand on hers and mutely made adjustments on her wrist-con. She held up her letter and kept her hand out when Tuya took the letter.

They shook hands. It was immensely underwhelming.

"I didn't keep you alive because I felt bad about Aguilar and Vampatella," Moore said, hand still clasped. "It's because in any unbiased analysis, the universe is better with you."

"And because I'm your best friend?"

She pulled her hand back. "I'll protect you when I can, just don't record my wrongs, I'll—" she doubled over, holding her head.

"What happened?" Jiao's voice was laced with pain and thinner than a gossamer thread.

Tuya froze. "Do you remember anything?"

"Everything." Jiao rubbed her head, scowling when she felt her shaved scalp.

"Calm down." Moore slowly sat on the floor.

Jiao reached for her weapons, and not finding them, her brace, but she was tied to the gurney and couldn't reach. "What's going on?"

Fix your kid. Moore laid on her back, massaging her head.

She's not doing anything.

Her mind is storming like the sulfuric rain on Venus. Stop using this, I'll black out.

"Jiao?" Tuya said. "We're gonna get out of here soon, rest—"

Moore pushed her aside and sat as far from Jiao as the gurney would allow. Jiao tried to shift away, but her hand was cuffed.

"Watch." Moore showed two lines on her wrist-con, tapped the shorter one so it filled the screen, then turned it down so it was only a dot thick. "Pull your sleeve down between the cuff."

Jiao glared.

Moore tapped the line. Jiao stiffened, rubbed her forearm against her leg to shift the sleeve. Moore pretended not to notice. "That's all I'll do unless you lose your mind and try to kill civilians or something."

"Untie me."

"I don't have the key, or a need to get stabbed again." Moore clenched her jaw. *Jiao, I have no problem with you—*

Jiao grabbed for Moore, who batted her arm aside. Jiao kicked her away. "Do that again and I'll kill you."

"You'd rather I shocked—"

"My mind is my own." She looked to Tuya. "I didn't agree to be aware of my own subjugation. What happened?"

Tuya glanced to Moore. "Science is hard?" ***Jiao, when Moore talks to you, I hear. Can you hear me?***

"People owed you favors, one paid up," Moore said. *I think this is the primary link. You can hear me talk to her, but she can't hear us.*

Leave her alone or I'll never give you your letter.

Taivan knocked twice and barged in, Strudel and Sophie still in the hall. He tossed Jiao the key and stepped between her and Moore. Moore retreated and held her IV pole for support, but stopped massaging her head.

"I don't know what number they gave you, but you're Admiral Jun Jiao. I'm your general and friend, Jochiin Taivan, and I'll explain everything once we're on our ship."

"General first, Taivan?" Jiao said, freeing herself and tossing Tuya the key.

He blinked. "No, but it was proper, and.... Forgive me, but what do you remember?"

"Everything. They can electrocute me, but the memory wipe didn't take."

Taivan laughed and carefully hugged her, gingerly with his left arm, but she squeezed him. Tuya was too glad to see them well to be jealous.

Taivan finally let go. "Strudel, we'll return to our ship. Just remember what I said before you try to double-cross me, yeah?"

"You're only throwing wood on your own pyre, Jochiin." But the man's hands shook.

"Then even in death, I'll burn you." He looked to Moore. "I'm glad you're alive, Chip. Do you remember what the sunset looks like on your planet? How your children felt in your arms? A single thing your parents said?"

She said nothing.

"Maybe if you kneel and ask nicely, I'll let you live after I've destroyed your planet. But I doubt it."

"You've given this some thought." Moore fought to stay vertical. "I haven't thought of you at all."

He tased her. She collapsed, and he shocked her again as she recovered enough to reach her knee. Even though Strudel wasn't restrained in anyway, he remained in the hall, playing with a wrinkle in his pants. Taivan looked to Strudel and electrocuted her again.

Moore's legs writhed, but she was otherwise frozen, the taser's crackle drowning any protest she might've made.

Her pain itched Tuya. There was no pleasure watching Moore splayed out on the floor, eyes bulged, muscles contorted. But if Tuya spoke, it would raise awkward questions.

Taivan stopped long enough to kick her ribs and tased her again. It was a show, letting them see he was in control, confirming Moore was his enemy and therefore a good UOD soldier. But he could accidentally kill her.

It hurt.

Tuya started to protest but Moore caught her eye, tried to send some message but it came across as a buzz. Moore, already demoted, already doubted, had to take it.

But she didn't want to see Taivan like this. He'd never been cold, but there was no emotion or exultation now. He studied Moore's spasms as if he knew exactly how much a human being could endure.

"General," Jiao, who was allowed to be decent, said. "We've had our vengeance."

Taivan crouched beside Moore, tore out the prongs, and dug the barbs into her neck. "Now you know what it feels like. I trust you to remember this next time you feel a need to hurt my soldiers, yes?"

She stared into space, struggling to breathe.

He shocked her again and stepped over her on his way out. "When you wake tomorrow too weak to get out of bed, you'll think of me."

Nothing Special To Report

THEY WERE TWO YEARS from planet 34RS12NE, where the Ito Arc Dilator was located.

With everything in all inhabited galaxies and countless disturbed time streams on the line, Taivan, Jiao, Davids, Aidan, Sophie, and Tuya each decided to stay awake and spend what time they could perfecting each plan and making dozens of contingencies.

It was the first time Tuya could remember being perfectly content.

Part V

Death be not proud; I know that I shall meet
my fate. Not as a child searching under
the bed, motto to mantra on repeat.

I will not quiver as a hunted fawn
wobbling through the woods on untested legs,
mewling for aid beneath my final dawn,

nor as a prisoner plead on bended knee
for final undue reprieve or lesser
agony, forgetting I was once free.

Let me not as a dying star, splinter
all I upheld, or as an annual
shrub wither without weathering winter.

Above all, don't die with lingering breath;
our frame may be weak but we have strength yet.
"Don't Flinch" Tamika Moore, 533 DH

The Last Party

"Is it starting yet?" Tuya called from the kitchen. Triumphant strings and heavy horns played in the living room, where the others—minus Buck, working still—lounged around the screen eating stuffed goat.

The Nadaam festival was their first break in two years.

"Opening ceremonies," Taivan called. "Don't worry, you've missed the speeches."

Tuya returned with airag and watched the parade, where children rode horses with wretched concentration while their parents cheered.

"This isn't one of those 'this is totally traditional' things." Sophie took her glass and flicked a drop to the sky, wind, and ground. "Only for it to be eggnog with hot sauce?"

"You fell for that?" Tuya asked.

"I knew it smelled disgusting, but Taivan seemed so pleased."

He grinned. "I was."

Aidan threw a pillow at his head. "There're artists at work."

A conductor's white mare bowed, signaling to the orchestra's synthesizer and strings, and in Irmeg's largest plaza the biyelgee begun.

The dancers started in a crouch and rose slowly, with shoulders swaying. Their feet didn't move, the motion of their knees and hips and shoulders and hands aligned. Everyone moved as a one for a few beats, then friends broke into clusters, playing a thousand variations that had been practiced for centuries.

"I thought you said dancing was for people too dumb to play an instrument?" Jiao said. "There's a class I use for flexibility, and—"

Aidan bopped her with a pillow and she accidentally spilled her drink on him. He looked back to the dance, growled, and took off his wet pants.

"Great Blue, children, avert your eyes," Tuya said.

"Why?" Sophie said.

"Ask your brother."

Aidan sat back down in boxers and would have stayed like that, but Jiao threw a blanket over his lap. "Modesty only makes sense if you're biologically over forty."

Taivan tossed a pillow at him.

Buck entered with three six packs. "Meeting went long, but I..." he stared at the dancers until Sophie cleared her throat. Yeah, Sophie and Buck were a thing now, so he really did prefer everyone over her, but whatever. "I thought we were watching horse races."

Tuya tsked. "As if our glorious culture were confined to horses, how dare—" Musicians strummed horsehead fiddles. "I'll take a beer."

Taivan took a call and left.

Wrestlers in spandex, boots, and padded arm braces shoved and leaned against each other. Despite the violence—though it looked like two heavy men hugging each other—Moore let her watch.

Moore hadn't shocked her since recovering from that peevish death thing. She was growing up with the enemy and their indoctrination spilled through her guard, in her verbiage if not her arguments. But she still challenged her own beliefs, most at ease when Tuya debated her with Aidan or Buck.

Jiao stiffened slightly. Her chip hadn't lessened the riot gun's pain. But Aidan draped his hand over the couch beside her without touching her.

By the time the preliminary wrestling matches were over, Jiao had loosened up. When the children's race finished, and the first five finishers and the crying last place finisher were awarded, Jiao sipped sparkling water and leaned against Aidan.

Taivan returned. "Buck, what did your people say?"

Buck tossed him a beer. "No unusual movement. UOD has ZAX tech, but they're hiring from multiple mercenary corps, so they're not indebted to anyone."

"Hoelun and Timur were attacked a lightday outside of 34RS," Taivan said.

It was nearly impossible to fortify an entire planet, but attacking the enemy fleet before it arrived served the same purpose.

"UOD dedicated most of their force to them and can only hit us with a skeletal force." Taivan switched from wrestling to a three-dimensional model of 34RS and its orbital space. Apparently, 'a skeletal force' meant three destroyers to their singular tired ferry. "We have to outmaneuver them long enough to land."

"And the *Osiris*?" Jiao asked.

Taivan shook his head. "We need everyone on the ground and our fuel's low."

"Then we have to blow it up," Tuya said.

It'd been her home. Even if her quarters were next to the rumbling laundry room, and the gravity spinners had degraded so she no longer trusted the dumbbell's labels, they'd been safe here. But they couldn't give UOD anything.

"We'll fly our landing craft out and blow up the *Osiris* as cover," Taivan said. "Aidan, work on the explosion pattern, make sure the ship blows toward their destroyers."

"It'll be an atrocious splatter, worthy of a museum," Aidan said sprightly.

"How much time to plan the ground assault?" Buck said.

"Twelve hours. Sophie, half our soldiers are watching Nadaam, get anyone drunk to de-tox, and check our sick and injured. Then help Aidan."

"Got it. Can I tell the soldiers why?"

Taivan nodded. "Jiao, have the officers start gear checks and hydrating. Have the keshig set an example."

"We need a contingency," Buck said. "If we fail and our allies are intercepted, entire galaxies depend on Aidan. That's absurd. We should broadcast the coordinates."

Bad idea. You can't put the Arc Dilator up to an auction of force.

"We've tried that," Aidan said. "Half the universe doesn't believe it exists, and those who do will do anything to get it."

"What do you care?" Sophie said. "You've got endless attempts. We've got one."

"I'd prefer not to continue as a connoisseur of failure."

"How did you try it?" Buck said.

"We limited the broadcast to government frequencies so a legitimate force would pick it up. UOD either jammed the signal or shut down the entire intergalactic communication system and dragged us back to the Terran age. The regimes strong enough to make out the signal joined UOD or lost the war before they even invented a reasonable pretext for it."

"So, it's settled," Buck said. "We tell the people."

Aidan laughed.

"States will learn immediately," Buck said. "But they won't have a monopoly on it."

Jiao straightened off Aidan's shoulder. "Buck, if empires can't recover the time-machine, how could anyone else? You'll get them killed."

"Maybe." Buck scanned available frequencies, clicking through robust galaxy-wide channels with reliable translating tech. "But if we give the people that knowledge, we give them a chance. Not only today, but as long as they remember. If nothing else, I'll tell Westley. He's a man now." Everyone knew since the kid was his favorite subject. "He deserves a choice."

"Who's this 'people' you speak of?" Aidan dismissed the channels with public funding, leaving Buck the weaker or locked channels. "Private militias defeated by a warlord? Some universal uprising that never materialized after a millennium of prophecy? They'll die for nothing."

For a moment, the only sound was Taivan scrolling through network diagnostics.

"They can decide what their own life is worth," Buck said.

"If they want to throw themselves onto bayonets singing revolutionary hymns, they can do it now," Aidan said. "But I won't beat the drum."

Taivan didn't react. Aidan never gave orders, but there was always a sense of an adult coaching a kid's soccer game. If he wanted command, no one could stop him.

"In power, I counted on democratic impulses," Sophie said. "It backfired. I counted on the servility of the masses, and it backfired. There are always variables beyond our control."

"Some outcomes are more probable," Aidan said. "There is a chance a plucky prodigy or stalwart government will trample UOD, eradicate their foothold in every universe, capture the time-machine, and never use it or only use it properly. Whatever that means. But in centuries, I've never seen it."

"Have you ever lived the same future twice?" Tuya said.

"Depends on how narrowly you want to define 'future,' but roughly speaking, no."

"And when we keep this information to ourselves, has it made a difference?"

"We've never had Timur and Hoelun's fleet before, or so many of us alive." Since Batu, they'd only lost Whiskey I and II, and Sophie was picking Whiskey III today. Now they'd have to get the puppy life-pods ready.

"If Timur and Hoelun make such a difference, it's worth recruiting others for next time," Tuya said.

"There is no next time," Aidan said. "UOD never took us seriously. It's too expensive to react to every threat across three galaxies. But they will now. They'll eliminate you, your ancestors, anyone close. Entire planets will be snuffed out."

"Then we have no chance, regardless." Taivan switched back to Nadaam and watched archers on snow-dusted horses loose at leather cylinders, cheered on by a million hologrammed spectators, and shut it down. A diagram of white dots and gray arcs around a fallow planet took its place.

"We have a few hours to think it over," Tuya said.

"And more pressing questions," Aidan said.

Taivan looked to her. "Before Temujin united the people, there was Khabal and Ambaghai, others who strengthened and protected them in what time they had. If we can't bring this home for them, let's at least remind them they need saving."

Ambaghai had been crucified.

Still sure you can't trust us baddies, Chipper?

Hot peace and twisting chastisement transmitted, and Tuya sent back her own pride.

I hope my doubt in him is misplaced. But he—Moore buzzed her three times, the old sign they were watched. It was always like that: always accusing, never any evidence. Was it too much to hope Moore was just jealous, blinded by her illness?

"Buck, send the broadcast," Taivan said. "Don't mask it. Let UOD know the whole 'verse has their number. Everyone else, send an update hourly, start hydrating and eat."

"Yes, dad," Tuya said, leading the exit. She could sneak a few minutes to watch the archers or grab cookies.

"Tuya," Taivan said.

She groaned. "Is it the name calling? Because there are definitely worse things I could've said. Like—"

"I need your permission for something."

What's Left Undone

BATU HUNCHED OVER, THE blue hologram squinting at the camera, burnt face looking like a glitch.

"Did you watch it?" She'd wondered about it this past week on the anniversary of his death. Jiao must have kept it.

"No."

Taivan offered it to her. She accepted it and since his hands were warm, kept her hands there. He squeezed gently.

How much they'd changed, and Batu was the same. She didn't want him speaking to who she'd been, dying for the old Taivan. "He probably didn't mention the time-machine. I can't imagine he said anything Buck could use."

President Davids was discredited decades ago, Taivan hoped people might believe one of their own. But mechanics and engineers wouldn't see themselves in Batu, they'd see a Khanate officer. And he wasn't the sort of man easily trusted, eyes downcast, mouth half open like a neanderthal seeing a highway for the first time, grease smears on baggy trousers.

"Okay," Taivan said. "Then I've got to go—"

"Stay." She patted the seat beside her. "Please."

Taivan sat as Batu tapped the lens, messing up the sound. "Is it on? Jiao, I don't think—oh, hi, everyone." He waved.

Since living through her memories, she'd seen him more recently in her youth and expected him to be the one to carry barrels of water or petrol. Even as she grew, she let him do it, both of them pretending he would be invincible for as long as she needed him.

"Khair."

Tuya itched her hat.

"I wanted to tell you about our folks but I'm not sure how much time—" someone said something off-screen. "Jiao says we have time. But I don't think we do; Coloma's ships keep coming closer. There's so much... you'll find out one day, somehow. Wish I was doing this in person, feels funny talking to a blinking light."

The emotion in his voice was too muffled to make out.

"Anyway, just wanted to say I'm gonna miss you a bit. Be careful. Tell Jiao not to worry, she's doing her best." He waved. "Bye. Make sure Taivan stretches when he gets out of the 'tube, or he'll get stiff. Bye for good now. Love you all."

The image froze with his hand a ray of blue, mouth still open.

Five seconds later, it started over. She kept tapping it to make it stop, on and off a dozen times, then chucked it across the room. It kept playing. "That's it? You want to galvanize the masses with a bumbling old man?"

Taivan said nothing.

"Why did I expect anything?" Tuya collected the chip, a scratch in its side she couldn't rub off. "Whatever else he was, he was a bleeding idiot."

"Enough." His tone stopped her, a remix of the boy he'd been. "What else could he have done?"

He'd died lying about Buck to conquer a city they had no claim on, and lost days later.

"He could've lived." Tuya slumped back in her chair, stomach knotting. Why couldn't she be grateful? "Couldn't he have been selfish once?"

He'd died twenty-two years ago. Two years ago for her. It should have been long enough to grieve, but he was still dead.

"He was," Taivan said.

She might've shoved him, but her arms were heavy.

"He loved you so much he would rather die than watch you suffer." Taivan leaned forward. "That's an easy choice. And that's why you have to leave."

"What? Why?"

"If we're able to take the machine somehow, they may kill you for it. I'll try to bargain for you, but—"

"But I'm not worth the time-machine?" She squeezed his hand so he couldn't pull back. "If I run, they'll kill me, but if I let Sophie put me on a chip and throw me in someone else, I'm already dead." She inhaled, blinking to keep her eyes dry. "Batu was right. This chance to build a home is worth it. You're worth it."

"You're worth more than this, baghatur. And I'm at my best with you. Makes it hard to confess, but there are things I've—"

"Don't. Let me believe whatever noble lie it is I have to until we meet again in victory."

"Victory." He said it like a curse. "And if we lose?"

There was so much she wanted to say, but it was a tangled fishing line; it'd take hours to unravel, maybe it was impossible to free. So she ran her hand up his arm, across his chest, held his collar and searched his lion-like amber eyes.

"If we win," he talked fast. "We can rest for a year on Imger, hike, hunt, take up something silly like kite-skiing or dancing, and prepare to take Jungang ju back."

She'd like to see him dance. "Or we travel back and see a megalodon, or wooly mammoths, or watch Hai Rui build a coffin and say goodbye to his family before he confronts the empire." She waved, releasing him. "Goodbye."

He kissed her. Not desperate or demanding, as if he had done so a thousand times. And stopped. She kissed him, pulled him closer, somehow up on his lap. Wait, she needed air.

She pulled back as far as she could manage, but stayed on his lap. "What was that, my goodbye present?"

"That was the Jochiin Taivan deluxe loyalty package."

She smirked. "Well, you're going to have a busy day, only an entire battalion to go."

"Already done, you're last. I was dreading it, had to put it off."

"Understandable. Quite dauntless overcoming your fears, but you should practice doing so. To prove it's not a fluke."

"It wasn't." He got a call from Jiao. "But wait till I tell you everything, and when we have lots of time."

This was probably their last chance, but she ignored her pounding heart, the rush in her blood, and pressed her forehead to his. "In victory, then."

The Charge of the Light Battalion

PLANET 34RS12NE, OTHERWISE KNOWN as Itoville, was dense and heavy like a bowling ball, if a bowling ball was made of lava and filled with sulfuric gas.

It was Tuya's job to find one of the four viable landing zones.

The enemy destroyer's guns could reach the surface, but the soupy atmosphere blocked their scanners and made it impossible to aim at the ground. If the Khanate captured the time-machine, they'd have to face whichever destroyers were still operational after they blew the *Osiris* up at them. The only way off the planet would be with captured UOD ships, or if Timur and Hoelun picked them up.

Or using the time-machine.

Tuya donned her insufferably itchy, reflective yellow suit. It'd protect against the planet's heat and poisonous air, but now the cooling filters laid awkwardly empty on her shoulders.

Stupid question. But you didn't see Batu when you died, did you?

I didn't see him, no. Moore loosened like a prisoner let out of confinement. *But I remember. It wasn't what I expected. Not a wraithy heaven, the colors were somehow brighter and darker, the air pure like in the forest after rain, all oriented toward Truth and Love and—*

Your Osiris 2.0, and screw whoever gets left behind. Moore knew she didn't mean it—the words, yes, but not the tone—but Tuya hated the pity cycling through their bond.

No one ever died confessing they had seen Osiris' resurrection.

That's not the point. You could've gotten pulled into another 'verse, like Aidan or Taivan, and Batu could be there. A good man shouldn't have a bad end.

None of us are good enough.

Sophie entered the locker room, carrying a puppy.

No, but some of us are kind enough to let our friends say goodbye.

"There's a minor emergency," Tuya said.

"Do we not have enough Explofit? You know it's never been tested in temperatures this high." Sophie wrapped a puppy's paws in the miniature boots. "We might all be sausages a minute after we land, yes we might, uh-oh."

"Then we have two emergencies." Tuya touched her toes, testing the suit. It was flexible at the joints for energy return but starchy and stiff elsewhere. "Taivan likes me, right? I mean, normally he doesn't care about women he's involved with, but he's more than a little fond of me."

And no, she wasn't normally that observant, but she noticed how his gait changed slightly after they passed solar flares, that these past few days he was drinking more coffee and working out more, touching Jiao's hand or eating with Aidan more often.

Sophie covered the puppy's ears with its paws. "They're so nauseating. 'Whatever you need, baghatur,' 'thanks, dad,' 'I'll need your help,' 'anything, anda.' Do you need a certificate of marriage or something?"

"It's probably too soon to say 'yes' if we haven't actually been on a date?"

"So old-fashioned. Buck too." She shoved a ring with a rock half the size of a moon at Tuya's face with such verve she nearly hit her.

"That's very…" the orange stone was flecked with reds and black, like how Tuya imagined the hellish landscape below. But she'd only seen the stone on their home planet. "Big. Expensive. He's rich?"

"Nope, I am. You can say you don't like it. It's not an engagement ring, it's for choosing Whiskey III together. Anyway, what do you need validation on now? Taivan? I thought you guys were pretending being together was a secret."

"We're not together. I introduced you to Daichi? Daiki? last week."

"That wasn't to make Taivan jealous?"

"No!"

"Normally you don't compare a one-night stand to the man you've loved for years to his face."

"It did seem awkward."

Sophie changed into the Explofit, and uncoiled the feeding tube before running it into the back pouch with salty, protein powder infused water. The filmy stuff tasted terrible, but it had all the nutrients and energy they needed. It was the only thing they would have once they reached the ground, since they'd have to keep their helmets on until they captured UOD's compound and checked its air.

"The only thing more cringy than you and Taivan are Aidan and Jiao, and they don't even flirt. They sit in the same room silently," Sophie said.

"Are you sure they're together?"

"Aidan's not done anything suicidal, so he's in a relationship. It must be someone he actually cares about or I'd get all the salacious details I never wanted. And Jiao's been talkative—a whole hundred words a day. Ug. Besides being snobby and dangerous, what do they have in common?"

Being alone. "An ability to eat unlimited junk food with absolutely no repercussions?"

"No, they run for hours like sociopaths." Sophie zipped up the last layers of the suit. She looked more like a beekeeper than a woman on the precipice of the multiverse's most ambitious invasion.

They didn't have armor that could protect against ZAX guns, so they didn't wear any. If they were grazed, they'd be exposed to enough hydrogen sulfide to poison their lungs, along with a fistful of other poisonous gasses Sophie had gleefully described. They carried extra polymer bandages to keep a scraped knee from becoming lethal, but if it went unnoticed, they were goners in minutes.

"Do you think she's happy?" Tuya said.

"That day you dropped in, Aidan told me I had to meet her like she was a recovered national treasure. She just lay in a closet, unconscious with an oxygen mask. It was awkward."

"Not with him, in general. You and Buck pick puppies, or dance, or work in the greenhouse together. Aidan could get a new life anytime he chose. Taivan's preparing and content with it, and I've gotten a far better life than I deserved."

Sophie fixed the oxygen mask to the pup's face. "She survived. Until tomorrow, let that be enough."

"Aren't you going to pack more? Doctubes or something?"

"They don't work in the heat."

"So, there's no medical treatment whatsoever?" They'd gone over this before, but there was something comforting about asking a question and knowing the answer.

"There's this." Sophie shook the puppy's foot. "Don't go, you have so much to live for! Like people getting fried in these suits and becoming yummy sausages."

"Everyone, board your transport," Jiao said over the intercom.

Tuya donned her helmet. It was clear all the way around with defrosters to keep her breath from fogging it, but its curve distorted distance slightly. The rebreather tasted stale within moments and her breath thudded against the glass. But it wasn't nearly as bad as the diapers.

"If I never apologized, for uh—" Tuya made a poking motion.

"No," Sophie said. "And you better not be miming it. Don't panic. I can identify time of death by the bugs eating a body; life goes on. The puppy's yours, from Whiskey's litter. Take care of him."

She squeezed Soph's shoulder. "Me and Scip will see you below."

"Scip?"

"So everyone will tease him for having a dumb name when I call him Scip, and then I'll say 'you dare mock Scipio Africanus?' and have him growl at them."

"It won't be the dog they're mocking."

"You're running away, so it's clearly working."

Sophie left with a mock salute. Tuya waddled out to her ship, and the Explofit's first layer stretched and tightened like a second skin as she moved, though it was a moment behind.

In the back of Jiao's ship, Taivan and Aidan studied the winds around the compound. Taivan had divided the transports into five pairs to guard each other's back; Jiao and Taivan would work with Buck and Aidan.

Aidan clapped Taivan's back and maintained a standoffish expression while Tuya let the puppy scratch his face, then left for his ship.

"Why's it in my cockpit?" Jiao pat her wheel three times, dusted clean instruments, adjusted and readjusted the seat, and placed a bronze bankhar dog in front of her.

"It's a 'he,' and he's moral support," Tuya said.

Taivan slipped on his gunner's glove and glasses. "Put him in the back. The door is soundproof if he starts barking."

"We could use that suit as extra bandages," Jiao said.

"There'd be a mutiny if we let him roast," Taivan said. "And would you clean that puddle?"

Jiao started the engines, a grunt as they woke, a tick as they finished the first rotation, then silent. The lights died. Scip barked once before the door closed and cut out the soldiers' baby talk.

They'd be vulnerable once they left the *Osiris*.

"Buck, radio check," Jiao said.

"Five by five, loud and clear," Buck said.

They couldn't sustain a radio network in this atmosphere, but as long as they stayed near their partner ship, they would have one connection. Missiles—theirs, the enemy dogfighters, and UOD's anti-aircraft—would be all but blind. Bombs, bullets, and other unguided projectiles would work perfectly.

As their landing ships slipped from the hangar, dozens of dogfighters rushed from the enemy destroyers, converging into five ship wedges. Khanate landers were bigger and better armored and their rail guns had a wider field of fire, but the dogfighters were faster and shot faster.

Cover your ears, Chipper, it's about to get loud.

The dogfighter formations layered themselves vertically to cover the most area while remaining in radio distance.

"Aidan, one minute count till *Osiris'* detonation." Jiao hadn't sped their lander; the dogfighters had limited ammunition and hadn't opened fire.

"Can I shoot yet?" Taivan said.

"Wait," Jiao flashed her lights, signaling to the other landers.

The dogfighters held fire as they closed in—close quarters favored them. There was nothing to do but wonder which ships they aimed at.

From here, Itoville was regal: the largest planet Tuya had ever seen, slow in its stately orbit, six moons in its retinue, an arresting black with glowing ruby bands, with white spots so bright they turned to pearls. Even the destroyers were dwarfed before it.

"We'll be in their range in a hundred meters," Buck said. Better that he was nervous than drugged.

"I'll cut under their top layer and work from there," Jiao said.

The dogfighter's guns were on their hull. In their formation they depended on each other for sharing shields and firepower, like a phalanx locking shields and hoplites stabbing at the diagonal enemy. Once they smashed through UOD's line, it'd be chaos.

"Three seconds till detonation," Aidan said.

Tuya looked back. There was nothing special about the *Osiris*. They'd never given it a fresh paint job, so it still sported a giant squid on the side from its old name. Tuya looked away before it exploded.

She'd wanted to leave Batu's hologram there and let him rest at home, but if Jiao had kept it safe for years, she should have it. She had kept Batu's hat and Moore's letter.

The explosion was silent, no disturbance in space so that she'd never know it was gone except for its reflection in the destroyer's darkened windows. The destroyers crawled back toward deep space. Gleaming glass and shards of steel rolled over their formation at the destroyers, a shielding cloud of silver hail.

Jiao flipped on the thrusters, but she didn't aim at the gap between layers of enemy dogfighters. She flew at the top row. Taivan instantly fired at the formation beneath them, but the enemy system fired first. They missed, their angle poor. Jiao kept her course, though the angle only got worse for Taivan.

"Jiao?" Buck said.

From the cockpit, Tuya could see Buck's ship darting after them. Aidan shot at a speed that should've been impossible, but half his shots missed; it didn't matter, while the bottom rows evaded his strikes, they opened themselves to Taivan's sudden blast.

Whatever Buck said next sounded like a sneeze—his translator or radio malfunctioned.

Jiao still flew at the top layer. They were only a kilometer from the dogfighters, both firing, neither retreating.

Sure, the landers were bigger and their shield was at full capacity, but if they collided at this speed, it wouldn't matter.

Jiao tapped the wheel three times, but her luck was gone, that formation holding fast.

"Jiao, duck," Taivan said.

She didn't move, bent over the controls, staring at the unflinching dogfighters with blank disbelief. So, that was what it took to beat Jiao. Suicide.

Jiao twisted their lander, her wings clipping on a fighter. The fighter burst into flame. That, at least, broke the enemy's formation.

But they were still in a tailspin.

Tuya couldn't see anything but their landers bumping through the dogfighter's line as Jiao released them into a free fall, dedicating all the ship's controls to patching the wing. Taivan concentrated fire ahead, but still, the lights flashed red and debris bounced off the cockpit window.

Buck dove too, Aidan fired ahead of them.

Smoke billowed behind them, but it slowed as Jiao kept them together long enough to breach the planet's atmosphere. Tuya's ears popped until she was deaf. There was nothing to see outside but a net of colored flames.

When the flame darkened and died, Tuya struggled to keep her head up against the crushing gravity.

The enemy dogfighters had entered the atmosphere too, lined again in their layered wedges like snake scales.

Tuya squeezed her seat and searched for the ground.

Their map filled the war room, full color, and with a three-dimensional elevation, but there was no steam rising from the map's surface. Itoville only retained one percent of its sun's light and vomited milky white sulfuric gas. Their lights pierced perhaps a hundred meters of cloud cover and only in a narrow beam.

Their ship jolted as the wing finished healing. Jiao spun them up, the dogfighter on their tail now in Aidan's range, shot down half a second later.

Tuya was sweating already, unable to wipe it away, chewing on her straw and drinking vanilla protein water until remembering she'd have to trek at least twenty kilometers without a refill or latrine break.

Below stripes of cloud lay a clump of rocks a darker brown than the surrounding terrain. They weren't close to a landing zone, so it should be UOD's compound, but the defenders didn't fire to confirm it.

Taivan spun and hooked an uppercut, the gun on the roof mirroring his hands, fired with a back fist. There were no extraneous movements, no blow harder than it had to. For two or three shots, his hands circled in fluid lines only to cut back and fire at a jet ducking into range.

As Jiao banked to the side, giving Taivan an angle to come to the aide of weaker teams, Tuya rubbed her thumb ring, her warrior's badge, and noticed Taivan wore the same.

Taivan downed a pilot on Buck's tail. Jiao veered down, away from the enemy formation. They had a moment's reprieve as the dogfighters hesitated to follow close to the ground and lava flare-ups.

Jiao swerved around the compound and raced beyond, toward lava pits and light. As they fled, dogfighters from the compound swarmed.

They must be passing the first landing zone. Between the islands of fire and obsidian gas, Tuya didn't see it. It wasn't a volcano range with magma bursting from mountains; the ground had never formed, the surface indistinguishable from its runny core.

Their scanners occasionally found blimps of igneous rock where some accident of air current had allowed the ground to cool enough to harden, but nothing large enough to land on.

"Losing more," Buck said, voice hazy.

There'd been no sign of anyone else up here.

"Mark zone two," Tuya said, noting a beige flecked patch.

Jiao gave no indication until Taivan swatted away a dogfighter. "Copy. Coordinates recorded."

They couldn't land until they'd dealt with the dogfighters. Their landers were equipped with anti-aircraft ground mortars and the men were trained enough to raise it quickly, but the enemy dogfighters wouldn't fight to the last man. They'd retreat, return in greater numbers, and fire on defenseless infantry along the road.

"Turn when ready," Tuya said.

Jiao flicked her rear lights, three long and two short bursts, and spun her ship up. No more retreating. They climbed higher. The dogfighters trailed below, their pilots not wanting to risk the dizziness of atmospheric re-entry again.

"Slow," Tuya said. The enemy dogfighters had broken off slightly, unsure if they were about to take to space.

Jiao leveled the ship out and floated toward the enemy compound. The dogfighters followed, closing into firing range.

"Now," Tuya said.

Jiao gave the signal, one long flash, and the Khanate released every bomb they had.

They hadn't bombed Albion. Even as they lost Coloma, they'd saved them, and they never would've made a difference against the mammoth *Hopper*. But in the darkness, with the dogfighters' scanners all but useless, they ran into a forest of bombs and it splintered them.

One second there was the whisk of following propellers, the deep belch of enemy fire, and the hissing path of missiles slipping past. Then a rumble.

There was a difference between the sound of thunder and explosions. Thunder cracked, let rain soften it, or roared and echoed out. This droned on. When it finally stopped, there was a breath of silence, waiting for an ambush or an enemy sortie, but still, nothing. Then their soldiers cheered, heard through a soundproof wall. Jiao sighed and righted her tipped bankhar with shaking hands.

"Ace in a day, Buck," Jiao said.

"Aidan's already bragging."

Jiao smiled.

Six of their ten carriers landed twenty-three kilometers from the compound. Tuya checked her suit for tears before stepping outside.

The surface was putty. She bounced on it, expecting to sink through one of the tentacle paths of barely dried lava rivers. Light died in the bulbous clouds and any survivors were culled against the ground.

Air burned through her respiratory system. When she drank, a green banner blinked "75% remaining."

But the biggest problem was gravity. They had cooling air blowing through their suits, their headlights reached fifty meters, but there was nothing to help suddenly weighing 150% of their body weight. They'd packed only water, guns, and ammo, but between that and the thick, insulated suit, standing was a chore.

"Stay close and watch your footing," Taivan said on everyone's channel. They operated on two frequencies, one for everyone and one for the officers. "Is this everyone?" He used the officer frequency.

"Counting this guy," a junior officer said, raising Scip. It bit at him and growled when their helmets bumped.

"Give it a second." Aidan consulted the platoon sergeants. "Seems like it. They got a good look at our numbers on that last turn. No sign of stragglers. About the expected number of casualties, survivors checking in now."

Sophie hadn't made it.

Regret It Either Way

BUCK WALKED IN A daze. Aidan searched the horizon for the ship that wouldn't come.

Taivan started to speak, but Tuya caught his eye and shook her head. They needed time. But a pillar of lava spurted up ten meters from her, and crashed down in a splattering heap just centimeters from her boot.

"We carry everyone we lost with us," Taivan said. "They'll be time to mourn, but not on ground that melts underfoot. We can make their sacrifice matter. Aidan, come up with me. Tuya, stay at the rear guard with Buck and Jiao. Keep in shouting distance in case the radios fail."

Tuya blocked Taivan Taivan walked on ahead, and within a few meters, Tuya lost sight of him.

The sun above was a clear puddle droplet. It gave no light through the sick yellow gas—making their reflective suits of the same color useless—but it must exist, because heat assaulted from above and below. There was no getting around it. Half the time Tuya didn't realize when she stood beside lava; red veins pumped by, yes, but most of the lava lay still and looked no different from a dirty cloud threatening storm. It radiated heat either way.

Sophie would say she was wrong and one type of lava was hotter than the other, but Sophie wouldn't say anything. Buck would never look up from work with that half smile he reserved for her, Aidan wouldn't sigh and change the subject when she proved him wrong, Jiao didn't have anyone to play Go or poker with.

Sophie was dead, and a part of them died with her.

The ground melted beneath a woman's foot. She didn't sink into the lava, the surface too dense, but her foot caught fire and even if they could put it out, the exposure would kill her.

Buck shot her.

He wavered, the woman's scream breaking an octave higher as he raised his rifle, but he was standing so close he could see her eyes dilate and couldn't miss.

"Enemies?" Taivan asked over the officer's channel.

"No," Buck said.

They walked around her. It wasn't the first body. There was no time for funerals and they couldn't scavenge; they'd have to take off their suit to replace the water keg, and few could carry extra ammunition in this gravity.

Jiao whistled through her teeth and grabbed her leg right before she collapsed.

Tuya caught her, but could barely hold her up. "Buck, give me a hand."

He looked back from the woman he'd shot, bracing his rifle against his shoulder so it aimed at their legs until he blinked and lowered it. "Taivan, slow down."

Jiao slung her rifle, held herself up between Tuya and Buck. "I just need a minute."

"We need to stick closer anyway," Buck said.

As people watched friends sink into the planet, they sped up. But with their overworked rebreather and the crushing gravity, they couldn't keep pace for long. The column spread out as people tired. The paths of hardened ground, its braids fraying like old rope, were only thick enough for three people at a time. When a group slowed, everyone behind them stalled. Stragglers rushed to catch up and stay within headlight distance, only tiring themselves out again.

"The ground weakens as we stand on it," Taivan said. "We can't wait."

Jiao leaned forward and tried to bear weight, but her effort pulled them down. The ground below Tuya's feet softened. Her boots stuck to the ground.

"Easy." Tuya ripped her boots up and pulled Jiao forward. Clouds of boiling mud billowed where they'd been standing. "We're only here because of you. Besides, Buck has to complete some great feat of strength to redeem himself for losing that pull-up contest to me."

Buck stared ahead.

The trail was steep. The ground dried as they marched higher, but it was no more stable. Chunks of rock grated down the mountain like sand swirling through an hourglass. Slow at first, gaining speed, leaving nothing behind. When it crashed at the bottom, it must've roared, but she couldn't hear it over the landslides crunching by.

Her helmet flashed—she'd drunk half her fluids.

"I can walk." Jiao didn't have her brace, it interfered with the Explofit, but she set her feet down and wouldn't be helped farther.

Tuya let her go. She hobbled a step, teetered. Tuya lunged for her, snagged her collar, but couldn't hold her one-handed and fell on top of her.

Jiao's breath fogged her helmet faster than the defroster could clear it. "I tore the suit, it's plugged now."

Tuya rolled off her without moving her. "I've got bandages ready."

No Sophie to tell them how much low-level exposure Jiao could take.

"Taivan, more people are falling behind," Buck said.

It wasn't just them. Forms lingered in the shadows beyond their lights, hunched in the clouds. They shrunk against the rocks, no longer able to stand, or pressed forward on four legs. In this dark mist, the meters between them were lightyears. Their screams and cries reached her clearly, but if she held out her hand, it would pass through them. There'd be no help from those shades.

Tuya wrapped the bandages over Jiao's hand and around the knee, loosely, caught Jiao's eye, and on her nod, tightened it as Jiao pulled her hand back.

"Lean on me until we reach the summit," Tuya said. But that was at least seven kilometers away.

"Our sergeants say they're managing," Taivan said.

"Then they're suffering from heat exhaustion and delusional, or lying," Buck said. "We're taking double the casualties we expected."

The soldiers contorted as they choked, their shadows gorged and distorted. This air attacked the nervous system. If Jiao hadn't caught the cut, her lungs would've failed no matter how hard her rebreather pumped.

The dying crawled from the group. One man's eyes had glazed, not noticing his legs caught fire, letting it climb unobstructed to the ammo strapped to his chest. The ground bubbled on the explosion and ate what remained. Lava flew five meters high and rained back down as a hard rock.

"We could switch with you," Tuya said. "You and Aidan take rear guard. Buck and I'll lead; Jiao needs help."

Aidan and Taivan were stronger than she and Buck, and the time it took them to walk back would give the battalion time to rest.

"That'll take too long, the ground will give out," Taivan said. "Jiao, accept help. Tuya, Buck, rotate shifts."

No one here could help. Those closest cried and laughed and prayed in their native tongue, translators overwhelmed by the cacophony. Their faces seemed bloodless, stone, part of the planet now. She hated them. She couldn't save them, couldn't accept any more loss, so she told herself she hated them and almost believed it.

"There's no one left," Buck said.

Taivan's 'uh' prickled over the radio, then cut off.

Buck screamed, a wordless cry that broke at the end. A crevice etched through the mountain. Rocks tumbled and globs melted into the ground below like rain splashing into puddles. Lava spit out of its disturbed bed, lighting the opaque clouds before it fizzled out into a grainy gray dark.

He sat beside her and Jiao, not checking for an errant sharp rock. "I wonder if that puppy's still—" he turned away, though the comm played his sniffling. "Sophie said that dog wasn't any good, took longer to house train than the others."

The cooling system in Tuya's suit wheezed, the taste of her watermelon toothpaste tinged with vanilla protein coated her tongue, her body warred to find a regulatory temperature. But she felt nothing for Sophie. If she was alive, Tuya would worry for her, but nothing could hurt her anymore.

"At least she didn't kick it out an air vent," Jiao said. "That's what I would've done the first time it messed."

Buck laughed, high and hollow. "Her favorite threat was turning it to a cyborg, but she just wanted to try it."

They fell silent. Around them, people died loudly.

Jiao handed him the bronze bankhar. "It's the only animal I ever liked."

"You sure?"

She nodded. The planet agreed this was an earth-shattering event and quaked, slabs flushing off it.

"We could go back to it," Buck said.

"We'd be shot down," Tuya said.

They didn't know the layout of the compound, what guns waited or where, if or how many more dogfighters they'd held in reserve. The compound's scanners were as weak as their own. They wouldn't catch infantry. But they had no chance attacking by ship.

"We could act as a med-vac," Buck said. "I could pilot."

Jiao glared like she was attempting to make him spontaneously combust.

"Or you could," Buck said.

The ground rumbled and light erupted. It didn't mean they could see. Instead of being surrounded by clouds chalky white in a world devoid of light, they were engulfed in a flashing, murky orange. But nine spheres, moving too quickly for her to follow, sprayed a dousing steam. It only provided a second's relief before gas filled its place, but it was long enough to see.

She had thought the piteous beings bound to all fours and croaking like beasts were their soldiers. And yes, some lay dead or dying. But hairless humanoids, faceless except for an incandescent eye half as big as their head, crouched over the corpses and nourished themselves through a sharpened flesh straw jutting from their clawed hands.

Tuya raised her rifle, cursing, but Buck grabbed the barrel. She stared at the darkness where they'd been, straining to hear above the hiss and splash of vapor as the nine spheres rushed past.

"That real?" It couldn't be a spyware projection in this atmosphere, but it seemed more likely her suit had leaked and her brain was dying than for those beasts to exist kilometers from galactic power's encroachment. Maybe they'd been made and abandoned here.

Buck nodded, motioned silence, and helped Jiao stand. Tuya wrapped her right arm around Jiao and kept the rifle nested in her left shoulder, able to shoot ambidextrously at close range. Jiao's slung rifle hung in front of her, hands around the other's shoulders.

Buck led them toward the creatures.

Their gray hide might be leathery skin or a short, bristled coat, covering everything but their eyes, claws, and hand-mouths. They didn't revel in their kills—if they had killed, rather than scavenged—or fight over pieces, but waited their turn and helped the little ones find a vein.

With the stable path so narrow, they had to march within lamp beam's view. When the light landed on the creatures, they screeched and growled and shied away, but otherwise, they ate the dead and ignored the living.

How long had they fed on her soldiers why she stood by? There was nothing to do for them, their suits cut. She couldn't even give a quick death; if she started shooting, the things could swarm.

So, she and Buck and Jiao limped past their soldiers as they screamed for help or mercy, called them by other people's names, reached out a quivering hand. She passed burned bodies and couldn't tell if they were human.

Her breathing echoed against her helmet, hammering around her. Needed to take it off, needed to throw up. But she kept walking, tried to concentrate on the mountain's incline, keep her footing sure though the crumbling gray rock morphed to the beast's blotchy skin. She closed her eyes and shook her head, but she couldn't unsee it.

Her rebreather could barely keep up, the defroster couldn't, her breath raced, heart strained in her sweaty suit. Jiao squeezed her arm.

Were they people adapted to live here or animals? They reacted to their companion's mewling, but even insects communicated. Their hands were strong and dexterous enough to use tools once they retracted their mouths. Perhaps they'd some moral code and only scavenged the dying, or never took more than they needed since they made no overtures of aggression, or none she recognized.

A soldier grabbed her boot. A dozen creatures held him, two dozen hands pressed against his limbs. His cries were no more intelligible than their warbling. Drool dribbled down his beard while the creatures made sure not to lose one drop of blood, so his suit was unstained. His fingers twitched, so it was easy to pull away, so Jiao and Buck never felt her slow.

Had these things gotten Taivan and Aidan?

Seven feasted over a body in their path. This one still fought, one arm and leg pinned, a tongue bouncing off his helmet.

"Buck," Tuya whispered, voice shaking. "I can't watch, let me sho—"

He fired.

Tongues curled back; giant, unblinking eyes stared. The seven closest whimpered, one carefully pulled back the skin around the wound back to retrieve the bullet. That one ripped apart the body and dragged back the biggest pieces into a cave.

The rest charged.

Aliens

THEY WERE SURROUNDED. TUYA stood back-to-back with Buck, Jiao beside them, and the beasts would be on them in seconds.

The creatures had thick legs and short, spindly bodies. Their bounding movement was like a kangaroo's, but their animalistic, squealing rage was human.

Tuya shot the mountain ridge above them. The ground popped as bullets sank into the mushy rock, and lava gurgled out with the speed of tapped syrup. The creatures didn't even glance up, accustomed to the explosions that made her hands shake.

They charged with raptor claws raised high, chopping down with bone-breaking force. The most disciplined legion would've collapsed with the casualties she inflicted. But their young were with them. They didn't slow as their comrades fell, only screeched louder and ran faster.

Tuya's throat closed as she squeezed the trigger in bursts, aiming at first, then spraying as they closed, corpses only meters away. She stepped back as she reloaded and bumped heels.

Too many.

Molten rock squeezed from its bed and stretched down the mountainside. Red faded to black as it gathered rock and bone in its wave, hardening as it wandered from its hearth. The smoother ground made a road for the impatient lava, each new tide sweeping out farther and faster.

Behind her ground snapped and screams silenced. Buck turned to her shoulder. She glanced back to an orange pool boiling ten meters away, lava filled crevasses creeping closer.

Seconds stretched, each the same—heat making her eyes water, her rifle recoiling and bruising her shoulder, rows of creatures falling and leaping over their dead.

She stood fast and shot at everything that moved. Though monsters bellowing war cries leaped at her, though almost-humans flanked and disappeared in shrouded clouds, though veins of lava pumped closer, she stayed shoulder to shoulder with Buck.

They'd dawdled too long on this weak, shuttering ground, but there was nowhere to go. Her feet might decide to run, anyway.

But she couldn't abandon Buck and Jiao.

Steam blew over her helmet and she didn't have time to wipe it, blindly shoot in the gloom. The creatures' mammalian blood triggered her blood aversion and vanilla powder churned back up her throat.

Jiao shot a creature so close Tuya hit its corpse aside before it fell on her. Her rifle jammed. Her gloved finger didn't fit in the ejection port, and shaking the weapon didn't clear the stuck bullet. She dropped it and drew her sword.

"Stay close," Buck said.

He replaced his empty magazine, the motion taking one hand and half a second, finger never leaving the trigger.

A mouth stuck to Buck's rifle. He reeled it back, pulling the creature closer and twisted back, smashing the buttstock against its skull.

Tuya lunged from the group and stabbed the closest creature. The blade pierced skin without resistance, but stuck in bone. She ducked under a shooting tongue, grabbed a rock, and batted it away.

She released the sword, shoving it down toward Jiao. "Free it!"

The mouth on its other hand flicked at her. She kicked it away and slapped the rock at the creature's throat. It fell. Purple ink squirted from its eye, the defensive screen missing as it stumbled.

She pinned its mouths with her boot, sawed and jimmied at its neck with her rock. The skin wouldn't break. She screamed as it rolled its wrists to find an angle for its needle tongues, beat its head until the skull cracked and gray matter—she turned away.

Jiao pulled her back as another closed in, shot it. Tuya took her sword back.

"Can't they just run?" Tuya yelled, begging them to decide that was a very clever idea.

Some had fled. But they took the quickest path from the impending lava—through them. Maybe if there'd been somewhere for her, Buck, and Jiao to stand, they could've bowed out. But there was nowhere to go and no quarter.

Let them be overgrown frogs and their spawn. Not people, not children.

"How many magazines left?" Buck said.

"Three," Jiao said.

Tuya tossed Buck another mag, stepped in front of him to reload, but he'd already made the switch and she ducked to let him shoot. Buck never turned from his target, brow furrowed, but no more flustered than shooting zombies at an arcade.

She grabbed an empty magazine case, hardened plastic, and used it as a club. It was only thirty centimeters long. She used every weapon, palm, fist, elbow, knee, foot, nearly head butted one but stopped herself before she shattered her helmet.

In this gravity, her blows were slow but heavy. Her knuckles might have broken beneath her gloves. The suit pumped in painkillers so she felt nothing beyond a growing side stitch, though the medicine shouldn't have been working already. How long had they been at this?

Where were Taivan, Aidan?

Buck swung a dying creature into the one behind it, kneeled with his rifle over the creature's shoulder, using its corpse to steady his shots and shield his body.

Jiao lay with her feet flat against the ground to steady herself, and still, the recoil pushed her back toward the lava. She pulled herself forward and shot again.

The early rush of adrenaline had dried, and her breathing had fallen into a deepening rhythm. Since her sword handle encompassed her hand, she didn't drop it, but otherwise, she couldn't have held on. Her injured hands deadened. But her arm still swung.

Buck loaded their last magazine.

Tuya slashed at a claw. The hand fell away, but the creature was already midair. She ducked and let it fly over, not quick enough, and was kneed in the head. Heat hammered her face. There was nothing to do but close her eyes so the poisonous gas would suffocate, but not blind her.

But within a fraction of a second, Jiao's gloved hand sealed the breach.

Tuya couldn't open her eyes, couldn't breathe though air hissed into her lungs. She groped for Jiao's other hand, trying to hold something as the ground protested beneath her. Jiao hit her hand aside and kept working to save her. Air smelled like manure, then there was no smell.

Buck kept fighting while the planet reclaimed its ground, but Tuya lay prone, tears burning and cleaning her face. Her lungs swelled, back curled, her body fighting the atmosphere.

Hopefully, Sophie's explosion had been better than this.

The pressure from Jiao's palm against Tuya's helmet loosened; the sword handle opened and her hand swelled. She held Jiao's hand, sucking on watery air, floating.

Swimming. Water, precious water all around. Batu grilling ribs and potatoes on the shore, warning her to stay close to her mom and Bataar and Tolui and Altani, though her friends raced out beyond the buoys.

The sun was bright against her face, blinding as it reflected off foamy green waves. She didn't bother shielding her face and swam toward the laughter of familiar voices, teasing taunts silenced in a splash. The sun warmed.

Buck said something, distant but firm, and Jiao's grip tightened once more.

"Breathe in for four seconds and hold," Jiao said. "Breathe out for four seconds."

She forced the motion, but dirty oil oozed through her lungs. No use. Tuya tried to swim past this interruption, back to her friends in the deep end beyond the bobbing line that swept in and out with the waves. The lake went on forever. Her friends stayed just out of reach, but their giggling guided her.

"I bet I can hold my breath longer than you," someone said, his voice more insistent than Batu had ever been.

And of course, she wasn't going to let them beat her, so she held her breath as long as she could, couldn't have been more than ten seconds, then released and gasped, breathing deep. Her puffy eyes opened.

Buck stood over her, holding her sword. Beyond him, the mountain had opened and lava stampeded down, trampling the creatures in its path. Yet the creatures had only slowed to grab their young and charge with them in hand, to kill, to escape. No difference now.

Jiao released the sealed helmet.

Tuya heaved, expecting immediate relief, but the air still tasted like lake water.

Jiao searched the ground, scattering the empty casings for accidentally discharged bullets they could still use. There weren't any. Tuya grabbed Jiao's arm. Didn't have anything to say, couldn't speak anyway, just wanted to see Jiao's face before her eyes melted.

Jiao, face flushed, hair pasted to her cheek, slowed long enough to meet Tuya's eye. She pressed her helmeted forehead to Tuya's. Then she used Tuya's shoulder to stand and held her rifle as a club, standing back-to-back with Buck.

Tuya let her eyes close. Let heat drag her toward that dream on the beach, the cool water against her skin, her body whole and rested.

It didn't come. There were only grunts and whacks and panting as Buck and Jiao scraped for life with asinine ardor. They would die here. Sophie had already died pointlessly, a victim of chance, with so many of their people. Maybe they deserved this after killing Albion's ministers and laying waste to Asa, sacrificing Batu, abandoning Coloma.

Maybe she deserved it.

Didn't matter now. Her rebreather had finally caught up, but her lungs were still rotten. She could keep her eyes closed, unyoke from this pain, never see Jiao and Buck fall. Light flickered at the edge of her vision. No need to rage and rave when gentle—

Nah.

Not gonna leave Jiao and Buck. Not gonna lay still while lava broke closer in paths of forked lightning. Not gonna wait for the big bad universe to divine its justice. She inhaled, embraced the stale air and the sting in her lungs, and wobbled as she stood.

Then she fell.

When she woke, the last of the almost-humans raced around them, giving them as wide a berth as possible. Not from any dread of them, Jiao bent over, using Tuya's sword as a cane, Buck with a bloody rock.

From the nine spheres that squirted water to clean the air scowling down at them.

"Taivan, Aidan?" Tuya ached like she'd gone over a waterfall in a rusty dumpster, but she could breathe.

The nine creatures—or nine headed creature?—above were worms. Maybe eels or snakes. But long, thin, ugly things with beady eyes and not much by way of a mouth, shooting burning water from their nose.

"Keep moving," Buck said, still panting.

Jiao offered Tuya the sword. She drank water—down to 25%—and took the blade. The ground still cracked behind them, but blasts of water from the worms hardened it to a congealed sludge. Jiao hurried her up.

Buck had stayed.

"Bucky?" Tuya said, her eyes stinging at Sophie's nickname.

He shook his head. Showing a sliver cut on his neck. When he moved to seal it, there was a long gash across his forearm. He inhaled slowly, breath crinkling, as he hid a grimace in a smile that just barely reached his eyes, and laughed. "Should've saved a bullet."

His words slurred at the end.

Jiao's hand dropped from Tuya's shoulder and took the sword back. Buck stumbled, a blood vessel in his eye popping. He swore and fell. Lava splashed from a nearby fracture and landed on his hand, catching fire before he padded it out.

Jiao started to toss the sword, but knew better and held back.

Buck grabbed his throat. Tried to look at them with bulging red eyes, clearing his throat, opening his mouth, but words didn't come.

"He knows," Jiao said.

Buck nodded and collapsed, eyes widening, kicking the ground.

Tuya couldn't look away though the nine worms spun around them, pumping water on the broken earth.

"Westley will—" Jiao's voice broke, but Buck's thrashing slowed with the mention of that name.

Tuya grabbed a rock. "Westley will be safe. We all will." She threw the rock against his helmet. He breathed three more times and stopped.

It was one lie she didn't regret.

Tuya's First Death

Tuya and Jiao struggled up the mountain, following the points Taivan had plotted for their wrist-con maps. She drank all her water within ten minutes, though they had kilometers to go. They passed bodies with water in the suits, but they couldn't connect those bags to their own without exposing their flesh.

She checked the faces of strong men, but stopped. Though static crackled over the radio, she tried to contact Taivan and Aidan every few minutes.

Jiao slung her rifle over her shoulder, and Tuya collected half empty magazines, unable to consolidate the bullets since her broken hands swelled against her compression gloves. The painkillers had run out and there'd be no medical attention until they'd taken the fortress. She carried her sword anyway.

Jiao didn't speak. Tuya traced her footsteps to stay on solid ground. Jiao often wavered. Once she needed rest, so Tuya pretended she was tired. Wasn't much pretending there.

"I miss them," Tuya said.

It had only been an hour.

"Concentrate on the path," Jiao said.

"The eight-fold path." Tuya panted, looking for a reaction. "First, understand four noble truths. Suffering exists." She meant it as a jape, but it sounded like old coffee, cold and bitter. "Because we crave what we cannot have."

She switched to Christianity. "You covet but cannot obtain, so you kill. You do not have because you don't ask God, but when you do ask you ask wrong, for your passions, and still don't get anything."

Back to Buddhism: "But there is an end to suffering: stop being attached. No matter whose rules you follow, stop loving anything, or everything will hurt."

Jiao finally turned. "Stop making things worse."

Tuya swallowed, even her saliva heavy, and traipsed up until she was level with Jiao.

Kilometers passed quietly: their steps shy, distant creatures slurping, lava burping. There was no change in scenery. They walked through darkness, headlamps illuminating bulges of fog, glowing orange slits in the ground, gravel sliding beneath their boots.

The days here were only twelve hours long. It'd been a day already, but there was no proof of it in the sky.

She looked for water. Those almost-humans might gather there. It churned above. There were no tracks on the ground, no plants either except a patch of dark purple mold—or maybe the burned suit of a previous failed invasion.

"How's the patch on your suit holding?" Jiao said.

She'd be dead if it wasn't, but it was a cue she could speak again. "Splendidly. Impeccably. Serendipitously."

Jiao rolled her eyes, easing wrinkles of concentration.

"According to Aidan, they're alive in another timeline," Tuya said. "I don't expect you to talk about them. But I..." if she kept it up, she'd cry and her rebreather couldn't keep up. "I'm being silly, I guess."

"Yes," Jiao said softly.

That was it. That was all she'd give them? "Did you love them? Because even if you didn't, Sophie was Aidan's sister and Buck—"

Jiao faced her. "Did you? Or do you just like the idea of love without a care for the person you project on? There's a difference between love and passion, love and possession."

No need for nitpicking. She longed for them like cool, clear water. "That's not an answer."

"Grief isn't a contest." She kept walking. "I loved them poorly; I loved them the best I could, and I will miss them as long as I exist. Hurry, before we fall further behind."

Tuya caught up and bore the silence as long as she could. "Have you decided what afterlife they're in yet?"

Jiao's jaw tensed. "It can't be worse than this."

Apparently, imagination was not among her talents.

"It's the countryside for Buck," Tuya said. "Up a mountain, but there's a city in the valley for Sophie."

"Very domestic, though they'll deny it," Jiao said. "Dogs, kids, probably goats or horses, hunting falcons."

She doubted the falcons. Even when Buck had been dying, he couldn't bear another to do his work. "There's a big garden, with a scummy pond Sophie finds interesting."

"Projects scattered," Jiao said. "Half crocheted blankets, lumpy pillows, uneven tables."

"And every time I tease her, it's the same excuse: 'I don't see anything wrong with it,'" Tuya said. "But there's always light traffic over there, clear weather, and a fast net."

Jiao's steps slowed. "You know it's not like that."

"No, I don't."

"Unlikely, then."

Very. But after all they'd done, there were worse fates than the embalming fond memories of loved ones. "Let's live well, and pretend till then."

Jiao snorted.

"Jiao," Aidan's voice echoed. "Khair! Buck!" He crested a little hill and jogged down, looking at them, not the shifting rock. He didn't ask about Buck. "No ammo? What was it?"

Tuya and Jiao exchanged looks.

"Let them eat the dead and they'll leave us alone," Jiao said.

"My hands are broken," Tuya said.

Jiao glanced at her. "You can still fight." It was a compliment, not an order.

"Taivan's scouting where to put the charges on the wall," Aidan said. "We'll need everyone. How's your water?"

"I've got fifty percent," Jiao said.

"Nothing," Tuya said.

Aidan groaned. "If we need to leave you, we will."

"She drank her water carrying me," Jiao said. "And we'll need everyone."

Aidan looked back to the hill. "Yes, good, we'll just hurry. We're only five kilometers away."

"Must be a good sign if you're nervous," Tuya said.

"We have two hundred soldiers left. Don't know how many they have. They'll probably have a failsafe, reset everything to when the machine was first built or something. I learned Latlish to mock Buck, and I don't know quantum mechanics!"

Jiao turned her translator off and spoke Jungang ju's dialect, close enough to Tuya's Irmeg that she looked away and whistled. Difference between love and passion indeed.

Jiao elbowed her, and Aidan smirked.

"Hate to break up your party," Tuya said. "But we have crashers."

The worms were back.

In the distance, they'd seemed frail twigs twisting in the wind, their heads moving so quickly they'd disappeared completely.

They were only ten meters away, and there was no mistaking them.

At the base of their bodies, they were indistinguishable from the ground except for the rock they displaced. Each worm was thick as a tree copse where they met the ground. Their segments thinned, a discolored band a few segments down from the snout holding up the gelatinous head, with a stubby tongue and huge nostrils.

"Turn your lights off and don't move," Aidan said.

They did.

The worms looked in their direction, rolled past. Their bodies cut through the semisolid rock like a carrier breaking up an iceberg, heads above the ground, shooting water from their nose. They moved in loose lines, banged heads and locked bodies when their scales brushed, broke off, abashed when the other squealed.

One moved under foot.

Fan-freaking-tastic.

Only a meter of pebbles lay between it and them, so long and slow that after a minute there was still no end in sight. They couldn't step off it, it filled the safe ground corridor. And it only thickened. How old was this thing? What did it eat to reach this girth?

It began to surface. There was no way off it and no way to fight.

Buck was right: they should've saved a bullet.

They were carried along as its hard, blubbered flesh expanded and contracted to pull forward.

"We could run along its back, reach our men faster, get off sooner." Tuya didn't whisper. If it had ears, they were kilometers away.

"It might feel us," Jiao said.

If it felt anything, she pitied it; its scales skimmed the surface of the lava pools without catching fire. Could anything pierce it? Did this giant live until its body gave out or did something hunt this?

The worm's back shifted up like a surfacing whale. It sped up. Something grated, vibrated, and the worm sped up. They could try to run to its tail and hop off, but it kept accelerating, so they'd only exhaust themselves.

Tuya sucked on the dry straw, cursing it and her.

The ground thundered. And here was what could threaten this beast: its own brethren. Their beast, bigger, knocked its head into the other and started to roll onto it. It'd take a minute for them to be flipped and crushed or flung into lava.

And there was no way off.

"Cut into it. Maybe we can chop our portion off." It would be like sawing through a skyscraper with a screwdriver, but Tuya tried to jumpstart the brainstorming.

Neither Jiao or Aidan bothered.

"Or run off it the other way." But already, a few segments ahead started to cant. "Or hack into it and hop into its innards." Though that was probably as hot as the lava.

"Both of you exist in your chips, like Moore," Aidan said. "I could cut off your heads, swallow the chips, kill myself, and find you a body somewhere else."

Without hesitation, Tuya said: "I'll pass."

She was more than this body, but she was it nonetheless. Her brain chemistry, yes, but the callouses on her hand, this lousy haircut mimicking a singer these ears appreciated, the remembrance when she smelled Sophie's favorite candle or drank Buck's favorite beer. Plus, if she was alive in that chip, she'd feel the decapitation.

Jiao shook her head.

"What does it matter?" Aidan said, almost shouting, landslides drumming around them. "They'd be dead enemies, and they'll be enough to shop around."

"One life is enough," Jiao said.

Two segments ahead spun in a slow curl, like a top winding down.

"Why? Why live a hundred years instead of a thousand? Why bow to arbitrary limitations?" His face fell. "Not that it's even in your top ten concerns, but I would love you no matter who you were."

Jiao said nothing.

He grinned sadly. "But you're mortal, so what does it matter?"

The ground beneath them tilted. Tuya tried to stab into the worm, to get a perch and buy them a few seconds. Her broken hand had no strength, and the scales were impenetrable.

"I could bring you through universes if you were willing to keep fighting." Aidan said. "It worked with Buck in Coloma, but it'll wear off eventually and that could strand you in another universe. And you'll never know which death will be final."

As the worm rolled, they jogged along it, pathetic oversized hamsters on their wheel. The blackened scales started to burn through the suit, patches of lava burning on the beast.

"Might as well," Tuya said.

They would die if they stayed. At least if they went with Aidan—or tried to—then they could come back again to finally destroy the time machine.

Jiao stepped from splattered lava. "Why didn't you tell us about it, or Sophie, or Buck?"

"Weakening the corridors between universes gives UOD more power." He sliced a knife across his arm, the breach in his suit long enough to kill him. "But this is the only time we've gotten this close."

Tuya held out her arm.

He slashed his blade through her neck. She felt her body stand, stiff, until it toppled off the worm and burned.

Through the Multiverse

SHE WAS STRETCHED ON a rack, run over by a tank, feet first, burned at a stake, her skin flayed and pinned back so her organs could be ripped out one by one.

But none of that really happened because she was in nothingness. Not dead, not asleep. Definitely not breathing and yet not needing air, suspended between her body and the cosmos if there was a difference, and beyond it all in some black matter/Tao/Logos—the underlying, organizing principle in chaos, the progenitor of existence.

It might be a black hole, a hazy darkness surrounded by an effervescent swirl of blue light. But no, she wasn't traveling out through space; she was moving in, through selves, through possibilities, through all that might have been.

No, not all. That was limitless. But through what was most plausible, through the footprints of history, nature's inclination, the fate of character.

The hurricane spiraled and tightened around her, flinging off light. Beams glowed around the eye of the silent vacuumed storm, sometimes filtered through an invisible prism to reveal the full spectrum of visible light, otherwise amalgamating into a blinding white.

Then her body squeezed and her ears popped and she was gone.

***

When the deafening pain stopped and she un-imploded, she gasped on chilly, steamy air. She lay on dirt under a weak gravity. Her hands weren't broken.

Tuya—she still had her mind, her memories—choked. A semisolid syrup filled her mouth, plugged her nose and ears. A clear, thick film blinded her eyes. She crawled, groping over dirt until she felt tiles, then nothing, and fell into a pool.

She expelled the gunk under the surface, breathed clear water and let it burn through her chest. Tuya surfaced, gasping, lukewarm water burning her extremities. Her fingers were a wine deep purple, shriveled black toes mismatched to pink swollen feet.

She lay in Albion's outer chamber, surrounded by graffitied walls, wind knocking on the door. Aidan, in a green and gold mask with a dead animal as a hat, marched inside cradling Jiao. Bandages wrapped Jiao's eyes—snow blindness, hopefully, since that would heal—and her legs were amputated at the knees. Aidan tried to set Jiao down, but she clung to his neck.

"Did it work?" Jiao said. "What went wrong?"

"It worked," he said. "The other you got hurt in a crash, but you'll live."

"And Taivan, Tuya?"

"Tuya's here. This Taivan is dead, but yours is back where we left him." He carried her to the door, clicked a button with his elbow.

"About time!" Sophie, seventeen, with wide blue eyes that sparkled silver at the edges, bounded inside. "What did you bring me? Ew, cool. Don't worry, Admiral, if you're willing to make a deal, we'll have you back to normal in no time."

This Sophie was what she'd been when they met, a different flower on her dress, a little heavier, but the same neon nail polish and dramatic makeup. She stood the same, swaying from side to side to examine the hurt stranger.

Aidan waved for a gurney. "Keep her close. Jiao, take painkillers. We'll get out of this."

"Don't leave me! What's going on?"

"We'll figure it out," Aidan said. "You heal."

She was still protesting when Sophie snapped her fingers and kilted guards wheeled her away, shutting the soundproof door behind them.

"You actually look busy," Sophie said.

He whispered in her ear.

She embraced him and slapped his shoulder. "Then I was right; you're very welcome. Did you try the Hypothermic Care Cream yet? Maybe don't. Anyway.

I really don't know why you think this is worth traveling with for millennium," Sophie waved toward her. "The cat knows more and smells better. You'll get stupid by association."

"The Arc Dilator is on—"

Aidan whirled and punched Tuya before she could finish.

She stumbled back into the pool. By the time she surfaced, Sophie was still laughing.

Was that her? The woman she had confided in and gossiped with, who would listen to a game for hours even if it was a blow-out, so she knew for sure how it ended.

"Let me deal with this," Aidan said.

Sophie gave a mock salute and headed toward the door.

"Soph," Aidan said. "Naguib will make a fair minister, and if you don't have to worry about Albion, you discover how to preserve people's consciousness."

"If you didn't want me to rule, you should've stayed. The crown fits nicely now."

"That's the only one of her I ever see," Aidan said as the door shut behind her.

"You could've just told me to shut up." Tuya rubbed warm saline water on her bruised jaw. "And we should spread the machine's location to everyone we come across."

He nodded without looking at her. "We don't know if you and Jiao can jump again; if I kill you, you may stay dead. This is the best world we could've hoped for."

"Not without Taivan." Not without trying to make Buck and Sophie's death meant something. They burned in death, soft and malleable into whatever mold she needed, yet untouchable. Taivan and life were tepid in comparison, but they were tangible, fixed points, coordinates on a map to guide her way.

Aidan offered his hand. "You'd find someone else, and odds are Taivan won't survive the day."

Tuya stayed in the pool. "If people were so easily replaced, you wouldn't be doing the grubby mortal thing and avenging whoever UOD took."

"Ask Moore what a God does while his child is murdered." He paused, stretched out his snarl into a cloy smile, barked a laugh, and sat beside her with his legs dangling in the pool. "Don't worry. I'm a good God and forsake all privileges of creation; she will never be born again, never suffer again."

"Jiao was the mother."

"Naturally."

"And she doesn't know?"

Aidan rolled his eyes. "One dead family is enough, don't you think?"

"You're afraid to tell her."

"What would I be afraid of? I need nothing, and there's nothing left for me."

Tuya studied him, his worn eyes betraying his boyish face. "And you're still not enough." It wasn't an insult; she felt it too. Even if they got back to their own timeline, how could they ever reach the Arc Dilator after so many of their soldiers, their friends, had died?

"No." He let the word linger. "Your time is coming. Let the end be fitting, a well-matched frame that highlights the portrait."

Tuya searched his face for a joke, but he was about as serious as a man could be with boots swaying in a pool. She splashed him. "Cute way to change the subject."

"Your death is my failure. I would die for you all if I could."

"You would die for a pinecone."

"Death sounds interesting. It's the only time we're alone before the unknown, something we've never experienced, can't take anyone's word on."

Moore had come back, but whatever she had seen, Tuya didn't trust her interpretation.

"But you're not really alone," Aidan said. "The little girl who wanted to explore the universe, the war criminal too scared to defy her general—all your past selves—are watching, waiting to see how they end. Temujin and Manduhai, Chuluun and Ito. Batu. Buck. Sophie." He smiled, and it almost seemed real. "Jun Hannah."

Reckless courage swelled, but it couldn't loosen the tightness in her chest or stiffen her legs. "I thought you never saw this far."

"There are patterns." He stood, water dripping from his slacks. "Let's do this quickly. You're killing your selves as you travel."

"You're not?"

"No. My existence is an essential feature to these 'verses while yours is contingent."

"Are you Ivan Ito?"

"Only somewhat."

She offered her hand. "I don't care about Ivan the Terrible. Aidan Riley will fight for us."

He pulled her up.

"So, we die again until we find our time." She said it before she realized it meant murdering her own selves. It would probably be a service in most universes, as would Aidan's death, but Jiao? "We're not telling her, are we?"

"She'll figure it out, but let her." Aidan handed her his pistol. "I won't do it this time."

A few minutes later, Aidan carried Jiao out and put his forehead to hers.

She shot them, Aidan first, his blood mingling with Jiao's. She rubbed his dust from the dirt, all that was left of them, and followed.

***

Transferring worlds hurt no less, but it wasn't as long.

Tuya sat in a restaurant, stomach warm and head light, coughing on something caught in her throat. White webs laid on her eyes, but she blinked them away. The plush booth was oriented away from the screens and bar, and the wall was a window. Batu sat with his head against the glass.

"Dad?"

He grunted and drank.

She stretched her legs, flexed her healed fingers. Outside lay Irmeg. No sign said it, but the language on the signs above empty streets was her language, Mongolian with hints of their conquerors.

It was a dump, the People's Republic of Greater China's last post and buffer against the wildness beyond. Everyone said so.

And yes, the parks were small and consisted of open space. The matchmaking board was mostly empty, the martial arts practice devolved into a fight. The roads were unpaved, and the buildings lay in a jumble.

But pastel colors swabbed dilapidated houses, upstart monasteries attempted wrinkled spires, and upturned roofs held tilted towers. The yards had doghouses, basketball hoops, sprawling red herbs, and trees crouched protectively over the homes.

Perhaps this was the best possible of all worlds, after all.

"Don't know why they're bringing the bitch," Batu said at his cup.

Tuya stiffened. Batu's breath stank and his nails were stained with tobacco, but he was there.

"Nothing on this planet worth seeing." His face was scarred still; their family was dead. He spat in his cup toward a glass carriage rolling down the street. It had tall iron wheels but no motor, pulled by people who were whipped but not chained.

They'd been her neighbors: Qaidu who played techno music too loudly, Ariqe who baked cookies, Borte who grumbled at anyone who passed by but would share a pipe and talk for hours.

Among them, matted red hair standing out like a flag, Aidan toiled. And atop the carriage, Jiao stood beside aged parents.

For half a second, Tuya hoped Jiao's parents had been this terrible, that they'd somehow deserved what happened to them. But they had been better, and Tuya was glad for it.

She drank the grapefruit soju in front of her, squeezed Batu's shoulder as she stood, and opened the door.

"Whadaya doing?" Batu said.

She stopped at the threshold, cheerful bell ringing over her head, but she had nothing to say. Batu was safe beyond this shadow. She let the door go, ringing the bell again.

"Jiao!" Tuya blocked the street.

Jiao's red dress stuck out half a meter around her feet all the way up to her collar with whitened human teeth as beads around the bodice and shoulders. Though she wore heels, she shrunk beside her parents. They didn't notice, her father smoking and her mother decrying his addiction as the worst decision since keeping the kids.

Aidan dropped the rope, his back bleeding into his white robe. "We go together."

None of them were armed. How were they all going to die at the same time? Two dozen guards with shotguns stood on the carriage. A bodyguard raised a gun at Tuya, another at Aidan.

Well, that was a freebie.

"Ready?" Aidan rubbed his blood on two rocks, tossing one to her and another over the carriage's walls to Jiao.

One parent squealed about the audacity, their voices the same. Jiao looked to them, head cocked, mouth half open, eyes soft, twenty-eight going on twelve. "Even here, I love you."

Jiao cut her wrist with the bloody rock and took her guard's guns. Tuya charged the monarchs directly behind Aidan, shotgun blasts blotting out the crunch of a crushed skull.

***

The tunnel of light once more, a flush of heat, air known by its absence, each beat of her heart an eternity.

Weeping. Then she was in Jungang ju's throne room. The elevated throne flowed into a staircase surrounded by golden pillars draped with diamond ivies, and a sheer silk veil separated the throne from the rest of the room.

Chuluun mounted the steps, caressing the curtain with bloody hands he'd wiped on his trousers.

It'd been Jiao crying, adult Jiao with three rifles aimed at her head, but as she blinked, saw Chuluun, saw her brother's tiny corpse, she stifled it immediately.

Chuluun kicked the throne, swearing in glee as he rubbed his toes. "Real gold. Considerate of the poor bastards, eh, Khair?"

She held her Dragoon and almost shot him, but she wouldn't survive it and Aidan wasn't here yet.

Jiao combed her brother's gel-stiff hair. He'd been shot—somewhere else, there was no blood—and dumped here, landing awkwardly. His eyes were still open.

"Yes," Tuya said.

He snorted. "You look like you saw a sun burn out. We have a problem?"

Who was this thing in her skin before her? She couldn't control it, but it had her thought processes, her mind. "I'm just tired."

He laughed. It should grate like scraping ice from a windshield, but it was inviting and warm. "Don't talk like that, or you sound like my wife." He elbowed her, nodded to Jiao. "Loosen her with a few drinks and she could keep you get over Toregene."

Even that couldn't wheedle a response from Jiao. She silently straightened her brother's crooked limbs, wrinkled out a fold in his high collar, untangled the fringe of his epaulettes.

"I'm fine."

Chuluun ripped down the veil, crumpled it, and threw it at her. "Your prize, then, and stop moping. Toregene was a stupid treasonous bitch who only lived that long because she made you happy. Jochi!"

Taivan's father had weathered skin, grey hair, and a lean frame. He cleaned his glasses only for his oversized helmet to sink and push them down again. Taivan stood tall to reach his father's shoulder, holding an automatic rifle and watching Jiao.

"The pilot's yours," Chuluun said to Jochi. "Don't let her kill herself. I'll build you a monument worthy of Sukhbaatar Square if you get her to fly for us."

Jiao didn't move.

"Hear that?" Chuluun said to Jiao. "Fly for us and you'll win next time. Taivan, what sort of prize do you think you earned?"

Taivan saluted. "There's nothing here that entices me, uncle. I would simply reserve a favor from you, who grants everything."

Chuluun laughed. "Presumptuous, boy. And very foolish of me to succumb to such flattery. But it's not every day we conquer an empire!" The rest cheered, but it was a tired, obligatory cheer. "You have your wish, Taivan. Just help keep track of the pilot for me."

Taivan saluted again and turned to Jiao. His face was rounder, pimples breaking out across his forehead, his voice only starting to change, but the rifle's shortened buttstock fit him. "You've served your people bravely, Admiral, serve us the same and we'll prosper your people for your sake."

Chuluun beamed.

Tuya tossed the curtain at Jochi and blocked the path toward Jiao. "Trade you."

"Who gave you permission?" Chuluun asked.

Jochi bowed, helmet knocking off his glasses. "It's no trouble, great Khan. This silk is finest—"

"Everything here was taken by my army, with my strategy, and weapons my conquest supplied," Chuluun said.

"All due respect," Tuya said. "I don't give a damn."

Shotguns aimed at her. Chuluun waved them off and skipped down the stairs, drawing a saber. No outcry from the men, her comrades. They had seen this before.

Where was Aidan?

"What happened to the king and queen?" Jiao said, voice flat.

Chuluun advanced toward Tuya, ignoring her. "The girl isn't worth your loyalty, Khair." He had a professor's tone, right and righteous. Just as when he was telling her to rape Jiao to make up for the girlfriend he'd killed. Had he ever considered he could be wrong?

And Khair had stuck to this parasite.

Chuluun pointed his sword. "You were—"

She shot his knee. Jochi raised his hand, and none of the other soldiers shot.

"What is this?" Chuluun tried to stand, using the sword as a crutch, the other hand out to steady himself. "After everything—"

"Where are my parents?" Jiao said.

He laughed, straightening, shoulders back. "They gave you up and fled. But my hunters killed them by now."

Tuya shot his other knee. Jiao grabbed the pistol and blew off his head.

Taivan screamed and charged Jiao, pressed his rifle to her forehead. Jochi grabbed his son, attempting to lower the rifle, telling him it was over, they could go home, but Taivan kept fighting and crying though he never pulled the trigger.

"Jochiin Taivan," Tuya said. "You were meant for more than this."

A dozen keshig rushed in, red hair behind one of the bronze masks.

"Aidan?" Jiao asked.

He pushed up his mask. "Here."

Jiao shot herself. Taivan stared and let his father take the rifle from him, rested his chin on his father's shoulder.

Another shot fired.

***

"What were you thinking?" Aidan shook Jiao. "You didn't use my blood."

They were in a shack in Asa, gravity and sun weak, air gritty. Corpses leaned in the corner without a mark on them, preserved by the cold.

"You said your blood could last awhile." Jiao flicked his hands away.

"'Could!'"

The door was barred, windows nailed shut, and a crowd mulled outside, but there was no sound of weapons or loudspeakers or screens or vehicles.

Jiao sat on the cobwebbed table. "Right guess or correct knowledge, no difference. Isn't that right, Khair, Tuya, Chip, Moore, whoever's in there today?"

The bodies were emaciated, yet they hadn't unlocked the doors. What was outside that it was better to starve? Yet when one died, they hadn't eaten each other. Smart, since by then there was no meat left, but they would've been too sick to realize it. Love or resignation had stayed their hand. Or maybe a disease.

Something scratched the wall.

Tuya grabbed the only weapon, a broom with a steak knife duct-taped to the end. "Aidan's right, let's be careful and get back safe."

"To the volcano planet that already killed us?" Jiao brushed back her hair. "I know we have to go back, but I'm not hurt here. Let me recover or I'm useless."

Tuya looked away. She'd utterly failed Jiao if she thought she could ever be useless.

"Easy," Buck whispered in the street.

Jiao pressed her ear against the window.

"We don't know what's out there," Aidan said.

Jiao reached for the makeshift spear, but Tuya shielded the weapon with her body.

"I won't listen to him die," Jiao said.

"You don't know them," Aidan said.

"I know me." She muttered 'I think.'

Aidan unscrewed a table leg for a club and raised it. Jiao whirled. Aidan scratched his head with it.

"I'll never speak to you again," Jiao said.

Tuya tossed her the spear. She tried the doorknob, but something heavy lay against it on the other side, so she pried out the nails barring the windows and started to squeeze through.

Something pulled her out.

She screamed on the other side, but it was a war cry. Tuya ripped out a wooden bar and followed, Aidan so close behind she kicked his head. She fell on a leprous, rotting corpse.

Jiao rubbed a bite mark on her shoulder and scooted away from the reeking, barely clothed body.

"What was—" Jiao's head exploded.

Tuya tried to put dripping pieces together, hands shaking, but every trace of her body disintegrated.

"No cure, ma'am," Buck said. But he was only armed with a rifle while ten-year-old Westley reloaded his shotgun.

Aidan charged Westley; Westley and Davids both shot him.

She rubbed Aidan's blood on her wrist and cut deep. It stung. She whimpered and cursed, trying to force her numbing hand to grip the knife, but it hurt so much she couldn't make herself do it again. This would take too long.

Buck grabbed her wrist, staunching the bleeding.

Precious seconds. How far behind would she be?

"If you let me live, I'll take revenge on you and Westley."

He gave her a merciful death.

***

An artificial dome pumped cold air with the fury of a sailor bailing his ship.

This was Itoville, inside UOD's compound.

The Best Chance

UOD's COMPOUND WAS A silvery alloy, unmoved by the heat.

Even the layout of a city could be a defense and these buildings, cubes stacked at odd angles like toddler's blocks, were a maze. They were distinguishable by shape but not by function; she could find each blocked crab or snail but had no idea what was inside. Between buildings, small tanks sat in the open, covered motorpool. The streets had no identification.

This wasn't a civilization, wasn't even a proper military post—a post had restaurants and bowling alleys. But still, its occupants had rolled out a patch of turf and hung cheap jewelry and toys on fake plants.

The outer wall was the same dense metal as the buildings, twenty meters tall with a clear dome like Coloma's. She couldn't see a gate.

The longer she stayed here, the more she could explore the enemy's layout. But she still needed to get back to her 'verse. How did time work between timelines, anyway? Aidan had never seemed to age, so that had to be a good sign.

"Hey!" Moore exited the closest building and the heavy door shut before Tuya saw what was inside.

She and Moore wore suits similar to Explofit, with gas masks in a Velcro knapsack on their hip. The air inside was safe. If they breached the gate, this courtyard area would be compromised, but what about the buildings?

Moore flipped her a hologram chip. "Ready to brief?"

It'd get her inside to look for the time-machine. "If you fill in the boring parts."

"So all of it?" Moore led the way, her back to Tuya without hesitation.

The streets swelled and condensed at random intervals and curved to protect the defenders. Automated, automatic rifles hung from buildings, too high to easily disable. And there was always an ultimate defense: they could sink the compound into the planet's core.

"The only thing worse than living here," Tuya said. "Would be trying to attack it."

Moore held the door for her. "Or having to write the reports after, acting like it was urgent to get fresh food with the reinforcements."

They must not be reinforced often. Good. It was hard to maintain discipline among bored, lonely, safe soldiers.

"Almost seems worth it." Tuya stepped into the building expecting cool air, and was immediately disappointed.

The building didn't have an inner wall. It was only a frame where fiberglass insulation and paint cans were jimmied away, and lighting wires were taped up. UOD had either ran out of supplies or the soldiers had melted when they attempted construction. A potted cactus had died, brown and tilted from its rotted roots.

Moore glanced down the hall, guided her to a corner. She managed not to flinch when Moore took her shoulder, thumb close to her neck and leaned in, lips to her ear. "We last a week, and we've got them. Relax."

Tuya held the hologram up between them. "I'm gonna be honest: I did not prepare for this whatsoever."

Was Moore still a revolutionary here? Had she been?

"If you were better at bouncing a ping-pong ball in a cup," Moore said. "You wouldn't have that problem."

"Sergeants!" Jiao had an officer's emblem on her chest. Tuya couldn't make out the rank, but too much gold had been wasted on it. Was this her Jiao? "The venue's changed. There were technical difficulties in the conference room."

"Yes, ma'am," Moore said. "We'll be there in a second—"

"With me," Jiao said.

Moore fell in behind Jiao, the awkward silence following indicating this was her Jiao, unsure of what to say in a foreign world. Or the Princess was an ass.

Jiao found a janitor's closet, empty save a mop bucket and a sink with backed-up sewage.

"What an innovative place for a conference." Moore unstrapped her pistol.

Tuya did the same.

Jiao closed the door behind her and looked to Tuya. "What did we rename the *Nautilus*?"

"The *Osiris*. Have you seen Aidan?"

Jiao shook her head.

"Aidan?" Moore sized them up, knuckles whitening where she held the pistol. "What've you done?"

"I'm from an alternate universe, and I need to learn everything I can about capturing this compound," Tuya said.

Moore blinked. "So, you don't know our mission? Where's Tuya?"

Soldiers didn't call each other by their first names, not unless they knew each other before they enlisted or spent considerable time together off-shift.

She looked to Jiao. Jiao cleared her throat. "This is the only Tuya in this timestream."

Moore scratched her wrist, releasing the pistol. "So, out of all the worlds in the 'verse, yours is the only one that matters?"

"I screwed up." Tuya said, more a revelation than an admission.

She shouldn't have threatened Westley, or attacked Jiao's parents where there'd be retribution and where Batu would have to watch her death replayed. Or played along with Chuluun in front of Jiao, or left young Taivan in that state. Just like when she'd woken on the *Osiris* and killed that liaison, or panicked through Coloma's streets.

Tuya shrank. All these lives, and she was still a fool.

"We believed we were creating these worlds," Jiao said. "Playing our role, but—"

"But this world was functioning perfectly fine," Moore said. "And you killed your counterparts here for your own convenience."

Had Jiao really not known what they were doing?

"We have the same mission as you," Jiao said. "Are those maps of the compound?"

"No, but I can pull them up." Moore sent it to Tuya. "You should stay. Otherwise, you'll flip through worlds killing strangers. And there's always unintended consequences."

"In our world, we're at the gate with hundreds of soldiers, guns, explosives. Now this map." Tuya waved it on her wrist-con, already uploaded so that it would remain with her through the different 'verses. "That's our best chance to stop UOD's interference in every world."

Chuluun had thought he was their people's best chance. Who didn't?

But they didn't actually know they replaced their self, maybe they were just never together. That was a stretch. So too to say she was killing herself and she didn't mind; she didn't know those other people. If nothing else, they were her soldiers, and she'd spend them as best she could.

True, but not totally true. If she had no army, would she still kill her other selves to get back to Taivan?

She studied the map.

"You're really not her," Moore said.

Tuya shook her head.

"What can you tell us about the compound's defenses?" Jiao said.

"Nothing you shouldn't already know." Moore looked to Tuya. "We only needed five days."

"We don't have that long. Don't panic." She drew her gun. "You should leave. I can't imagine this being easy to explain."

Moore gave her a wide berth, turned around. "If you win, you won't be able to use your desperation as an excuse, or say the enemy is worse. You'll have proven you can be great; try to be decent."

"Mediocrity is my specialty," Tuya said.

"It wasn't hers." Moore blinked back tears. Tuya offered Moore her hand, but Moore shook her head and stepped back, letting tears fall. "You've left me without my conscience."

By now, she really hated the sound of gunfire.

***

Jiao kicked her, thrashing, then stilled. Tuya started to fight as Jiao did, but strong arms held her, though she couldn't feel them through her suit.

She looked up and relaxed. Taivan, her Taivan, held her on a burning planet outside the enemy compound.

"I have their map." She managed to send it to him before she fainted.

Nothing is So Difficult As Not Deceiving Yourself

WAKE UP.

Tuya groaned, still aching from the transition. She was back in her own universe on Itoville, UOD's compound looming nearby as a murky shadow. Jiao rested beside her, awake, but limp. Aidan and Taivan sat beside them, her head on Taivan's thigh while he held her hand and studied the map.

Tuya might be back in her world but her scars were gone, and her hands weren't broken—they hadn't healed, it was an entirely new body even if her hair was cut the same and she had the same muscle memory. "Moore's here, so the *Hopper's* reinforced this compound."

"I haven't found a gate," Taivan said.

"I'm not sure they have one," Tuya said. "Thought they might change things between 'verses."

Ask Jiao if I can talk to her.

What do you want with her?

This Moore—what was left of her after the memory loss—had helped her recruit Buck, and then by not executing her on the *Nautilus*. And that was enough for her to break down, get slapped in cuffs, interrogated, demoted, and take it out on Khair the next day. Yet the Moore from that other world would have drawn a weapon on an officer to protect her revolution. That Moore had thought they could win and been willing to take risks, been a real friend.

The line's secret. Moore could tell her superiors it meant secret from Tuya, but she meant the secondary link escaped scrutiny somehow.

Tuya nudged Jiao, tapped her own forehead. "You've got a call."

Jiao gritted her teeth and nodded.

She agrees.

I won't hurt her.

Jiao sat in silence for a few moments, eyes out of focus and blinking rapidly. She turned to Taivan. "Is the army ready?"

Their little band was a mockery of the word, but Taivan nodded.

"Then we have to go. Timur and Hoelun flipped teams, and they land soon."

Even if Moore had used the other channel, anyone could figure out what she'd said. After all this secrecy, she'd given herself away with nothing but a cosmetic cover? Maybe she was a friend or thought they could win and would finally take a risk. Or maybe she was aiding UOD and luring them into a trap, keeping her cover for her precious rebellion.

Tuya opened Moore's letter to herself, still safely uploaded to her wrist-con.

Tamika Ruth Moore,

All will be well. One day, your memory will be restored, your nature will be redeemed. Until then, remember your husband, Zion, and your children, Marty, Tommy, and Jordan, are waiting for you. Don't look into them; your time is limited and once you start tracking down your great-grandchildren, you'll endanger them.

You swore an oath to defend your country, the United States, years ago. To that end, you're part of a group that has infiltrated the United Oversight for Democracy—which was once part of the US, but hasn't been for centuries. The US is mostly gone. Don't look into it; you have enough misery without reading about the end.

Your current mission for UOD is to conduct surveillance through Tuya Batuyin of the Kerait, a high-ranking member of warlord Jochiin Taivan's Khanate and probably his lover, although she gained her position by merit. You mistreated Tuya (that she was a horrible person at the time is irrelevant), do better. But do not lose your cover. Make excuses, feign incompetence, allude to technological errors.

Tuya will try to recruit you. The moral clarity she offers will be appealing. But it's a lie and your US command forbids it. Taivan inherited a contract from his Khanate predecessor, wargaming against UOD to expose their weaknesses, spread fear that will garner them intergalactic support, and make them look good by comparison. To help Tuya is to help UOD.

Her hand shook, but she kept reading.

(Tuya, you might not believe me, but Taivan used UOD to kill his uncle, and UOD has wired his Chief Keshig money for years.)

Taivan watched her, impatient but unconcerned.

For Tuya's help safeguarding this, you will give her an hour alone every day ~~for a month.~~
Remember these people around you, Tuya, Jiao, Strudel, Juarez, are decent people. Whatever history will write of them or you, you have thousands of decisions to make each day, opportunities to be undoubtedly honorable regardless of the uncertainties surrounding the greater good. Treat these small things with reverence, as they are the most obvious, perhaps the only, absolute on the wrong side of paradise. Gal. 6:9.

She sent Taivan the letter. "Tell me we haven't been walking in Chuluun's footsteps."

"What?" He scanned it, and sent it to Jiao. "No. What's the gal thing?"

"Probably some reason not to die, definitely not what you're thinking." Tuya looked it up anyway. "So, why are they paying you?"

Aidan looked to Jiao. "I'm Ivan Ito's clone. He made me as a test subject for the Arc Dilator, and when I tired of being his lab rat, I left. Eventually, I became his enemy, but that's another story. He's a patronizing bastard, sends me money because he believes he's so invulnerable that this is nothing but a cheap test for his defensive protocols."

Taivan and Tuya exchanged looks.

"And that didn't come up over your little tea-times?" Tuya said.

"I don't normally talk about my genetic material, no," Aidan said.

"We could've bought a faster-than-light ship," Taivan said. "Avoided Coloma entirely—"

"Then you would have gotten to the *Hopper* without crossing UOD, and they might have recruited you then. You've seen it."

Taivan burned red. "I also saw you as a king, but that was a different 'verse, with far different men."

"They hired Chuluun to weaken rival powers, make themselves look like the victim," Jiao said. "Why are we doing what they want? We need to regroup."

"We can't," Taivan said. "Unless you're willing to kill versions of yourself in other 'verses."

"We've done worse."

Hey, Ruthless, it's not true.

Even if he's not UOD, Jochiin has proven to be—

Consider a deed in and of itself. You should keep your oath, that means destroying UOD. We will destroy it. Test your work so that you don't deceive yourself, and help carry this load. Tuya summarized that from a few verses before Moore's selection.

Still Moore resisted, but it was a natural inclination, not a conscious rejection, a stream flowing where it had run before.

Your rebel command has done nothing, so screw their orders.

Moore leaned toward Tuya, but her habits and surroundings still rooted her. *It's not their fault they left me; they're not the ones out of their minds.*

Either way, they're not a factor. If we prove no better after we've won, take us on. We'll be an easier target. But if you're waiting for that absolute solution, it won't come. None of us are good enough, remember? Do what good you can and accept grace.

"Killing ourselves in other worlds limits our opportunities," Aidan said. "They spare themselves at all costs."

Moore had made no commitment. She just cared for her friend when she said: *Don't kill yourself. You have no guarantees about when or if you'll come back.*

"Let's not risk it," Tuya said.

"Agreed," Taivan said. "Our primary concern is the machine. If they've known we were coming since Chuluun, is this where the machine is, or is it an entirely hypothetical scenario?"

"I don't know," Tuya said. "But my buddy does."

But answering meant doing something on the verge of being useful, so heaven forbid.

If Taivan attempts to misuse the machine, I'll kill him.

Moore grappled for excuses. For some perch from which to protect Strudel and Juarez, a foothold to keep her grip on the life she had and hated, but was accustomed to suffering.

But she'd known this day was coming. Had looked for her countrymen's revolution for years, and they were yet to crest the horizon. To let go of her crumbling rationale and accept she was no longer the woman she'd been, the woman who'd sworn the vows that bound her still, who had loved and been loved to make such vows worthwhile.

It was no leap into faith; it was just falling when she said: *I'll hold you to that.*

Through The Gates

AIDAN SQUATTED A HUNDRED meters from the compound's wall. On a normal planet, they would have been shot three hundred meters back, but even with the stadium grade beams over the fortress, they were all but invisible. When Aidan put the charges against the wall, he wouldn't be.

They'd all taken another dose of his blood to inoculate themselves against death, Jiao grudgingly so.

"I don't know when I'll be back." Aidan's hands fluttered. No more courage than a student presenting a project thrown together minutes before. "They put something into my blood for the machine to identify and transfer between 'verses. The most useful thing I can do is attempt to isolate it with Sophie in another 'verse. Don't count on my help."

He walked toward the compound and turned around. "Are we sure there's not a better idea?" He laughed. "No, or I would've thought of it. Well. If we succeed, I'll probably never see you again, so good riddance."

"Why not, will you die?" Tuya asked while Taivan nodded serenely and Jiao tipped her head.

Aidan ran toward the wall. The hundred meters between them seemed like the thousand kilometer derby in this gravity, on animated footing, with light beams circling.

'What ifs' plagued her. They should've invented a planetkiller missile. They should've used the *Osiris* as a bomb and flown into the base, though its sensors would've been blind. Should've stayed in their boarding crafts and attacked by air, or at least a two-pronged attack, but they hadn't had enough experienced gunners to fire without scanners.

Still, she didn't want to watch.

A light caught Aidan within fifty meters from the wall. He sprinted, not wasting effort swerving, every step carrying the charges to the wall.

Bullets punched through Aidan's chest.

She expected him to keep going. He'd run quick enough to shame Olympians. He'd had centuries to train. But he hit the ground and stayed down, the instructions in his tattoos obliterated. And the bombs hadn't detonated.

Static jumped over the radio. Aidan hadn't moved, hadn't talked, but he'd opened his line.

"You made it," Jiao said.

She fired one shot, and the comm fell silent. Aidan's burned corpse dimmed and shriveled to dust, leaving nothing but the bomb.

Jiao shot it.

Light flashed but not heat, or if it did, it made no difference. And the wall stood. They didn't have the water or ammunition to retreat and regroup. Their weapons wouldn't scratch the walls and they couldn't dig or climb.

Another friend gone for nothing.

Moore, you have to—

Lava murmured. Magma fizzled from where Aidan had laid, and the earth cracked. They should run, but where to? Roots of fire grew through the ground, shedding dirt and steam, and sheets of rock tumbled into growing caverns.

The compound beams turned red.

"We need higher ground," Taivan said.

As the core reclaimed the surface, the lava surging up cooled, and the planet recreated itself with hisses and groans. They ran for as long as they dared before smoke smothered their head lamps and suffocated the compound's high beams, leaving them in a comforting, uniform darkness.

She clutched Taivan, or at least who she hoped was Taivan, and he held her.

But the world wouldn't fade. It pressed closer, the rocks at her feet bouncing, her suit wheezing, her skin itching under a blanket of sweat, Taivan's gloved hands interlocked with hers.

Time passed, and she didn't move, didn't speak, just leaned against Taivan while he traced circles on her back. Landslides still rippled, but there were minutes between them now.

"The wall must be compromised," Jiao said over everyone's comm.

They cheered, barely heard, more relief than elation.

"Stay close and move fast." Taivan's hand lingered in hers a moment more before he marched toward the compound. Everyone fell in behind him.

Their maps of the surrounding ground were useless now, and their lights pierced only a meter of darkness. But the ground glowed. She didn't see the wall until she banged her toes against its melting foundation. Most of it was intact, just sunk a few meters. They circled it until Taivan found a tear in the wall.

"How many are on the other side?" Tuya faced Jiao, but asked Moore.

"They're in disarray," Jiao said. "No idea."

The breach was thick enough—and their numbers depleted enough—for one third to rush in at once. Some had used up their ammunition against the humanoids, others had lost magazines in the seething dark. They fixed bayonets.

"It's dark and the ground's unstable. Avoid friendly fire," Taivan said. "Don't conserve ammo or fluids; this is it. I could give a speech, but you know who we are and what we do. Let someone else have their speeches. We conquer worlds."

Taivan leaped over the rubble and into the compound.

Chuluun had done so once. This time, Tuya didn't need to threaten anyone to follow; no one hesitated. Not even her. She was first in, no human shield this time.

Automated rifles fired from the street corners, shooting at falling walls and swaying wires—anything that moved. Tuya knocked out the first unmanned rifle and looked for living targets as she ran in a crouch toward cover.

Every UOD soldier on the streets was dead, most of the gas masks at their hip still in the bag.

Moore, where are you? What do you see?

Tuya's soldiers screamed and died behind her, but there was nothing she could do; by the time the wounded were carried to safety, they were poisoned beyond recovery. She pressed in, shooting automated rifles and hiding in the buildings' odd ridges built to shield the defenders.

Moore dulled the sharp pulse of her heart, released an even breath. The smell of carbon and oil, and the kick of a rifle not properly locked into the meat of the shoulder, bounced between them. Recoil lessened as Moore's form improved.

The automated rifles turned off.

They see you. I can't turn off their infantry's rifles, but the guns attached to the building are disabled both inside and out.

The compound jolted with the grind of rock and flush of sucking lava. The ground tilted.

Any additional safety measures against the planet?

We're using them.

The vacuuming sound thrummed on, but the ground remained firm, the compound interior untouched except for the corpses. It seemed bigger than in the other 'verse, the barracks painted differently with a tantalizing beach, with newer vehicles, but the city blocks were askew in the same design, rifles in the same place though they were double stacked here.

They cleared the first block without reaching human opposition, reached where Jiao's group would split off to the building that almost certainly held the Arc Dilator. It was most heavily guarded. Because the halls were narrow and crooked, the rooms small, they couldn't bring their entire force or they'd shoot at each other.

She and Taivan would assault the headquarters and there turn off UOD's infantrymen rifles.

They had only a hundred soldiers left. Seventy-five would go with Jiao.

"We could search the motorpool," Tuya said. "Find a tank or something, blow things up." Blasting open the building with the time-machine would kill any unmasked soldiers inside. Maybe they could destroy the machine without taking the building.

"It's too open in the 'pool," Taivan said.

On open ground, numbers were a bigger advantage.

"Keep your line open," Taivan said to Jiao. "If you need reserves, fall back to a defensible position and we'll come."

"Be quick." Jiao fidgeted with her wrist-con, injecting herself with painkillers. "We can't stand against Timur and Hoelun."

They left Jiao and brought their twenty-five troops to headquarters. They circled it, looking for another door to open a second line of assault, but there was only one. The front door was sealed.

It unlocked.

Thanks, Babe Ruth.

Taivan kicked the door in. She entered as three grenades rolled past her feet.

To Whatever End

BULLETS WHIZZED PAST, SHARDS of wall exploded, Taivan doubled over his bleeding arm. As the grenades spun down the stairs, their soldiers scattered, Tuya tackled Taivan inside the building and kicked the door shut. The grenades exploded.

She listened for whimpers, cries. There were none.

Taivan drug her into the janitor's closet, and kicked her his gun as he tightened a tourniquet over his wrist. She lay half exposed in the doorway, balanced both rifles on their magazines, and shot both. They bobbed against the hard floor. She didn't slow, laying down fire to keep them from getting close enough for another grenade.

She expected the door to burst open and her soldiers to pour in. But as her shoulders ached and the barrel heated, as Taivan fought his suit and she controlled her breathing, they never came.

"Jiao, we can't help," Tuya said.

"What?" Gunfire popped on Jiao's end in controlled pairs.

"It's just me and Taivan."

Taivan's right hand was only technically attached, a string of skin holding it outside the Explofit. He'd looped the tourniquet five centimeters above the wound and tightened it till the bright bleeding stopped, though a dark ooze still dripped. At close range, he could shoot with his left.

"Join me," Jiao said.

"Our suits are compromised. We can't go outside."

Jiao said nothing.

"Yes, we can." Taivan reclaimed his rifle. The end of his right sleeve was tied and sealed with a second tourniquet so he could go outside, to Jiao, to the Arc Dilator.

He'd pulled off his hand.

"Motorpool wasn't so bad of an idea," he said.

"We could break through the wall." The building was an unfinished outer shell and frame with spots of drywall and insulation. "See what tools we can find."

He nodded. But it was the sort of nod where she ran while he stayed behind doing something stupid and heroic.

"You promised not to lie to me, Jochiin Taivan."

"I'll cover you, then you cover me."

"Be quick." She smashed against the wall shoulder-first and the plaster wall collapsed around her.

In the motorpool, soldiers fumbled to start overheated, under-used vehicles. They stared at her, covered in dust, sticky fragments pasted on her suit.

Jiao was just across the street. But the soldiers raised their guns.

Tuya scrambled out of the debris and slid behind a truck, bullets ricocheting at her feet and the vehicle's undercarriage. She shot back, angling bullets off the metal of the armored vehicles to shoot those behind cover.

A man screamed a war cry behind her. She kicked his knee without looking, didn't have time. Feet pattered around the truck. She shot them.

All the while, Taivan kept firing.

Whatever miracle she'd been looking for in here didn't materialize. Boiling, dirty, sudsy water ran through a truck-wide door to the street and evaporated. Cheap hand tools, loose receipts, and broken screens lay in the middle of the room like a shrine to useless things. There was a flimsy lockbox with the truck keys on the other side of the motorpool.

Tuya climbed onto the closest truck's roof, exposing herself for a millisecond as she slithered into the armored carriage with the rail gun. The truck sank as its wheels were shot out. The engine caught fire.

She shot everyone she saw, but dozens hid. "I'm set, Taivan!"

He hurled himself through the hole in the wall, firing backward as he did. Soldiers in the motorpool repositioned to escape fire and hit him, but her gun was bigger and she was faster.

The fire reached the windshield.

"Taivan, you set?"

"Not yet." He pressed out the words.

She tried to pull the railgun off the truck, but it was screwed down. She picked up her rifle, managed two shots, felt the magazine was too light and stopped shooting, let them think she was out. A few bolted to the door, but most advanced to a closer concealed position. She shot them before they reached it.

And ran out of ammo.

The truck's engines and seats burned.

"Taivan, I need you!"

He didn't answer.

She rolled off the roof, snapped off a burning windshield wiper and chucked it at the truck a few soldiers hid behind. The fire fizzled out harmlessly.

A soldier crept behind her. She swirled under his crowbar and stabbed him, kicked him off her bayonet.

"Jiao. Status?"

Tuya's hot breath echoed too loudly, her boots were too loose, her mouth was dry and her water was gone, while her wrist-con buzzed about her problematic vitals. A scratch thinned the fabric around her collar.

Everything was wrong.

"Low ammo. Low men. Close to the room," Jiao said.

Tuya swallowed, looked at the outline of the building where Jiao was, not a hundred meters away, the turmoil within lost amid the present gunfire. "Once you take the room, lock it down. Get out of here with it and destroy it."

Jiao fired. "Copy."

Moore. When I'm gone and Jiao's safe, tell her... There was nothing that meant enough. ***What did you tell your children that last day?***

A soldier ran at her, but he dragged the man she'd stabbed to safety.

Something about their lunch. They took me before I could say goodbye.

Three more soldiers joined the man, bent over his injured comrade, armed with wrenches and screwdrivers.

Tell her I'll love her in whatever world, to whatever end. And you. I don't hate you too much.

Slicing fear found a gap in Moore's armor, but it was a shallow wound. *Godspeed, Tuya.*

"Manduul!" Friends tried to wrap the stomach of the man she'd stabbed, but his lungs were failing.

Manduul was just a mercenary—her countryman, by his name. What had UOD paid him to venture to this forsaken corner of the 'verse? He must have imagined his most exciting assignment would be taking stims to stay awake for night guard, and now he was dying.

How did he have any right to fight for strangers, to die for nothing, to leave everyone that loved him? Why couldn't he be content to make his own corner in a backwater world and leave everyone else to do the same?

Why, Taivan?

"On your knees!" A man with a wispy beard pointed a flathead like it was a rapier.

The only one who looked like he'd been in a fight before, one ear flattened, held a wrench. "Just kill her!"

"What did UOD give you?" She asked. "If you know what's here, they can't let you—"

Manduul stopped trying to breathe, and his friend dropped his head as if death were contagious.

All three mercenaries charged.

She faked a blow at the first one, spun back to the one with the wrench. He was quick, smashed the wrench against her wrist—would've been her ribs, if she hadn't sacrificed her forearm and stabbed him.

She didn't have time to draw out the knife. The second smashed her against the car. Flames flickered. He grabbed her helmet and dragged her face toward it. She elbowed his chin and flipped him through the window into the fire.

The last stabbed her own bayonet at her neck. Tuya dropped. He stabbed his comrade as the burning man tried to crawl out the window.

She hooked a punch into the last one's kidney and kept battering his side. He raised his arms to defend himself. She yanked the bayonet from the dying man and smashed the buttstock into his gut. He doubled over and she cracked his skull.

"Jiao, status?"

"No change."

They'd stopped Jiao's progress, but she still had limited ammo.

Tuya braced herself behind the burning vehicle, set her feet, and pushed it toward the largest nest of soldiers. They crowded together like they could save each other, like her boys had done before the grenades got them.

It'd kill these kids, too.

The first step was the hardest. She wasn't sure she could move it, but once the truck inched, she surged forward, screaming her frustration, and picked up a run. The burning truck, wheels flat, rumbled across the concrete.

Bullets pinged against the truck, but she kept her head low and her legs behind the wheels, and shoved it the last meter. They scattered. Blood ran to the concrete.

They saw her bayonet was dripping, figured she'd no ammo. They didn't even take cover, raising their rifles, their only concern that they didn't shoot each other.

A row of bullets flattened everyone left standing but her.

Taivan opened the passenger door of his truck. He was pale as frost, eyes rimmed with oppyin yellow, his rifle slung out the window. "Let's get our girl."

Tuya collapsed into the truck.

"Tuya?" Jiao said. "We're down to seventeen soldiers. No ammo, just outside the room."

"We're coming," Taivan said.

"Taivan?" Hope flickered. "Hurry."

Tuya brought up a map, hopped up to the railgun turret on the truck's roof, and shot a door through the wall a few hundred meters from Jiao's position.

How many UOD soldiers were left? How close were Timur and Hoelun?

The truck slowed and bullets popped over her head. The lead shelter around the gun protected her, but she couldn't see anything. "Taivan, what's going on?"

"Energy bars got shot. The reserve leaked out on the way over."

Jiao yelped over the radio. Taivan floored it. The truck's engine rattled, but they slowed. She could hop back and push, but that left Taivan without cover and the reinforced glass of the front shield wouldn't hold forever.

"Cover me." Taivan slid out through the truck's back window and pushed with his remaining hand, the truck between him and the men shooting at him.

Tuya kept shooting, but there were too many, and boots pattered toward them from behind. They would be surrounded.

"Taivan, get to cover!" Tuya said.

Jiao's slow, wet breathing carried over the feed. "In the room. Down to four. No ammo. Fifty of them."

"Taivan, get in the truck!"

He kept pushing. But his head had drooped, and a bullet blew off his prosthetic. He sat on the bumper and pushed with one leg, though the truck slowed to a crawl and stopped.

"Taivan," Jiao said, voice distant. "Get to cover."

He wormed into the back and disappeared inside the front seat. The engine huffed, didn't start.

UOD soldiers raced down the hall from behind them. Tuya swiveled the gun to face the new threat while the remnant on the other side kept shooting at her. They couldn't hit her through the turret's armor, but she had to keep her head down and couldn't aim.

"I can hear you," Jiao said. "You're fifty meters away."

There were at least twenty soldiers between them. And there were no rooms to duck and hide in, nothing to conceal them, nothing to shield them once they left the immobile truck.

Tuya spun the gun around and shot at the mercenaries between them, but there were too many rifles to find them by sound alone.

Moore, I need your camera.

No words. Not even an emotion or the suppression of one. Tuya would've felt her die. What was this?

"Just hold a minute, Jiao," Tuya said.

The windshield shattered. She didn't hear if Taivan was hurt, didn't hear him at all.

"You won't make it," Jiao said.

There was a lifetime of failure in those words. Everything since she'd helped kill Jiao's family, abandoned her, set off to sacrifice against UOD but became their tool instead, letting Jiao get shot with that riot control, playing along with Chuluun in an alternate universe this very day.

There had to be a way to make it right. She could shoot through the roof, hoist herself up without getting shot, run on top of it and—no, they'd shoot her through the roof. The walls then. She could break through and—still, she'd get shot. She couldn't move.

Moore, if you can't get me those cameras, take care of Jiao.

"Taivan!" Tuya said.

"Please stop yelling," Jiao said, half a command. "I've got to try...."

There was nothing left.

"Don't worry, you've done your best." Tuya said. "You'll wake feeling better. Aidan and the others are waiting on a beach somewhere. We're all due for a decent world."

They shot out the roof above her. Tuya dove into the bed off the truck, knocking her head against hardened plastic.

"Still pretending?" Pain threaded through Jiao's voice.

Tuya's gun was buried in rubble, and this truck bed wasn't bulletproof.

Jiao's breath wheezed through. "Tuya—"

Her rasping stopped.

The Time Machine

TUYA LAID IN THE back of the pickup while bullets ripped around the bed. Taivan was only meters away, but whether he was unconscious or dead, she couldn't reach him, couldn't help.

It'd taken twenty-three years to get here, in shouting distance of the Arc Dilator.

It hadn't even taken an hour to fail.

All the evils UOD had done, would do, and they would win. It didn't matter how much Batu, Sophie, Davids, Jiao, Taivan, even Aidan, had sacrificed. End visions didn't matter, methodologies didn't matter, all that mattered was who could impose their will. They would've been better off staying with Chuluun.

That was all she let herself think about. Rage against the universe, complain about abstractions but don't dwell on the moment, on the individual.

On how Jiao's only concern was for the mission as she lay dying—as she died alone, surrounded by enemies. She had gathered up strength to say one thing more, but her body failed her. Now it was gone.

The one time Jiao needed her, and she hadn't been there.

"Hey!" Aidan spoke over Jiao's comm. "It's me, I'm back with Jiao, we—" he laughed. "Nah, it's Ivan Ito. Game's over, come clean up your dead."

Some evil hope pressed when the soldiers stopped shooting. But whatever Ito's sportsmanship, it was only because he thought he was their employer.

"Bring Moore," Tuya said. "And I'll be there."

Tuya had overestimated her ability to move, chest burning, limbs spent. She fell out of the truck. The worn spot on her neck was threadbare, so she cut a protective suit from a corpse and wrapped it as a scarf.

Taivan lay in the driver's seat covered in broken glass. He was cold with shock. She turned down his suit's AC, checked his tourniquet, and plucked slivers of glass from his suit, using his bandages to wrap it.

His vitals slowed, but in these suits, she couldn't feel his pulse, couldn't mop the sweat from his hair or massage the phantom pain from his wrist.

She wouldn't carry him. Even if she had the strength, she wouldn't lay him at UOD's feet. She sat beside him, waiting for his temperature to regularize, for him to wake. A minute passed.

"Hurry up," Ivan Ito said. "This is unsanitary."

She didn't move.

Taivan gasped and tried to sit, knocked his head against the steering wheel. He howled but kept moving, reaching for his weapon. She shook her head.

"Jiao?"

She couldn't bear to look at his face, his lips a thin line, wrinkles stamped in his forehead, a drugged glaze over his eyes. She embraced him. His arms hung limp, but he tucked his chin into her shoulder, the fabric between them thick.

It would almost be worth it to take off her helmet and kiss him, to die feeling their breath mingle but their bodies separate, their own but not alone.

Taivan pulled back, searching her eyes. "That thing I had to tell you." His stripped voice was gruff and ancient.

"It doesn't matter." She cupped his helmeted face in her gloves, but he looked away. Her hands dropped. "Taivan, I'm s—"

"I'm sorry." Tears leaked down. "Years ago, when you were in the 'tube for the first time, I put a bomb in your head."

She froze.

All that time he'd kept her close, it was no different from Ito sheltering with his machine.

And yet there was no strategy in letting her blast her heavy metal during their workouts, or bringing her in on his pranks, or watching Nadaam with her when he didn't care about any tradition he couldn't eat.

"Wanted to tell you, but I didn't want you to die for me." He tightened the bandage around his arm. "I'd already lost my army getting you. That was why I put it there in the first place, I wasn't sure how you'd react to the program and

I needed to make sure it wasn't all for nothing." He sniffed and held back tears. "It's always all for nothing, but we—I—needed you there along the way."

How was she so already making excuses for him? As she'd done for Chuluun. Chuluun too, had been brave and stupid enough to lead from the front, might've laid down cover fire for her in Taivan's place.

"So, Batu died instead of me. Who else has one, Jiao, Aidan? You?"

"No one since Batu. And I've had no power over it since then. If you think this code," he pressed paper in her hand, "it'll detonate."

It was folded, so she didn't accidentally trigger it.

"Sophie wrote it in her language, so if you turn your translator off, it's harmless."

She bit her lip. "Did everyone know?" Moore had warned her for years not to trust him, and she'd only doubted Moore.

"No, Sophie didn't even know."

She'd so often lost herself in his goals, his strength, his crooked smile at any compliment as if he should be above such mortal things, that if she stopped fighting, she'd forgive him in an instant. Say that because he shouldered the blame, that was difference enough from Chuluun.

But she couldn't.

"You said you trusted me." It'd been twenty years ago, but she'd repeated it to herself thousands of times. "I would've detonated if it might've saved Jiao or gotten us the machine. I might—"

"Let's gooooo," Ito said.

She stared at Taivan, waiting for him to say something, to fix it.

"There's nothing I can say, Tuya."

She shrugged, shoulders heavy. "Ito won't wait forever."

He braced his wounded forearm against the wall and hobbled on, his rifle in his free hand resting against his shoulder.

Whatever else he had done, he had taken nothing more than he was willing to give.

She offered him her hand, and he took it. They shuffled down the hall.

"I'm still mad, y'know."

They entered a room that was empty except for corpses, three cloned Aidans with tattoos of varying quality, a victim of plastic surgery, and Moore. Moore's wrist-con was sliced off and her bandaged forearm bled, her hands cuffed, with a shock collar around her neck. All but the freak—presumably Ito—wore helmets, the building breached and air poisonous.

Tuya didn't look for Jiao, couldn't yet. There was no sign of the Arc Dilator. From here there was nothing more interesting than Ito, of indeterminate age in a tee-shirt, boxers, and flip-flops.

"There you are!" Ivan Ito clapped his hands, his voice projecting more than Aidan's mumblings. Humanity was stretched off his features, his eyes and lips swollen to impossible proportion and his chin chiseled to a stump, his fat sucked out to reveal all the muscle of a snail. She half expected his hands to be fins. "Don't be alarmed. These ugly lumps are Brayden, Caiden, and Dan, and you know your sergeant here." Ito tapped Moore's shoulder.

Moore shrugged off his hand.

"Where's Jiao?" Tuya said.

Ito gestured to the room. "Which one is she? There's a lot."

Had Tuya seen the Arc Dilator, she would've detonated.

"Don't look so glum," Ito said. "In a couple centuries, you'll be beyond caring."

"Where's your wrist-con?" Tuya said to Moore.

There was nothing martial in the sergeant now. Her posture had relaxed, and she seemed smaller, but steadier, hair grown back from her surgery and in a braid that may or may not be within regulation.

Ito waved the wrist-con. "This is nothing. Look here." He flicked a switch and the wall behind him turned into the Arc Dilator.

Within a glass steamed a liquid jewel. Water pumped into the cube through clear bubbled pipes like a rat's maze, and a super-coolant dripped in, shavings of its condensation simmering below in a vat with blood and brain matter.

Her legs numbed.

Even after seeing how time travel worked, she had expected a clunky machine. But it was a barely controlled bio-based transit between universes. Even if they'd destroyed it, as long as UOD had people with whatever that thing created and injected into their blood, they controlled—as much as people could—the passage between universes. But destroying it would contain it.

Right?

She stepped back, poised to bounce at Ito, but Taivan squeezed her arm. Ito's clones had guns, and she had to see if Jiao's body was here, if she was dead or floating off in another 'verse. If she lay here, Tuya would give her Batu's hat, the only marker the galaxy's best pilot would get besides the bodies of the comrades she'd led and enemies she'd killed.

"How long does the serum last?" Taivan said.

Ito gave an exasperated sigh, resembling Aidan for a moment. "Be grateful, you're the first to earn it. What do you say about the chip? Should we start it at birth or would it make the populace too unstable? Sergeant, what do you think?"

"You're deranged," Moore said.

"Hm. That's more like an insult. Can we move to constructive criticism?"

"What Moore means," Tuya said, "is that if you don't tell us what happened to Jiao, we'll blow you up."

Ito flicked the syringe. "Wait, this was for real? Spooky. Go on. I can't die, my clones are irritating—Aidan especially. That's why I shipped him to my dumb friends. I was actually hoping for you to win, but," he shrugged. "That's not possible."

"If you blow up this room, you'll destroy the chip," Moore said. "You'll be free."

Tuya had been shot in the head before and that didn't work, but it could've missed the chip.

Ito waved his hand. "This is turning irksome. You could permanently kill yourself and your friends if the trace has worn off. Moore's almost certainly has."

Ito would lie. But most things in the body were constantly dying and remade. Foreign matter was probably quickly absorbed.

"Sucks to suck," Tuya said.

"Go on, then." Ito balanced the syringe on one finger.

Tuya didn't do it.

"I've always suffered from boring enemies." Ito threw Moore her wrist-con. "I like the chip. I'll keep it. How about double or nothing next round? I'll let you choose one person to get the trace with you if you can reach this point again. But if you fail, I'll cut you off."

"We'll make our own way," Taivan said.

Moore didn't put on the wrist-con, but she pressed a few buttons on the screen. *I cut it out, didn't want anyone using it on you, but I guess it doesn't work like that.*

Where's Jiao?

I don't know. There're four groups currently gunning for UOD, but actually in their employ and probably coming after you. None of them have the trace. You need to destroy it before anyone else gets it.

If the explosion destroys your body and my chip, it destroys you.

I have an immortality of my own.

Maybe we can recruit Timur and Hoelun for real. And—

Trying to go 0-3 for that heroic sacrifice? That's not even good in baseball.

I don't want to kill you and Taivan.

Or die with them. She wasn't a good person. If she took the serum again or charged and died from bullets with most of her body intact, she'd know what it meant to transfer worlds, what the time machine was, and she'd do better. If she stayed dead, she'd never make things right with Taivan and Jiao, never help all the people she'd hurt.

"Tuya, the *Karokorum* landed," Taivan said.

Timur and Hoelun had arrived.

Sacrifice looks different for us all.

"They'll be here in ten minutes," Taivan said.

No one's death is a sure thing. And even if it was, I'm better for knowing you; you've done more than enough for me.

"If he says something else annoying," Ito waved toward Taivan. "Shoot out his knees."

"Taivan, just do it for me," Tuya said.

"I locked myself out; I can't. Here," Taivan removed his glove, atmosphere poisoning him, and took her hand.

He was dying now; she had to do it. Had to. And yet, watching him suffer didn't stiffen her back, it just shattered her heart.

Dan raised his hand. "Who defines 'annoying?'"

Caiden shot Dan. "Stupid questions."

Moore flinched, forced herself to look Tuya in the eye.

How had she ever thought of this woman as some sort of unstoppable force when she wanted to read in the corner during work parties, whose initial rebellion was sending a strongly worded letter?

Not some giant with statues in the park from whom greatness was to be expected. Just a patriot and a traitor and an idiot trying to do better.

She squeezed Taivan's hand but didn't take off her glove. He stood close enough to take a bullet for her, not noticing he leaned against her for support.

"I want to," Tuya whispered, only Taivan hearing. It was the worst lie she'd ever told, contradicting everything she'd ever done, the rushing blood in her veins, the tightness in her chest, her hand in Taivan's aching for more—more time, more trust, more life. And it was the greatest truth she had ever known. "But I'm so weak. Help me."

Taivan steeled himself and stepped in front of her. "Hoelun and Timur are—"

She caught him as he collapsed, three bullets in his knee, and bullets kept riddling through him, bleeding her. "Take me to another world, baghatur, my anda." He pulled himself up, still shielding her as pink slobber ran down his chin.

Moore smiled grimly, pulling at the collar on her neck. *I don't hate you either.*

'I will not wear a collar, Ms. Batuyin, or leave a world where my son wears one in my place,' Buck had said. And he had given his life proving his words.

Aidan was a genetic facsimile of a galactic tyrant, but had forsaken his inheritance and fought his family and biochemistry for his dead daughter.

Sophie had known her time was short and spent it defying the laws of nature, even death itself, for her friends.

Though surrounded by his nation at its worst for years, Batu had risen above and remained loyal to that germ of good.

And Jiao, the memory of her still so raw, a kaleidoscope of images and feelings. Jiao, who'd survived so much until she'd spent herself here for a 'verse that had done her no favors, had found refuge flying free, a queen in the sky.

Her people, who she knew so well, whose foibles had helped make her, had given everything. How could she do less?

Hadn't she lost enough?

Taivan's clouding eyes searched hers. She took off her mask and kissed his hand as he died and his hardened, glorious body crumbled to nothing in her hand.

Moore, one of them, itched against the collar. Not so different from the cangue even Temujin had worn once, but that was ancient history—their own history was a millennium ago too, weighty, forming them, but without its sharp edge.

Tuya opened Taivan's note with trembling hands, relaxed as she saw his familiar handwriting before her translator gave her the self-destruct code. She closed it again, looked Ito in the eye for a moment, but it wasn't worth it.

We're free.

She breathed in and closed her eyes, enjoyed the air in her lungs, the clear uniformity and soft rest of darkness.

Fire flared out, but Tuya didn't feel it.

The explosion left no bodies or machines, only an odd-shaped crater and a wave of energy before lava oozed in and creatures resettled their righted ecosystem.

Epilogue

My friends, I'll love you through eternity.
   Here we'll drift, float back, wander, and bind fast.
   But now, take my trembling hand, walk with me.
   My anchor when I drift off aimlessly—
   and the rowers, the winds, the sails, the mast.
   My friends, I'll love you through eternity.
   I'll step up and take the charge willingly,
   the throbbing back will heal, scraped legs pass.
   But now pull me to my feet, run with me.
   You're a moment of quiet energy,
   harmony too heavy, too true, to last.
   My friends, I'll love you through eternity.
   Ours is no peaceful, easeful melody,
   we've crossed that river, the die were cast,
   so now guard my bleeding side, fight with me.
   My friends, I'll love you through eternity—
   now, bear my mournful mind, wait for me.

"Goodbye For Now" Kerait Batuyin Tuya, 555 DH

The Bastion

FOR THE FIRST TIME in years, Westley Davids Bennett pouted. He sat in his apartment, flicking through propaganda to see if there was any news, or barring that, a hockey game.

He'd graduated with Agriculture and Political Science degrees a few hours ago. It had taken five years to do it with his Reformatory Public Service duties. He had no land to farm and there was no need to study the art of leadership when he'd tested into a managerial position in middle school. But he'd expected Anna Nkosi or his parents to show up. Or at least leave an apology note with store credits.

He poured moonshine, turned off the screen, and stared out the window. Smog poured from the factories that made clean energy. The illusory facades that, so he was told, had cloaked the city in color and light were dismantled for security purposes, revealing cracked rock and ripped tents and apartments squeezed into old alleys. Coloma University had been his only bastion from the gloom—though everyone had their own—its gothic towers overshadowing the city.

He'd been happy there. Known he was being babied and monitored, directed away from inconvenient facts or outright lied to, but the classrooms had been warm, the food plentiful, the professors amicable, and the women pretty.

But he'd never step inside again, never access those records, not even papers he had written—so careful that anything subversive was packaged in six levels of sarcasm or hidden in footnotes. His life ahead lay in the factories, pacing through clicking aisles and yelling at workers to be heard over the machine scratch, itching at his sweaty mask and hoping it prevented lung cancer. No people even made the product, monitoring the machines that made the machines that would monitor them.

It was the sort of thing that made a man want to walk out his window. But he was only on the second floor. Which made him better off than most, closer to the ground in case of fires.

His wrist-con glowed with a message from his birth father, though it wasn't a birthday or holiday. Wes had never told Davids about Bjorn Bolivar.

Bjorn wasn't half the revolutionary he thought he was, but was twice the father he feared. Since his mother spent her time traveling, officially ensuring Albion met their quotas and unofficially helping Hassan Naguib kick the embers of rebellion so they didn't go out entirely, Bjorn's fathering seemed the only quality she concerned herself with.

Normally, Wes would humor Davids, but he wasn't in the mood to let anyone pretend he was a child.

"It's been a while; some of you may not recognize me," Davids said.

Wes checked his wrist-con, but it was still on hold, Davids' voice carrying from the room above.

Davids had been declared a traitor, a drug addict and a coward and a collaborator by UOD, his comm banned. His mom had said Davids was loyal except for being a womanizer, the prophet no one believed until they needed a scapegoat. Wes knew him as the one whose careless message had gotten him re-educated and enrolled in Reformatory Public Service. If Davids' message played nearby, they'd blame him.

Since he was going to be punished for it, Wes played it.

"Some of you may blame me for United Oversight for Democracy's takeover."

This must have been days, maybe even weeks, ago. Whatever he said was long fixed, but Wes still watched it as if he sat across the table.

"I should've been more proactive in our defense. I should've gotten help. There're a thousand things I wish I could change. Chief among them is leaving you."

Wes had always measured himself against Davids, the man only a decade older now, though sometimes he seemed ancient. If he had ever been a father, he certainly wasn't one now. He was dressed for war.

"But today, I'll make that right. I and the Andromeda Khanate have located UOD's Arc Dilator on RS34NE12, guarded by three destroyers."

He'd taken a class on Einstein, the only class late enough to fulfill his science requirement after his RPS hours. Time travel had been disproven every which way. But they'd only looked at it from a physical perspective, ignoring biological or chemical possibilities, and laughing off questions.

Whatever else Davids was, traveling with imperialists terrorists, he was no fool. Would he die for a lie? No. But he could be deceived. If he wanted to be taken seriously, Davids ought to share his evidence.

"If we get it, you know where we are. Hold us accountable." He said it with a smile, eyes glistening at the joke; he knew he would never get it. "If we die in the attempt—and that is the only option when facing an evil of this magnitude, submission or defiance unto death—then you know where it is."

Wes opened his link to the net, looked to see if Davids was available. He wasn't.

"I hope we can take this burden from you, or at least lessen it. But even if we do win this victory today, your home will still be under occupation, and you'll have difficult choices ahead."

If they had won, they were lightyears off. Davids could be sleeping after the battle, wounded, drunk. But no, if they had won, there would have been punishment here. And Davids would've called him.

"There's some who value the length of days over the quality. I don't speak to you."

His father was dead. He'd been gone so long it was almost a relief to cut through that last tenuous tie.

Bjorn was a good man, had taught him how to shoot before guns were turned off, how to plant and cook and play guitar. His mother had never been apt to overpraise, but she'd few complaints. Had returned late from work on Friday nights, cast off her shoes, laid aside her riot control, and said 'You spoil the boy too much,' while sneaking him chocolate.

But he'd always assumed there would be a day Davids returned. He'd tell of his adventures and Wes would match him. Davids would nod to Bjorn and Bjorn would take a graceful exit.

Then he and Davids would talk about baseball in the way old men talked about sports—the friends they'd watched it with in the easy days of youth, the possibilities of human greatness, how they couldn't catch a break but they'd be back at it next time.

He drank with shaking hands and wiped his misty eyes.

"But to the fighters—for UOD and Coloma both, I speak to you. Don't look to the past and accept present failings because things were worse then. Don't look to the future and accept present failings now in hopes of a distant utopia. Look around. Your people are suffering now."

Even if Wes was better off with closure, without UOD waiting for another message to intercept, Coloma wasn't. The universe wasn't.

"Fight for them. Even if all you can do is spare half a ration for your neighbor, fight for them."

Wes should be running, UOD would assume he was responsible. But Davids was dying for these words. Did his mom know, would she care?

"Westley."

He had no reason to cry for a dead man, much less one basically a stranger. But he knew what came next, the charge he'd be given, that he'd been born into no matter how his parents tried to hide their work.

He'd always imagined he'd die to the applause of gunfire or frozen in a work camp, but it had been for his deeds, not his name.

"Whatever happens..." Davids laughed at himself as he teared up and Wes chuckled too, an embarrassment shared across galaxies. "I love you, and I'm proud of you."

Knocks on the door. He glanced out the window. There were soldiers on the street. His parents had a hidden bunker in their room but it only had a week's rations, and if they didn't find him, they'd post a guard.

Wes grabbed a kitchen knife and cursed himself. There could be a dozen out there, armored and with riot control guns. If he hid in the bunker, there'd only be a few guards, and they wouldn't be as prep—

Gunshots, pieces of wall exploding. Wes dove behind the kitchen table and kicked it over as a shield. The door knocked open.

Jochiin Taivan waltzed in, dripping blood, middle-aged now, but with the poor sense to barely age and remain recognizable. "You're Westley Davids?"

"Wes Bennett." He was much taller than Jochiin, but even at his age Jochiin was stronger, better armed, and looked like a bullet would bounce off him. Still, Wes held the knife in front of him, hoping his eyes weren't red.

Jochiin nodded to Davids, the dead man's voice no longer strained.

"—in some kinder universe."

"I can't leave you here," Jochiin gestured to the bodies outside his door. "I'll bring you to your ancestral home in the Milky Way; we faked papers for you. Or you can come with us. Clearly you can't fight. What can you do?"

"I box," he said, though only been for PE credit and they hadn't actually been allowed to hit anyone. "UOD wanted me making spyware, but I got a degree in farming."

He snorted. "Should've known."

"I'm not him. If I'm going with you, I need Anna Nkosi, Cassia Bennett, and Bjorn Bolivar safe. Hassan Naguib can help us."

"To flee or fight?"

Westley didn't know how or in what way, but he would find one. "To fight."

Afterword

I almost don't want to write this, because then there's nothing else to write for this book. You'd think after so many rounds of edits I'd get tired of these characters and all their issues, but hey, they're (usually) trying their best.

I'd like to thank Grace, Michael, and Nicole, my primary beta-readers, and the professionals in my publishing team: Fiona, Heather, and Melissa. This book is far better for your contributions. I'd also like to thank my family for their support, and teaching me how to read; this whole book writing business would be much more difficult otherwise.

Lastly, I'd like to thank the readers. (Unless you're one of those weirdos that skip to the end, what are you doing? Go back to the good stuff.) If you have the time, I'd appreciate a review on Amazon or Goodreads. I have a potential sequel clattering around in my head about Jiao and Aidan, but I'm working on an epic fantasy series and my thesis novel, so I'll only write it if there are readers for it. For the same reason, if you liked the book, I'd appreciate a shout-out on social media.

If you want to read short stories set in either this world, or the upcoming epic fantasy world, you can sign up for my mailings list on my website: https://www.laurapaquette.com. If you sign up, you get my dystopian novella, *The Pre-Corpse and Mortician* free.

About the Author

Laura Paquette is currently working towards a Master of Fine Arts in Creative Writing at Southern New Hampshire University. Although born and raised in Pennsylvania, she now lives wherever the United States Army sends her and her long-suffering dog. Her hobbies include working out and choreographing her fight scenes with real swords, which may have resulted in unintentional redecorating.

9 798988 395041